HISTORY OF WITCHES

COVEN OF SHADOWS AND SECRETS

CROWNS OF MAGIC UNIVERSE

ASHLEY MCLEO

MERAKI PRESS

GLOSSARY

* *Abscondita* Coven - a coven hidden in the woods of England tasked with keeping information about the *Vindix* and *lapis caelesti* safe.

* *Arcacustos* - the eight members of the ultra secretive *Abscondita* Coven.

* the Beinecke - a library at Yale

* the Covenant - the supernatural ruling body of the human world. It's made up of three individuals from each supernatural order (example: three vampires, three witches, three phoenixes and so on).

* the Darkborn - people in the human world who follow the Princes of Hell. Some are Hellblooded, but not all.

* Hellblooded - individuals with demon blood. They are usually born in the human world and are forced to register by the Covenant.

* Hellborn - individuals who were born in Hell. Nearly all of these creatures are demons.

* Isila - another realm where magical beings live. It's comprised of nine kingdoms (four fae kingdoms, mage,

dragon shifter, elf, vampire, and wolf shifter). Many characters in the Coven of Shadows and Secrets have direct ties to Isila's courts.

* *Lapis caelesti* - the sacred stones made by angels thousands of years ago and given to seven witches to protect. They are great sources of power that can defeat the darkest evil.

* Ordo Aeternum - Also known as the OA, Ordo, or the Order. An elitist group of supernaturals who believe those of magical blood should rule the world (many believe they should enslave humans too).

* Ouroboros - The symbol of the Coven of Shadows and Secrets. It is a snake, formed in a circle, eating its own tail.

* Wolvea - royal wolves of Isila

* *Vindix* - the chosen seven individuals who can claim and use the *lapis caelesti* to their highest potential. The *Vindix* all have witch blood in their line.

* Vow of Intent - an vow between supernaturals where the person loses their magic if they break it

CHAPTER ONE

TOBIAS

Rage unlike any I'd ever known boiled through me, scalding, vital . . . dangerous.

Meredith had just vanished, clutched in the talons of a hideous, bull-faced demon. I stared at the spot where she'd soared over the top of a New York City skyscraper and began to vibrate, the need to find her, to hunt the demon who'd taken her, overcoming me in a way I'd never experienced. Even someone like me, a vampire with superhuman strength and speed, couldn't reach her now.

I roared, my hands digging into my hair.

"Tobias!" Luca's voice, normally calm and smooth and lilting like the Mediterranean Sea on a sunny day, called out. Fast footsteps followed as the mage sought me out. "What's wrong?"

I tried to reply, but words wouldn't form. My hands remained stuck in my hair, my nails digging into my scalp and drawing blood. Unexpectedly, a growl worked its way up and out of my throat to rumble through Central Park.

The violent noise should have acted as a warning to others,

an alert to stay away. Luca, however, wasn't like most people. It did not surprise me when he appeared around the corner, brown eyes wide as he took in my crazed state.

"Tobias? Where's Meredith?"

Her name hit me like an adrenaline shot straight to the heart, snapping me out of the all-consuming fury. I turned to Luca, staring him in the eye.

The mage jerked back.

Bloody hell. I must look like a madman.

"Tobias? Is Meredith okay? Did you . . .?" he trailed off, unable to finish the question of if I'd drained her dry.

Just days ago, that concern would have been insulting yet valid. But since I'd shared my blood with the witch, everything had changed.

Me.

Her.

The air between us, which often crackled with energy, potential, desire.

The way I saw her and wanted to be near her, to protect her but no longer dominate.

"They took Meredith," I ground out with effort.

"Who?" Luca barked, shoulders stiffening.

"The demons."

"Was it the prince? Did he return?" Tension laced his voice as he scanned the area.

"Not him." I considered the winged monster who'd clutched our coven's seeker in its talons. I had no name for such a beast, but he was certainly not a Prince of Darkness. Those vile royals looked all too human, but also somehow *more*, much like vampires.

"But the creature must work for him," I added. "I don't know what kind of demon it was, but it had gray skin, wings, and horns. Looked like a bull. She went that way." I pointed and noticed that my entire arm was shaking. "Over the buildings. I lost sight of her within seconds."

I swallowed, the worst part not having been said yet. "Luca, they know what she is."

"*Merda*," Luca swore in his native tongue. "*Veni con me*."

He took off, and though my body hadn't seemed to work properly before, just the knowledge that I wasn't alone in finding her, was enough to set me in motion. As the coven master requested, I followed.

The mage stormed through the park, calling out names, magical messages flying from him as balls of light that would deliver his directives. He led me to the edge of the greenspace, and one by one, members of our coven appeared from where they'd been looking for humans caught in Prince Wrath's reign of terror on the city.

Harper was among the last to join us. Her gaze landed on me and then scanned the area for Meredith.

My jaw tightened, my teeth grinding together so hard that, if I were human, they'd surely crack.

"Meredith was abducted," Luca announced. "Half of us will search for her, the other half will remain here and continue to assist any injured humans you find."

"But how?!" Harper cried, her face crumpling.

"A demon grabbed her and soared above the buildings," I spat out. "Took her away."

"Likely one of the prince's peons," Luca added.

"I'll help search for her," Harper stepped forward.

Luca nodded, pointed out a few others, and then repeated his order for the rest to continue helping the humans. The coven master's choices went unchallenged, and those who would remain near the Park were dispersing to fulfill our duties, when Shay and Hans rounded the corner, sweat beading their faces.

"We saw the texts about the prince and got here as soon as we could!" Hans shouted. "What's happening? Where is he?"

I closed my eyes, ignoring the way my muscles trembled with the need to act. The last thing I wanted to do was go over the issue *again*. I'd stood here long enough and needed to move. Meredith might be miles from the city by now. The Prince of Darkness might have—

No . . . A lump lodged in my throat.

Prince Orien had seemed far too smug before we fought, even for a prat of a prince. He'd offered us a place in the Darkborn, but when Meredith denied him, the saucy minx, he'd snapped.

"We'll use your power, whether you are with us or not, and when we're done with you . . . Well, then you'll learn what Hell is really like."

Those words, coupled with the fact that Josiah was gone, sent my usually still heart racing.

"They have a necromancer," I blurted out, the pieces coming together, pummeling rage through me so hard that, again, I found myself immobilized.

What the bleeding hell? I didn't freeze! I was a vampire. A royal. Once a sailor and a fighter. A *hunter* of the highest order. Freezing like prey was not in my nature.

What was going on with me?

"How can you be sure?" Shay asked.

"Nicoleta told Prince Orien about Meredith," I said for the benefit of everyone save Luca, "and he threatened that they'd use her power whether she joined them *or not*. Clearly, they have a human in play to absorb her magic. And if they transfer her power to someone they can control, the Darkborn can find the other *lapis caelesti* with greater ease."

"How so?" Shay's eyebrows pinched. "Meredith didn't know where the stones were when she found the Pearl. And she hasn't known where they are since then either. Seeing as she's touched one, more than almost anyone else, *she'd* know how to find them. But she hasn't."

"We don't know much about the stones, but some lore tells us that the stones wish to be together," I reminded her. "Now, the Darkborn have two *lapis caelesti*, that could make it easier to find the others. Particularly, if they can control a seeker's magic."

It was all theoretical, of course, but from the looks of horror on the others' faces, my idea made sense to them too.

"And Josiah did just escape from the coven dungeons and disappeared. I hate to say this, but it could be him." A muscle in Luca's jaw twitched.

One of our own, against us.

"Time is of the essence," Luca said. "Josiah still hasn't been found guilty of the murders of those in The Night Circle, but if he *is* guilty, and determined to take Meredith's magic too, her life is on the line."

Supernaturals rarely survived the barbaric process of necromancers for hire stealing their magic to place it within another being. Usually a human who wanted power. But Luca was referring to something even more horrific. For whatever reason, the murderous necromancer ripped the heart clean from their victims' chests. Using those methods survival went from rare to impossible.

The gaping hole in Lola's chest would haunt me for the rest of my life. If Josiah was guilty—which I was quickly coming to terms with as a genuine possibility—Meredith might meet that fate.

The urge to attack and dominate the necromancer burned so hot through me, I could barely breathe.

"How can we track her, though?" Harper asked, and I wrangled my attention back to the group, watched her sniff the air, trying to catch the scent of her roommate. "She flew."

"Shay?" Luca twisted.

Shay normally did not fly, in order to avoid human attention, but who would care now? The city was already in shambles. No humans walked the streets of New York. They were too busy hiding and fearing for their lives, and rightfully so. Before the humans retreated, Wrath had targeted their kind, terrorized them. Used his peons to possess them.

The Covenant would already have a hell of a time covering up the events of the day—erasing memories, cleaning up the prodigious damage. Why not add a half-angel soaring about?

Shay clearly agreed, as she leapt into the air and took flight.

Her white wings gleamed as she flew above the skyscrapers, and only then did I realize the sun was setting. This day, one that had started with an undercurrent of fear that had exploded into sheer mayhem, was slipping away.

Would Meredith vanish with it?

We all watched the nephilim with hope, though mine was mixed with that same pulsing fury that had gripped me since I'd watched the demon fly away with Meredith.

Shay soared from side to side, seemingly examining all angles of the sprawling metropolis, before descending. She landed lightly on the cracked cement.

"I didn't spot her. Or anyone in the air," Shay said, tone tight. "When exactly was she taken?"

"No more than ten minutes ago," I growled, sure of my estimate, though I had not glanced at my watch when she'd disappeared—hadn't thought to do such a thing in my panic.

"That probably means they didn't take her too far, right?" Harper piped up. "What if they're hiding away in a building? So many places nearby look like they've been ransacked. What if they're using one?"

"It makes more sense than traveling a great distance for the procedure," Luca admitted. "And I still think the Prince of Wrath would love to place a permanent headquarters somewhere like the city. There's prestige here."

"But we can't search all of New York," Hans said. "We need a lead."

"And you can't sense *anything*?" Luca asked him, his bushy eyebrows arched.

"No!" Hans shouted, his face turning red. "I'm Hell-blooded but not a fucking demon detector."

At that, the tide of rage that had been sloshing through me broke.

I stepped forward, fists clenched. "I don't bloody well care *how* we find her, but we have to move! *Now!*"

The others backed up. Luca's magic flared, Harper flinched, and even Hans blinked in fear.

Shockingly, though, Shay did not respond to my aggression. Instead, the nephilim moved closer, her blue eyes searching me. She cocked her head, like a dog listening, but I didn't know what for. I had excellent hearing, and no unusual sounds met my ears.

"Tobias," she breathed, "can you sense her?"

"What?" I gritted out, sweat dripping down my face from stress.

"Meredith. Can you sense her?"

"She *flew*, Shay. I can't hunt in the air."

What sort of idiotic nonsense was this?

"I don't mean can you *scent* her." The nephilim swallowed, and her hand moved slowly to her heart before falling away. It might have been an innocent gesture, but the look in Shay's eyes was too intense for that. "She drank your blood."

Pursed lips hinted that the half-angel suspected what I'd been feeling for days now. That the exchange of blood had changed things between Meredith and me. That, though I'd not been the one to take the witch's blood, it had changed things *inside* me too.

From the moment I'd met her, the witch had rubbed me the wrong way—she felt off. Too hard. Too opinionated. Most of all, too close for comfort, despite not knowing me at all. After Luca freed her magic, that sensation mounted to the point where, if I didn't drink liters of blood a day, I could not stand to be around her.

But since that fateful night in the New Haven Museum, when the witch drank my blood, I hadn't so much as *needed* the blood I drank as I had *used* it. A precaution for her and for me. Perhaps even for everyone around me. I didn't know. Bloodlust hadn't affected me for many years, but I knew one couldn't be too careful.

After all, Meredith was part of the coven now. I'd vowed to protect and assist those of my coven, which included not sucking blood from their veins.

Had there been more to the blood exchange, though? Something that tied us together in a way I hadn't expected? Or had that tie already been there?

Shay had hinted that she thought so. More than once, in fact. Giselle, my sire, had hinted too—that a bond was already in place. How were these women sensing these things? Oftentimes, where Meredith was concerned, I was too confused to discern one emotion from the next.

"Tobias?" Shay prodded, head tilted as if she was listening to words on the wind. "Meredith drank *your* blood. Can you sense it in her?"

"I—" My mouth slammed shut. Where only anger had boiled through me before, now something else took over.

My blood, so hot, so dangerous mere seconds before, was vibrating, just like the rest of me. No—not just vibrating. I blinked as the rage took a turn and stark realization sailed through me.

My blood is singing.

The song keened low, a chorus of hums that sometimes sounded like words, but most often not. Shay arched an eyebrow.

Had the nephilim heard it? But how?

"There's something inside you, isn't there?" Shay asked.

I didn't know what she was doing—if she was using angel magic, which her kind kept very secret, or if this was all in my imagination—but without a doubt she knew something had shifted.

My rage was broken, and the song of my blood, a vibration I did not understand but that had to mean *something*, took over. The force washed through me like a tsunami, significant, undeniable.

And it pulled me in one direction.

"North," I said, though that wasn't the precise direction the demon had gone. "I think, somehow, my blood bonded to her. Or maybe I do sense my own blood in her. I don't know, but we have to go north."

Shay exhaled. "I think you'd know best."

My brows knitted together, but this was no time to ask

questions. Ask what made her feel this way. Instead, I took off.

I ran slower than my vampiric speed would allow, but only because I was focusing on the pull, the song inside me. We did not have time for errors, so I needed to make sure I made none.

I'd gone two blocks when something yanked deep inside me, veering me right. A soft breath left me. Was the sensation growing stronger? The odd humming of the song louder?

I turned the corner, focused on my body.

Yes, the hum had amplified. I was on the right track.

"This way!" I yelled, aware that the others chased me, and Shay flew above.

We're coming, Meredith. Just hold on.

CHAPTER TWO

MEREDITH

THE RINGMASTER'S PEON, A GANGLY WIZARD WITH A RAT-LIKE face, tightened the straps around my wrists for the third time.

As if relishing my captivity, ravens cawed from where they perched on the open windowsills of the abandoned office building my captors had set up shop in.

The wizard moved down to my ankles, tightening the straps there with such force that it shook my body. I grunted, the straps digging in painfully. "If you're going to kill me, why not just knock me out?"

He sneered, "I suggested the same, but your old boss was against it." His eyes flashed to the side of the room, where Josiah and the Ringmaster spoke in hushed tones. They stood next to a table by the windows. The surface of the table was littered with bottles and other items, some sharp and glinting in the room's faint light. "Not so bright of you to work for her."

"Looks like you're doing the same thing," I spat back.

"Fuck no. I'm just on loan." He shook his head. "She's the type to enjoy the screaming as life drains from a person."

Ice slithered over my skin. He spoke like he'd heard that sound firsthand.

I wouldn't be surprised if he had. Unmasked, the Ringmaster might not be at all like I'd imagined her. Thanks to the hired bodies she'd sent to discipline me and the ominous black-silver mask and voice synthesizer she'd used when we spoke online, I'd always thought the Ringmaster was actually a man. As it turned out, I had never been face-to-face with the *real* Ringmaster. Still, I knew how she ticked.

She was brutal. Power-hungry. Sadistic. A woman who took revenge on those who had slighted her, with zero shits given. The person who'd owned me for years did not allow herself to be made a fool of . . . which was exactly what I'd done when I'd walked out on my debt.

Now that she'd found me, she had one aim. The Ringmaster intended to make me pay, with my magic *and* my life.

The wizard, done with me, turned and crossed over to the door, where the sulfur-reeking demon who'd lifted me off the streets stood guard.

Taking my chance, I pulled at the binds restraining me, trying to slip my slender wrists from them. They didn't budge, so carefully, I called on my hedge magic. That didn't work either. My teeth ground together. Of course, I wasn't great with my hedge magic yet—hell, I'd only known I had it for a couple of weeks—but I was sure it should have done *something*. There had to be magic on the restraints, nullifying my power.

Footsteps sounded, and I turned my neck to find the necromancer walking toward me, the Ringmaster at his side. The ravens by the window stayed put, watching Josiah, their master. A dozen more soared outside.

Maybe someone would see the birds and realize who controlled them, but that hope was only a sliver. We'd flown here, and I did not know where I was being held in the city. Far from Central Park, where the demon had swept me off the sidewalk, that was for sure. How would the coven track me in the air? Was that even possible?

"How about you let me handle this?" Josiah said in response to a whisper from the Ringmaster. Tension riddled his tone, as if my old boss had been trying to push him to do things her way.

She frowned. "It would be faster if I assisted."

At her words, the scars on my back tightened and my heart rate spiked.

For a long time, I believed she'd been the one to give them to me. Though, now that I learned she'd used a decoy to hide her identity, I knew that wasn't true, but I remained certain she was to blame. The marks I'd lived with for years, the lines made by a cane, were ordered there by her.

She was responsible for so much of my pain.

"Remember what happened before? I couldn't work with those witches if I wanted to." He arched an eyebrow and lifted a feather he'd been clutching, pointing it to his heart.

She shrugged. "I wanted to ensure the women were ready for you when you arrived."

My tongue went dry. I hadn't seen Lola or the other witch after they'd died, but I *had* seen the way Tobias and Luca reacted to finding Lola's body.

A shiver ran through me as I recalled Tobias's tense jaw, his roaming gaze as he assessed each person at the party as a threat or non-threat. He'd been handsome as ever, but there was no denying that Lola's death freaked him the hell out.

Rightfully so. Who expected to discover a body with a cavernous hole in her chest at a birthday party?

From what she'd just said and what I recalled from the

party's timeline, I gathered that the Ringmaster had torn open their chests before Josiah arrived. Perhaps she'd even pulled out the witches' hearts too. Apparently, she'd straight up murdered them under the guise of preparing their bodies for Josiah to do magic.

That woman was insane. I bet she relished slaying those witches.

"Like I said," Josiah replied after a prickly pause. "Let me handle it." He broke eye contact with the Ringmaster and caught me watching him. "Actually, I forgot something. Can you grab the bottle of sage oil?"

"Why?" the Ringmaster asked, lips pursed. "You never asked for me to have that on hand before. What's its purpose? Are you hiding things from me?"

My jaw tightened, an old, fearful reflex. If there was one way to piss off my old boss, it was to withhold information.

"Not intentionally. I told you I'm still learning about this," Josiah replied, annoyance lacing his tone. "Using sage oil is something I've heard about before and think we should try it. Some say it clarifies the area where magic is being performed."

"Which does what?"

"Ensures no power escapes." He paused. "You understand that even when you hold her magic, none of what I do will apply to you, right? You won't be a necromancer, you'll have seeker magic and that's it. We made a *deal.* I won't do this again. Not to anyone else."

She glared at him, glacial eyes seeming to glow dangerously. I had no idea what she was pissed about, but clearly Josiah had struck a nerve. "Don't put your limitations on me."

"I won't do this to anyone else," Josiah repeated. "One type of magic is enough."

She scowled. "I'll get your damned oil." She turned and marched back to the table.

The moment he was free of her, Josiah rushed over to my side.

"Meredith," he whispered. "I'm so sorry."

I scoffed. "Screw you."

"I'm going to keep you alive," he added.

My eyes narrowed. "Is that possible?"

"If the necromancer is very careful. And skilled."

Well, I was screwed.

"You killed Lola and that other witch," I growled. "Forgive me if I doubt your skill as much as I doubt your word."

He cringed. "*She* did that. They were both dead before I could even touch them. She was sure all I needed was the heart—the seed of power—but that's not true."

He checked that the Ringmaster was still at the table, searching for the vial. "I have to do this, but I can spare your life."

Maybe.

The word hung in the air between us, unsaid, light as the black feather in the necromancer's hand.

"Meredith," Josiah whispered. "She has Sara, the love of my life . . ." his voice cracked when he spoke his girlfriend's name.

A bigger person might have felt sorry for him, but I couldn't muster such pity. I'd barely had a chance to experience my own life, to know who I could become, and now it was all being taken away.

He's a weak-ass douche-canoe.

Josiah had the power of an elite coven behind him. Yes, the Ringmaster had, somehow, taken Sara and was threatening her. Perhaps the psycho was even threatening to try to steal

Sara's magic, in addition to my own. That would track with what I'd just heard, though how she expected to convince Josiah to do that for her was beyond the limits of what I could fathom.

Truly, I felt for Sara. She was sweet and innocent—a necromancer by birth and a healer at heart.

But the question remained: why the hell hadn't Josiah asked S&S for help? The option was there. As it had been when the coven offered to pay my debts to the Ringmaster.

Of course, I'd declined that help, but the circumstances were different. I'd only been gambling with my own welfare. Josiah, on the other hand, was gambling my magic. In all likelihood, my life too.

"She's crazy, you know that, right?" I said. "If you give her my magic, there's no telling what she'll do."

"I know," Josiah gulped. "But I have to. I—"

His excuse died on the back of a breath, as the Ringmaster appeared at his side, a brown bottle in her hand.

"Saying your goodbyes, Meredith?" My boss smirked down at me.

"As if I would waste my breath on him."

A wounded expression crossed Josiah's face, but no remorse cut through me.

We all made choices. His decision had been to screw me over. Now he had to live with it.

"Even as a girl, you had a sharp tongue. Let's hope your power is just as biting." The Ringmaster held up a bottle. "The sage oil."

Josiah took it. "Do you have the scalpel?"

"You didn't ask for that." The Ringmaster glared at him, and damn, if looks could kill, he'd be a goner.

It was so clear to me that, while she needed the necromancer, she did not enjoy being bossed around. After all, she was usually the one commanding others, most with deadly skillsets.

As if her thoughts were in line with mine, instead of moving to retrieve the blade, the Ringmaster snapped her fingers. "Jazco! Get the instruments!"

The wizard detached himself from where he'd been lingering at the doorway with the winged demon and walked to the table the Ringmaster had been perusing. The way he moved was cat-like, loping, but not nearly as graceful as most felines. He was too tall, too gangly for grace.

"What do you need?"

"The scalpel," the Ringmaster barked at him. Then she turned to Josiah again. "Anything else, necromancer? A saw, perhaps?"

I tensed, and the corners of her lips pulled upward, the word having hit its intended mark.

"I told you, we don't need to cut deep," Josiah murmured.

"But it's so much more fun."

"Psycho," I snarled.

"*Revolutionary,*" the Ringmaster corrected me, and for the first time, I glimpsed what might motivate her.

I'd assumed she wanted power, but did she want to use that power for something she really believed in? Had she been doing so behind the scenes while I worked for her?

As Jazco's slender fingers plucked up the scalpel, and he came our way, my questions disintegrated.

What did it matter what her motivations were or that she was working with the Darkborn to fulfill them? Josiah might hope to spare my life, but even if he could—which I doubted—the Ringmaster wouldn't allow me to keep breathing.

I owed her, and I didn't believe my magic would be

enough to cover my debt. For the Ringmaster, blood would be the only suitable payment for my betrayal.

"Here you are." Jazco offered the blade to the Ringmaster.

Before she could take it and plunge it into me, Josiah snatched it from the wizard's hand so that the implement joined the black feather he carried.

The Ringmaster snorted delicately. "Any last words, Meredith? Messages you'd like us to pass on to your loved ones?"

What a bitch. She knew I had no one in my life. Why would I sign on to do her dirty work if I had even a single fallback?

But I couldn't let her know she got under my skin.

"As if you would."

"I've always been a monster to you, child, but I'm not without my reasons. Nor humanity." Ice-blue eyes I'd seen a million times behind a black-silver mask glinted down at me. "I'm making the offer. Don't stomp on it with that defiant little heel of yours. People you love might need closure."

Tobias's face—the way he watched me as I'd woken in the coven's infirmary—flashed in my mind's eye. I blinked, and a strange vibration trilled through me. Before it could latch on, though, I shook the sensation away.

I'd known Tobias for little more than two weeks. Though we stood on more solid ground than before, and I was certainly attracted to him, the vampire wasn't what I'd call a loved one. Hell, he was barely a friend—more like someone I was starting to trust.

For me, trust took a long time to grow. The only exceptions to that rule remained Harper and Shay. Probably because the latter wouldn't take no for an answer when it came to being friends. The nephilim had shoved her way into my heart and pulled the more serious wolf along with her.

Besides, even if Tobias was someone I'd consider family, why have the Ringmaster send whatever macabre note she had in mind? What would be the point?

Knowing who murdered me would only torture anyone who loved me.

"I don't want that," I said. "It's kinder to let them think I vanished."

The Ringmaster smirked. "Spoken like a true shadow in the night. Get to work, necromancer."

A bead of sweat trailed down Josiah's face as he lifted first the feather and then the scalpel, the latter aimed at my heart.

CHAPTER THREE

GUNNER

DEEP IN THE RAINY WOODS OF ENGLAND, SILAS AND I FOLLOWED three witches toward a house in the distance.

These witches were connected to a *lapis caelesti*, the Opal of Heaven specifically. Did they know more of the other sacred gems too? They were largely a mystery but one thing was plain as day; these ladies reeked of magic.

They also had to be at least seventy, and the elders in my pack were the ones with the most information. Wise Ones we called them. Those wolves were revered, though they could no longer run far and fast or fight, and were just below the alpha in importance.

Pa, the Alpha of the Blood Moon Pack, had two primary betas who he trusted with his life, and he'd shown me time and time again that he trusted the Wise Ones just as much.

I hoped that when I became alpha, I'd have the same strong relationship with the Wise Ones.

"How many live out here?" Silas asked, peering about. It was dark and rainy, though the fae was protected from the water by a magical shield. The witches were too, actually. I, the shifter of the bunch, was the only one soakin' wet.

But I didn't care 'bout that. There were more important things. Like was he asking for numbers because the fae sense more magic around us? A potential attack?

I scanned the women. I'd been trained to assess threats since I was a pup. Far as I could tell, there was no scent of magic in the air. Just the smell of rain and greenery, ferns and damp bark. These ladies were doin' just as they said—showing us to their home. They'd claimed we might be able to help, and seein' as we'd come here for their help too, I was pleased as moon punch to oblige.

"At all times, eight wardens exist to protect lost knowledge," Miriam Black, the very woman with access to Meredith's vault in *Le Bastion*, replied.

My ears perked up. She hadn't quite answered my partner's question. Did more live here? Or just the eight?

Time to dig.

"Do you all live here, though?" I asked. "It's a big place. Could fit more."

Then again, my family's home was just as large and our plantation home didn't seem near big enough for five. When my Ma or my brother went on a tear, it was all Pa, my sister, and I could do to stay outta their way. No need to talk about that though.

"It suits our needs," Miriam replied, not bothering to look back at me.

Another non-answer.

I shot Silas a warning look. The fae nodded, his silver-white hair shining in the moonlight.

In less than a week, that same moon would be full as a

summer peach and calling to me. By then I'd be home, runnin' through the forests of New England, singing her praises.

The only thing that could be better would be being back in North Carolina, with my own pack, racin' my sister through our land and scarfin' down Pa's beta's famous barbecue and homemade vinegar sauce the day after our full moon fun.

A pang ripped through my heart. I loved being surrounded by other wolves, loved the camaraderie and how we understood the others' need to be together. But as much as I missed those days, I didn't go home too often. What I did was important, and I wanted to make a name for myself before I inherited the honor of alpha.

I needed something apart from the Bryant name to show others I deserved the power bestowed on my family. Something to make Ma believe I was worthy of followin' in Pa's footsteps.

"Touch nothing," the short witch with the raspy voice said as we approached the door to the home. "And say nothing."

"You hidin' us from your roomies or something?" I gave the witches a cheeky grin.

"The others are *sleeping*," Miriam replied, twisting so we could feel the full effect of her steely blue stare. "We do not wish to disturb them."

"Oh, right."

I guessed it was late, though I didn't know exactly what time. We'd traveled so long to get here, and I hadn't been concerned with the time when we'd been searching for this place.

I patted my pocket, hopin' to peek at my phone. It wasn't there. Aw, hell. I'd left the damned thing in the car so it wouldn't give away our approach.

A frown pulled at my lips. What if Luca was trying to contact me?

My questions fell away as the witches led us inside their manor, and the stoutest witch with the smoker's voice motioned for me to stop.

"We don't want water all over our floors. You need drying off." She extended her hand, whispered a spell, and warm air blasted me, drying my clothes.

As the magic worked, I locked away the fact that this woman was probably a caster, like Hans. His type of witch used spells to work anything more than basic magic. The more spells a caster knew, the more powerful they were. I'd bet, given her age, that this woman had learned a whole heck of a lot of spells.

Once I was dry, the spell fell away, and I could focus on gettin' the lay of the land. I sniffed. Scents of their craft—honey, sage, rosemary, and the faintest hint of something darker—filled the air. My eyebrows screwed together as I tried to discern what that last aroma might be, but I couldn't focus for long before the crones took off down the corridor.

"Follow us closely," Miriam barked, as if that wasn't the very damned thing we'd been doin' all along.

"Bossy like my sister," I muttered low enough the grannies couldn't hear.

Silas let out a dry laugh. "Don't go mistaking them for family."

In other words, don't let the wolves into the henhouse.

And this time, I ain't the wolf.

I smirked at the private joke, but nodded to the fae. Silas and I were ideal partners, as we balanced one another well. Where I was more the wheelin' and dealin' type, he was careful, calculating.

The witches led us to a room dominated by a circular table ringed with eight chairs. In the center of the table, a small tree grew, and on it gems gleamed. I took them in, recognizing the colors and deciphering a pattern.

"Are those meant to represent the *lapis caelesti*?" Silas asked, beating me to the punch.

"They are," Miriam replied, pushing a lock of short gray hair out of her glittering blue eyes. "How much do you know of the sacred stones?"

"Others in our coven research them, and I have basic knowledge, but nothin' too deep," I admitted.

"I can't imagine that those researchers find information readily," Miriam replied, arching a gray eyebrow.

"No," I answered, thinking of how many times I'd heard Toby cussin' a blue storm about the *lapis caelesti*.

Sure, he'd found information, but most of it was basic. Toby was used to knowing *everything* and getting what he wanted. The fact that so much about the stones evaded him, pissed the vampire off.

"That's as designed," said the witch with long gray hair. She had an accent but it was faint and I couldn't tell what it was. "We're the keepers of the most important knowledge surrounding the *lapis caelesti*. It's our job to ensure that little is known on the subject."

"But people know about the Pearl of Hell," Silas pointed out. "So why are there tales of that stone?"

"Sometimes, secrets simply cannot be kept, no matter how hard we try. Now, take a seat." Miriam gestured to the table and then nodded at the long-haired witch. "Can you get the wine?"

Miriam and the shortest crone swept to the table as the other witch poured two glasses of wine. My partner and I took up seats, waiting for the niceties to be over so we could get down to business.

Once the goblets were good and full, she handed them to me and Silas with a smile. "I'm Claire. If you want water, we have that too."

"How 'bout a beer?" I asked, hopeful.

"Afraid not."

"This'll do." I toasted her and sipped the wine, which was actually pretty darn good. For wine.

"And I'm Gloria," the third said, her voice deep and raspy, fitting her stout frame and stern gaze.

Claire settled into her seat, the wood creaking beneath her. "We were on watch tonight."

"Do you have a watch every night?" Silas asked carefully, taking a sip of his wine as he leaned back in his chair.

"Perhaps you'll find out," Miriam replied. "But first, what are your names? Unless you prefer us to continue calling you Wolf and Fae? Or the intruders?"

"You haven't called us anything," Silas said.

"Not that *you* can hear," Gloria laughed dryly. "This coven, though small, has very particular gifts."

So, they could speak mind-to-mind, like my kind could do in wolf form. I'd not heard of a group of witches who could do that before. It set me on edge.

Silas leaned forward, propping his elbows on the table. "How did you manage that feat?"

"We've been around a long time, boy," Gloria grunted.

"As have I," Silas retorted. "Three hundred years."

The stout witch arched an eyebrow. "Well, if *we* learned how to mind-link, you certainly should have figured it out by now. You're positively ancient!"

A roar of laughter burst out of me, which earned me a glower so fierce from my partner it could peel paint off a barn.

Gloria softened a touch, but my laughter didn't do anything to loosen up the other women. Actually, Miriam seemed mighty inclined to pretend things were business as usual.

Kinda like an English vamp I know. Must be a redcoat thing.

"Sorry," I whispered to Silas as my mirth faded. "She caught me off guard."

"You and me both," Silas muttered beneath his breath. "But a show of solidarity is appreciated."

"I know, man. Got carried away."

"If you're quite done," Miriam's voice rang out, "perhaps you can finally tell us your names. Then we can proceed?"

"Sure thing, Miss," I said, momentarily returning to my schoolboy days, when I'd been reprimanded for talking outta turn too much. "I'm Gunner Ray Bryant."

"Silas Aztraca," my partner said tersely.

"Do you live here now, Silas?" Claire asked.

"I do."

"Which Court? The fae often cross over in my homeland. I'm always curious as to where they came from."

The Irish lilt in Claire's voice grew a little stronger, maybe cause talkin' about her home brought it out of her. She musta lived in England a long time for it to fade that much. I'd been outta North Carolina for nearly five years, and most of the time I still sounded like I just came back from a fish fry.

"I relocated from the Winter Court two hundred years ago."

I listened with interest. I hadn't known all that about Si.

The witches' eyes widened.

"How?" Claire asked. "From what we've learned, no one has entered or left that court in nearly five hundred years."

"That's untrue," Silas said. "The royals travel, though not much. My mother and father worked for them, and traveled too. On one trip, they took me with them and paid someone to smuggle me into this world. They wanted a fair chance for me, one I wouldn't get in the Winter Court. I've observed parents doing the same here."

"Of course," Gloria said. "But why not remain in Faerie, or at least Isila? Why come to the human realm?"

She sounded like so many mortals from this world did when they spoke of the other realm. Awed. Wistful. To me, Isila didn't deserve that, but witches and many other supernaturals never visited Isila.

I'd only been on one trip to the other realm, and never wanted to go back. It was a hard place. Dog eat dog. Or on the island I'd visited wolf eat wolf.

"If you lived in the Winter Court, you'd understand." Silas folded his hands on the table, hintin' that the matter was closed.

Gesturing to the tree in front of us, I chimed in, ready to change up the topic. "So, we know these represent the sacred stones, but why?"

Miriam's expression softened as it fell upon the center-piece. "That is a reminder of our wee coven's purpose."

"I'm a simple man, so I gotta say, I'd love to be enlightened a bit more about that."

Miriam's lips quirked upward. "As Claire said, we're keepers of knowledge of the *lapis caelesti*. We are also responsible for training the seven chosen to hold and protect the stones when they're ready."

I blinked. "You're tellin' me there's been a coven of women

like you around for . . ." I trailed off. I had no idea when the *lapis caelesti* had been hidden away; that was much more a Toby fact.

"Thousands of years, yes," Miriam supplied. "Women of my bloodline have always served. The same can be said of Claire and Gloria."

"Is it always the ladies who do this?"

"No, but it is in my family. We have one male *Arcacusto* in our coven right now."

"*Aracac—*" The word got stuck in my throat.

"We are *Arcacusto,*" Gloria hissed. "Derived from 'secret-keeper.' Is everyone in your organization such a simpleton?"

"'Fraid not. Just me." I shrugged, used to such talk. Toby, Luca, and Hans were the scholars in S&S and they often had to enlighten this old Southern Boy.

"It's been the same families? Always?" Silas looked intrigued by the idea.

"Yes," Claire answered.

"Might I ask . . ." Silas interjected. "Does your rather unique coven have a name?"

"The *Abscondita,*" Claire answered.

"The Hidden," Silas translated.

"Precisely. We are tasked to wait here for when the seven arrive."

"Do they have a fancy name too?" I asked, 'cause it seemed like they must. Wolves in this world preferred more straightforward names, but mages, vampires, fae, and witches liked puffed up titles.

Like *Abscondita.* What a mouthful.

"Of course they do," Miriam scoffed. "The seven to whom the stones are entrusted, can wield the stones in times of danger. They are the most important people on the planet."

"We call them the *Vindix*," Claire added.

"Champions," Silas told me.

"Now you're just showin' off," I muttered.

"You live by Yale," the fae retorted. "Take advantage of it."

I did, just not the same way many of my coven members did. So I brushed off his remark and soldiered on.

"Alright, so they're the *Vindix*. Since you recognized her name, it seems like y'all already know about Meredith and think she's one of the chosen ones. How 'bout the others? Are they here?"

Miriam eyed the other two women for a moment before a sigh parted her lips. "Unfortunately, Meredith is the only one we're familiar with."

"How can that be?" Silas asked, his eyes wide.

"Her mother's line were the keepers of the Opal of Heaven and they are the only ones who kept in touch with the *Abscondita*. There were a . . . number of catastrophes in history that had to do with the *lapis caelesti*. After that, some families hid from us, thinking they'd be safer. As the world grew larger, they had an easier time of concealing themselves."

"You and Mrs. Stone spoke, and that's how she knew to put your name on the vault in *Le Bastion*?" I pressed, needing to put the pieces together.

"In case of a disaster." A look of exhaustion crossed her face before vanishing. "Because unfortunately, disaster tends to follow the seven families of the *Vindix* lines."

"But if you lost touch, how do you know that all seven *Vindix* are alive? What if the family lines died out?" Silas asked, sipping at his wine faster. I followed suit. If ever there was time for a drink, this was it.

"There were signs," Gloria replied this time. "Ones we knew to look for."

"Like?" Silas prodded.

"The night of the first *Vindix*'s birth, a shower of stars filled the sky in seven key locations around the world." Gloria's narrow eyes shone with the memory. "That same phenomenon occurred six more times afterward, all within the span of seven years."

"We were to look for a rare celestial phenomenon repeated seven times in rapid succession," Miriam added. "That fit the bill. And when I learned of Meredith's birth—she was the fifth *Vindix* born, according to the astrological signs—I knew it was true."

"So did you know about the Pearl being unearthed when we did?" I asked.

"We too felt the magical phenomenon when the Pearl came to light," Miriam said with a nod. "Of course, most supernaturals would feel it but have no bleeding idea what it meant. Only those who were looking for the signs would recognize the significance. Which brings me to the question . . . Why is your coven looking for the *lapis caelesti*?"

I leaned back, crossing my arms over my chest. "We're dark artifact hunters, and our coven master knew that if they got in the wrong hands, the stones could be real bad for the world. So he wanted to be the one to find them. I don't think he knows about the *Vindix*. Or any of this." I gestured to the room at large.

"Are you sure he wouldn't use them for evil?" Miriam asked.

"Luca? *Never*."

There was more I could add, that Luca wished to keep them out of the mitts of very powerful people who weren't even in *this* world, but that wasn't my tale to tell.

Miriam, Gloria, and Claire stared at me, as if assessing whether I was tellin' the truth. Finally, Claire stood.

"I think that's enough for tonight. We should show them to a room," she said. "You're staying for the night, correct?"

A surprised glance passed between Silas and me.

Not that I didn't appreciate the gesture. After all that travel, I was flat beat. But really, I hadn't been expecting these ladies to offer us anything, so a bed was above and beyond.

The sweet British gal manning the inn we'd planned to stay at flashed through my mind. I coulda had a lot of fun with her, and the wolf inside me was already whining for that kind of touch and affection, but I nodded. S&S business had to come before pleasure.

"If you're offerin', we're stayin'," I replied. "We have many more questions, but you're right, they can wait until morning."

"Remember the other members of our coven are sleeping," Gloria said as the women rose, as if anticipating that we'd start yammering—which, actually, with me . . . was probably a pretty good guess. I hated too much silence.

A hush fell over the group as the women led us through their home. The deeper into the manor we went, the more I discovered I'd been wrong about its size. It had seemed large from outside, but I was pretty damned sure there must be a spell on it. There were too many hallways. It shouldn't have been possible.

We took one more turn, and the crones began to descend steps. A damp smell filled my nostrils, and the nape of my neck tingled.

"You showin' us to the suites?" I joked.

"Of a sort," Miriam replied, turning and smiling.

That curl of her lips should have been my first sign that

something was up. But I brushed it off, and when we got to the bottom of the stairs and Claire pointed out two doors next to each other, I exhaled.

They probably just didn't want outsiders sleepin' too close to them. I could understand that. You had to protect your own.

"Your rooms. There's a connecting door, should you two wish to hold a meeting." Claire raised an eyebrow like maybe she thought a *meeting* might be something more.

"Guys can be good lookin', but I'm an admirer of females only," I said to set the record straight.

Claire looked to the fae.

He shrugged. "We're far more fluid, but Gunner's a bit muscle-bound for my taste. And talkative."

Claire smirked. "What a shame."

Okay, things were officially gettin' weird. Time to hit the hay.

I went to the door and stepped into the room. A grin spread on my face as my eyes raked over it. This was nice, something even my Ma would like.

I was about to thank the witches, when a cold chill cut through the warmth budding inside me.

Magic.

I spun in time to see Miriam slam the door in my face. To the right, another door slammed shut, and I heard Silas yelling through the wall.

Lunging forward, I gripped the handle and twisted. Locked. And not just with metal, but with a spell.

"You'll only hurt yourself if you try to get out," Gloria's gruff tone seeped through the door. "Or shift."

"How?!" I growled, pissed that their hospitality was takin' a mean turn. Especially if it affected my ability to shift.

"Your wine will make shifting excruciating. And the wards will keep you in place," Gloria replied. "We must be sure that you are who you say you are. If Meredith comes here looking for you, if she can find us, we'll release you."

"And what if she can't?" I asked, recalling how long it had taken us.

Seekers could use their magic to find *things*, but not people. What if when we didn't return to New Haven, Luca decided not to risk sending her?

"Then measures will need to be taken," Gloria said. "Memory erasure. Perhaps more."

My fists clenched, but I knew better than to fight back. Already, the magic in the room was working against me, suffocating my inner animal.

Isolation. A wolf's worst nightmare.

This coven had gotten one over us, and though I hated it, it seemed like I'd have to sit tight and wait for S&S to make a move.

CHAPTER FOUR

SHAY

I soared high above the streets of New York, relishing the air that ruffled my feathers. Below, I tracked Tobias's movements as he searched for Meredith. It would soon be night. Would we find her before dark?

If anyone can, it's him.

The certainty in my thought shook me. I wasn't sure how I'd known he'd be the one who could find her. Some angels had great intuition, though I'd never claimed that power. But as I'd studied the vampire earlier, I'd felt something, *heard* something, and somehow, I'd known it was a connection to Rooms.

That Tobias was the key to finding her.

Once that girl was safe, I was abso-freaking-lutely having a talk with the vampire, because I was getting the sense from him that I wasn't the only person feeling something was off.

Plus, I just wanted the DL on how he felt about Rooms. I was pretty sure he had a thing for her, and I was getting likey-likey vibes from her too. She tried to hide it, but I had a tried-and-true radar for romance. There was *totally* something there.

I glanced down, checking that I was still soaring above Tobias, and then twisted to verify that the others ran behind. I was the bridge between the vampire and those who lagged, so I had to stay within their line of sight.

As it did every time I looked back, my gaze caught on Hans, his blond hair gleaming in the setting sun. Before I could stop myself, my attention dipped to take in his arms, the tats climbing them, how his muscles bulged as he ran.

Inwardly, I groaned at the tragedy of it all.

Lilith! Of all the demonesses, why did he have to be related to her?

I might be able to overlook his dark side. Heck, I might savor it even. Who didn't like a bad boy? But his mother and the power she possessed . . . the power she might have passed to him . . . that was too dangerous. Even if he didn't act it, having Lilith's blood in his veins was some seriously bad juju.

Dad would be furious. If he ever bothered to pop into this world . . .

Before I could go too far down that road, I pulled myself out of those thoughts. Considering my parents would only cause me misery.

Luckily, a distraction presented itself right away, as Tobias veered closer to a building and stopped. My heart began to race. Had he found her?

I swooped down, waving my hands to catch the others's attention. Of course Hans was the one to see. He shot me a thumbs-up and a hopeful look.

Instead of reciprocating the gesture, I merely dove and landed on the cement next to Tobias. He stared up the side of a dilapidated building that, judging by the bold geometric motifs typical of art deco, had once probably been stunning.

"You think she's here?" I asked skeptically.

"My body says yes. And it's the perfect place to hide out," the vampire replied.

"Looks unstable."

"All the better. Who would suspect?"

If he said so. Personally, if I were to hide out somewhere, I'd like there to be Egyptian cotton sheets and room service.

"How do you know, though?" My gaze raked over him, trying to pinpoint what I observed earlier.

Tobias tore his attention from the building and arched an eyebrow, so I rushed to continue.

"Back by Central Park, something was telling me that you would know. And now you feel different, more vibrating-y or something. What does it mean?"

This was freaking hilarious. I was basically asking him to explain my own intuition.

"I thought you'd be able to explain that yourself," Tobias replied slowly.

"I . . . can't."

He sighed. "I'm not sure I understand it either, what I felt or what you sensed. All I know is that my blood sang, and something inside pulled me in a specific direction."

"*Sang?*"

"Yes. It was rather odd."

I snorted. "Just a touch."

We said no more because at that moment the others arrived, their breathing deep, chests heaving.

"*Here?*" Harper asked, her tone high with disbelief.

"See?" I said to the vampire, "I'm not the only one who thinks this is a horrible place for a hideout."

"This is the place," Tobias confirmed. "I—"

Suddenly a cacophony of caws rang out. Everyone looked upward, and I gasped. A flock of ravens had soared up to the building and now circled as if they were just waiting around. The behavior might not draw attention normally but I took it as a sign.

"Josiah," Tobias growled.

Luca cocked his head, the question of how in the world the vampire could possibly have known to come here was written clearly on his face, but instead of asking, the mage rolled with it, showing his trust in Tobias, and turned to the others.

All together, we had a team of eight, each with a strong set of skills for their species, which ran the gamut of two wizards —one with demon blood—a mage, a vampire, a nephilim, two shifters, and one siren.

"I think we should split into pairs," Luca said, "and each duo sticks with another until you can't any longer. But always, and I mean *always*, stay within view of your partner."

"I'm with Tobias," Hans said.

The vampire didn't even turn. His neck remained craned upward to stare at the building, but he did nod slightly, accepting Hans's bid. The two weren't friends, but they were among the strongest in the coven.

From how Tobias had reacted when Meredith was taken, we all suspected he'd go in guns-blazing. Hans could keep up, and if there were demons in there, his dark magic might be able to battle theirs.

"Shay and I are together." Harper came to stand by me.

Luca agreed and chose the other wolf, Avon, to fight alongside him, leaving the final pair to be a wizard and siren. Then he pointed to my team and Tobias's. "You four, stick together. If anyone will find her, it's you. We'll have your backs and do our best to search."

"Ready," Tobias said, looking seconds away from jumping out of his skin.

The only reason he was still even standing here was that he respected Luca and the coven so much.

"Go," Luca said. "We'll follow."

We rushed into the building, Tobias and Hans taking the front, Harper and me right behind. My roommate remained in her human form, but I already sensed the wolf in her just begging to come out. There was always a strange tension around wolves before they shifted. Harper was exhibiting that in spades.

Inside, a run-down office building with an astonishing amount of space spread before us. The lobby boasted forty-foot-high ceilings, and the floor was made of white marble with onyx streams running through it like arterial rivers. On the opposite wall, a staircase switch-backed its way up three floors. A busted-up desk that had once probably accommodated three security people was positioned in the middle of the lobby.

"This way." Tobias moved toward the staircase. "I doubt this place has electricity, so the elevator won't work. She's on the top floors."

"How sure are you?" Did we have to search all the floors on the way up?

"Quite sure. I feel—bloody hell!"

He skidded to a stop as six winged demons fell from a level above to land at the base of the steps, fangs bared.

Light flashed through me, and I cupped the beam in one hand. In the other, a sword of flame and light—a token of Archangel Uriel, my father—flared to life. Harper shifted, a snarl ringing from her lips, and Hans's magic was at the ready.

"What the hell are those?" I barked, watching the beasts who blocked our way.

"The same kind that took her." The vampire caught the half-wizard's eye. "What are they, Hans?"

"How should I know?!" he snapped, face reddening. "Let's just kick their asses!"

But before we could launch an assault, someone yelled, "Behind you!"

I spun to find our adversaries had doubled, and another batch of demons was attacking the other team.

"No more distractions. Fight your way up the stairs," Tobias growled, his irises tinged red in a way that only happened when a vampire was either really hungry or super pissed.

The demons might be hulking with muscles and have four-inch-long talons, but if they had a shred of sense, they would also be scared.

One roared and lumbered forward.

Sweet, they're idiots. I lifted my flaming sword. *Should be easier to beat.*

I leapt into the air, thankful the building's high ceilings would give me a chance to pummel them from a different angle. The others had the floor covered; already, two demons lay dead from a mage strike and one from vampire fangs. If I could pull a couple away from the main group, that would be a huge help.

Unfortunately for me, I attracted a bit more attention than I'd hoped. And not from below.

Another waterfall of demons fell from whatever floor they were amassing on above. Three of the brutes beat their wings to come to a halt mid-air right in front of me. Drool dripped down the chin of the closest one as he broke into a horrible smile.

"Ang," he grunted, swiping his meaty hand at me.

Jagged claws came within inches of my face, but I jerked back in time and retaliated, slamming my sword of fire and light straight into his gut.

He roared, and blood spurted, dotting my sleeves as he writhed. But no matter his size and strength, it was only seconds before the angelic magic in my sword took hold and the beast fell.

"Watch your heads!" I hoped my team could hear my warning over the fight now raging below.

The other two monsters from the underworld struck quickly, and again, I swung my sword. They seemed to have learned from their buddy's swift death, because they were careful to tag team me, one approaching from the front while the other closed in at my back—or sometimes surging from below or diving from above. Always, they were quick to retreat.

Within ten seconds of our aerial dance, however, I learned something important: whatever type of demon this was, it didn't seem to have magic. If they did and they weren't using it, these creatures were stupider than I thought—and I already believed them to be of base intelligence.

Though I was much smaller, I had the advantage. I just needed to maneuver myself so I was not getting bombarded from both sides.

I veered right and barely dodged a set of claws ripping into my wings. Predictably, the other swooped in right away, striking from the front.

I swung my sword, and managed to graze his shoulder. The demon howled in pain as my heavenly magic blazed through him, and he clutched the wound, soaring upward.

A quick glance behind told me the monster was still in retreat at my back.

I spun in the air and backed up, ensuring both demons were in front of me. Then, calling on my inner angelic light, I extended my hand to send a beam from my palm, straight into the closer foe.

My assault seared right through the demon's chest, and he fell with a shriek of pain. A grin spreading across my face, I turned my attention to the one above. His red eyes were wide as he worked out what was coming.

Too slow, bucko.

I blasted him, the power surging from me, lighting me up from inside. My palms glowed white, and the veins shifted dangerously from blue to crimson as the magic traveled through me. Heat followed, flooding me, and I swallowed down the building pain. Burning out wasn't too far away. I had to hurry.

Thankfully, my opponent had slowed, and I had enough strength to hold onto my beam of light, fighting my own pain as I followed him with the light until it cut him in half.

As the pieces fell, I released my magic with a sigh of relief. Immediately, my veins returned to normal, no longer red and glowing beneath my skin. Any longer, and I would have been on the edge of burning out.

Just like in Le Bastion. I shook my head. I needed to be more careful.

Angelic magic was dangerous, only pure angels could handle it without repercussions. As a half-breed, I used my light minimally and trained mostly with my sword. Using great blasts of power in rapid succession could literally burn me to death from within.

More than one nephilim had met that fiery end.

Though I'd always been scared of that, now that we were at

war with demons, I wondered if my reliance on my sword had done me a disservice.

I'll have to practice more wi—aargh!

Claws dug into my wings, and the putrid stench of sulfur flooded my nostrils as yet another beast from the underworld fell from a floor above.

Using all my strength, I twisted, calling my sword of fire and light, and slammed it into his chest. But I was too slow to avoid blowback, and the brute managed to get in another strike, his talons piercing my non-dominant arm. I dropped the sword, which disappeared into the aether, leaving me wide open as I beat my wings to stay aloft.

The demon growled, the hot stench of his breath rolling over me before the hole in his chest did its work. He fell like a boulder, leaving me alone in the air.

An exhale parted my lips, and relief sailed through me—but only for a moment.

Suddenly, stars began to appear in my vision. I tried to blink them away, but to no avail. When the reason for them hit me, I swore.

My shoulder throbbed like hell, but adrenaline had seen me through, so I hadn't thought it was too bad. How wrong I was.

Blood poured from the wound, which somehow seemed inches bigger than it had seconds before. My wing, too, looked ragged, and with each beat, pain pulsed through it with a little more intensity.

I was bleeding too much. And I was thirty feet in the air.

As if to hammer that terrifying point home, a cloud of darkness crept in on the edges of my vision.

Freaking out, I descended as quickly as I could with an

injured wing. It wasn't fast enough. I made it only about halfway before my compromised wing gave out.

"Help!" I yelled as I fell, my other wing fluttering madly to slow my descent.

"Got you, Shay!" a voice called out above the guttural roar of a demon and the defiant howl of a wolf. "Stop trying to fly!"

Though I was close enough to hit the marble floor and not die, broken bones weren't out of the question, so I did as the person asked, allowing my body to free-fall as I wrenched my eyes shut.

"*Oof!*" I grunted as, seconds later, hands caught me, and I jostled a little.

"Oh, thank God," I opened my eyes and tensed.

Hans stared back at me, sweat trailing the thin scar along his jawline. "You good?"

"Uh, yeah," I croaked. Why did he need to be the one to save me? "Thanks. I can stand."

He set me down gently so that I stood on my feet. I took a step, but it was no good. I collapsed to the ground, right on top of my injured wing.

"Mother effer!" I gripped my shoulder, slapping wetly at the blood there.

"That's *your* blood?" Hans asked incredulously. "Why did you say you're okay?"

"Of course it's mine!" I snapped. "Why do you think I couldn't fly?"

"I didn't think about that. There's so much . . ." He trailed off. "I thought maybe it was all demon blood. Your hair covered the wound."

"I got cut with a talon, after it attacked my wing." I gasped and tears pricked my eyes when I tried to roll off my wing.

"Let me see."

"I can do it my—" A whimper left me as I tried to sit up, and I collapsed again, right into Hans's tattooed arms. I groaned. Good grief, it was like the heavens were testing me!

But despite being super uncomfortable, I didn't protest when Hans maneuvered me to the side of the room, away from the rest of the fighting.

"Are we winning?" I asked, trying to take my mind off the fact that a demon was touching me. That I didn't know how to handle this scenario with the grace my kind should exhibit.

"Yeah. Luca and Tobias just left to go upstairs."

"But Tobias is your partner!"

"He saw I had you and they pivoted. Luca's partner is still here, so the numbers are even. All the demons are almost gone." A shadow dripped in his voice, and I wondered if he felt for them. "I'm going to lay you down."

He did so gently, putting most of my weight on my uninjured side. "Let me have a look at your wounds."

"Fine," I murmured, no longer possessing the strength to fight his ministrations. Those stars had returned, plaguing my vision, the darkness creeping in from the edges.

Hans bent over me, and his scent, freshly clean with a hint of motor oil, washed over me. Part of me relaxed, but then I caught myself and tensed.

"Chill," Hans muttered, prying my wet, blood-soaked hair from the wound.

He sounded annoyed. Surely, he'd noticed how uncomfortable I seemed. Yet, he was still helping. Why didn't that make it any better?

"Shay, this is bad," Hans whispered a second later. "We're going to need a—*oh no.*"

"What?"

The word was just out of my mouth when the reek of sulfur hit me, and yet another demon dropped from above to land mere feet from us.

We were too far from the others for them to help in time, and I cried out in pain as Hans maneuvered himself out from where he'd been supporting my weight and leapt to his feet.

My heart rate spiked as the demon lunged, and a new round of stars burst in my vision, obscuring everything.

Panicking, I tried to rise, and a scream wrenched its way up my throat as I fell back to the ground, right on my bum wing. My head collided with the marble, and darkness began to descend in earnest.

The last thing I saw before unconsciousness took me were black tendrils soaring through the air, wrapping around the demon's neck, and choking the life from the beast.

CHAPTER FIVE

MEREDITH

My chest ached something fierce.

Though the line Josiah had cut into my skin just below my collarbone was fairly shallow, it stretched all the way from shoulder joint to shoulder joint, curling up at each end in a macabre smile.

And as if the gash in my skin wasn't enough, the necromancer was waving a raven feather over the wound, 'cleansing' the area. Like I was dirty or something. Plus, the process kept wafting the strong aroma of sage oil, dripped all around my body, right up my nostrils, making me feel nauseous. Between the laceration and the knowledge of what had happened to the Night Circle witches, I should be terrified, but the strange actions of the others in the room had sparked a flame of hope.

Just five minutes ago, Josiah had barely anointed the table with oil when the demon at the door began grunting. That got the attention of the wizard Jazco—talk about a douche-canoe name. Somehow, the wizard understood and spoke to the damned thing and he'd called over the Ringmaster. Since then, her movements had been hurried and tight.

Perhaps most telling, the demon guard had vanished, leaving only the wizard at the door.

Had the coven come for me?

The hope grew hotter, and I couldn't resist casting a glance at the door every few seconds. This, of course, caught the Ringmaster's attention, and eventually, she repositioned herself so that she stood directly in my line of sight.

Bitch.

"Waiting for someone, Meredith?" she hissed.

"Just for you to keel over," I replied lazily, not about to let her know I was scared to death. If my magic would soon be stolen, and I'd probably die in the process, I planned on going out looking like a badass.

"Keep dreaming, child. Come morning, only one of us will be dead."

"I'm not a child," I gritted out.

"If you say so."

"Will you shut up?" Josiah growled, but he directed the comment at the Ringmaster, not me. "I'm working here and need to concentrate. Actually, you need to step back anyway. Meredith's magic won't want to be freed, and you're human with no means to protect yourself against its backlash. Give me six feet so I can contain it before the transfer."

She shot the necromancer a look of pure contempt but didn't reply. She only gave him the space he requested and watched as he set down the black feather, poured a liquid smelling faintly of flowers on his hands, and held them over my collarbone.

I'm sorry, Josiah mouthed for what felt like the billionth time.

I turned my head. Actions spoke louder than words. He was *choosing* to do this. Plain and simple.

"Meredith," Josiah whispered, his voice pleading.

"Get on with it, or don't," I snapped back.

Silence prickled between us, and for a moment, I dared to hope he'd take the second option.

But then pain struck, sending my breath hissing between my teeth, and I knew I was dead wrong. Maybe, literally.

"Calm down," Josiah muttered.

"Hurry up!" the Ringmaster yelled behind him, her tone frantic.

"*Arrgh!*" I screamed as dark gray streams of magic rushed inside me and seemed to wrap around my heart, squeezing the life from it.

Back arched, my fists curled so tightly the palms grew wet, slick with blood. Another scream wrenched its way up my throat as the necromancer bore down, pushing his power deeper to the center of my being. I'd never felt anything like it. The necromancer's magic was constricting and threatening. It pressed inward and, like scissors, cut at my very soul. Or my power. I didn't freaking know which, but did it matter?

I whimpered. It hurt so badly, I wished I could just pass out to not feel it.

Then, something far worse happened.

Josiah's magic was inky gray, nearly black, but from the cuts he'd made in my skin, wisps of white began to emerge, right as weakness overcame the pain.

My magic! It was leaving!

Panic tore through me, and I strained against the binds on my hands and ankles, but they held firm. As did the wizard's invisible restraints on my magic.

Tears stung in my eyes. "Stop! Please, stop!"

"Stay still, Meredith!" Josiah yelled.

I dared to meet his face. Tears shimmered in his eyes.

If I wasn't in so much damned pain, I might feel a sliver of pity for the guy, but I was freaking dying here, so screw him.

I opened my mouth to demand once again that he stop, when a roar from the other side of the room and the banging of wood on wood caught my ear.

"Touch her again and you die!"

My heart skipped a beat. *Is that . . .*

Tobias appeared in a flash, grabbing Josiah by the head and pulling back. The ravens on the windowsill loosed a cacophony of caws, but Tobias paid them no attention. His eyes flashed menacingly at the necromancer, the irises crimson. "If you don't stop, I'll sink my fangs into your neck and drain you dry. There will be no fair trial."

The necromancer's magic stopped flowing. The white wisps coming from my chest vanished.

I gasped, sucking down air, and feeling deep within for my power. It was still there.

"Get away from him!" the Ringmaster snarled, and then the foolish woman snapped up the blade on the table and stabbed it into Tobias's arm.

The vampire glared at her, fangs descending. "Step back, mortal, or court your own doom."

For the first time since I'd been in her presence, the Ringmaster paled. She took a step back, only to be stopped by someone—*Luca!*

"This was a poor choice, Josiah," the mage said. "We could have—"

A blast of light from the side of the room cut him off.

Tobias swore. "The door didn't knock the twat out."

"I'll handle him," Luca replied. "Unbind Meredith. Get her out of here."

"No!" The Ringmaster launched herself at Tobias.

Not missing a beat, the vampire tossed Josiah to the side of the room and protected my bound body from the crazy woman. When she landed, he grabbed her and hurled her away too. She slammed into the far wall and slumped against it, apparently too dazed to move.

But before Tobias could release me, Josiah was back.

"Please, Tobias! I'm sorry!"

A snarl ripped from the vampire. "Back away!"

But Josiah came closer. "I didn't want to do it. I promise, I was going to try to spare her. I—"

"You'd steal her power? Who is that woman?!"

"I—they have Sara!"

Tobias must have reached his limit, because he grabbed Josiah and sank his fangs into his neck. The necromancer screamed and thrashed, throwing blood all over the place. Second by second, Josiah's umber skin paled, took on a sickly hue.

My heart started to race. Would Tobias really kill Josiah? Did I care?

"Stop! Don't kill him!" I yelled, before I even made a conscious choice.

Tobias stilled, and slowly lifted his head. Blood coated his face, and that should have repulsed me, but it didn't. He'd attacked Josiah to save me. I couldn't find a damn thing disgusting about that.

"Are you sure?" the vampire asked. "You would have died at his hands."

"I was going to keep her alive!" Josiah wheezed.

"If you were capable, which I sincerely doubt," Tobias spat. "Stay quiet."

"Yes," I answered the vampire. "Let him go. He needs to face a trial for killing those witches—or at least being an accomplice. And I don't want you to kill him on my behalf."

"I'd do it gladly."

Why the hell did my stomach flutter when he threatened to off someone for me? And why did that feeling just get stronger as Tobias's eyes continued to bore into mine, waiting for my word?

Be reasonable, body!

"Let him go. A trial is what I want, what the other witches deserve."

Tobias glared at Josiah. "Count yourself lucky."

He released the necromancer, shoving him across the room, and I watched in horror as the ravens on the windowsill soared at the necromancer and began circling him until we could no longer see his body.

Oh no. What was happening?

Again, I tried to rise, and again, the binds around my wrists and ankles made it impossible. So I lay there, helpless and fearful, as the storm of ravens grew to hundreds.

"What are they doing?" I called to Tobias over the loud cawing.

"I'm not sure." He leaned over me, protecting me.

"I—oh my God!" Clouds of birds moved toward the window, Josiah with them. "They're going to help him escape!"

"Not without me!" a shrill, feminine voice cried. The Ringmaster had shaken off the discombobulation of being thrown against a wall and was sprinting toward Josiah. "I have Sara!"

I gasped as the Ringmaster, in a display of lunacy, bravery, or both, ran into the swirling conspiracy of ravens and disappeared as the birds soared out the open window to join a hundred others darkening the sky outside.

I listened. No screams. Just cawing.

"The ravens are . . . flying with them?" I asked, unable to believe what I'd just seen.

"It seems so," Tobias shook his head. "They do whatever Josiah wishes, and he clearly wished to escape."

"And to keep the Ringmaster alive, so she could tell him where Sara is!" My hands formed tight fists. "Dammit!"

I pulled at the binds, furious that the Ringmaster was still at large, and desperate to get to her—to pry Sara's location from the psycho and then put an end to my old boss. If she wouldn't stop until she got my magic, then getting rid of her was the only way I'd survive. Of that much, I was sure.

Tobias glanced down and, perhaps for the first time, noticed the straps. Quickly, he undid the leather. "Careful, Meredith. You—"

Not heeding his caution, I shot up. The world spun, and the nausea returned. I grabbed for the table, folding in half, about to hurl my guts out.

Damn, I'd been horizontal for way too long.

"Are you okay?" the vampire asked. The low rumble in his throat hinted he might tear out someone's throat if I said no.

"Yeah, the cut hurts, and my wrists and ankles sting like hell, but more importantly, I can't use my magic. I thought it was the straps that kept my magic from working, but now that they're off, that can't be it. The wizard did something to me."

Tobias's eyes narrowed before he twisted to face the door. "Luca!"

"*Un secondo!*" the mage called back.

The whole time Tobias had been fighting off Josiah and the

Ringmaster, our coven leader had been preoccupied with the wizard. Now he had the man cornered and delivered a blow of magic that hurled the wizard to his knees.

The moment that opponent was out of play, the coven master gave us his full attention. "He might be a criminal, but he certainly knows his defensive spells. What's up?"

"Meredith's magic is bound," Tobias answered.

"*Again!*" I inserted, because he was right. I hadn't considered it while I'd been strapped to the table, but that was exactly what the wizard had done.

My parents had bound me to keep me safe, so I'd never considered it as an offensive tactic. I needed to learn how to prohibit a similar attack from ever happening again. I hated that someone could so easily disarm me, take away part of who I was.

Luca approached, his brown eyes scanning the laceration from one side of my collarbone to the other. "How much did Josiah take?"

"Not a lot," I answered, sort of stunned he knew the process had already started.

"May I?" Luca raised a hand and tilted his chin to my shoulder.

I nodded, and repressed the wince burning through me when he laid a soft hand on my shoulder.

He exhaled. "Thankfully, the wizard is not nearly as strong as your parents were. This will be nothing like your first unbinding."

"Good, 'cause I don't really feel like blacking out today."

The coven master chuckled. "Sit tight."

I closed my eyes, preparing for a twinge of pain, so when Luca released me a second later, I was confused.

"That's it?" I asked.

"Done," he said. "Try your magic."

I went basic, pulling a small ball of light into my hand, and it flared to life right away. "I didn't even feel you unbind me at all!"

"Like I said, your parents were strong witches." Luca turned his attention to Tobias. "Is the area outside clear?"

The vampire nodded. "Safe."

"Grab the wizard and let's leave. Hopefully, the others took care of the demons in the lobby."

"More demons?!" My heart raced.

Luca's eyebrows pinched together, so thick and hairy they resembled a caterpillar. "You didn't hear the fighting? There were dozens of them in the lobby."

"Lobby? We arrived on the roof. I thought I sensed something, but I couldn't hear a thing. The wizard must have soundproofed this area. I had no idea fighting was going on! Is anyone hurt?"

"Shay was injured," Tobias said. "Hans is caring for her."

That probably wasn't going well.

Tobias scooped up the wizard and threw him over his shoulder, fireman-style, before we exited the room. In a line with me in the middle, we rushed down a hall to a stairwell that opened into a lobby littered with bodies.

Demon bodies.

I swallowed, taking in the carnage. Luca hadn't been joking when he said they'd fought many. There had to be two dozen demon corpses!

Thankfully, the rest of the people, and one wolf I recognized as Harper, seemed okay. They milled around, some collecting samples from the demons, others healing minor wounds.

As we got to the bottom of the stairs, Luca broke away

from Tobias and me. "I need a word with Avon," he gestured to a man I hadn't met yet, but from his build and thick chest hair, would guess him to be a wolf. "See to Shay?"

"We will," I assured him, rushing to the nephilim's side.

As I neared, Hans glanced up, his eyes lighting up when he saw me. "We weren't too late."

"Not to save her. But that bloody necromancer maimed her," Tobias grunted, clearly pissed off.

Hans's eyes dipped, the blue of his irises darkening. "He'll pay for that."

"He will. Take watch over this wizard." Tobias dumped the wizard next to Hans. "Meredith, I need to speak with you."

Ignoring the vampire's request, I knelt by Shay. "How is she?"

My eyes told me she was in a bad place. Her wings, which I hadn't seen much of before today, were matted with blood. And there seemed to be a gash in her shoulder.

"She lost a lot of blood, but I think she's fine. Do you mind watching her?" Hans asked. "I don't think she'll want me here when she wakes up."

Throat tightening, I nodded. "Sure, I—"

"No," Tobias growled. "Come with me, Meredith."

I twisted to face him, incredulous. "Dude! Shay is my friend. Why do I need to go with you so badly?"

"*You're* wounded, which I can fix. I *need* to take care of it. "

Before I could question why, Harper rushed over to me, now in her human form, and knelt at my side. She threw her arms around me. I was surprised to find that she was shaking. So un-Harper like.

"Meredith!" Harper said, voice tight. "Thank the Old Ones you're alive. We were so worried."

"I'm okay," I assured her, trying not to get teary. Harper

was more stoic than Shay, but over time that veneer had cracked. She really cared. They all did.

They'd come here *for me*. Fought *for me*. Bled *for me*. Even Tobias's insistence that I come with him was semi-sweet—despite his growly, bossy-as-hell tone.

"Meredith," Tobias insisted, and this time, something in his voice made my heartbeat kick up. Not in a scared way, but in a way, I didn't quite understand and couldn't name. *"Your blood."*

Suddenly, his insistence clicked. Oh, right. He'd always had trouble around my blood. That must be why he wanted the wound closed so quickly.

I looked at Harper. "Can you stay with her so I can put Tobias out of his misery?"

"Of course," Harper replied weakly. She often gave Shay a hard time for . . . well, being Shay, but there was absolutely love between the shifter and the nephilim. "Heal up fast, Meredith. We just got a message that Covenant Seats have arrived in the city and they want a word."

Tobias led me away from Shay, to a corner where no demons sprawled on the ground.

"Are you trying to pull a fast one?" I teased, trying to loosen the tension in his shoulders.

"Pardon?"

My lips curled up. There was a lot about Tobias that put me off, but his proper sayings and turns of phrase from the past didn't make the list. I found them charming.

"You're taking me to a corner, like a guy would at a bar when he wants to suck face with a girl. Or maybe—"

"I would never disrespect a woman in that manner." Tobias's eyes narrowed, and the green in them intensified as if alit from within.

"It was a joke," I said quickly, because clearly, I'd hit a nerve. "So, how are you going to heal me?"

He quirked a brow at me. "You say it like I haven't already done so."

Oh right. The blood drinking.

I tried really hard not to think about that, to pretend it had never happened, but the blood in Tobias's veins *had* kept me from dying in the New Haven Museum. Obviously, there were major healing benefits to vampire blood that I knew practically nothing about.

"Do I have to drink it again?" I was seriously pleased I had been passed out last time.

At that, Tobias cracked a smile. "You're not one of those girls who wants to be turned?"

"Heck no." I wrinkled my nose. "You get to keep all the blood to yourself. I'll stick with pizza and tacos and whatever else Harper cooks for me."

He laughed. "Then you'll be happy to know that you do not always have to drink vampire blood to heal quickly. I can apply it topically. It might not heal as fast, but," he eyed the trail the scalpel left, "that doesn't look too deep."

"It's not," I assured him. "He just needed an opening to siphon magic out of."

I felt like I was defending Josiah, which was pretty strange, considering all that had just happened.

Tobias nodded and lifted his wrist, biting into it.

My mouth dropped. "You said—"

"Shhh," he breathed, licking the red from his lips in a way that made a shiver trail down my spine.

"Here," Tobias murmured, dipping his finger into his own blood. "Move your hair."

I did so, pulling the pieces that had fallen out of my ponytail behind my shoulders. He inched closer, and I inhaled his scent of spice and soft leather. Then, ever so softly, he placed his finger on the cut in my skin, trailing it lightly all the way across my collarbone.

The touch sent a wave of goosebumps down my arms, and I rubbed them so he wouldn't notice. I didn't think he did, because the vampire was not looking anywhere but at my eyes.

"How's that?" he asked, his raspy tone making my mouth go dry and heat pool in my belly.

How the hell was his blood on my cut turning me on? Was he really asking about the wound? Did he notice my goosebumps?

Oh my God, can he tell that I'm turned on?!

Heat flooded my cheeks. I wasn't an innocent little virgin, but right now, I was freaking mortified.

Without success, I tried to dampen the electricity racing through me as Tobias continued to stare into my eyes. What was he thinking? Am I overthinking this? Is he just trying to see that I'm really alright?

After only a few seconds, I found I couldn't take the intensity, the questions that arose—the feeling of being alight under his gaze—any longer. I broke our stare, glancing down to see my skin was already knitting together a touch. The pain had lessened too, becoming barely noticeable.

"Better."

My words acted like a spell, and the air began to crackle between us, electrified.

I breathed out in awe. "Thank you."

"My pleasure, Miss Stone," he replied, hooking my chin, so that I met his eyes once more.

It was then that I knew I wasn't crazy. The vampire looked

at me like I was water in a desert. There was totally something new there, an attraction that had been growing between us for days.

I exhaled a little of the tension riddling my body. I didn't know what was going on between us, but one thing was certain—it was something I desperately wanted to explore.

CHAPTER SIX

TOBIAS

I wanted to kiss Meredith. Yearned to do it. Needed her lips on mine, her body crushed against me, her—

Bloody hell, man. Stop it.

I blinked, trying to center myself. What was going on with me?

What if Giselle had been right all along?

My breath hitched. *Impossible . . . Isn't it?*

But as I stared into those mismatched gemstone eyes, I had to admit it didn't feel impossible. Not anymore.

I'd been on the verge of killing Josiah for what he'd done. He deserved it, of course, but I knew as well as anyone that wasn't how things were done in our world. People died in the heat of battle, but I'd completely overpowered Josiah. He couldn't have stood up to me. There was no battle between him and me.

And yet, had Meredith not spared him, I would have drained the fucker dry for hurting her. For even touching her again.

"Tobias! Meredith!" a voice called from behind, breaking the spell perfuming the air between me and the witch.

Equally thankful and frustrated by the disturbance, I pulled away and found Luca marching toward us. "Everything alright?"

"For now," Luca replied. "But the Covenant officials are waiting. They want to speak with as many people in S&S as possible."

I stiffened as the possible repercussions of meeting the supernatural ruling body rolled over me. They would want to know why we were here, how S&S knew to be in the city before anyone else. They'd also want to hear about the Prince of Hell and his minions.

All roads led to the Pearl and the Opal, and they'd want to know how we knew about that too. I took in Meredith once more, her attention now on Luca, oblivious to what this could mean for her.

If they learn about her . . .

"We're not telling them about Meredith, are we?"

"Absolutely not." Luca glanced at the witch. "Meredith, the Covenant is the ruling body among all supernaturals. Just say you're a witch, don't mention seeking."

"Won't they ask?" Her brows pulled together. "S&S has powerful members, so won't they assume I have a specialty, too?"

The bird was smart. The Covenant *would* want to know her skills, but we had to minimize others knowing of her power for as long as we could. It was bad enough that we'd have to tell them about the stones and Wrath's invasion of Earth.

"I'll take care of any prying," I said. "We stick together."

There was no way in hell I was letting her out of my sight.

"Okay," Meredith said, surprising me.

No sass. No raised eyebrows or defiant chin tilts. Just . . . *Okay.*

I was sure she'd felt that heat between us, but had she felt more? Had her blood sung as I searched for her?

Could I ask her that? It sounded so crazy.

"Shay's awake, so we should get moving," Luca commented, waving at Harper and the half-angel, who was now sitting up. "Tobias, carry the wizard. I want Hans to be ready to fight any straggler demons from afar. I'll have others help Shay."

A second later, though, it became apparent Shay didn't want to be helped. The moment the nephilim could stand, she staggered over to Meredith. "Rooms! Are you okay?!"

I winced, watching her move. Her wing was covered in blood. She needed to see a healer.

"Better than you." Meredith looked hesitant about embracing her friend, and turned to me. "Can you give her your blood?"

"No effing way," Shay said.

"What? It works, though!" Meredith gestured to the line below her collarbone. "A minute ago, this was a cut and it's nearly totally healed."

I cleared my throat. There was a reason I hadn't offered. "Vampires are considered damned, and Shay is nephilim. Angelic. We mingle, can be friends even, but no one with angel blood would accept vampire blood."

"Yeah, sorry, Tobias. It's too deeply ingrained in me," Shay said. "I'll be fine. The Covenant will have brought healers. Just need to get there."

"Then let's go," Meredith said. "'Cause you look like crap."

Shay snorted. "Pot, meet kettle."

"We can create a club."

The girls devolved into chatter, which only grew more frenzied and ridiculous as Harper joined. I resigned myself to carrying Jazco over my shoulder and walking behind the trio. I needed to stay close to Meredith but could see she needed time with her roommates.

As Luca led us through the city, I assessed the landscape. It looked like a bloody warzone. How would we convince the humans nothing had happened here? The Covenant was filled with powerful supernaturals, and commanded squadrons of people to assist them at the drop of a hat, but even they would have a hell of a time covering this up.

Would we have to bring in mages from Isila to help?

The idea, while full of merit, did not sit well. The mages in Isila were extremely powerful, but most despised the human realm. When asked to travel here, they would only do so for a steep price.

For Luca's sake, I hoped the mages would remain in the mirror world. He did everything he could to avoid the mages of Isila. While I never asked exactly why, I knew it had to do with the royal court. I felt the same way about the Court of the Blood, so that gave me a fairly sizable hint.

At that moment, the lump of a wizard that I was carrying groaned. Without hesitation, I punched him in the head. He fell limp, and I didn't feel at all bad.

"That's for Meredith," I muttered low enough so that she couldn't hear.

I remained half determined to tune out the women's chatter and half lost in thought until we reached a street lined with people and tents. Magic filled the air and people walked about without fear, full of purpose. We'd found the Covenant.

Luca marched straight up to a recognizable man wearing a red beret.

Artem Kovalenko was one of the three Covenant Seats for the witches. He had a reputation among witching kind as a no-nonsense wizard who got things done. Like Hans, the Ukrainian wizard was a caster, and it was rumored he had acquired a prodigious lexicon of spells in his sixty years, one of the largest ever mastered. Seeing him here brought me hope that the city really might be restored and the humans clueless as to what had occurred.

"Looks like you need a healer." Someone spoke nearby, jarring me slightly so that Jazco slipped. I repositioned the arsehole over my shoulder. He wasn't heavy, but I couldn't wait to be rid of him.

I'd been so intent on watching the coven master and Artem, I hadn't noticed another person approach. I twisted to find a woman; the scent of rosemary and honey coming off of her in thick waves indicated she was a witch.

"I do," Shay replied, cringing as she had to maneuver her wing around Harper so that she could turn. "Are you a healer?"

"I am. One from a local coven. The Covenant called on me for the crisis." The woman gave a kind smile. "We're setting up a station over there for any humans we might find with injuries. Best to get you in there before they start arriving. We'll need to fix those wings before you can hide them."

Shay nodded and made to walk toward the tent. Meredith started to follow, but I reached out, wrapping my hand around her wrist to stop her.

"We have . . . other matters to attend to," I said, though at the moment, there was no task on our plate. I simply didn't want her socializing with anyone close to the Covenant.

"Much to be done," the healer agreed. "Is anyone here a shifter?"

Harper stepped forward. "Wolf."

"Oh, wonderful! They need your kind to sniff out humans." The healer cast a wary glance at me. "Vampires are welcome, too, if they can resist drinking blood. We expect there will be lots of it."

"As I said, I have another matter to attend to, but if I can help I will." My first priority was to keep Meredith safe.

The healer nodded, relief sweeping across her face. "The wolves are meeting over there." She pointed for Harper's sake, and our group split up.

For a moment, Meredith and I were alone, and by how her shoulders stiffened, I suspected she wasn't entirely sure what to do about that.

Nor was I, for that matter.

Thankfully, Luca returned, dissipating the tension before it could mount to unbearable heights.

"A few members of the coven will stay to help," he said. "I don't want Meredith to, but . . ." He looked from side to side, "I had a thought."

"What do you need?" she asked, her expression suggested that, despite all she'd just been through, she was eager to assist.

"Since you seem fine, I wondered if perhaps you might be willing to do a search for the Pearl before you leave?" Luca asked softly. "Just to see if it's still in the city? I suspect not, but I'd like to be sure before S&S disperses."

"But we can't have the Covenant realize what's happening," I reiterated as I shifted Jazco again. "They would want to use you, Meredith. And some members of the ruling body are not as pure of heart as others."

One ruthless, traitorous vampire, a two-faced wizard, and a cruel siren were top of my list. Though I had not seen them milling about yet, it was best to proceed with caution.

"Absolutely," Luca agreed. "You can seek, but you must be careful about it. If you sense the Pearl or the Opal, let me know immediately. Only when S&S members are around me, though."

"Got it," Meredith said, looking completely unbothered by the scenario. "I'll check it out and text you."

"Perfect," Luca said, his lips curling up. "I'll take the wizard to a holding cell. Tobias, stay with her."

"Obviously," I replied as Jazco levitated off my shoulder, now under Luca's control.

I didn't need Luca to request that of me. Even standing here, I knew I wouldn't be able to leave the witch's side. Not yet. Though she was safe and, according to her, fine, my protective instincts were still too strong. Separating would send them into overdrive, and banish reason from my mind.

"Once I dispose of this one," Luca gestured to the unconscious floating wizard, "I'll be with Artem. Ask for him if you need to find me." With that, he left and again I was alone with the witch.

This time, Meredith turned to me, purpose burning in her gaze. "Maybe we should veer down a side street? Get out of sight?"

"Yes. We want no suspicion regarding what we're up to."

"That's what I was thinking too," she replied, her full lips spreading in a smile. "Look at us! Agreeing like a team!"

Something inside me warmed at that, and the soft singing in my blood returned.

Meredith cocked her head, and I blinked.

Did she hear that? How?

Or did she feel it?

I swallowed. Before, the question had sounded too crazy to ask, but now . . .

"Let's get out of earshot," she said, halting the words in my throat as she marched down the street.

I followed, stunned. We were associated as colleagues, but if she felt the singing too, then I'd have to admit to myself something deeper was happening.

That perhaps, Giselle was right.

If Meredith and I were mates, this was no normal blood-bond between vampire and vampire. In my magical order true mates were rare, but often, instantly recognized. That hadn't happened with Meredith, and I wouldn't have expected it. She was not a vampire. This should not be happening at all.

But no matter what the laws of fated mates were *said* to be, the attraction, the pull, was quickly becoming too much to deny. Would it continue to grow with time? With our acknowledgment? Would there be a trigger?

How can I deal with this?

Aside from my original concerns, many more presented themselves. Like how, if it were true that we were mates and we went public, the target on Meredith would expand.

I was a royal vampire, and though most of our kind fell in line around us, many other creatures hated the Laurents. They'd view anyone I cared deeply about as a prime target. It was why, aside from my family and supernaturals who could take care of themselves, like Luca, I rarely made close friends.

Being a friend of the Laurent family was a risky position.

"How about here?" Meredith piped up after we'd gone a couple of blocks. "This has to be far enough, right? Or can your kind smell and hear things miles away?"

Trying not to let on that fear raced through me, I managed a small smile. "This is good."

We slid down a narrow side street, the kind that one often saw on films portraying a tight-knit New York neighborhood. There was even the quintessential Italian pizzeria and a brightly colored beauty salon that was undoubtedly filled with women on a daily basis.

"Cute street," Meredith commented. "Homier than where we were earlier."

"Manhattan isn't very warm," I agreed.

"I doubt the Prince of Wrath will be anywhere nearby—this isn't flashy enough. He looked like he'd be flashy, right?"

"Agreed." A memory of the dark smoke rolling toward us came back to me. "He's certainly a showman."

"Yeah . . . still, we have to try," Meredith shrugged. "So should we get this show on the road?"

I scanned the area, and after determining that no one was, in fact, around, I nodded. "At your leisure."

She smirked and turned to face the street. The moment she called her magic, her scent intensified in the air, the aromas of jasmine and pine mingling with the sweet honeyed aroma of witching power.

However, this time, something was different. As Meredith worked her magic, the honey became cloying, almost overwhelming, and again, vibrations wracked my veins. Then, suddenly, my blood began to hum.

Meredith spun to face me, eyes wide. "Okay, what is that?!"

I pressed my lips together. "What do you mean?"

Was it wise to speak of this? Were we experiencing the same thing?

"Don't play with me, Tobias." Meredith scowled. "You

heard that!" Her hand fluttered to her heart, but it dropped almost as quickly.

My eyes narrowed. I didn't sense *her* blood singing, but perhaps it was just too faint. Who the bloody hell knew? This was firmly in the realm of the uncharted.

"What exactly?" I pressed, because I had to be sure before I laid out my own feelings.

"The . . . humming! There's a song I hear when I'm around you, and—" her mouth snapped shut, and I knew.

"And your blood seems to sing?" I asked.

She gasped. "Yes!"

"Mine as well," I admitted, somewhat relieved, somewhat fearful. "I don't know what it means, but I believe that it's a result of you ingesting my blood."

She nodded, licking her lips in a way that made me want to cup her face and take her lips in mine. "That does make sense. But it feels like something *more*, too."

Giselle's belief nearly launched off the tip of my tongue, but I held it in. Because even if it were true, even if Meredith and I were fated mates, my reasons for not wanting her to know remained valid.

For now, probably forever, it was better that she did not entertain such thoughts. Even if with each passing second, it grew more difficult to deny my growing attraction to her.

"I doubt it's more than that," I forced the words out. "Blood exchanges can be quite powerful. Otherwise, you wouldn't have survived that night."

I sensed a hesitation in her, but the next second, her magic flared to life again, perfuming the air with honey, and Meredith turned and began to walk slowly down the street, seeking.

I remained quiet so as not to distract her, and though I

usually found comfort in silence, after our conversation the quiet felt prickly.

Or perhaps it was just the fact that I had, at worst, lied to her, and at best, omitted information.

It's for the greater good, I thought, increasing the distance between us by two steps, hoping that would help stave off my discomfort.

After three blocks, she sighed and stopped. "Nothing. Like seriously, *nothing*. Not even a hint of the Pearl."

"Then Prince Orien must have fled," I said. "If I'm being frank, that's what I would have done."

"Still sucks," she replied. "We came here for one thing and totally screwed it up."

"There will be another opportunity. We—"

"What have we here?" a man with long black hair and moon-pale skin appeared from an alleyway some ten yards ahead.

No, not a man. A vampire.

One I had hoped to avoid.

Egor Drago—a vampire Seat in the Covenant, and unofficial peon and spy for the Court of the Blood of Laurent.

"Keep back," I whispered to the witch.

The only indication she heard me was the half-step she took to remain behind me.

It was the best we could do. The rest would be a show, a farce to hide Meredith's magic. I had to hope this vampire fell for it.

"Egor." I tried to infuse some enthusiasm into my voice and found it impossible as his shrewd eyes, gray like his morals, raked over me. "What are you doing here?"

"Searching for injured humans," he purred, a cunning smile on his thin lips. "What else?"

What else indeed?

"Have you found any?" I asked.

"None in these blocks. Most are holed up in their homes." Egor craned his neck to glance at Meredith. "Who's your partner, Tobias?"

"A colleague in the coven," I replied. "We, too, are looking for humans to assist."

"Were you?" Egor arched an eyebrow. "Because I thought I smelled magic. Rather strong magic, too. Are you a caster, witch?"

Meredith cleared her throat. "No."

"She's a warder." I flung out the first witching specialty I thought of to throw him off, again stepping closer, blocking Meredith's body with my own.

"Why would you need a warder to escort you, Tobias? Afraid of humans leaping from their homes and throwing themselves at you?" He snorted. "Giselle's children always were vain."

"Precisely." If he thought my maker and her offspring—a branch of the Laurent family he'd never quite taken to—were that pompous, then so be it. As long as it got him to leave, I'd lean into it. "She's here for my protection."

The other vampire let out a low hum. "And do you have a name, witch?"

"Meredith."

"Lovely name." Egor inched forward, eyes trained on what he could see of Meredith. "But I'll be honest, it didn't seem like she was protecting you, Tobias. In fact, if I didn't know better, it seemed to me that the pair of you were searching for—"

"People," I cut him off. "As we've already told you."

"Then why would a warder lead *you*, a Laurent? No witch is better than a vampire at *seeking* out humans." He craned his neck once more to peer at Meredith, and though his emphasis on the word 'seeking' made my heart thump, I did not let the growing fury I felt show on my face.

Let him try to question Meredith, to take her. I'd rip his throat out and throw it to the royal court of vampires he worshiped.

"I don't know when you began spying on us, Egor, or why you'd bother, but I simply was returning to Meredith's side after scanning a building." My tone was low, warning. "Now, if there isn't anything else, I believe we all have a job to do?"

After a prolonged pause, Egor shifted his attention so it was solely on me once more. "You're right of course. I should be getting back to the meetup place, tell the others what I've seen."

"Who you've helped, you mean?" Meredith spoke up, her tone challenging.

Though I largely wished she would have kept quiet, a small part of me relished the look of outrage on Egor's face. A young witch well-versed in this world would know better than to take on Egor, but Meredith knew little of this world.

"Of course," the vampire gritted out.

"Great," Meredith snapped back. "See you later, then, bud."

She stomped past me and Egor, who I was sure would whirl about and try to wring her secrets from her.

"Pardon me." I moved around him, again putting my body between him and the witch. "My partner grows impatient."

"I see that. You'd do well to *educate* your partner."

"Actually, I believe I'll let her continue her self-study." I glanced back in time to see outrage flicker across his face. "Until next time."

The vampire's chin tilted up, and for a heartbeat, I thought for sure he'd follow us. But instead, he turned and blurred away, using his vampiric speed to run down the street.

Who was he really going to inform? The Covenant? Or someone else?

Not the time to dwell on that, I thought as Meredith disappeared around a corner.

I chased after her—and skidded to a stop when I found the witch leaning against the wall, gasping for air. Hyperventilating.

Inside me, a monster roared, and in three strides, I closed the distance between us and placed my hands against her cheeks, steadying her. "Look at me. Meredith, look at me."

"H-he—that man! Tobias! Who was that?" Her right hand flew up to land on top of mine, and suddenly, my skin was alight.

Desire burned through me, nearly as hot as the urge to chase after Egor and rip his head from his body for scaring this woman.

He courts his doom.

"Tobias?" My name, whispered off her lips, ripped me back to the moment, and she became my entire focus once again. "Who is that person? He felt so . . . wrong."

"Egor Drago is a Covenant Seat. One of three vampires on the council."

She shuddered. "There was something off about him. Like, evil."

Her eyes filled with tears, and I pulled her close to me, wrapping her in my arms. Shockingly, she accepted the embrace, her breathing calming as I held her.

Meredith was as tough and headstrong as the oldsalt sailors who'd taught me to crew, and they did not take an ounce of shit. Yet, Egor terrified her. What was it about the man? Why hadn't I sensed it?

Before I could make sense of my thoughts, Meredith pulled away, and I loosened my grip on her. She looked up at me, one blue eye and one green staring into me so deeply, I thought she could see my soul.

And then, her lips parted, she leaned closer, and desire flooded me, a deluge.

I fought against the tide, and at the last second, sense took over. Remembering the Laurents' many enemies, I leaned back, releasing her. "I'm sorry, Meredith. I—"

"I don't know what came over me," she blurted. "I'm sorry too."

I looked away. "We should keep searching. Just a few more blocks."

We needed to do something, anything, to take my mind off that almost-kiss.

"Right." Meredith sighed and then she whisked past me, back into the street.

I followed, my whole body alight in a way I hadn't felt in years. In a way I wanted more than anything to ignore.

The problem was, I didn't believe I'd have the strength to do so for much longer.

CHAPTER SEVEN

HANS

I sat on the sidewalk, watching those of the Covenant mill around. Of those in the group of ruling supernaturals, only Artem Kovalenko had acknowledged me. As I was one of his kind—as far as he knew—and had even voted the man into his position, I appreciated that.

Just as much as I appreciated it when he left me alone to think.

Because, as I stared down at my forearms—the veins still darkened but largely hidden by my tattoo sleeves—I couldn't believe what I'd just done.

My head fell into my hands.

To protect Shay, I'd called on my demon magic. And somehow, after being dormant for years, the powers that had once plagued me cropped up, ready and willing to do my bidding.

It had been so easy. *Too* easy. As if I hadn't been ignoring that side of my magic for well over a decade.

Would my veins stay that way? Or would they fade?

Something told me my gray veins were a sign of the Hell-born powers inside me wanting out. Was pushing for it.

Thank the Goddess I'm inked.

The Covenant was supposed to be there for the supernatural community, but they had a history of being draconian with Hellblooded individuals. Seeing as Lilith was my mother, I suspected that would shift me out of the wizard camp and into the demon spawn one.

Luca didn't have to tell me to stay quiet about my bloodline; that was second nature to me. I trusted everyone in S&S not to spill, too. Largely because Luca had decreed it, but also because many were friends, and hadn't treated me differently since the truth came out.

Well, except for Shay.

She'd been on the verge of passing out when I sent those black ribbons out to protect her, but as she'd been shooting scathing looks in my direction since then, I was certain she'd seen them.

Thinking about her regular disregard sent anger trickling through me, and with it, a push of darkness. I slammed the latter down, aghast.

Since I'd basically tortured that demon with black ribbons, the dark magic remained closer to the surface than ever, simmering just beneath my skin. I didn't know what to do, or how to deal with myself—and for a guy who'd been in total control for years, that was fucking terrifying.

"Hans!" Luca called out.

I lifted my head to find the coven master walking my way, his strides urgent.

"What's up?" I stood and brushed the grit of the city off my pants.

"I have a job for you."

"Ready for anything." Seriously, *anything* to get my mind off my own woes was welcome.

"I need you to search for possessed people. And handle them." Luca cleared his throat.

"Okay . . ." I sort of understood why he'd want me to search. Though I couldn't follow the trail of demon magic like some thought I could, I was a strong enough wizard to keep a possessed human in check. But that was about all I could do.

"Shay will be going with you," he added quickly, as if he thought it would be like ripping a bandage off or something. "I want you to be her eyes while she works on the exorcisms. Make sure she doesn't burn herself out."

"Dude! Are you serious?" I barked.

"I'm not too pleased with it either," a voice said from behind.

I whirled to find Shay approaching. No longer bloody, her wing and shoulder looked a million times better.

"But I need someone with me," she added. "They cleaned me up, but my wing is still throbbing, and you're the only one from the coven left."

The nephilim was right. Every other S&S member who'd congregated here had already been sent off to help deal with the catastrophe that was the city.

"We can be adults, Hans." Even as she said the words, her lips pursed in disgust.

Can we, though?

"The Covenant needs help cleaning this up. And aside from two nephilim representatives, I'm the only one of my kind here right now. That's not nearly enough for how many people might be possessed."

A long exhale left my nostrils. She was the one who had a problem with me, so if she was willing to work together for the sake of the city, I could suck it up and do so too.

After all, what were a few judgmental looks compared to how hard I judged myself?

"Fine," I muttered.

Luca's shoulders loosened. "Excellent. You two will be working with the Covenant for as long as it takes to settle things here. Could be a day or two, but we hope not. Memory witches are on their way."

The coven master paused, as if he wanted to add more, but then he clapped his hands together. "Call me if anything strange arises."

"Where are you going?" I asked.

"I'll remain here through the night, then head back to New Haven," he replied. "I'm not sure we'll see each other before I leave."

So it was basically me, Shay, and the Covenant—a bunch of elected officials, some of whom were pompous assholes.

Wonderful.

"Best get started, then." Luca marched off, leaving me and Shay alone for the first time since she'd woken up.

An edgy silence fell between us. Shay fidgeted with her healing wing, and I swallowed thickly, still not sure how much she'd seen.

"Are you going to keep those out?" I asked.

She remained staring pointedly at her wing. "For a while. The healer said I can retract them once the tingling stops."

"Oh. Okay."

Where the hell to go from here?

A huff left the half-angel, and finally, she deigned to look at me. "Look, Hans, I know we're at odds—"

"I'd like to point out that you're the only one of us who thinks that," I said quickly.

"I am?"

"Yes."

Shay's lips compressed, and for a moment, I thought we might be able to get through this right here and now. But then she shook her head. "Maybe. But what I was going to say is, even though I do not approve of the means you used to keep that demon away, I wanted to thank you for saving me."

The backhanded apology stung, and I couldn't let it slide. "You don't approve of the . . . *means*?! What are you saying, Shay?"

"I saw your dark magic. Why did you lie to us about it? You said you *never* use it."

"That was the first time since I was a kid!" I roared.

People walking by stopped to stare, and my cheeks heated.

"My vision was blurry," Shay hissed, "but you seemed pretty skilled for that to be your first time in years."

I snorted. "I can see that no matter what I do, I'm never going to be anything but a Hellblooded devil to you. So why don't we just go and do our job?"

I didn't even wait for her response, I couldn't—I was too pissed off. So before she could get another word in edgewise, I stomped past her, down the street, sure she'd follow so we could complete our mission.

"He went around the corner!" I yelled. "Hurry!"

"Coming!" Shay gritted out. "Just tackle him!"

She sounded annoyed, just as she'd sounded for the last two hours that we'd been searching for people possessed by non-corporeal demons.

Two *long* fucking hours of silence interspersed by bouts of verbal sparring.

Thankfully, we finally had a distraction. We'd spotted a man with red eyes, indicating that we'd hit gold in the possession department. I hoped that if we managed to successfully work together as a team, it would dissipate the black cloud of tension hanging between us.

Shit, at this point, I'd settle for the cloud shifting to gray.

So I bore down and put on a burst of speed, lunging at the man as soon as I was close enough. I just caught him, and together we fell and rolled across the litter-strewn cement.

The man snapped his teeth at me, the fucker.

"Hurry!" I yelled as we rolled to a stop and I struggled to pin down the man. He easily had thirty pounds of pure muscle and four inches on me.

"Almost there!" she shouted back. "He needs to be still!"

"What do you think I'm trying to do?" I shot, grabbing at the guy's flailing arm and slamming it to the pavement. "Dance with him?"

The man snarled and snapped, but after a few more seconds, I managed to straddle him.

"*Gelditi.*" I pressed my palm to his chest, and the man grew stiff and still.

"Why didn't you do that spell earlier?" Shay asked, huffing and puffing as she caught up.

"He was sprinting! If I immobilized him while he was in motion, it could really hurt the guy. It's not his fault he's possessed."

"Like he's not scuffed up now," Shay retorted.

Unfortunately, it was true. The tumble and roll had opened a gash in the man's cheek, and I was pretty sure my leg was bleeding. Still, I preferred this method. At the very least, he didn't faceplant and break a few bones or shatter his teeth. Seemed more humane to me.

"Just pull out the demon, okay?" I hauled myself up off the man.

"You might want to step back."

I ground my teeth, but I did as she said, giving the nephilim her space. I didn't want her claiming that she couldn't work her angelic magic with my Hellborn influence nearby, or some other shit like that.

Once I was far enough away, Shay began to work.

Though she hated me, I found watching her use her power a delight. Her magic was so unlike mine, so different from anything I'd ever seen. Among the supernaturals in both realms, there was no direct parallel to angel magic. They were in a class of their own—which made sense, seeing as her ancestors had created all other supernaturals.

The light bloomed from Shay, growing ever brighter as it entered the man. Paying close attention, I watched for an intense glow around her veins, indication that she was pulling too deep, but it never came. And when a dark cloud exploded from the man, who began coughing up a storm, I knew it wouldn't. She'd succeeded, and done so without threatening herself.

"What the hell?!" the man cried out. "Who are you?"

"My name is Shay," my partner said calmly. "I mean you no harm. Just calm down and listen to me, okay?"

I took a few more paces back, knowing that Shay's angelic influence would lower the man's pulse. I didn't need to be hovering over them, potentially distracting her patient.

Useless for the moment, I turned slowly, taking in the area. The street was dark now, night having fully fallen. For once, the city was eerily quiet, non-threatening. The humans still seemed to want to huddle in their apartments and hide.

Good. That would make everyone's job of erasing signs of a supernatural battle so much easier.

Hopefully, they stay that way all nigh—fucking hell!

My heart rate spiked as black ribbons of magic teased beneath the light of a streetlamp some thirty feet down the street.

Nicoleta!

I broke into a run, chasing the ribbons, just like I had the first time. This time, though, I swore I wouldn't leave this street. Or Shay. Since being in the city, I'd already broken one S&S rule—leave no covenmate behind. It wouldn't happen again, but I couldn't resist the lure of seeing if my sister was nearby.

Did she want to speak to me? To apologize?

It seemed too good to be true.

That belief panned out when I reached the streetlight and followed the ribbons to the side of a building, where they disappeared into solid brick.

But they didn't leave me with nothing.

Atop a windowsill, to the side of where the strands of darkness had danced, an envelope bearing my name sat.

I exhaled, picking it up.

"What the heck are you doing, dude?!" Shay yelled, making my heart stutter.

Quickly, I pocketed the letter. "Thought I saw more flashing red eyes!"

The lie slipped off my tongue easily. It was that or become even weaker in Shay's eyes. I had to stop jumping at any sign of my sister.

Though, of course, that was easier said than done. Nicoleta was my little sis, the only sibling I'd ever had, and despite reason, I felt like I owed it to her to bring out the good in her.

No matter how unreasonable it was to want to speak to Nic, to convince her to leave the Darkborn, I couldn't stop trying. I couldn't give up on my own blood. It simply wasn't in me.

"What was it?" Shay yelled back.

I twisted to find her approaching, and I made to meet her, not wanting her to get too close to where the letter had been, in case she sensed dark magic.

I didn't think she could, but I wasn't about to take the chance.

"Lights from an electronic," I said. "The guy's okay?"

"As good as a person can be who was just possessed."

Absentmindedly, I patted my pocket. The paper crinkled, drawing Shay's attention, and I bit back a curse, wishing I wasn't such a nervous screw-up.

I cleared my throat. "Let's keep on keepin' on."

She eyed me warily, but I steered her down the street, keeping an eye out for my sister with each step.

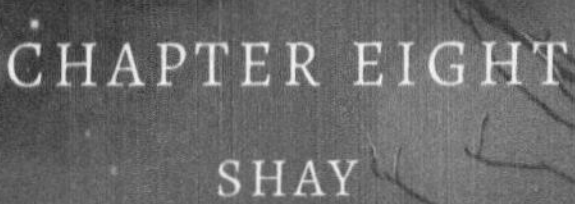

CHAPTER EIGHT

SHAY

My palms pressed into the supine woman's shoulders, and sweat poured down my face, getting in my eyes. Through all of it, though, I watched my forearms carefully.

My skin was warm, indicating that I might be reaching my edge.

Hans and I had been trekking through the city for hours. So long that the sun was rising over the New York skyline. I'd freed a dozen people from possession, but I sure as heck wouldn't be able to go on for much longer. Not without burning out.

The idea of my own magic lighting me on fire drew a shudder up my spine.

This is the last one.

"You doing alright?" Hans asked.

I didn't turn, but could feel the blaze of his blue eyes as he watched my back, both literally and figuratively.

"Fine. Almoooost . . . done!"

An explosion of black smoke reeking of sulfur and mold

burst out of the woman. Predictably, the victim gasped and clutched at her throat as she began coughing.

Though the non-corporeal demon rarely made a clean exit out of the mouth, 99% of people coughed after an exorcism.

"Wh-who are you?" the woman asked, her eyes widening as she stopped coughing and found me straddling her.

Magic washed over us, and though the recently-possessed couldn't sense it, I knew Hans was undoing his immobilization spell. This human would be none-the-wiser that she'd been paralyzed.

I got up and held my hand out. Surprisingly, she took it.

My wings were healed, and I'd been hiding them for hours, but still, most people usually slapped my hand away like it was a snake, and ran for their lives. Especially the women.

"I'm Shay. We found you here, passed out. Your heart had stopped, so I did CPR to revive you." A small smile graced my face, and I allowed a little angelic influence to seep out and make her feel more relaxed.

As it always did, it worked like a charm, and her shoulders loosened.

"Sorry I had to get so close," I added.

Her hand fluttered to her heart. "No . . . thank you. I-I've always been so healthy. I can't believe that happened."

"Maybe you saw something that affected you? Trauma responses can be really intense." I fished for details. "Do you remember what you were doing before you fell?"

The last two humans I'd exorcized had not recalled coming upon a demon, hinting that the Covenant and other local witches were probably already bathing the city in memory-reversal charms.

"No, I—" She craned her neck to see around me. "Is he with you?"

"He is," I replied firmly, hating the words. But they had to be said. Anyone would freak out if they were being watched by a guy like Hans—tall, muscular, tatted, and, after a night of scouring the city, filthy. "Don't worry about him."

Or should we?

I frowned at how easily the thought popped into my mind. Though logically, I knew Hans was a good person, and always had been, it was nearly impossible to turn off my angelic distrust. Especially after his demon magic had made an appearance earlier.

Plus, I was feeling justified. I was pretty damned sure he was hiding something from me. Something I intended to figure out.

"Okay," she murmured, still watching the demon-wizard, though now with something more like desire in her eyes.

I feel ya, girl. He's hot. But run—run fast.

"Anyway," I said. "It's early in the morning, and I don't know how long you were out before we found you."

"Oh my lord! My family is probably worried sick!" The woman gasped, looking down at her watch and then began digging through her bag, which miraculously no one had taken. When she looked back up at me, her cheeks where pink. "I'm so sorry. I don't have cash to give y—"

"I don't need anything." I assured her with a smile. "Just glad to help."

"The world needs more people like you two in it," she replied. "Thank you."

The woman left, and I waited until she was out of earshot before turning to Hans. "I can't do any more."

"I didn't see any signs of burnout," he frowned.

"Not any outward ones, but they'll come if I keep it up. My skin is getting hot. I don't want to get close to that mark."

"You know yourself best," he nodded. "We should probably—"

His phone chimed, interrupting him. "That's Luca's ringtone."

He answered the call. "Hey, man."

While they spoke, I scanned the area. Morning light was spilling across the concrete now, threatening to consume the city.

I was glad the Covenant had, most likely, put memory reversal spells in place, but how much more was needed to right New York? Had they brought in more nephilim to exorcize demons? Over the hours, I'd done twelve by myself, but there had to be more people in danger. This city was too big, the job couldn't be done by just a small group.

"Okay," Hans said, bringing his attention back to me. "Luca is returning to New Haven with Tobias, Harper, and Meredith. He's leaving his car for us to take back, and he's gonna catch a ride in the Stiffmobile."

I snorted at the nickname. The term pissed Tobias off, but damn if it wasn't the truth. "Why is he leaving? It's still early."

Hans shrugged. "Something cropped up with Scroll and Key that requires his attention, and he wants to check in with Night Circle and tell them about Josiah."

Oh. Freaking-A, that'll be a nightmare.

"He said we should return to the Covenant's camp and see what else they need, assist them in any way possible." He paused. "And he mentioned that your mother was there."

My throat tightened, and the sense of heaviness that had descended over me when Luca assigned Hans as my partner weighed me down a little more.

It was no secret Mom and I had a strained relationship.

After the other two nephilim seats arrived to help the city, I had been wondering if she'd show.

My mother held one of three nephilim Covenant Seats and always liked to be in on the action. She also had a habit of claiming credit for positive outcomes. Even if she didn't deserve it all.

I exhaled. "Thanks for the heads-up. I say we go back now. I don't think we're far."

After quickly pulling out my phone, I confirmed we were only seven blocks from where the Covenant had set up camp; basically, we'd traveled in a huge-ass square.

"This way," I said, and we started hoofing it to the camp.

It was easy to dismiss the uncomfortable silence between us as we walked. The city was being repaired, and along the way, we did what we could to put it in order. For Hans, that meant magically scrubbing blood from the streets, whereas I picked up dropped items—groceries, phones, bags, whatever I could find—and tossed them in the trash. Anything we could do to make the city a touch more normal would be useful.

When we arrived at the camp, the area was even more bustling than before. As promised, Luca was nowhere in sight. Neither were Rooms and Tobias.

"Artem has Luca's keys." Hans gestured to a bear of a man in a red beret. "I'll go get them and see if they have more for us to do."

The unsaid hope that maybe we could just go home too hung on his lips.

"I'll be around here." After exorcizing so many people, I just needed a moment to chill.

Hans strode off to speak with the wizard Covenant representative.

As soon as he was gone, an ease I hadn't felt for hours

swept through me. Really, Hans had been doing all that he could to keep me comfortable, but it just wasn't working

And I knew for a fact that a lot of it was down to me. I hated that, but it was true.

Usually, I was a people person, happy to get to know pretty much anyone, and I could chill with most of S&S's members. But since the moment I'd learned Hans was half-demon, things had changed inside me. I was still crushing on him, for sure, but a loathing coated that desire.

Some of that loathing was targeted at myself—an angel lusting after a demon?!—but part of it was for him too. Though I told others it was because we were on opposite sides of a Heaven-Hell divide, that wasn't the whole truth. There was something more, something internal that I couldn't describe and didn't understand.

Mom might know.

As soon as the thought cropped up, I cringed. Not only did Hans want to keep his ancestry a secret from those outside of S&S, but me admitting to my mother that I had a crush on a half-demon was just asking for her to be disappointed in me.

Not that that took much.

"Shaylina!"

Shoot me. I scowled at my horrible given name. One only a single person in Heaven and Earth used. *Speak of the . . . nephilim.*

Pasting a fake smile on my face, I turned and found my mother: a tall, blonde, Mexican woman who still drew many stares, despite appearing over fifty years in human age. Basically, she was still a bombshell, and I was glad to get my looks from her—all except my blue eyes, which were purely from Dad.

"Mom!"

Her brilliant smile dimmed for a moment before she realized where she was and who was around, then it returned. Only I could see the annoyance lining her eyes.

Oops. I'm in for it.

"Call me Angelina, my darling," Mom said once she stood in front of me and had taken my hand—again, probably for show. "I'm here on Covenant business."

Like that would matter. Since I'd turned fifteen, she had insisted I call her by her first name.

"Sorry," I muttered, not meaning it. I wished she could be like a normal mother. "Have you been scouting the city?"

She nodded. "I've performed twenty exorcisms."

Oh, great. Three, two, . . .

"You, darling?"

"Twelve. I had to stop because I was in danger of burning out."

Her full lips pursed. "But you've been out here far longer than me. I'm proud that you're helping, but really, Shaylina, have you given it your all?"

"I have," I gritted out, trying to keep my cool, though she always made it difficult. "Maybe your possessions weren't as intense."

She shrugged. It was obvious she considered my lower number a personal deficiency. That annoyed the hell out of me. "Perhaps. Walk with me. There's so much to do still."

As we strode through the camp, Mom left little chance for us to catch up. Instead, she filled the awkward silence between us with commands for others. Apparently, she'd brought her whole business team—all nephilim, save for one excellent vampire accountant—to assist the Covenant.

A favor I was sure she would not let anyone in the ruling body forget when it came time for re-election.

"So, I hear you arrived when the demon prince was still in the city?" Angelina asked, finally speaking directly to me. "Did you see him? How many demons did you come across during the battle?"

"Uhhh."

Unease trickled through me, thinking of Hans. There was no way I'd out him to my mother, but she'd flip her shit if she knew that, for most of the battle, I'd been working *with* a demon.

"Shaylina?"

"I saw a lot of demons, but not the prince. Got there too late."

Disappointment flashed in Mom's eyes. I bet she would have loved it if her daughter was responsible for vanquishing a demon prince. She'd always wanted me to follow more in my father's footsteps. To be extraordinary.

"I did see hellhounds, though," I added. "A pack straight from Hell. They were huge!"

She gave a nod, slightly mollified.

In the background, I caught sight of Hans, and suddenly, I had an idea. One that could earn me more of my mother's respect, and give me more information on why my feelings toward Hans were so intense.

"Actually," I said slowly, "I got really close to a couple of demons. One was a Hellblooded girl. She must have had a powerful parent, because her magic was astonishing."

"She wasn't a full demon, then?"

"At first, I thought she was just a teen who needed help." I lied to avoid tossing Hans under the bus. No matter my personal feelings toward him, coven members didn't do that. "She was really playing it up, and I was full of compassion for her."

Liar, liar, pants on fire.

"But then she showed her true colors. As soon as I realized what she was, this sense of *deep* loathing filled me. It came from the inside, and it was like I couldn't even see the little girl anymore. That didn't happen with the possessed people I came across, though. Is that normal for us?"

My mother studied me, as if she sensed there was something I wasn't saying. And yet, instead of prying, which was normally her way, she nodded. "It is. I worked hard to shield you from the Hellblooded as a girl, but those with stronger blood—of which there are not many—affect nephilim."

"But why couldn't I sense it before? It was so weird. Like the moment I knew she was a demon, that switch flipped, and loathing filled me. She was one the whole time, though, so I should have felt it from the start."

"It's ingrained in our souls to despise anyone with demon blood, Shaylina. However, they can wear convincing costumes."

I pictured Hans. A bad boy wizard who I'd lusted over many times without once feeling gross about it—at least, not until recently.

Tell me about it, Mom.

"Is there a way to turn that off?" I asked.

Mom cocked her eyebrow.

"It was so distracting when I fought her," I added, hoping she'd think the excuse was good enough.

"I'm not sure, but I do not believe you would be able to stop it. Not that you should wish to anyhow." A shuddering breath left her. "Did you put the girl out of her misery?"

"I—no," I said, stopping there.

Mother's lips flattened. "Shame."

Another disappointment.

"Seat Ramos!" a voice called out, pulling my mother's penetrating gaze away from me.

As she turned, the frustration she felt for her daughter disappeared, and a brilliant smile blossomed on her face. "Yes, Gigi?" Mom asked, taking in the short, plump nephilim who worked for her.

"We've finished our sweep of this borough. As far as we can tell, there are no more possessed humans. What would you like us to do?" Gigi, my mother's assistant, spared me a smile as she approached.

The nephilim appeared to be in her mid-thirties, so she was probably nearing a century in age. She was gregarious and ambitious and I liked her, despite how much she kissed Mom's ass.

"Move on to Brooklyn. No one has burnt out?"

"We're being careful." Gigi's dark eyes found me. "Would you like to join us, Shay?"

"I—"

"Shaylina informed me that she came close to burnout. So no, she will not be assisting," Mother replied for me, regret in her tone.

Really, it was fine with me if I didn't help. I was dead on my feet and seriously didn't want to risk burning out. But I still hated how the words sounded on her tongue.

"No worries," Gigi said with a shrug. "We've got it under control."

"My team always does. It's why I brought you." Mom turned to me. "It was good to see you, darling, but I fear I must go. There's much work to be done, and I have energy to spare!"

Mom pulled me in for a brief hug, and then she was off to continue saving the world.

In her absence, the annoyance I'd been holding back since the start of our conversation bubbled through me freely. I loved my mother, I really did, but she expected so much from me. And I never, *never*, met those expectations.

Even when I could do things she couldn't, like wield a sword of fire and light, she'd simply wish I was more like my father. That my sword was bigger, brighter, *better*—like his.

Dad was an archangel! It was incredibly hard to top that.

The frustration surged, and seeing as no one was paying attention to me, I let my fists curl into tight balls, the only outward sign of my anger I'd show. Angels were supposed to be happy, light, to keep negative feelings away—and usually, I could do that, but sometimes . . .

Breathe, I told myself, and inhaled deeply. A few more rounds of breathing exercises proved beneficial, and I'd nearly gotten through the deluge of emotion, when something caught my attention.

About a city block away, Hans marched down the street, away from where the Covenant members and those taking their orders congregated. And then, with one cautious glance over his shoulder, he slipped unnoticed into an alley.

What's he up to? I wondered, sweeping around the larger group and following.

As I neared where he'd vanished, I slowed my pace, not wanting to be heard.

Was that . . . Did he just tear a piece of paper? What is going on?

Carefully, I poked my head around the corner. Hans's back was to me, so he didn't see, but I could see the letter plainly. Just as I could see the name scrawled across the bottom of the page in large, bold letters.

Nicoleta.

"What is that?" I snapped.

Hans whirled, shoving the letter in his pocket, just as he'd done after our first exorcism.

"Is that what you've been keeping from me?" I yelled, not at all caring if someone else heard. My vexation after talking to Mom was too fresh, and this was making me burn hotter.

So hot, in fact, that before I knew it, my sword of fire and light flashed in my hand. "What. Is. It?"

Hans took a few quick steps backward, his eyes trained on the sword.

We were an even match and both knew it, but my sword was mythical. My father was the only angel who could call such a thing, and I'd inherited that gift.

"Shay." Hans raised his hands, a gesture of surrender. "Calm down."

When had saying that to an upset person *ever* worked?

"I saw your sister's name! And I know you went across the street to get something after that first exorcism, Hans. Do *not* treat me like an idiot. Are you turning to your dark side? Did Lilith ask you to align with the demons?"

"No!" he shouted. "Nothing like that!"

"Then what is that? Tell me, or . . ."

"You'll what?" his chin tipped up with defiance. "Luca said to keep that quiet."

Yes, and normally I'd do anything Luca said. He wasn't the leader of a ruling supernatural sect, like those in the Covenant, but sometimes, I got the sense that the mage cared for magical beings more than some in our ruling body.

Still, I needed to know what was in that letter, and I was just fine with Hans thinking I might betray S&S. Even if I'd never actually do it. So I just held his stare, my eyes blazing into blue ones that were trying to work me out.

Finally, he sighed. "It is from my sister. I'll let you read it, but you can't tell anyone here."

"Fine," I agreed. "Hand it over."

He fished the paper from his pocket and smoothed the crumpled paper out before extending it to me. My fingers had just grazed the letter, when he pulled it back.

I snarled at him. "I'm not playing, Hans."

"I know. I just want you to be warned that you're not going to like what you read here."

"I'd expect nothing less from your demon sister," I spat, and immediately regretted the words.

Hurt cut across his face, and even though Hans recovered quickly, I felt like an ass for saying them.

"Take it." He shoved the paper at me.

I read each line hungrily, my incredulity growing. This girl had major balls.

"She wants you to kidnap me and bring me to Prince Orien?" I said, reaching the end of the letter. "What the actual hell?!"

"For the record, I have no intention of following through," Hans said. "I'd just started re-reading this when you interrupted."

"Well, it's a relief that you're not going to give me up to your demon kin."

"Stop saying that!" Hans threw his hands in the air. "I have no say in what I am, Shay. I—"

"You have no say," a male voice boomed behind us. "But you certainly should have mentioned this, Hans."

My breath hitched, and I spun in time to see Seat Artem Kovalenko, wizard of the Covenant, rounding the corner, his arms crossed over his barrel chest.

CHAPTER NINE

HANS

MY BODY WENT RIGID, AND SHAY SEEMED TO DISAPPEAR FROM sight as I zeroed in on Artem. The elder caster stared me down like a bull in a ring, and I was the red cape, waving frantically in the wind.

"I-I—" Before I could continue, I zipped it.

What the hell was I going to say, anyway? It wasn't like I could claim to be naïve to my parentage. Nor did I want to lie to this man, the most steadfast and trustworthy wizard I knew. Someone I looked up to.

Equally as much, though, I didn't want to become a pariah. Unable to help myself, I glanced down at my arms again. Over the hours, the gray tint of my veins had lightened a touch, which seemed to support my theory that the hue was a product of using my dark magic.

The more time I went without using that magic, the less noticeable it should be. Still, if one looked hard enough, they might see. I swallowed thickly. Would they know what it meant?

It was all good and fine for those in my village to know what I was; they were small-town folk. The longest journey any of my neighbors had taken was to London. Plus, the only supernaturals in Minim were the wolfpack, and they wouldn't give us up to the supernatural ruling body. They didn't even trust the Covenant, or anyone outside of our village.

But the Covenant? The supernatural world at large? Nicoleta might sing her bloodline from the rooftops, but I wanted no part in that.

"I'm not mad." Artem's muscular arms dropped to his side.

"But now I have to register." I sounded so fucking small, so unlike myself.

"Perhaps not, if we play this right." Artem eyed me thoughtfully.

My heart rate slowed. "How do you mean?"

Shay remained silent. Though she'd stepped out from between Artem and me, her blue eyes were ping-ponging between us.

"I overhead almost everything Shay said," Artem admitted. "Is it true that your mother is Lilith?"

"Yes."

"Do you not think the demon prince would be interested in that sort of power? I assume you inherited some of her dark magics?"

"I did."

Before yesterday, I could have claimed that my demon powers no longer worked, that they had died since I shoved them deep inside me. But they hadn't. Just last night, those demonic powers had helped me save Shay.

"Don't you believe we could use your lineage to get close to him? The Prince of Wrath wishes to conquer Earth, Hans.

You would be helpful in this."

"Y-you want me to play spy?!"

Artem glanced around the corner, as if worried someone would overhear us. "It's a possibility. However, I believe we should speak with the rest of the Covenant first."

For the first time since the wizard appeared, Shay's attention landed solidly on me, the question plain in her eyes.

Though it seemed impossible, I did have options. S&S ensured its members were not powerless. And while Luca was not a political figure, he *was* a powerful mage, and S&S had major clout among those of the Covenant. I could claim to need to discuss this with the coven master. Artem would most likely agree. He was, after all, one of the most reasonable Covenant members.

In the end, it would be my choice . . . and I had to admit that the idea, though fucking terrifying, had merit.

"Before you decide, I should add that I believe Shay should come too. If the contents of that letter is any indication, to a Prince of Darkness, she is nearly as valuable as you." Artem glanced at my colleague with discomfort. "I hope you take my meaning, my dear."

"You're talking about using me as bait for the prince," Shay spat. "I get the picture."

"You are your mother's daughter."

Shay straightened, and for a moment, I thought she'd deny Artem, even hoped she would. She was an angel, so seeing a demon prince would be even more dangerous for her. Plus, a denial from her would buy us time.

"Fine. Let's speak with them," Shay said, astonishing the ever-living fuck out of me. Why would she want to do this? Did she not realize how perilous this was? Of course she did.

Shay was a smart woman. . . so what was motivating her? "Hans? You in?"

Now that she'd agreed, how could I say no? It would look weak and like I had more to hide. But I didn't. My secret was out and sure to spread.

Seeing as that was all but inevitable, I wanted to make very certain others knew they could trust me. No matter how powerful I was, or how renowned my mother, I needed others to understand that *I* wasn't *that* kind of Hellblooded.

"Sure," I breathed finally, hoping it wasn't a huge mistake.

"Let us go, then," Artem said. "The Covenant members who made the trip to New York are convening to discuss what to do next. This will be an ideal time for you to speak with them." He turned and left the alley, sure that we would follow.

Before we did, I glanced at Shay. "You don't even want to talk to Luca about this?"

She shook her head. "This has nothing to do with S&S." Then she strode out onto the street after Artem.

I snorted, still not sure where the hell Shay's head was at, but went along with it because right now she was my partner and in our coven we didn't leave a man or woman behind.

Instead of leading us back toward the camp like I'd guessed, though, Artem turned down a side street. It was empty, and if he'd been a shady sort, that would have had me questioning his motives. But Artem wasn't that way.

"Where are we going?" I asked.

On the other side of the wizard, Shay leaned forward, curious too.

"The Covenant is borrowing a local coven's meeting place," Artem replied. "It's quite kind of them to share."

The wizard marched another two blocks in the same direction before turning down a street filled with brownstones. He then climbed up the steps to one and knocked.

Right away, a Latina woman who looked exactly like Shay, but with blonde hair and brown eyes, opened the door.

"Shaylina," the woman said. "This is a surprise." Her eyes trailed to me. "Who's the young man?"

Shaylina?

My lips twitched as Shay scowled. Someone else had secrets too.

"I'm Hans, Ma'am."

"Please don't call me Ma'am. I may be this lovely, young one's mother, but it makes me feel old. Do I look old?"

"No."

And it was the truth. Now that I knew for certain that this was Shay's mom—who I'd heard of but never met—the resemblance made sense. Still, there was no way in hell I would have guessed this woman was old enough to have birthed Shay.

"Good boy," Shay's mom purred, which made her daughter's nose wrinkle. "Call me Angelina." She turned her attention to her wizard counterpart. "Now, Artem, why are these two here? This is Covenant business."

"I believe they will be able to help," he replied.

Angelina raised an eyebrow but stepped aside. "If you insist, but this had better be good."

Shay began coughing, her face turning red as she covered her mouth. Though she'd been the one to agree to this scheme, I got the sense that, in the face of her mother, she had doubts.

No surprise there. What mom would want their daughter to give themselves up to a demon prince?

Angelina led us through the brownstone, which appeared larger inside than it seemed to be on the outside. Magically enhanced, no doubt. The coven who owned it was also wealthier than I'd imagined. Or maybe they were just more ostentatious. Our coven's tomb was grand in an Old-World way, but this home-turned-meeting-place put headquarters to shame.

Cream and gold were the colors of choice, making me cringe. They were too pale, too difficult to keep clean for someone like me, who was so often covered in machine grease in his spare time—which, technically, I hadn't had in a while.

We took a turn down a hallway, and suddenly, images of the famed witch Circe were everywhere. My eyes widened at the blatant display of supernaturalness. So now we were deep enough into the magically enhanced home that the coven felt safe showing their true colors, their witchy nature. And who they held on a pedestal.

Not every witch coven worshiped a powerful predecessor, but those that did were usually the strongest of our kind. Powerful and, most often, secretive. Which hinted at one thing: this coven likely wasn't allowing the Covenant to use their space out of the goodness of their hearts.

I was proven right a second later when Angelina let us into a room dominated by a circular white marble table large enough to seat twenty. The damned thing must have weighed hundreds of pounds!

Around the table sat a few recognizable faces. Two annoying ones, Egor Drago and Richard Brons. The latter was a wizard, bald as an egg, and with a pretentious, pointed beard he loved to stroke.

Douche, I thought, moving on from Brons.

Aside from them, a smattering of vampire, siren, necromancer, nephilim, shifter, and of course the third witch representatives were present. Not every Seat was present, but almost every magical order that held a position on the Covenant was accounted for. Most Seats I was somewhat familiar with by sight, though there were four people I couldn't name.

And one woman I couldn't place at all. She was a mature woman of about eighty, dressed in an expensive-looking outfit. Her attire felt incredibly pompous, given the state of the city outside the front door, but she held herself like a queen, unbothered by the fate of the world. Her steel-gray hair had been pulled into a bun worn at her nape, and blood-red lipstick colored the elegant woman's lips.

My own lips curled into a smirk. That had to be the representative for whatever coven this was. They wanted in on the action.

A part of me didn't blame them; New York was their home. A larger part of me, however, was on guard.

Artem knew my most closely guarded secret, and we were about to expose it to these people. The Covenant was one thing, but any witch or wizard on the street . . .

"Artem," I whispered. "Who is that?"

"Grand High Priestess Rebecca Knox of the Sisters of Circe."

I stiffened. I didn't make it a rule to familiarize myself with many covens, but I actually had heard of this one. They weren't just rich and powerful, but *very* influential in the Covenant elections. I suspected they were responsible for getting Richard Brons on the board three years back.

I shuddered, despising the wizard and what he stood for.

"Does she have to be here?" I whispered.

"It was a stipulation of using their space." Artem swallowed, clearly not totally comfortable with the idea either. He turned to me first, then to Shay. "I should have mentioned this earlier. I apologize. Do you two wish to change your minds? Or put off speaking of this?"

Shay shook her head emphatically. "I'm all-in."

I exhaled, still not sure where her mind was at, but I agreed that doing this later wouldn't be better. I just needed to put a few rules in place. "No, but I have a few stipulations of my own for the Sisters of Circe."

"We will all do our best to accommodate your wishes," Artem said seriously. "Do you trust me?"

"If I didn't, I wouldn't be here," I replied.

Shay nodded, and the wizard's shoulders loosened.

"Thank you," Artem said. "I value that trust. Now, we should sit."

Four seats remained. Shay and I took up chairs flanking Artem, who leaned forward and placed his folded hands on the table.

"As everyone can see, I've brought two members of S&S with me."

"And why is that?" asked Egor Drago, a vampire and one of the most unlikable people I'd ever come into contact with. "I didn't get the memo that this was an open meeting."

"It isn't," Angelina said. "But Artem claims to have a good reason for my daughter and this man, Hans, to be here. So let's hear it."

The Ukrainian wizard cleared his throat. "As mentioned, these two are members of the Coven of Shadows and Secrets, and are therefore trained to undertake dangerous missions. They have agreed to go on one for the good of the Covenant and all supernaturals. That said, before I go further, I must request secrecy from all members regarding Shay and Hans. What they are about to share is quite personal."

Angelina snorted. "Shaylina is my daughter, Artem! What could she have to hide from me?"

From the corner of my eye, I caught Shay shift in her seat.

Did Seat Ramos know her child as well as she thought?

"I must have assurances from each person here, Angelina," Artem pressed. "If Shay and Hans wish to divulge their personal matters to others later, that is their choice. But as their elected officials, we should honor their wishes."

Angelina rolled her eyes, a delicate gesture that I'd seen on her daughter—though often more exaggerated. "Of course. I will keep secret whatever they wish to share."

Everyone else in the Covenant nodded their acquiescence, and then Artem turned to Rebecca Knox.

"And you, Grand High Priestess? We request your silence too, and while I cannot bind you to Covenant rules of conduct, I ask that you submit to them willingly."

Rebecca's gaze fell first on me, then Shay, as if assessing if we were really worth so much trouble. Then, like she was doing us the biggest favor in the world, she heaved a sigh. "I will remain quiet, until otherwise notified by my Covenant representatives."

"Very good," Artem leaned back in his chair. "Does that suffice, Shay? Hans?"

"Yes," the nephilim replied.

I nodded. It would have to do. Only time would tell if these people would stay true. I, for one, would be keeping my eye on Egor, Richard, and Rebecca.

"Very good," Artem said. "Then I'll proceed."

"*Finally,*" Angelina huffed. "You'd think you were about to tell us that you were in league with the Princes of Darkness."

"It has come to my attention," Artem continued, his tone stronger than before, "that Hans here is not only a wizard."

"Have a little human blood, then?" Angelina snorted derisively. "Welcome to the club."

If only.

"He is, in fact, a Hellblooded. Related to the Queen of the Underworld herself."

"Lilith?!" Richard Brons shot out of his chair. "B-but how?"

"I don't wish to share that information," I spoke up, not about to throw my father under the bus. If it came out that my mother could slip into our world, and had been doing so for years, and Father knew, he'd be in deep shit. "But what Artem says is true. My father didn't know who she was when they met. Not until after my sister was born."

"There are *two* of you?!" Brons's eyes went wide. "You know the law, Hans. All Hellblooded are required to register."

It took everything I had not to glance at my veins, to check on how gray they were. I knew about the registration and I'd avoided that racist-ass law for years. Even now, I had no intention of willingly putting my name on the list, though I was definitely more demon than 99% of those on the list. Far more powerful, too.

"I'm aware." I looked at Artem.

He nodded, as if to say *'if you wish, go on,'* so I did.

"I have my reasons for not registering, and if I'm to help you out, I request that I maintain my status as only a wizard. My sister too." I hadn't considered such a thing before, but that was my limit. I was sure that, once they heard what I had to offer, they'd buckle.

"You'd better be willing to give prime information, boy," Egor Drago growled. "Lilith killed my maker, and I would absolutely love a little retribution."

I swallowed. I wasn't about to apologize for my mother's actions, but this new information would make it harder to bargain for her safety—which I belatedly realized I should do too.

Failing Nicoleta had been out of my hands, but this wasn't. And though my sister was making all the wrong choices, I loved her and didn't want to see her hurt. Not when I truly could provide a better life for her—if she'd just give it a chance.

"My sister has fallen prey to the Prince of Darkness's sway. She gave me this letter," I pulled it from my pocket, "which requests that I bring Shay to a specific place at a specific time. I believe this might be the Prince of Darkness's way to gather more power—as Shay's father is a well-known angel."

Angelina's chest puffed out.

"Perhaps he wishes to transfer Shay's, or her father's, power to another using a necromancer," a female shifter representative raised an idea I had not considered.

Clearly Luca had told them about Josiah. He'd probably had to do so. I assumed the Ringmaster was in cahoots with the Prince of Darkness, since there'd been a shitload of demons in the fight.

"Shaylina's father would never stand for that," Angelina said. "If he heard his own blood had been taken, he'd offer up much to get her back."

Shay squirmed again. Did she agree? We all knew that her father was the Archangel Uriel, and the pureblooded angels did not make appearances on Earth often. In fact, Uriel's coupling with Angelina was the last known occurrence. But wouldn't he come to the aid of his daughter?

"Actually, I believe there's another reason for this," Brons said slowly. "If the Darkborn can't get all the sacred stones, this is their backup plan."

I blinked. *Wait . . . what?*

"What do you mean?" Shay asked, leaning forward in interest.

"Very few things can open the Eyes of Darkness, the gateway from this world and Hell. The *lapis caelesti* are rumored to be able to do so," Brons replied, his bald head glistening under the bright light of the room. "But so is pure angel blood. An archangel's blood would be even better. It might open all the gates at once, it's so strong."

I sucked in a breath. I hadn't known that, and was curious as to how Richard Brons learned the information. There was not much written on the *lapis caelesti*, and most of it was in the Beinecke's supernatural section. How had he gotten such information? And how did he know of the uses of pure angelic blood? Angels weren't exactly forthcoming with information on their kind.

From the looks on the other Covenant members' faces, they didn't doubt him, so it must be valid.

Was the Covenant hiding information from the public?

"Do you wish to do this, Shay?" Another nephilim representative, a woman I didn't know with long blonde hair and piercing green eyes, studied my partner. "Even if your father came to save you, you likely would not survive. We are dealing with *demons* here, child."

"I do." Shay's voice broke slightly, hinting that might not be the complete truth. "I want to help," she finished and looked to the wizard at her side.

"As others have mentioned, the demons are surely setting a trap of one kind or another," Artem interjected, "However, I believe we can turn the tables on them, with or without the archangel's help."

"An ambush?" Angelina scoffed. "On the Prince of Wrath? He's a General of Hell, a master tactician, and you think we can get one over on him? You do recall Luca informed us that he's been hiding here for decades, correct? Just biding his time?"

"It's an *option*," Artem replied. "That is, unless you have better means to find him?"

The room fell silent, and I had a hunch that Artem's plan, risky as it was, would see light very soon.

CHAPTER TEN

MEREDITH

I THREW OPEN THE DOOR TO SHAY'S HOME, WEARINESS thrumming through my bones. Tobias and Harper marched in after me, the wolf letting out a groan of relief that I felt all the way down in my soul.

"I might skip classes today," she announced.

Might!? We'd been up all night long chasing demons. Going to classes hadn't been at the top of my list.

"You should rest," Tobias nodded. "There's no telling when we will have to act again."

"I'm fully aware of my obligations, Tobias." Harper turned, a hand on her hip. "S&S first, Yale second."

I blinked, because that really put things into perspective. And it made a ton of sense. Luca had gotten a few of us into Yale, he could surely maintain our enrollment if we needed to take time away and flunked out as a result. Not that I wanted that to happen, but with the Prince of Hell on the loose, it seemed likely that classes would be postponed.

When would I have to search for the Pearl next? When would I even be able to? Nicoleta had let Wrath—I rolled my eyes at the pompous name—in on my secret. Surely, he'd be more careful when he planned to use the Pearl next. Was it possible that he'd even figure out how to cloak the stone?

And what about the Opal? Had he used it before?

It grated that no one knew what the other *lapis caelesti* could do. What if Prince Orien *had* used the Opal of Heaven already and we had no idea? What if its effects were even worse than those of the Pearl?

Something told me that wasn't likely. Just the full name of the Pearl indicated a more ominous nature. But still . . . No one *really* knew, so nothing was off the table.

"Anyway, I'm going to pray to the Old Ones for those in the city, then I'm hitting the sheets. Night you two." Harper threw a wave and disappeared down the hall, shutting herself in her bedroom.

Suddenly, the vampire and I were alone. I inhaled slowly. Was it just me, or was it already getting warmer in here?

"Are you going to rest too?" Tobias's hand landed on my shoulder, sending chills up and down my spine.

On the drive home, I'd noticed him glancing at me in the rearview mirror many times as he and Luca discussed the events of the night. Maybe it was just me projecting my own desires onto him, but it almost seemed like he'd wanted to connect with me.

"I'd like to," I answered. "Do you just want to . . . stay down here? Or I can show you to the spare room? It's next door to mine."

"I'll remain on the couch," Tobias replied, though I didn't miss the shifting of his gaze up the stairs. Nor the bobbing of his Adam's apple.

"Okay. I do have classes today, in the afternoon, but I'll

skip them. Unless I wake up feeling amazing, of course. I'm going to play it by ear."

"Don't stress yourself," the vampire replied. "You've done quite a lot the last twenty-four hours."

I nodded. "Then I guess I'll head up. See you soon."

With that, I began my slow trudge up the stairs, my aching muscles wincing with each step. When I got to the top, I peered down, over the banister, only to find Tobias's intense attention, still locked on me.

I waved awkwardly, unsure what to think or do with myself, and went to my room.

The moment I opened the door, Benedict hissed.

"Where *have* you been, Meredith?!"

Oh crap.

Benedict leapt off the bed, where he had been expressly told not to perch, and stomped his little cat paws all the way over to me.

"I was worried sick, Meredith! You didn't come home! None of you did." Light amber eyes glared at me, demanding an answer.

"I'm sorry!" I held up my hands, a plea for forgiveness. "New York was under attack by a demon prince, and—"

"And you didn't get me to help?!" Benedict let out a yowl of anger. "Did you even think about me?"

The truth was, I hadn't. I'd been so caught up in finding the missing stone in my ring and then being called to S&S's head-quarters, driving to the city, and dealing with the demons that I hadn't spared my familiar a second thought. But I couldn't admit to that, it was too mean.

The expression on his face told me I didn't need to. He looked equally crushed and pissed the hell off, and I felt like a super-asshole.

"I'm sorry, Benedict. It won't happen again."

"Too right you won't. I'm sticking to you like glue!"

Awesome. Now I'd not only have a vampire shadow that I was feeling increasingly conflicted about, but an invisible cat. One who didn't know how to shut the hell up. I was pretty sure conversation with my invisible familiar on campus made me look totally insane. Wasn't looking forward to that happening daily.

"Tobias is still my guard," I told him. "He's actually downstairs right now, so I don't think you really have to follo—"

"Oh *yes*, I *do*, Meredith." Benedict turned around and gave me an unashamed view of his butthole. "Your parents said that when I was called back to your side, I was to protect you. I had thought the vampire would be good enough to assist while you're out, but from the looks of that scar, I no longer think that's true."

My fingers went to the line on my collarbone. Tobias assured me that, thanks to the healing powers of his blood, the scar would fade. That despite it being made by a necromancer's blade, it should be almost invisible, if not completely gone, in a day or two.

As much as I wanted to argue with the cat, I found I couldn't. Benedict was only showing he cared, and he'd always honored his word to my deceased parents. Whether it made sense or not.

"How did it happen?" Benedict strolled to his cat bed and sat on the cushion like it was a throne.

Oh boy, here we go.

"I had a run-in with the Ringmaster."

"Excuse me!?!"

The story of the last twenty-four hours spilled from me. With each beat, Benedict grew stiffer, ramping up my own stress. Only when I got to the point that Tobias and Luca arrived to save me, did he loosen. Sensing his relief, I did the same.

"Josiah is guilty," the cat murmured. "That no-good—"

"He is," I cut Benedict off, not wanting to think about Josiah anymore.

The necromancer had his reasons for selling me out, but I still believed he could have asked for help. The coven would have assisted him, and Sara would likely already be safe.

Now that he was on the run with the Ringmaster, that could only spell trouble. Until he was caught, I'd be wary of every raven I spotted.

"Is the Covenant still in the city?"

"To my knowledge," I said. "It was a war zone, Benedict. I bet it takes them forever to clear up."

"You'd be surprised what magic can accomplish in a short period of time," Benedict remarked. "This isn't the first time supernaturals have gone on a rampage and the Covenant had to cover it up. And having members of S&S to assist will make the process go even faster."

I blinked. "This isn't the first time?"

Benedict's features softened. "Far from it."

I wanted to ask what other sorts of magical disasters had occurred throughout history, but when I opened my mouth, a yawn escaped me instead.

Benedict reared back, disgust evident on his face. "You need to brush your teeth."

That was saying a lot, coming from a cat that ate tuna daily. Still, rude!

"Thanks, *Benny*," I shot Shay's favorite nickname back at him. *Tit for tat, jerkface.*

He glowered, but instead of reminding me that he didn't

do nicknames, he just stood and stretched. "Someone did a perimeter sweep when you returned home?"

"Actually, no." I gaped, unable to believe Tobias hadn't done so. He'd been so focused on getting me inside, on watching me, on making sure I was okay . . .

"Well, since the vampire—who I'll be speaking with about his lackluster bodyguard skills, by the way—is downstairs, I'll take up that mantle." He gestured to the window, which I'd left open yesterday, totally oblivious that it would be a full day before I returned home.

"Okay. But I'm going to wash off." Though it was impossible, I'd definitely been imagining the stench of demons on me on and off for hours. "And to be honest, I don't feel comfortable with it being left open right now. I saw too much in the city."

And the Ringmaster had peons who were masters at breaking into places. Sure, the wards around the home were better protection than a cheap lock, but if I was going to sleep any time soon, I needed every extra reassurance.

"Everything is just freaking me out a little," I added, feeling like I needed to justify myself.

"Close the window after me," Benedict said, not a trace of judgment in his tone. "I'll either be waiting outside when you're done, or let you know when I get back so you can open it."

"Sure," I agreed, touched by how much he was showing he cared.

Benedict slipped outside a moment later, leaving me alone for the first time in over a day.

I closed the window behind him, latched it shut, and shuffled to the bathroom, more than ready to be clean and sleep the day away. Removing my filthy clothes, I stepped into the shower.

The hot water felt heavenly, and I allowed steam to fill the en-suite. Once done, I grabbed a towel, wrapping it around me. I felt a million times better and after sleep, would be good as new. Ready to take on whatever came next.

Just some face lotion, and I can collapse. I moved to the mirror and wiped the condensation off with my forearm.

The moment the mirror was clear, I stared at myself. The woman there was one I knew but was also just discovering. Someone capable of thieving but also learning to love and trust others more. A woman claiming control of her life.

I closed my eyes, exhaling deeply at the thought that once had seemed so far away.

When I opened my eyes again, I screamed. A flash of black and silver, a person wearing a mask glimmered back at me.

The Ringmaster!

Fast as I could, I scampered out of the bathroom—and ran right into Tobias's broad chest.

He gripped me tightly. His fangs were already descended, and his brilliant evergreen eyes locked on me. "What's wrong? What happened?"

"The Ringmaster! I saw her!" I pointed to the bathroom.

Tobias rushed past me, into the steamy room. But when he emerged a moment later, it wasn't with my nightmare in tow. "No one is in there, Meredith." His tone had softened, as had the steely look in his eyes.

I groaned as what I'd done, how crazy I'd just been, washed over me. I'd imagined her there, in her mask.

I shook myself, a chill still creeping over me. The vision of her looking over my shoulder had seemed so real. So dangerous.

"Meredith?" Tobias asked softly. "Are you okay?"

"Obviously not. I just imagined her there." I huffed out a breath. "Sorry I scared you."

Tobias nodded, and then his eyes dipped. A sheepish expression came over his face as he cleared his throat and looked at the ground. "The towel."

I glanced down, and my cheeks burned. The towel was still on, but a part of it must have slipped when I ran into him and now one of my boobs was hanging out.

How mortifying.

I pulled the towel up to cover me. "Shit. I'm such a mess, I can't believe that happened."

"You were just kidnapped by a person you fear." Tobias came closer, his words rumbly but in a reassuring way. "Additionally, someone you thought you could trust—a coven member sworn to have your back—sought to steal a piece of you, and endangered your life. If you weren't experiencing some form of PTSD right now, I'd be worried that you had no heart at all."

Tears pricked my eyes. It wasn't just what he said, but the way he said it that was getting to me. I was still getting used to a social network that cared about me as a person, rather than just what I could do for them.

"Thank you," I breathed and, unable to stop them, the tears began to fall. I bowed my head, not wanting him to see my weakness, hating that I was crying in front of this man. "You have no idea how much that means to me."

In two steps, Tobias was there again, wrapping his arms around me, pulling me close. "Believe it or not, I do."

I leaned into him, allowing myself to be held, supported, and for the tears to seep from me.

I'd had one hell of a night, and though I didn't normally

find relief in crying, right now, I did. I let the tears flow. With them, some of my pain, fear, and anxiety leaked out of me too.

When the waterworks finally ran dry, I drew in a big sniff and lifted my head. Tobias stared down at me, his gaze intense and soft at the same time.

We'd rarely been as close as we had in the last day, and as my skin tingled and heat rushed through me, I found myself wanting to get closer.

As if he felt my desire, he tilted his chin downward, his lips parting slightly.

My heart skipped a beat. This wasn't the first time I'd felt like the vampire might kiss me, but this time felt so real. So much *more*. I could hear his breath, feel his heart beating inside him. It seemed to pulse with mine.

"There you are!" a sharp voice called out as Benedict rapped on the window with a paw. "Let me in! I need words with you, vampire!"

Tobias twisted to take in the cat, and when he turned back to me, I swore disappointment flashed across his face.

"Umm." I pulled back, my teeth digging into my lower lip. Regret tore at me with every inch that expanded between us, but the moment was gone. Shattered. "Benedict is pretty pissed we didn't bring him along to the apocalypse."

"And it appears he wishes to give me an earful," the vampire said, a smirk pulling at his lips as a mask descended over his face. "Perhaps you should let the cat in so he and I can go downstairs and discuss all my shortcomings? In the meantime, you can get some rest."

I snorted as his attempt to lighten the heady sensation swirling between us worked. "Just don't call him a cat, or it's your funeral."

CHAPTER ELEVEN

GUNNER

I STARED AT THE CEILING AND SIGHED.

I couldn't remember the last time I'd gone so long with nothin' to do, but I was going damn near stir-crazy being cooped up in this manor like a chicken. One more day, and I'd begin to wonder if S&S cared about me at all.

A clamor from outside snagged my attention, and I rolled to the side, off the bed. Must be a feeding hour.

"Si, my man! Time for grubbin'," I called out, but when Claire opened the door to my room, she held no plate in her hands.

Her eyebrows were pulled together in mild amusement, her long gray hair disheveled, like she'd been caught in a windstorm, and she looked pale—which was saying somethin', 'cause these ladies didn't seem to get much sun as it was.

"You finally lettin' us out?" I drawled, not even trying to push my way through. Physically, I could overpower the witch in a second, but there were wards around our rooms. Fresh ones. I smelled 'em.

And considering Claire didn't look at all worried that I'd escape, they were probably dang good protections too. Better to save my energy.

"Read this." Claire pulled her shawl tighter around her, shivering as she handed me a phone already open to a webpage.

"You get the internet out here?" Silas asked, coming into my room through the adjoining door. "Miracles do happen."

I swear, if I hadn't had him to talk to for the last day and a half, I'd have gone insane. That seemed to be a mercy the witches had given us. They coulda put us in separate spaces, not allowed us to see one another, or to speak. But they didn't.

Not so sure Si felt the same about bein' so close to me all the time, though. I talked a lot and could tell that sometimes, I wore the fae out. Try as I might to be mindful of that, I pushed his limits, and every few hours, he'd retreat to his space to . . .

Well, I didn't know what the guy did. Read? A bunch of books were about all the witches had left us.

"Hurry up then," Claire hissed, gesturing down to the phone in my hand.

I started skimming the page she had open, but got only two sentences in when my mouth fell open. "This is on the internet?! But what if humans read this?"

The witch shook her head. "They can't. The Covenant has been posting on secret supernatural message boards, making sure those around the globe know what happened."

What had happened, it turned out, was a full-on apocalypse in New York City. Though the article didn't identify S&S by name, it did mention that a small group led by a mage had helped the Covenant restore peace.

That has to be us. Luca wouldn't let something like this happen so close to home and do nothin'.

"That must be why no one has come!" Silas said.

Apparently, he'd been feelin' just as put out as me, though the fae was better at hiding it. Hell, I'd asked the guy to snuggle, and I didn't even feel embarrassed by the request. It was a wolf thing. We weren't meant to be alone or cooped up in one place.

"We believe so too," the witch said. "And I regret to inform you that means you'll be staying here longer than we thought."

"What?! You're not gonna let us out after readin' that?" I thrust the phone at her, which she took with a shake of her graying head. "But we can help!"

"There's no mention of the stones, or anything that has to do with our coven. Nor yours. Not by name, anyway," Claire gestured to the device. "So we can't trust you completely until Meredith arrives. Not to mention, we must be *absolutely certain* that Meredith has the power we believe she does. That she's capable of finding this place on her own and . . . other things."

"She'll come here," I growled, gettin' pissed.

We'd said she was a seeker, she'd found the damned Pearl of Hell when she shouldn't have been able to, and her name was on that fancy-ass vault in Switzerland! What more did they want?

And what were these *other* things?

"You gonna test her when she gets here or somethin'?" I asked, trying to sniff out the direction this was going.

"That's none of your business," Claire said. "I came down here as a courtesy to you two, knowing your type can get *antsy* if cooped up too long."

I closed my eyes. Too long had been hours ago. I was dying for a little bit of fresh air and people time.

I shuddered, and when I opened my eyes again, the witch was watching me carefully.

"We're not doing this to be cruel," her tone softened. "Just cautious. The *Arcacusto* hold a special place in this world, and we can't trust you until one of the seven arrives and we hear from her lips that she trusts you. No matter how much your story aligns with recent events, we must be certain. I'm sorry."

With that, the crone shut the door again, trapping Silas and me inside.

My hands flew up, fingers winding through my shaggy curls as I spun, releasing a low growl.

"Gunner," Silas spoke softly, his tone mimicking the pitch it took on when he used the magical influence he was known for —almost like a vampire's compulsion, but not as strong.

But because we were in a prison meant to nullify our powers, his voice didn't calm me or my wolf, which was struggling to break through my skin. Unfortunately, whatever they'd put in my wine was still in effect, so even the stirring of my wolf caused pain to ripple throughout my body. Shifting to relieve the animal inside was a no-go.

I was imprisoned in every sense of the word.

An exhale parted my lips as I tried my damndest to calm my other half, but only succeeded in making my skin itch painfully and my muscles tighten.

I had to get out of here soon, get outside. Had to interact with as many people as possible. Had to let my wolf free. If I didn't, I wasn't sure what would happen.

Unable to stop it, a soft whine escaped me.

Silas sighed. "Bring it on in, big guy."

"You mean it?" My gaze flashed up, hope thrumming through me. "I know fae aren't huggers."

"True, but I don't want you going crazy in here. We need

to keep our wits about us. So come on." Silas held out an arm, and I went to him, snuggling into the crook of his shoulder.

The effect of touch was immediate, and not surprisingly, my greedy wolf wanted more. Silas wasn't even my type, but to my inner animal, he was looking pretty damn good right about now.

Chill, man, I spoke to the other part of me. *We don't bat for that team.*

The wolf howled, not giving a hoot.

I rolled my eyes. He might not now, but I wasn't that desperate. Not yet, anyway. Give me a few more days in this cramped space, and Silas would probably be looking more like a real option.

"Let's talk," Silas suggested. "Take your mind off things."

"Sure, man," I gestured to the seats at the far side of the room. They were placed in front of a fireplace that I hadn't lit, since wolves ran hot.

"You want me to make a fire?" I offered, figuring that since Claire had looked chilly, Silas might be too.

"Ice flows in my veins, so I'm well used to the cold," he replied. "However, a fire *would* be a welcome distraction."

Fire was primal; most supernaturals were drawn to it, just like humans. The trance of the flames might calm me more, so though I hadn't thought about it, I was glad Silas encouraged it.

"Happy to oblige." I set to tossing wood in the hearth.

Five minutes later, the flames were roarin', and we were settled in the chairs, Silas with his arm draped lazily on the side table between us in case I needed more touch.

Greedily, I laid my palm on his hand, a sigh tearing through me as I did so. "I really appreciate this, Si."

"No problem. I was getting a little bored too. The witches don't have the best of libraries."

I nodded. I hadn't been at all tempted by the books, but that wasn't a surprise to me. I'd rather be out doin' things than inside readin'.

"Did you mean that bit about ice flowing through your veins?" I asked.

"All Winter Court fae are born of snow and frost."

"Guess I just never thought of it that way." I cocked my head, thinking back to the other night, when he'd told the witches that he'd snuck into this realm. I was curious about that.

"Also didn't realize you were a refugee," I said carefully, testin' the waters. I'd known Silas a while now but he didn't talk much about himself. I didn't want to scare him off with this tricky subject. "That musta been hard."

"The most difficult thing I've had to do in my life." Silas turned his silver eyes on me. He was open to talkin' about it then. "You've been to Isila, no?"

"To Wolf Island. None of the fae courts."

"You wouldn't have been allowed in," Silas said with a shrug. "Well, perhaps to Spring or Summer. Certainly not Winter or Fall."

I nodded. That's what I'd learned too. I hadn't been in Isila long, but those weeks had been a whirlwind of teachings and stark realizations.

"Do you wish to return?" Silas asked, flippin' the conversation back to me. It seemed that he didn't want to get into his past much. That was fine by me. Maybe one day, he'd tell me a tale, but not now. "As a Royal Wolvea, you'd have certain privileges."

"Nah." I removed my hand from atop his to give the guy a

break and waved it dismissively. Right away, my wolf awoke and begged for more contact with another person. A few minutes of touch wasn't enough after being deprived for so long, but I didn't want to test my luck. "People there are too hard, too—"

"Cruel," Silas finished.

"You got it."

Though that wasn't the first word that came to mind when describing the magical beings of Isila, there *was* an undercurrent of cruelty in the mirror realm. Isila was a dog-eat-dog realm where royals always battled for power and commoners wanted it too. That was why S&S gettin' the sacred stones, and not the OA or one of the royal houses—be them fae, vampire, dragon, or other—was so important. Humans didn't know it, but they had lots of enemies who'd do shitty things to them.

"I got no desire to return to the other realm," I added. "I'm happy here, with the coven now, and one day back with my pack."

At the mention of my pack, my wolf howled. I squirmed as he pressed on my skin, begging to get out, for comfort, for room to roam.

Silas held out his hand again, and I thanked the moon for the fae who was putting my comfort before his.

"How does that work, anyway?" Si asked as I gripped his wrist. Again, my inner wolf calmed down, settling inside me like a dog showin' their belly for a rub down. "Wouldn't they want their future alpha with them?"

It wasn't the first time I'd been asked that question. At first, S&S had doubted my motivations for joining. My role as future alpha to one of the largest and most influential packs in the United States was one huge reservation for Luca. He'd suspected I might be in the dark artifacts hunting game for the wrong reasons and would take whatever we found back to the pack. Not just magical items, but information, which was the most valuable currency the coven possessed.

So, like Meredith, I drank the potion that revealed any harbored bad intentions, and had a trial period before being accepted. All through that time, many had doubted me, but I'd proven myself over the years, and now Luca was my main man. A pal and a leader who I saw as another mentor.

I owed a lot to the mage, and one day, I knew my pack would work hand-in-hand with S&S to make the world safer for all supernaturals. Humans too, 'cause unlike the OA and many in Isila, I liked the non-magicals.

Still, the question of why I'd left my pack always made me uncomfortable. It revealed one of my largest insecurities, and no one liked to show those. Least of all an alpha wolf.

"They wish I was there, sure," I said slowly. "But I needed to get out for a bit, to do something other than follow Pa around."

"But won't they want their next alpha to learn from the current one?" He brushed a strand of silver-white hair from where it had fallen in his face.

"I shadowed him for years," I assured Silas. "I know in my blood what an alpha has to do. Put the pack first. Pa believes in me and approved of my choice to leave."

For a time, anyway.

Silas cocked his head. "But others didn't."

Nope, not one bit. Not that it surprised me.

I exhaled. "Ma wasn't too happy 'bout it. We have . . . conflicting opinions on . . . well, just 'bout everything."

The fae's eyes flashed with understanding. "That was my father. The only thing we agreed on was that I needed to leave the Winter Court. I wished he'd gone about getting me out a different way, but . . ." He shrugged and trailed off. "Here I am. Doing what I need to do to survive."

He didn't elaborate, and I didn't push. We were all entitled to our secrets.

"Families are hard sometimes."

"They are," Silas agreed. "So why didn't your mother agree with your choice to leave the pack?"

"I love her, but Ma's a hard woman." Though I normally wouldn't go into this tricky territory, I was feelin' warm toward Silas and wanted to prolong the conversation. Anything to not be alone. Even talking about Ma. "She's always wanted my younger brother to be alpha, so she took my leavin' especially hard."

"Aren't you firstborn? The heir?"

"I am," I replied, hedging the truth a touch.

No one except my family knew my greatest secret, and though Si and I were bonding, I couldn't spill it. "She just likes my brother more, I guess. He's the calculating type."

Silas snorted. "You say that like you're not."

"Not like you. Or Toby. Or even Kaleb."

"Who's Kaleb?"

"My little bro."

Silas fell quiet for a moment. "What's your sister like?"

The tension that had hitched up my shoulders eased. This was much safer ground. My sister, the baby of the family, was loved by everyone.

"Kate is . . ." I smiled and leaned forward to stoke the dying flames. Silas probably needed a break from my touch. This time, my wolf didn't stir as much, feeling sated. "She's a peach. Love that girl to death."

Silas grinned. "Your whole face changed when you spoke of her."

"Well, I'm her favorite too, so the feelin' is mutual."

Silas barked out a laugh. "How does Kaleb feel about that?"

"Not great," I admitted with a shrug. "But he doesn't treat her right. Didn't even stand up for her when a boy broke her heart last year. I had to fly down and tell that pup thinkin' himself to be a man what was up."

I'd taken pleasure in it, actually. No one treated my baby sis like that and got away with it.

"He 'bout near pissed his pants."

The fae laughed harder, which gave me pleasure. I always liked making people laugh.

Outside, bells chimed in the distance. Were those coming from the village we passed on the way here? I didn't think so, we were so far away from the village, and hadn't heard the chimes before.

"Not to change the subject," I said. "But I'm curious. You think they got other buildings on this property?"

"I wouldn't be surprised," Silas replied. "If their history is to be believed, they've been here a long while, waiting for—"

The door opened, and we twisted in our seats so fast that, had I been wearing a ballcap, it would have flown clean off.

Claire stood in the doorway again, a nervous expression on her face. "I felt bad. Here."

She stuck out her hand, and my eyes widened. The witch was offering up my phone.

"I found it in your car. Charged it too. You get one call to someone—which I'll supervise. Don't make me regret being kind, and no word of this to the other *Arcacustos*." She raised an eyebrow. "Understood?"

I leapt up, eager to get my hands on a line to the outside world. "Got it."

Before I could take the phone from the witch, she inclined her head. "Might I suggest, Gunner, that you make this lifeline count, for the both of us? The sooner you get a hold of Meredith, the sooner you can leave."

"That's exactly what I was gonna do," I assured her and pulled up Luca's number.

CHAPTER TWELVE

TOBIAS

My watch proclaimed the hour to be 9:00a.m when an alarm blared to life inside Meredith's bedroom.

The witch had slept for an entire day, save for three toilet breaks—which I only knew about because, despite her familiar's insistence that he could handle the guarding, I had been sitting outside her bedroom door for hours.

The door cracked open, and a cry of astonishment met my ears.

"How long have you been out here?" Meredith asked, staring down at me with eyes that were glossed over from sleep. Her hair stuck out at odd angles, and yet somehow, she still managed to look appealing.

"For the duration of your rest."

Just the idea of the Ringmaster entering her room riled the dominant, protective side of me. There was no way I could have waited downstairs.

"That was . . ." She paused to do the mental calculations.

"A while," I shrugged, saving her the math. "You needed the sleep, and I wished to prove myself to your familiar."

The witch snorted. "He reamed you good, didn't he?" She glanced over her shoulder into the bedroom. "And guess who's fast asleep now?"

"Bloody cat," I drawled, rising to stand.

"You got that right." She stretched her arms over her head, and the thin fabric of her nightshirt revealed more of her than she likely knew.

My mouth went dry as I recalled just yesterday, her bare skin staring at me from above her fallen towel, her nipple pert and tempting.

How I'd yearned in that moment to take it in my mouth. How I wanted to do so now.

"I need a pot of coffee," she said. "I'm so groggy."

I hauled myself out of the tide of desire rushing over me and leapt at the chance to put some distance between us. "I'll make it."

Meredith eyed me. "You don't like coffee."

"True."

"So do you even know how? Or will I be forced to drink crap because you did something nice?"

I chuckled. "I won't serve you swill. Believe it or not, I have learned a thing or two about making coffee in my years. I've even made it for S&S."

Once. People had complained that day, but I was certain I'd improved since then.

"I'll give you a chance," she said, as if the witch was doing *me* the favor. For some reason, this charmed me. "Did you see Luca's text about the meeting?"

"I did." In the small hours of the morning, the coven master had sent out a coven-wide communication. "We don't have to be at the tomb for hours, though, if you require more rest."

"I want to hit up my classes today," Meredith said, sounding excited.

While I understood her quest for knowledge, I felt obligated to inform her that things may not go according to her plans.

"I hate to say this, but you might be asked to drop your classes this term. It wouldn't be the first time a coven member has had to do so for the sake of an important mission."

Meredith frowned. "And what's happening now is pretty serious."

"Indeed."

"I wonder if I could do online courses?"

"Perhaps." My lips quirked up in a teasing manner. "If you wish to be obstinate about it."

"When don't I? I'm a Taurus," she teased back. "Now, aren't you supposed to be making me coffee?"

"Yes, Mistress." I gave a low bow, which drew an amused sound from her throat.

"I like the sound of that."

A dry laugh left me as I turned to do as I was bid. "Don't get too used to it. I'm merely in a good mood."

"Use the green bag of grounds, please!" she called back and shut the door.

A grin tugged at my lips.

I didn't understand this new dynamic between us, and truly, I feared the possibility that Giselle might have pegged us correctly, but I couldn't deny that, more often than not, a feeling of lightness came over me when Meredith and I spoke.

It made wanting to stay away—to prevent us from ever knowing if Giselle was right—far more difficult.

When I got downstairs, Harper was up, studying at the

table. She glanced at me, a smirk on her face. "So, you're gonna make us coffee?"

"I can't by chance convince you to do so? I'll pay handsomely." I'd been feeling confident upstairs, but when faced with a person who surely could make a good pot, why not go with it?

"I'd rather lap up the days when we have a butler." Harper's eyebrows raised.

Bloody wolf ears.

"Shay didn't come home," I said, changing the subject and turning to the coffee pot, which had all the necessary brewing materials laid out next to it. Including a green bag of beans.

I didn't recall the countertop looking like this before, which meant the wolf had gotten it out for me. I supposed I should be happy that I didn't have to rummage through the kitchen for what I required. I put the filter in place and scooped grounds into the machine.

"I know," Harper replied. "I checked her room late last night and called. She didn't reply right away, but I woke up to a text. Apparently, she and Hans stayed in the city with the Covenant all day yesterday. They were too tired to drive back last night, but are on their way back now."

"Do you know what the Covenant wanted with them?" I filled the pot with water.

The shifter shook her head. "She didn't say, but I hope it's the topic of today's meeting."

"It must be."

The pot was now full, so I transferred it back to the machine and pressed 'brew'.

There. Done.

The machine sputtered to life, heating the water, and I smiled at it as though I'd just solved a riddle for the ages.

"Don't get too cocky, Stiff," Harper said. "Let's see how it tastes before you celebrate."

A retort tipped my tongue, but died before it could be born when my phone vibrated. I extracted it from my pocket to find a text from my maker.

She must be around others if she can't call.

I unlocked my phone and opened the texting app.

Giselle: *The OA just got word of New York and the Covenant's presence. You were there, weren't you?*

I sent a reply. *Much of the coven assisted.*

The text bubble appeared.

Were you successful?

A frown pulled at my lips. We'd had successes and failures, but Giselle would only be worried about the sacred stones. *No. They remain at large.*

A long pause passed in which I imagined my maker swearing gloriously in French before she responded.

That's unfortunate. I have another meeting with a Blood representative today. They know who you work for. Expect them to contact you.

I hadn't considered it before, but the coverage in the supernatural news—which royalists relayed to the Blood religiously—would make pinpointing my coven, and hence *me*, easy.

Sighing, I replied, *I will.*

Giselle: *Do not trust them. I must go.*

"Who's that?" Meredith asked, whisking into the kitchen with a grin. "Your French mistress?"

"*Who?!*" Harper exclaimed.

"Inside joke," Meredith replied.

She'd been furious when I ran off to Paris. At the time, she'd claimed it was because I owed her an apology—which was reasonable. But she'd also brought up a mistress, and clearly, that idea had stuck.

My heart thudded against my ribs before I could rein it in.

"Stiff actually jokes?" Harper teased.

"I despise that nickname," I inserted dryly.

"Why do you think we all use it?" The wolf stood as the coffee pot beeped. "On a scale of one to palatable, what do you think this coffee will rate, Mer? I'm giving it a hard one."

"Harsh, Harp."

"He made it once at the tomb. It was awful."

Meredith shot me an amused glance. "He did mention having experience." Then she pursed her lips, studying me. "But you know what, I'm gonna give him the benefit of practice. I think it's going to be good."

"Like, with no cream good?" Harper asked.

"Are you a heathen?" Meredith asked, picking up the pot and pouring herself a steaming cup. "There will be cream."

Meredith shuffled to the refrigerator in slippers bedecked in hideous neon green claws, fished out the creamer, and poured a hearty dose. The cloying smell of artificial vanilla sweetener filled my nose.

I shuddered. As if coffee wasn't horrid enough, they added *that* to it?

And yet, as Meredith took her first sip, I couldn't help but lean closer. Would she like it?

She glanced up at me, the cup still hovering at her mouth. A pause pressed in on us before her lips slowly curled up.

"Well, what do you know? You can teach an old dog new tricks," Meredith singsonged. "Don't lie, Harp, it's good, isn't it?"

"Passable."

"Is that better than palatable?" Meredith egged her on.

Harper rolled her eyes. "It's good, okay?"

I rolled my shoulders back, feeling like a bloody prince, and immediately recognized it was vaguely ridiculous that this was all over coffee. "Glad you enjoyed it."

Meredith shoved off from where she leaned on the counter. "I missed Bio Lab—not that I'm crying about that—but I don't want to miss Women Who Ruled. I'll get dressed, and then we can go to class, Tobias?"

"I'll wait down here," I assured the witch as she breezed past me, filling my nostrils with her heady scent of jasmine and pine.

"See ya soon."

The moment she disappeared up the stairs, I inhaled deeply, savoring the hints of the witch in the air.

"You have a crush!" Harper hissed.

I looked up to find the wolf watching me carefully.

How long had she been doing so?

"I do not," I shot back, my tone a touch too indignant.

"I think you do," Harper replied, amusement lacing her words. "But don't worry, Stiff. I won't tell her."

"I'll be in the living room," I growled and turned my back on the much too observant wolf.

***

We filed into Meredith's last class of the day, Women Who Ruled.

"Are you sure about this?" she asked. "This is a relatively small class. You're going to stick out."

"The professor is a siren. Alexandra knows me and won't say a word."

"A *siren?* What do they do?"

"Shall we discuss this later?"

Too many humans were about, and as a vampire and a witch walking together, we already drew attention. Talk of sirens would surely garner notice that we did not need.

"Sit with your partners today!" the professor called out as she entered the small classroom from a side door that I assumed went to a private space for the instructor.

"You've got to be joking," Meredith moaned, but I grinned.

"He won't do anything."

The twat Bentley Sloan was enrolled in this course. He'd attempted to terrorize Meredith before, but I would ensure that he stayed in line. In fact, I relished the idea.

As the professor caught my eye, she waved. I gestured to Meredith. As I'd expected, the professor gave a single nod and went about studying her notes.

Meredith turned, analyzing me. "Just because you threw Bentley across a lawn, you think he'll behave? He was publicly embarrassed, which means he'll probably be even more of an ass today."

"Perhaps."

I'd never told her that I had a chat with Gerard, an elder bonesman from Skull and Bones, who might have perceived my words as a threat to keep Sloan in line.

"We'll see," Meredith replied, though she didn't look convinced.

Bentley still wasn't in class when the professor took to the lectern, and I scowled, somewhat pissed that the Sloan kid wouldn't have to squirm beneath my glare for an hour.

And then, as if I were a witch and capable of conjuring, the idiot strolled in five minutes after the class began, a grin on his face.

One that fell straight off when he saw me sitting next to Meredith.

"Bentley, if you can't show up on time, don't come at all," Alexandra snapped. "Now take a seat by Ms. Stone. You'll need to discuss your project with your partner today."

Bentley paled further, which gave me the greatest satisfaction, and he scampered over to claim the spot on the other side of Meredith, slumping back in his chair.

As if that will stop me from watching you. Bloody arse.

Meredith turned to me slowly, her eyes wide, and raised her eyebrows, impressed.

The predator inside me roared with delight, and to counteract Bentley's attempt to hide, I leaned forward, pinning him with my gaze.

The lecture progressed, and I half listened as the professor spoke of Empress Wu Zetian. While I was quite interested in the material, I focused mostly on Bentley. The professor might oblige me with a chat on the subject later—or better yet, Meredith would regale me with notes from this course—but I might not get another chance to terrorize Sloan.

So take advantage of the hour, I did.

By the time the professor ended her lecture so the students might go over their project with their partners, the New York senator's son was sweating profusely.

Meredith winked at me before switching her attention to Sloan. "So, I think we should do our project on Queen Victoria of England because she's a recent ruler. She's on the approved list."

"Whatever," the pompous prick mumbled. "You choose."

The witch smirked. "Are you just giving in because Tobias is here?"

"Look," Sloan spat, "you're both abominations I want

nothing to do with. Especially the vampire who narked on me."

"What?" Meredith's pitch went up.

"Then you best watch your actions," I growled, ignoring Meredith's scowl. "That starts with not calling anyone in S&S abominations, you twat."

Bentley huffed and began to write on a piece of paper that he then thrust at the witch. "Whatever, bro. Meredith, Queen Victoria is fine. Here's my info. Just text me or email me, and we can work that way."

"Works for me," she replied.

The senator's kid scooped up his books and scurried off with his tail between his legs.

When he was out of the classroom, Meredith turned to me. "You told someone about that day on the green?"

"Gerard. I didn't want Bentley coming at you in class."

"You know I can fight my own battles, right?" Her chin tilted up.

"Anyone who doesn't know that hasn't passed a glance your way," I snorted. "The point is, being part of this coven, you don't have to fight your own battles all the time. We want to help you. *I* want to help you."

She blinked three times, momentarily stunned into silence. "I see."

A heated pause expanded between us, and again, I felt an inclination to lean forward, to take her face in my hands, to—

"Tobias Aston, so glad to have you in class today," Alexandra Lambeau, the professor, and a siren of moderate powers, approached with a smile on her face. "Did you learn anything? Or were you too busy scaring the pants off my most privileged, and frankly, most obnoxious student?"

"Good afternoon, Alexandra," I replied. "He has been aggravating my charge. I wanted our displeasure to sink in."

Alexandra laughed, the sound musical. "Seemed to me that he got the message." She paused. "Are you up for a drink later? I've been meaning to call you up, get to know one another better . . ."

Meredith stiffened, and I felt the wave of unease that washed over her.

I cleared my throat, disliking the dynamic. Like all sirens, Alexandra was exceedingly beautiful, but I didn't find myself swayed in the slightest by her offer.

"I'll have to pass. Coven business. I'm not sure when I'll be available next."

The professor nodded but didn't seem all that let down. As a siren, she could have whomever she wanted and, in all likelihood, I'd simply caught her eye in the moment. "Shame, but I figured you're busy. I read the Covenant's message boards." She looked at Meredith. "You were involved?"

"I was, Professor Lambeau."

Alexandra gave her an approving look. "I knew you were a good student, but now I like you even more. Professors shouldn't play favorites, but . . ." She winked, and Meredith's cheeks grew a delicious shade of red. "I'm a friend to the coven, so feel free to call me Alexandra."

"Thank you," Meredith replied, a hint of surprise in her tone.

I knew how much she loved this class, and was glad to see her blossom, but as the clock struck the top of the hour, I turned my full attention to her. "The meeting."

"Right." The witch collected her things. "Thank you, Professor Lambeau. See you next class."

"You too, Meredith. Later, Tobias."

My charge remained quiet as we left the room, but the moment we were out of the building, she ground to a halt and turned to me. "You flirted with my professor!"

"I did no such thing."

"Liar."

"She flirted *with me*." My lips curled up at the indignation on her face. "And I declined."

I could practically see her running through the conversation again in her head, and when she realized I was correct, her cheeks grew pink.

At the sight, a growl of pleasure warmed my insides.

"I was just so taken aback," she said sheepishly. "Professor Lambeau has never singled me out like that."

"She must not have realized what you were. From now on, I expect she'll pay you more attention."

"Why?"

"Because you're part of S&S, and though few on campus know who we really are, those who do treat our members in high regard. And she spoke true. She is a friend to the coven."

"She told me to call her by her first name. I don't know if I can do that."

"Why not?"

"She's a Yale professor!" Meredith replied with awe. "I guess I just feel like she's above me and deserves the respect."

"Do you feel the same reverence for Luca?" I asked, somewhat surprised. Meredith was a grown woman, capable of taking care of herself and accomplishing extraordinary things.

"Even more."

I shrugged. "You call him by his first name."

Meredith's mouth opened a fraction of an inch, but she nodded. "True."

"You don't have to refer to Alexandra as such if it makes

you uncomfortable, but you should know she likely sees you as an equal in many regards."

The witch shook her head. "That's so weird."

"I suggest you try and get used to it," I said. "To head-quarters?"

"Yeah, sure," she replied, still in shock.

We fell into silence, which I assumed Meredith was using to come to terms with this new aspect of her life.

When we arrived at S&S's tomb, we followed the tide to the Shadow Room, to find the meeting space full to bursting with members. Even Lisha, another vampire, who'd been on an extended mission, was present.

She threw me a wave, which I returned as I made my way to my seat by Luca.

"There's a spot for you," I murmured to Meredith as she attempted to veer left, toward Harper.

"Alright," she grumbled and came with me.

Hans was already there, nestled between Luca and Shay, the trio speaking in hushed tones. Once I took my seat, and Meredith next to me, Luca looked up.

"Now that you two are here, we can start." The coven master stood and called the room to order. "There's no time to waste, but I called this meeting because everyone needs to be filled in. I'm sure most of you have read the message boards about the city?"

Everyone affirmed that they had seen the news. Many here received the paper—digitally or the old-fashioned way—and stayed up-to-date on current affairs. Since the Pearl had been released, everyone had been scouring the articles, hoping to spot hints of its whereabouts.

"Good. Then I can be brief. Prince Orien, the Prince of Wrath, has attacked New York and he has the Pearl of Hell and the Opal of Heaven. It's our job to find it, and to cull the demons he's brought over. Basically, anyone who is not already assigned a mission has just officially become a demon hunter."

A few people looked terrified—and for good reason. We were dark artifact hunters, but that did not mean everyone was well trained in fighting. Or knew much of demonology. Why would they? Pure-blooded demons, especially the most powerful among them, had been locked in Hell for years . . . or so we'd thought.

"What about the city?" asked Dan, a bear shifter more inclined to be proficient in tech than demon hunting.

"The Covenant has that handled from here on out," Luca replied.

A siren leaned forward. "I have no idea how to fight a demon. And I don't usually need physical skills on my missions, so I gotta say, I'm feeling pretty not okay with this."

Dan nodded, and a few others murmured their agreement.

"If you need assistance, come to me. No one will go untrained," Luca assured the crowd.

"Now, for the more specific missions." He turned. "Hans and Shay will be going undercover for the Covenant. I can't say much on that, because there's still the possibility of a traitor in our midst."

It rankled that we still had not sussed out the culprit who'd sent a shade after Meredith on her first day here.

Of course, there *was* a chance that had been Josiah, but we couldn't be sure until we captured him.

"I'm only telling you that much of their business because if you see them acting strangely, that is why," Luca continued. "Do not interfere. Do *not* offer to help. And as ever, do not pry into their mission."

My spine straightened as curiosity streaked through me.

Luca then turned to me. "Tobias and Meredith will also be leaving us for a while. I'm sorry, Meredith, but you will likely have to drop your classes."

Though I'd warned her it might come to this, she still frowned. "I really don't want to give up on this opportunity. If possible, I'd like to take online classes—even if just for one course."

Luca nodded. "I might be able to pull some strings. We'll discuss your options after the meeting. You see, we need you to go to England tomorrow morning. It's the first flight I could book."

My head tilted. "Why?"

"I received a call from Gunner. It appears he and Silas are being held hostage by Miriam Black." Luca's eyes darkened. "And the only way our guys will be released is if Meredith arrives in person to claim them as friend, not foe."

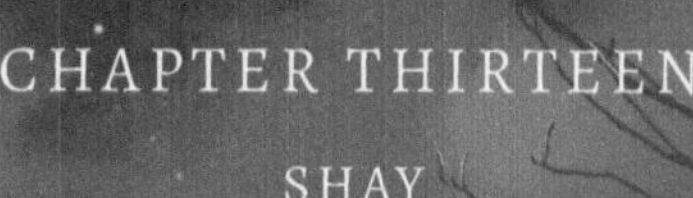

CHAPTER THIRTEEN

SHAY

I STEPPED FOOT IN MY HOUSE, AND IT FELT LIKE A MILLION POUNDS lifted off my shoulders. For a moment, I had refuge.

"Tonight calls for wine," Harper said, which was usually my line, but my wolfy roommate couldn't have missed the tension rolling off me in waves as we walked home from the coven meeting. "Want me to call for pizza?"

It was my last night in my house for who-knew-how long. Tomorrow, Hans and I would meet up with the Covenant in DC, Nicoleta's chosen location for Hans to take me.

"Only if you put pineapple on it," I replied, glad Harper understood no one was cooking tonight.

"*Half,*" she said, disappearing into the kitchen.

"Tobias, do you want anything?" I asked, still not totally sure how to treat a vampire houseguest.

"No, thank you. Lisha will drop off blood for me later."

Though the rest of us had already kicked off our shoes, and Meredith had sprinted upstairs to put on her comfy-cozies, he remained standing just inside the door.

For a moment, the temptation to ask him about Rooms rose

in me, but I didn't even have the energy for that. Maybe after a couple of slices of pizza, I'd be able to muster it.

"Kay. You should just chill on the couch. I'm going to shower." I still hadn't done so since New York, and the grime of the city mixed with the blood of battle had probably seeped into me for good by now. I shuddered, grossed out by the thought.

"Here's your shower wine." Like a beautiful goddess fairy-wine mother, Harper appeared with a glass.

"Thanks." I gave her a weak smile.

Harper acted tough, but she was really a nurturer. Pretty spiritual too. Meredith and I knew that, but the rest of the coven definitely saw her differently. I wasn't sure why she put up such a front and kept those parts of her private. She was great as she was.

"I'll be back once I'm clean," I promised again.

I disappeared into my room, swathed in shades of cream, sky blue, and gold. The canopy bed was wrapped in gauze to give off the impression of clouds. Basically, I'd decorated my room to be celestial, angelic, a reminder of what I *should* be, while also providing me great comfort.

Finally standing in my personal space, a long exhale parted my lips. The last few days had been crazy . . . and it wasn't going to get better any time soon.

Luca had told Hans and me not to let anyone know the details of our mission, but I'd already decided I was going to tell my roommates. I needed someone to know the truth if the demons destroyed me. Someone other than my mother, who, after she got over the shock of me offering myself up as bait, hadn't stopped reminding others that we were related.

I was sure she was proud—but was she worried? Or did

she just see me as a potential success that she wanted to attach herself to?

What would Dad think? Would he really come?

Honestly, I wasn't so sure. Even though it might be better if he didn't show, because we didn't want Prince Orien to use pure angel blood to open one of the Eyes of Darkness, not knowing if Dad would come to save me sucked.

My roommates, however, would definitely care about my future. They'd care about *me*. And while Harper wouldn't agree with me going against Luca's demands, she also wouldn't say anything. Tobias might, but I'd risk it. I needed to get it off my chest before Hans picked me up tomorrow.

I grimaced. *Hans.*

"No. I refuse. For one night, you won't haunt me." I gathered up my stuff to use the shared bathroom in the hallway.

After a quick shower and extensive moisturizing that was paused only for the sipping of wine, I felt like an almost new woman. I pulled on my jammies, tossed my filthy clothes into the hamper, and wrapped my brown hair up into a wet bun. I'd regret the bun later, when the kinks were murder to get out, but screw it.

When I emerged from the bathroom, the scent of pizza welcomed me.

"Whose firstborn did you promise to get that here so fast?" I entered the kitchen and toasted Harper with my nearly empty wine glass.

"Just gave a huge tip online." Harper winked as she set out the plates, and Meredith placed paper towels next to them. "Worth it."

"I'll say." Meredith pulled a slice dripping with cheese from the box. Because she wasn't afraid of showing self-love, there was pineapple on it.

"Save me some, Rooms." I set my glass on the counter and stretched. My body, though healed, was still sore from all the running and flying of the past days.

"You'd better hurry, then," Meredith teased, grabbing another slice. "I think Tobias might be convinced to try one too."

"I most certainly will not," the vampire said from where he sat at the table, which had been cleared of school stuff. "It's all yours."

"Oh, come on, Stiff," I winked. "There's tropical fruit involved!"

I did a little hula dance, which got a giggle out of everyone. The sound was like heavenly harp music to my ears, and a smile bloomed on my face. I was gonna miss these ladies.

Done showing them my sweet moves, I grabbed a couple of slices for myself. "Harp, can I have a refill?" I nodded to the glass I'd set on the counter.

She obliged with an easy grin, and a few minutes later, we were all sitting around the table as the sounds of soft munching filled the room.

Tobias, the only one not totally engrossed in the pizza, stared at his phone.

"Whatcha looking at?" I asked him.

"A map of England." He glanced up. "We know the general area where Miriam Black lives, but it's merely a forest. A small road runs through it, and a village is nearby, but there are no notable structures."

"Why would there be?" Harper bounced back at him. "She's clearly hiding."

"Not for long. We're going to find her." Meredith held up her moonstone ring. "I bet this will help."

"Where was the missing stone, anyhow?" I asked.

I'd noticed that it was whole now and the stones were different—representing the *lapis caelesti*—but I had no idea how she'd transformed the piece Tobias and I had found in *Le Bastion*.

"The library's supernatural section." Meredith shared a look with Tobias, and my romance radar went off again. The urge to egg them on struck, and I couldn't help but roll with it.

"Did you two make out in the stacks?"

Meredith turned red, but Tobias just glared at me. He knew I was on to them.

"We did nothing of the sort," he gritted out. "I'm her guard, Shay."

I snorted out a laugh because it was so obvious that they were into each other but neither would admit it. "Whatever."

"I don't care about kissing," Harper added, "but what does a girl gotta do to get an invite to that library?!"

Before Tobias could answer, Benny chose that moment to grace us with his presence, strolling into the dining room and leaping onto the table.

"By the Old Ones! Down, fleabag!" Harper waved him off. "Ugh, that is so gross. You walk in your poo!"

He hissed. "In case you hadn't noticed, there is no litter box in this house."

"That doesn't make it better. You're probably just shitting in our neighbors' yards."

Benny didn't respond, and I took that to mean Harper was probably right.

Apparently, so did she, because Harper rolled her eyes. "Wonderful. Don't let them see you. I don't have time to go digging up cat crap while these two are gone."

"How 'bout you take the empty seat at the head of the

table, Benedict?" Rooms suggested, clearly trying to keep the peace.

"Yeah, Benny," I cooed. "We're having a nice night. No fighting."

"Tell that to the wolf," he huffed, but strolled to the open chair. "What do you mean by you two being gone?" He stared at Meredith.

Uh oh, Rooms.

She hadn't told Benny yet, and he'd been angry enough that she'd gone to New York without mentioning it. The cat was about to blow a gasket.

"I meant to tell you earlier," the witch said once she'd swallowed. "But you were . . . out."

"Crapping in yards," Harper muttered.

"*Hunting* for pleasure," the cat snapped back. "Tell me now."

Meredith took a rather large gulp of wine. "I have to go to England."

"But it's so cold there," Benedict whined. "Can Luca send you to, say . . . Arizona? I prefer a warmer climate."

"I'm not sure you can come, Benedict," Meredith replied slowly. "I'm sorry, but—"

"And what makes you think I won't just slip onto the plane?" he retorted, tail twitching.

Cat had a point. That was exactly what he'd done when they went to Hell via Romania.

"You could," Meredith replied, "but you should know that where I'm going might be dangerous. They're holding Gunner captive."

"Did Luca say anything else about that?" I inquired.

I was so curious. It shocked me that anyone could trap

Gunner, especially when he was with Silas. Miriam Black must be clever and strong.

"I guess Gunner is in a dungeon, his words not Luca's, and was only allowed a few minutes before the call ended abruptly."

"Hmm." I took another bite of heaven.

"Well, if you're going somewhere with danger, then you really will need me," Benedict sniffed, not at all swayed.

Meredith let out a huff. "I can see this isn't up for negotiation." Then she paused, spine straightening. "Actually, I don't think we got to talk about this yet. Do you know anything about Miriam Black?"

Benedict shook his head. "Doesn't ring a bell."

Meredith slumped. "Bummer."

Seeing that he'd won that argument, the familiar turned to me. "I take it that you're leaving too?"

"I am." I took a fortifying bite of pizza. This was the moment I'd been waiting for. "I'm not supposed to say anything, but—"

"Then you shouldn't," Tobias cut me off, his eyes narrowed. "There's a reason missions are secretive, Shay."

"And I have my reasons for sharing." I rolled my shoulders, releasing the tension pinching the sides of my neck and trying not to be annoyed that the vampire had pushed back.

I'd known he would. Tobias and Luca were thick as thieves.

"Hans and I are going to seek out the demons—his sister and Wrath, too, probably. We're going to use me as bait."

"What the actual hell?!" Meredith shot up from her seat, sending a half-eaten slice of pizza flying to the floor with a *splat.*

Harper stayed in her seat, but her entire body had gone rigid. *"Explain."*

I lifted my hands in what I hoped was a calming gesture. "First off, I should say I had the option to say no to this. It's my choice, just like Hans also chose to do this."

"Okay, I understand, but we still need details," Harper said, looking not quite mollified, but slightly less tense.

I bit my lip, then began. "Hans's sister somehow got a letter to him." I brushed past how shady he'd acted when it happened. "They want me. We think that's partially because I helped kick Nicoleta's butt, but also because a pure angel's blood can open the Eyes of Darkness. We suspect the demons want to use me as bait to bring my father down to Earth."

Meredith picked up her fallen slice and sat down slowly. "Who's your father?"

I inhaled slowly. Rooms didn't strike me as the type of person to be religious, but then again, a lot about the witch surprised me. "The Archangel Uriel."

"What?! Whoa. Shay!"

"You've heard of him?"

Meredith snorted out a laugh. "A little. That's . . . crazy."

"To be honest, since I was born, I haven't seen much of him," I said with a shrug. "When he graces me with his presence, my mom is so proud." Bitterness seeped into my tone.

"I take it she's a hard woman to please?" Meredith asked gently.

Harper stayed quiet. She knew how much it hurt me that I never seemed to be good enough for Mom. She even understood it. She had similar struggles with her dad, a brutal alpha from the West Coast. Harper and I were different in many ways, but our family issues was a topic that bonded us.

"You could say that," I said finally. "She's on the Covenant, and runs a billion-dollar company. She attracted a pure-blooded angel, which for nephilim is, like . . . a *big deal,* because it strengthens your line's magic. Mom is accomplished, to say the least, and she wants the same for me, but we prize different things."

"Our relationships with our parents can be some of the most difficult we ever have," Tobias spoke up, and I wondered if he was referring to his human family or his vampire one. "But cherish them, if you can."

"I do," I said quickly, not wanting Rooms to get the wrong idea. "It's just . . ."

"Hard," Harper finished. "I get it."

I smiled at her.

An umbrella of silence fell over the table for a moment, before Meredith reached for the bottle of wine.

"Well, I can't say I love your mission," she grumbled. "Actually, it pisses me off that the Covenant would ask that of you, because it's freaking *insane*—"

"Can't argue with that," I interjected before she could get on a roll. I wanted to bring the vibe back up, not crash it into a chasm of despair.

The witch inhaled, nodding. "But I *do* understand and accept that you chose to do this. I hope that if you lure the demons to you, the Covenant can stop all this madness."

Meredith poured herself a glass of wine, filling it to the top. "Until then, what do you biotches say we eat, drink, and be merry? Who knows when we'll see each other again."

"So am I a biotch now?" Tobias asked, eyebrows arched as if he wasn't quite sure he wanted to be in the cool kids club.

"And me?" Benny piped up, sounding way more hopeful than the vampire had.

"Honorary biotches, both of you!" Meredith lifted her glass.

I dissolved into laughter and set to relishing the night in front of me, knowing full well that it might be my last with those I cared for.

CHAPTER FOURTEEN

MEREDITH

"Tobias, I'm seriously starving," I said as yet another pub flew past the car window. "I know you want to find this place, but if you want me to be alert when we get there, I have to eat dinner."

"And I wish to relieve myself," Benedict chimed in from the back of the rental.

In the driver's seat, the vampire let out a huff, as if mortal needs were the most annoying thing in the world. "Fine. The GPS says there's a tavern up ahead. We'll stop there."

It was only a couple of miles more before a sweet little thatched roof building came into view. One of those signs pointing to dozens of well-known locales on the globe stood in front of it, as did another sign proclaiming *'The best fish and chips in the village!'*.

I grinned. "Is that it? Looks quaint."

"I expect it's quite old. Most likely it was once used as an inn."

As we got closer, I could read the sign. The tavern was

actually *still* an inn. "Is it common for bars here to also offer rooms?"

Tobias shrugged. "It's not as common as in the past, but also not unusual."

"Have you ever been here?"

He laughed. "No. I grew up in London and have not spent much time in England since I left. The west country, particularly this far north, is new to me."

"That's too bad. Could have been good for us if you knew your way around."

He parked and we got out. Right away, Benedict bolted into the bushes.

"You want us to wait?" I asked, glad no one was in the parking area to hear me since I was very clearly not speaking to Tobias.

"Not necessary! I'll be on the lookout for your return, but I'd like to hunt."

I wrinkled my nose. He got fed the best canned tuna I could buy, but Benedict still loved to catch mice for the thrill of it.

"Gross," I murmured.

"Just be glad that I don't bring them to you as presents," Benedict shot back from somewhere in the greenery.

"If you do, you're no longer allowed in my room," I retorted.

The cat didn't reply, so Tobias and I left him to it, making our way to the tavern door. Inside smelled strongly of fried food and ale. A few patrons sat in booths or around tables, and they all twisted our way when we crossed the threshold.

A busty server sashayed up to us, her gaze roving over the vampire in a way that made my fists clench. Catching myself, I loosened.

Anyone with eyes could see that Tobias was devastatingly handsome, and this woman was allowed to agree. It wasn't like I had any claim over him.

"Evening, loves. I'm Deb. You visitors?"

"We are," I replied.

"We don't get many tourists in these parts. Where you headed? The coast?"

"Actually, we're looking for someone a local in this village."

"Well, you're in luck. I know the whole village. I can point you in the right direction." Deb grinned and batted her eyelashes at Tobias, who gave her a polite smile.

"Her name is Miriam Black," I said, wanting to pull the server's attention back to me

The woman blinked. "Black? You don't say?"

"Do you know her?"

Hope rose in my chest. Could it be this easy?

"Not at all, but you're the second person to ask after her. Strange, that."

"Oh." Tobias and I shared a glance, and I asked, "Was the other person a big, muscly man with longish hair and a twang from the south of the U.S.?"

Deb beamed. "He was! Handsome as the devil, and a charmer too. I always was a goner for that accent. Wish he'd have come back this way. . ."

Someone called to her from the back of the tavern, their accent so thick, I couldn't decipher what they said.

She turned, threw up a hand gesture that told them she'd be right there, then focused on us again. "So, you staying for a meal?"

"Yes, table for two," I replied.

Deb led us to a small booth in the back of the pub, where

Tobias took the bench seat—probably so he could keep an eye out for threats while I ate. He'd been watching for demons this whole time, and while I hadn't considered an attack until we landed in Heathrow, he was right to do so. What was to keep Wrath from sending peons for us? Specifically, for me?

"The special is fish and chips," the woman informed us. "We make them right good. There's also vegetable soup, if you fancy a healthier option."

"Thanks. I'll have a lager, whatever you think is best, but I need a moment for food." Really, I was already salivating over the thought of fried fish and french fries, but I wanted a word with Tobias first.

"And you, handsome?"

"The lady required a stop. I'm not hungry."

Thank God for that.

"What a gentleman," Deb cooed, only to be interrupted when a table called her over. "I'll be back for your order, love."

She disappeared to tend to the other tables in the tavern.

"That had to be Gunner," I said.

"Agreed. But she didn't seem to have a clue who Miriam was. In a village this small, that's odd."

"Well, if she's old, maybe that's not *so* strange. Deb is, like, what? Maybe thirty? Miriam has to be way older. She might be a hermit."

"Still, in villages like this, people know one another. Many families have likely lived here for generations."

Suddenly, a pint landed in front of me, sloshing everywhere.

"What'll you be having, love?" Deb asked, not at all bothered by the spilled beer.

"Fish and chips," I replied.

"That's all?"

"Yup. Actually, though, we were wondering. You don't know Miriam, but she's an older woman. Is there anyone here who's been around a while that we could ask about her? I'd hate to have come all this way for nothing."

"I was born and raised in the village," Deb said. "But so was Samuel over there." She pointed to an elderly man wearing a tweed jacket a few tables away. "You might ask him."

"Thanks. We will."

"Ta. Your lunch will be out in a jiff."

And she was off again.

I watched, amazed, as everyone smiled and laughed when she checked in on their tables. Deb had an easy, friendly way about her. That skill set was so opposite of everything I knew how to do.

"She keeps busy, and she's entertaining," I murmured, somewhat envious.

"I suspect Gunner appreciated her as much as she did him." Tobias's evergreen eyes followed the curvy server.

I rolled mine. "And you, apparently."

The vampire's attention veered to me. "She's pretty."

He said it slowly, as if testing me. From the way my jaw tightened, I knew I was failing the test.

"Yeah, she is." I took a glug of beer and once it was down the hatch, coughed.

Tobias snorted a soft laugh. "Too warm for your tastes?"

"Caught me off guard," I admitted, and though I should have been pleased with the change of topic, Deb laughed, the booming sound drawing my attention once more. My hand tightened around the pint.

Tobias noticed, and a smirk tilted his lips. "Gunner probably adored making Deb laugh, but she's not really my type of woman."

I blinked. He'd pivoted back to her . . . And explicitly said she wasn't his type. Did that mean . . .

"What is your type?" I blurted, unable to stop the words.

He didn't respond right away, and I could practically see him reaching back into the recesses of his mind. Was he sifting through the hundreds, perhaps thousands, of women that had thrown themselves at him over the centuries?

Or were we finally going to confront that something between us? How the air electrified? How sometimes he took my breath away, and I was pretty sure I did the same to him?

My heart skipped a beat, hoping.

"It doesn't matter," he said finally. "The women I fall for usually meet tragic ends. It's why I've forsaken romance."

Pain cut through me, making my throat tighten and something in me cry out.

Though I was really not one to talk, having exactly zero real relationships and a string of semi-regular sexual partners in the past, that was just so sad. And it made me feel empty.

"Here you are, love." Deb appeared again. The woman spoke and laughed loudly, but she walked as silent as a cat. "Brought you some vinegar and ketchup too."

"Thank you," I said, swallowing because I'd already begun to drool.

Before Deb left, I'd already dug in. Not only was the food delicious, but its arrival eased a bit of the tension between Tobias and me.

Though, when he stood, I went back on alert.

"Where are you going?"

"To speak with Samuel. I can't abide the smell of fried food. I'll be back."

His loss, I thought, digging into the breaded goodness.

Just a few minutes later, probably too soon for his olfactory senses, Tobias returned to sit across from me. "Bad news."

"What's that?" I asked, dread settling in.

Were we in the wrong place? It didn't seem possible. There was little in this part of the country. How could we have messed that up?

"He didn't know Miriam by name, either," Tobias replied. "However, he did know of a group of senior citizens who live in the direction we need to go. Apparently, they do not get out often and stick to themselves."

"Sounds like our people."

"I'm inclined to agree, though we can't be sure."

Tobias glanced at a motion behind me before continuing.

"Unfortunately, the road that cuts through the forest is even longer than the map notates. It runs for nearly a hundred miles, and no one seems to know exactly where the elderly group lives."

"Which means someone in that tribe of senior citizens is a warder."

"Precisely," he sighed. "And you're not trained to magically suss out wards."

I swallowed. "Nope. But there have to be other signs. Gunner can't do magic. Or would Silas be able to do that too?" I knew little about fae magic. Hell, I'd barely scratched the surface of witching magic.

"They'd be searching for the general feel of magic, and the wolf's senses are excellent for that. The fae's are quite good too. Vampires can sniff it out, but not as well." He nodded to my hand. "I believe our success rests on the ring showing us the way."

I peered at my hand, the fingers glowing with grease. A

frown tightened my lips. "I hope so, but it hasn't done anything since the stones changed."

Tobias leaned back in his chair. "In that case, I'd suggest that you eat heartily, because we may be in for a very long afternoon."

———

THE SUN'S DYING RAYS LIT OUR WAY AS THE RENTAL CAR JOSTLED down the road, which was in need of some serious repairs.

Then again, it's probably pointless. By the time the workers got to the end, they'd just have to start over again.

I stared out the window at the forest. It was our second pass down this road, and while there'd been a few pullouts and streets pointing to hiking areas, none of them looked promising. The offshoots were all even worse than the road and, thanks to the climate, overgrown with ferns as wide across as an average umbrella.

Only one area had a different sort of feel to it, one that might be magical—but we had to get closer to be sure.

"This pullout has got to be it," I said, looking down at the ring.

It hadn't exhibited strong magical signs like we'd hoped, but there had been a *tiny* tug within me when we drove by a single lane.

"It's worth a look," Tobias agreed, maneuvering to the side of the road and parking in front of a closed gate. We wouldn't be able to drive through, but the gate didn't extend into the woods, so it would be easy enough to get around.

We exited, and I dropped into a forward fold, the backside of my legs begging for a stretch. It was in that position that I noticed something strange.

"Tobias." My eyebrows pinched together. "There are tire marks here. Really faint footprints leading down the drive, too. A couple of sets, one is enormous. Think it's Gunner?"

The vampire rounded the car, and Benedict joined us, sniffing at the tracks.

"I cannot smell Gunner or Silas," Tobias said, "there must have been a rain lately to wash away the scents. It seems to me the car tracks are more recent."

"They could have parked and walked in, like we are, and . . ."

"Someone else moved the car," Tobias finished. "Perhaps to hide it? We know Gunner and Silas are being kept locked in a room."

"Hmmm."

I lifted my hand to look at my ring. It still wasn't doing a darn thing, but that inkling that this was the place, that very pull I associated with seeking, was present. Since seekers could not search for people with their powers, there had to be an item, or items, around here that was magical.

"But," Tobias turned, closing his eyes and sniffing the air, "now that we're no longer in the car, I do sense magic. Very faint, but it's there. I believe Miriam might be a talented warder, skilled in hiding her own power."

"Then I guess we follow the trail?" I gestured down the drive, which, from this vantage, appeared to be a flush tunnel of greenery. Pretty, but it would also make catching threats hard.

I knew from my days of thieving and tomb-raiding that a clear line of sight would have been far preferable.

"I'll go first," Tobias said.

"We'll go *together*." I fell into step with him. "This is my journey, vampire. You're just on it."

His lips lifted in a smirk, but he didn't deny it, so together, with Benedict trailing a few feet behind as always, we tramped down the gravel lane.

The street grew ever narrower as we went. Soon, it was no wider than seven feet across, and ferns waved about in front of my face every few seconds.

"If their car is down here, it must be covered in plants!" I hissed.

Trying to dodge a fern, I ran face-first into a branch. "*Yeesh!*"

"Is your ring doing anything?" Tobias gestured to my hand.

I focused on the moonstone set in a band. "Not a darn thing."

"I'm beginning to think they've warded the area specifically to *you*."

I halted as realization poured over me like rainwater.

Tobias mimicked me, his shoulders tight. "Did you hear something? Feel something?"

I shook my head, unable to believe we hadn't considered it earlier. "Tobias, this is a test! Miriam had to have made this harder than it should be, otherwise how would Gunner and Silas have found it in the first place? They might be able to feel magic in the area, but this ring should basically lead me here! But she nullified it somehow. This *has* to be a test for my powers—after all, Miriam should suspect I'm coming."

"Bloody hell," the vampire rumbled, as if Miriam had slighted him personally. "If this is a test, we need to expect an attack."

Did we? I hadn't thought to go there, but then again, why not? More than likely, Miriam had something to do with the *lapis caelesti*, and that information should be well guarded.

"Proceed with caution," I said.

Tobias nodded, and we set off again.

It didn't take long for us to come across the first hint that I was correct. The lane diverged—unnaturally so, for how small it was—and provided eight trails from which to choose.

"Totally a freaking test," I whispered, walking from the mouth of one trail to another.

Tobias joined me, and his green eyes widened. "Undoubtedly. This area has been recently enchanted."

"So she wants me to find Gunner, but also to see how well I do it."

"Cheeky bugger."

"I'll say," I grinned, up for the challenge. "Well, you just wait, Miriam. I'm coming for you."

I paced past the openings once, and then again, paying attention to how they made me feel and if the ring reacted.

The ring didn't do jack, but my seeker magic did.

"It's one of these," I pointed to the paths in the direct center. The pull was equal between right and left, but I could only choose one.

"I think it's the left," I said finally. "Guess there's only one way to find out."

I stepped down the path, and immediately, a vine reached out and wrapped around my neck.

Benedict loosed a hiss, which was almost immediately drowned out by the roar of the vampire.

"Meredith!" Tobias leapt forward and ripped the vine from around me.

I gasped, but the relief was short-lived, as another snapped out, then another, and another.

"Retreat!" Tobias shouted, pulling me back to the opening.

No vines followed; rather, they retreated back into the woods, as if they'd never been there in the first place.

I sucked in a breath. "If that's the way, Miriam is a straight-up psycho."

"Agreed," Tobias replied, shaking his head as he examined the other path.

"The right lane it is, I guess."

"Slower this time. And I'll go first." Tobias's tone held a dangerous note I didn't dare argue with.

He looked predatory. Like he did that one time in training, when he'd basically attacked me—back before we'd come to . . . whatever sort of agreement there was between us.

If Miriam knew what was good for her, she wouldn't try another attack like the first.

With caution, Tobias took a step down the other path. Then two. When nothing sprang out at him, he darted forward ten feet.

Still nothing.

"I believe this is the way forward."

I nodded. "Stay close, Benedict."

For once, my familiar did as I asked, hugging my side. Apparently, all it took was a little threat of strangulation for him to shape up.

"Something is wrong with these woods," Benedict said after we'd gone about a half mile. "I sense no prey."

"Like mice?" I asked. That would be prey for him, but in a forest like this, one would expect deer and other larger animals.

"Anything. There are no sounds."

"The cat is right," Tobias said. "It's too quiet."

I swallowed. "Do you think we're walking into another

trap? Maybe this isn't the right place after all. Maybe—oh my God!"

From the dense woods, a thirty-feet-tall, and powerfully built person, appeared. He carried a club and wore a loincloth, like a caveman, an image added to by his protruding brow and jutting chin.

Benedict scampered up a tree, and I wished I could follow.

"Tobias, what is that?" I asked, my voice shaky.

"Giant," Tobias confirmed my fears. "But they are supposed to be extinct."

"No," the giant grunted and pounded his chest. "Here."

"We can see that," I said softly. "But why?"

"Protec'!"

The giant swung his club at Tobias. Just in time, the vampire zipped out of the way.

"Brute strength," Tobias rasped, eyes wild. I'd rarely seen such fear in him, but the giant really was something else. "We have to knock him out."

"What?! Why?"

"He said he's here to protect. Someone has even taught him English, so he's not just here by sheer chance thinking it's his territory. This challenge must be to get past him. Unless you'd rather kill?"

"No!" I shouted.

I might be scared of the huge creature, but that didn't mean I wanted it dead.

"Just steer clear of the club and aim for his head," Tobias instructed, springing up and ripping a medium-sized branch clear from a tree.

No . . . is he going to—

Without sparing me a glance, the vampire leapt at the

giant's face, swinging the branch. The giant dodged with shocking speed, and my partner missed.

"Why not just bite him?" I yelled, astonished at what I was seeing. Wasn't there a more vampiric way to go about this? One with more finesse?

"What do you think I am?! A leech?! It would take ages to weaken him!" Tobias called back, rounding the giant and drawing its attention. "I can't even hold that much blood inside me."

Though inappropriate, I couldn't help but snort out a laugh.

"Instead of mocking me, why don't you help?" Tobias hollered, leaping up once more to pummel the creature, this time hitting his mark and whipping the huge man across his face.

The giant's roar ripped through the woods, its ferocity making my knees buckle.

"I'm not joking, Meredith!" Tobias shouted.

I had no clue if my hedge magic would do a thing against such an opponent, but I had to help my partner so I took a chance, blasting a beam of light at him. The attack struck his arm, and the giant dropped his club and howled in pain.

"Mean!" he roared.

"Not mean!" I yelled back. "Just—Oh crap."

The giant picked up his club and, this time, hurled it right at me.

With quick reflexes, I managed to dive out of the way, landing in a thick bed of ferns.

Well, that sure as hell backfired.

A grunt of pain from a certain surly vampire had me quickly ripping myself out of the bed of greenery, and when I saw the cause of the sound, I gasped.

The giant had grabbed onto Tobias's shirt and was holding him aloft. The vampire flailed, trying to get in a strike, but in this instance, none of Tobias's defenses could help him.

"Up here!" Benedict called out.

I searched to find the cat on a branch, above the giant's head.

"Aim between the eyes, Meredith!"

With that, the cat leapt from the branch, his claws digging into the giant's head.

Flailing, the giant released the vampire and sent him flying through the woods. My instinct was to run after him, but Benedict was still holding on to the giant, like a tipsy college girl riding a mechanical bull.

"Hurry!" my familiar yowled as the giant tried to bat the cat away, but somehow, Benedict just kept clinging harder to him.

A pang of pity for the giant rippled through me, but I needed to look out for my own, so taking aim, I blasted another beam of light, this one stronger, meant to knock the giant out.

As intended, it struck just between his eyes. I watched with bated breath while consciousness slipped from the creature and he collapsed to the ground.

Upon impact, the earth beneath us shook. I waited, not willing to take my eyes off the oversized man. But after ten thundering heartbeats the giant did not rise—not even when Benedict trundled over his face and chest on wobbly legs.

"That was a close one," my familiar wheezed.

"I'll say," I murmured, looking around for the vampire and not sighting him. If he wasn't on his way back, something was wrong. "We have to check on Tobias."

I trekked through the thick woods to find the vampire

slumped up against a tree, blood seeping from his head. His shirt was torn too, either from impact or how violently the giant had been flinging Tobias around.

As I knelt at his side and gingerly touched his face, his eyes blinked open slowly.

"Tobias? Are you okay?" I asked quietly.

"It's been an age since anyone has rung my bell quite like that," he grunted.

"I can't believe there are giants."

"There aren't," he growled, shoving himself up off the ground. "At least, not according to the wider magical community. Which means we must proceed with even greater caution as we seek Miriam Black."

CHAPTER FIFTEEN

HANS

"There's a spot." Shay pointed to the left of a crowded, car-lined street.

"Fucking finally," I muttered, turning on my blinker to claim the parking space before the oncoming car could. "I hate DC."

My dislike of the large, pompous city had only been compounded by our journey. We'd spent hours in the car—three more than we'd bargained for, thanks to traffic and a rainstorm pummeling the East Coast—and most of it had been shrouded in a prickly silence.

Shay hadn't tried to start a single conversation. For someone who yammered as much as she did, that was saying something. We may be partners on this mission, but we weren't friends, or even friendly. Not anymore.

Once upon a time, we'd been able to talk to one another without growling. Hell, we even used to flirt. Those days of lighthearted teasing at the bar, or even friendly waves at the S&S tomb, were long gone. It pained me more than I liked to acknowledge.

I pulled into the parking slot and turned off the car. "We're not too far from the house, right?"

Shay nodded. "My phone says we're actually closer than before that wild goose hunt. Only about a block away."

"Let's go, then. They're probably pissed we're so late."

Originally, we'd intended to arrive in the capital hours ago. Surely, the Covenant Seats who'd journeyed from New York and further to assist us in this ambush would be angry by our delay.

Then again, did I really care?

The Covenant was just fine with serving us up to the Prince of Wrath, like little demon playthings. A few hours of inconvenience on our part was nothing by comparison.

So, side-by-side, but with at least two feet separating us, Shay and I strode down the rain-soaked streets of D.C. When we reached the address Artem had sent me, her phone pinged.

"Arrived."

"Yeah, we got it," Shay murmured, turning off the GPS as we climbed the stairs.

The door opened before we got to the top, and the stunning Angelina Ramos, Shay's mother, stood before us, decked out in a gold and white cocktail dress with a neckline that plunged all the way to her navel.

Though I couldn't see anyone else, voices and tinkling laughter came from a side room. What the hell? Were they having a party?!

The nephilim Seat's deep red lips spread into a wide smile. "Welcome, Shaylina! Hans! You two finally made it! We were worried the rain might force you to turn around." Her eyebrows pinched together daintily. "You didn't bring your bags so you could change?"

"B-bags?" Shay cleared her throat, eyes narrowed. "What are you talking about? Why are you dressed like that?"

"Appearances, darling," Angelina hissed. "Hurry inside."

We did as the nephilim said, and immediately found ourselves in an expansive foyer that smelled like a spiced candle; not quite the pumpkin spice that was cropping up everywhere as Fall progressed, but close.

Craning my neck, I found about sixty people, all dressed in finery, milled around a living space just off the foyer.

Angelina shut the door and waved for us to follow her as she marched right past the party. "Come with me."

"Why are these people here?" I pressed.

She'd never answered Shay, and this seemed off. Suspicious. There were *so* many people. They couldn't all be Covenant members—who were really the only people I was cool with knowing our plan.

"Hans, the Covenant Seats cannot meet in the same city where your sister has chosen to claim my daughter and not draw attention. Particularly one where we do not have a Lodge," Angelina replied. "We're all powerful, and surely, there are demons watching us. As mentioned earlier, Prince Orien is rumored to be a brilliant tactician. He will certainly have eyes on people of power."

I blinked. Thanks to my sister, I'd already considered that demons were watching me, but I hadn't thought much about the ruling body of supernaturals. Though, Angelina was probably right. Why *wouldn't* Wrath keep an eye on the Covenant? All he'd need was a peon or two stationed in the area.

"So it looks like we're just popping into a party?" Shay asked.

"Exactly. And because I'm your mother, one might assume that Hans is using this party as a cover for himself before he takes you to his sister." Angelina arched her eyebrows. "Less suspicion."

"Fine." I gestured back the way we came. "But do those people know what's going on?"

"Of course not. We gave our word that we wouldn't out you," Angelina replied, her nose wrinkling. She had never done that before she learned I was Hellblooded, and that stung. Although it hurt way less than the times Shay had used the same gesture. "Those people are local supernaturals who wish to do their duty when the Covenant comes calling. They asked no questions."

"Is that because of Egor?" I pressed.

As one of three vampire Covenant Seats, Egor was powerful. Not as gifted as Tobias in compulsion . . . but then again, he wasn't a Laurent.

"Perhaps."

So, yes.

I wondered how those people would feel when they learned their elected representatives were cool with hoodwinking them. Or if they would ever find out.

The nephilim Seat led us to the back of the home, where about thirty people milled. The room oozed an old-fashioned type of wealth. Dark woods, leather furniture, and gold embellishments drew the eye as they caught the light of strategically placed candles.

I didn't know whose home this was, but someone influential for sure. Perfect for the type of cover the Covenant was trying to pull.

After raking across the room as a whole, my attention paused on Artem. He waved, and I returned the gesture, but didn't linger on him.

Save for mages, who wanted no part in being ruled, every

major supernatural order had representation in the Covenant. Even fae and phoenixes, arguably the rarest orders in this world.

Shifters were the most abundant in the ruling body. Each animal type required their own representation . . . because Goddess forbid a lion be represented by a wolf, or vice versa.

From what I could tell, more shifters, at least one phoenix, and a fae had arrived since I'd met a portion of the Covenant in New York.

My attention latched onto the flaming-haired phoenix for a long moment, taking in the backless dress she wore, displaying with pride the scorch marks where her wings could appear at any moment. It was a sight to behold. Though S&S consisted of many supernatural orders, this room was even more diverse. We had no phoenixes.

Then again, the Covenant has no Hellblooded. So maybe we're even.

Before Angelina could maneuver us deeper into the room —details of the night and who would be present during the ambush still needed to be hashed out—Egor appeared.

"You actually showed up," the vampire sneered at me.

"Of course, we did," I replied. "Why wouldn't we make good on our word?"

Egor drew in a long breath. "It's difficult to trust your kind."

"Many would say that of vampires too."

"Egor," Angelina cooed. "Leave these two soon-to-be-heroes alone, would you? We've all heard your fears. I assure you, there's nothing to be worried about. Shaylina and Hans are trained in escapades such as this." Her eyes went to her daughter, filled with pride

Shockingly, Shay shrank beneath the weight of her mother's stare.

My eyebrows pulled together. I still hadn't figured out their dynamic, but I didn't like knowing Shay had agreed to this without seeming all-in.

"It's not the mission I doubt. Nor your daughter, Angelina," Egor growled. "I do not want to put the full weight of the Covenant behind a Hellborn. Others agree, you know. Not everyone wants to put their life on the line to save the boy."

I stiffened. If the Covenant didn't come with us, there was no way I would meet Nicoleta tonight. I couldn't offer Shay up as bait without the knowledge that others had our backs. For sure, Nic wouldn't arrive without other Darkborn on her side.

I chanced a glance at my forearms. Hour by hour the gray in my veins had faded. Thanks to my ink, the coloring born of using my demon magic was practically invisible, especially to the unaware eye. Sure no one else would notice, and knowing that I had to make a grand gesture or risk losing the Covenant's support, I rolled my shoulders back. "Would you be more trusting if I underwent a Vow of Intent?"

Egor blinked. "You'd do such a thing?"

I gave a single terse nod. "Artem can bind me."

"What about Brons?" Egor replied with a cunning smile.

Revulsion surged inside me, but I should have suspected the vampire would suggest his buddy.

Artem had a soft spot for me and it was apparent to all. If I were to undergo a Vow of Intent, and break it, Artem would be more likely to go easy on me, spare me in some way. Perhaps even return my power.

With Richard Brons, one wrong word, one wrong move, and I'd never be the same.

"Not so keen now, are you, Hellborn?" Egor sniped.

"Brons is fine," I spat out, not meaning my words, but knowing that if I wanted to rely on the backing of the whole Covenant, compromises needed to be made.

Angelina sighed. "I take it that puts off our planning. You'll want to do the Vow now, Egor?"

"Those who have reservations would prefer the demon be bound sooner rather than later, yes."

"And here I thought *some* of the evening could be pleasant." The nephilim gave a dainty twirl of her hand. "Go on, if you must."

"Come, Hellborn." Without a glance back at me, Egor stomped across the room, heading right for Richard Brons.

I exhaled a long breath, hoping I hadn't made a stupid-ass choice. But before I could take a single step, a hand wrapped around my wrist, stopping me.

"You don't have to," Shay said gently.

I glanced down at where our skin touched, shocked at the connection.

The nephilim could barely bring herself to *look* at me since she learned the truth. And now she was telling me not to bind myself to Brons? Why?

"They already said you could maintain your status as a wizard," Shay continued. "Even if it's not the truth, they should honor that promise and not require more from you. It's risky, Hans."

I agreed, and her sticking up for me cut to the quick. It was so much more than I'd expected—the right thing to do, but clearly against what she thought.

And yet . . .

I pulled away. "You're right. But you know we'll need their help to keep you safe."

"We're trained. We might—"

"'*Might*' isn't good enough." I gestured to the room and brought my face closer to hers so only she could hear. "Look, Shay. There's a phoenix and fae here. This is *big*, and we want all the varied power we can get. Don't you agree?"

A part of me wanted her to say no—to back out. I was still wrestling with the idea of her even committing to this. I wouldn't back out, but if she changed her mind, we'd have no choice but to devise another plan.

But Shay just nodded. "Fine. If you really want to, go ahead and bind yourself to him."

Though I wanted to clarify that I didn't *want* to bind myself to Brons, I simply turned. Egor was already waiting on the other side of the room, brows raised. There was no need to give anyone in the Covenant more reason to suspect me.

Before I reached Egor and Brons, however, Artem stepped in front of me. He put a hand on my chest to stop me, as though he thought I might walk right through him.

"They're out of line," he insisted. "We promised—"

I laid a hand on his shoulder. "I know, but I can't risk not having as many strong supernaturals as possible behind us." I tossed a glance at Shay over my shoulder. "There's too much on the line."

Her blue eyes glittered, watching me closely. For a moment, my heart stuttered. I'd have to be a blind man to not realize she was beautiful, but at that moment, it almost seemed like she didn't hate me. Like we were back to normal.

But more . . .

Tingles wracked my body.

We'd flirted in the past, but my body had never reacted to her in this way. So heightened.

"I don't like this," Artem grumbled.

"I don't either. I offered you up to bind myself to."

The Seat's eyes widened. "Egor would never allow such a thing."

"Brons was *his* choice."

"Be careful of the wording, Hans," Artem warned softly. "I do not wish for your power to be locked inside you, yet unusable, at the discretion of Richard Brons. I've seen such punishments done in the past. It looks like a living Hell."

I hadn't actually seen anyone lose their power due to breaking a Vow of Intent, but I'd heard of it happening.

Making such an oath put one under a magical binding. If I broke the Vow, the person I betrayed—in this case, Brons— would lock up my magic. I'd still feel it inside me, but never be able to use my power again. Not unless he released me—and the chances of that happening were about as good as the Prince of Wrath taking up a halo.

"I'll be careful," I promised.

Then I rounded Artem and walked up to Egor and Brons.

Beside them stood the phoenix, and again, my gaze went to the burn marks where her wings could sprout from, if she so wished. A jacket would easily cover them up, but in this company, she didn't need to hide her true nature.

"About time," Brons said. "I was beginning to think you'd changed your mind."

"I don't go back on my word."

"We'll see about that."

Brons held out his tanned hand, and I clasped it.

"Ready?" he asked.

"As ever," I replied, somewhat smug that I'd been right and he hadn't noticed the discoloration of my veins. "Do you need me to cast for you?"

I smirked when his face hardened.

Brons had been born an air elemental, but had learned to

cast too—a feat that, as much as I hated to admit it, was impressive. Still, he wasn't as good as me, a natural-born caster. And I couldn't pass up the chance to rile the bastard.

"As if I would trust you to cast during a Vow of Intent."

Asshole.

Artem had come up behind us, as had Angelina, and others watched not much further away. Activity in the room had ceased, because nothing was as interesting or important as this.

I searched for Shay and found her in the corner, still watching me intently.

Catching my eye, the nephilim shook her head ever so slightly.

Again, I was touched, but there was no going back now. For this to work, for her life not to be in danger, nor mine, we needed support.

When I turned back to Brons, it was to find his eyes closed, magic pulsing all around him. He'd already begun to call on the power of the Goddess.

"Goddess, hear me," Brons spoke loud and clear. "Bind this man's word to me. Ensure his intention is true. His promise of the light, not the dark. Should he go against his promise, tie his magic within him to be released only at my will."

Wind surged around us, creating a funnel as Brons chanted the words again and again. My hair lifted and the skin on the back of my neck prickled. I fucking hoped this was the right thing to do.

Finally, Richard Brons opened his eyes. They glowed from within, a brilliant gold color.

My stomach lurched. The Goddess had accepted the bargain. Now I only needed to give my word to bind us.

"Do you, Hans Novak, agree to do everything in your

power to catch the Prince of Wrath? Do you agree not to betray the Covenant, and in turn, give everything you have to aid in catching the creatures of the underworld, namely Prince Orien?"

"I agree," I said without hesitation.

Light wreathed our hands. It came from neither of us, but from a power we were both connected to, one so much bigger than Brons or me. The Goddess—the creator of magic.

The illumination seeped between our fingers and then blossomed to fill the whole wind funnel, taking it over so that the air petered out to nothing. The Covenant wizard tilted his head back, as if experiencing some type of miracle, and I had to admit, as the light swirled around us and the power of the Goddess encompassed us, it was the closest damn thing I'd ever felt to a divine moment.

The moment that power left, just vanished into the air, I felt hollow . . . like I'd never been whole in the first place.

Brons's eyes met mine, his no longer glowing. "The Goddess has accepted the bond. Forsake us, and you will live forever without your magic."

I released his hand. "I have no intention of betraying anyone."

"We'll see about that," the wizard replied. "Now, let's begin our planning, shall we?"

CHAPTER SIXTEEN

MEREDITH

NO ONE IN OUR TRIO THOUGHT THE GIANT WOULD BE MY LAST test—I just hoped there weren't many more.

Three is the magic number, right?

"Keep your ears open," Tobias ordered softly.

I was pretty sure he took the appearance of a literal giant out of nowhere personally. The oversized man had knocked Tobias flat into a tree.

I nodded, though I had no doubt that he or Benedict would hear something before me. Still, we were a team, and—

Suddenly, I stopped short. Hot air, so out of place in the English woods under the cover of the moon, washed over me.

"The magic." I barely dared to breathe. "It shifted. Feels weird."

Tobias closed his eyes for a moment, as if digging deep to sense what I did. "You're right. I wonder why."

From where he waited near my feet, Benedict eyed the trail, which, thanks to the angle and the incredibly thick foliage, took a blind turn not too far away. "I bet we'll discover why around that corner."

My heart lodged a lump in my throat, and yet, I managed to stretch my magic out the way Hans had taught me. As I did so, I focused on the bend, searching for a difference of magical power to see if Benedict's proclamation had any merit. Seconds later, my shoulders sagged.

The cat was spot on. The strange heat, a shift in energies, was coming from around the blind turn up ahead.

The question was, what was emitting it?

"Stay together," Tobias directed, as if Benedict and I were likely to run into the woods and frolic like assholes.

We prowled forward as quietly as the gravel allowed, preparing ourselves for yet another horror to come. And though I knew something was about to happen, I wasn't even close to ready for what we saw when we turned the corner.

"A *dragon*?" I breathed, taking in the creature with green scales and wings. It was smaller than I'd always imagined dragons, and only had two legs. "I thought those were in the other world."

"Those in Isila are mostly dragon shifters," Tobias corrected. "But this is no dragon. It's a wyvern, rare, even in the mirror realm. Although, they're supposed to be extinct here."

I believed it. The vampire looked as astonished as me. Just like when he'd seen the giant.

"What sort of sorcery is in these woods?" he murmured softly.

"The kind that we *extinct* creatures keep under tight control so that we may persist," the non-dragon said, shocking the crap out of me.

It was one thing for the giant to speak—albeit poorly—but this was a dragon! No, a wyvern!

Then again, I had a talking cat next to me . . .

"But people live here." I pointed out, wanting more information on the creature.

"Witches of ancient and trusted bloodlines," the wyvern clarified, standing on two legs and watching me carefully with neon green eyes. "Since times of old, they have granted other creatures sanctuary. In return, we protect the *Abscondita* Coven."

So that was who we were searching for.

"We mean them no harm," I said.

"Nevertheless," the wyvern said, his tone rasping like he had to fight to speak. "This coven must be protected at all costs."

"I'm *supposed* to come here, though. To see Miriam Black."

How had Gunner and Silas gotten past these creatures? And why hadn't the wolf said anything about them? Had he faced them at all, or had the vines, the giant, and this overgrown lizard seriously been put here just for me?

"Perhaps you are meant to be here," the wyvern said. "But are you *worthy*?"

"How should I know?"

"The Seven are worthy, and they must also be clever. If you really are one of them, you must answer my riddle to pass."

The road stretched beyond the wyvern, and I couldn't help but peer past him—an action that did not go unnoticed.

"Do not try to cheat me by running by. You will not lose me. Not even the vampire." His tongue flicked out, snake-like. "And you do not want to feel the wrath of my venom."

"No," Tobias breathed.

I gave him a wary look.

"Wyverns have only to spit their venom on a person and they die," the vampire explained. "The riddle is the way forward."

"You're sure?" I asked. A few moments ago, he hadn't even known this creature existed.

"Positive." He eyed our riddler. "So let us hear it."

"Only one of the Seven can answer it," the wyvern said.

Well, blazing balls of shit. I'd much rather have Tobias's brainpower on this one, but apparently that wasn't an option.

"What happens if I fail?"

Something dangerous glinted in the wyvern's green eyes. "Then you'd better run."

So don't fail.

"Okay, what have you got?" I asked before I could chicken out.

"As you wish," the wyvern's claws dug into the ground, as if he were readying himself for this moment. "What must you first give in order to keep it?"

I waited, but when the wyvern added nothing more, my heart began to thud harder. "That's it?!"

"It is. Would you like me to repeat myself?"

"No, I got it," I grumbled, cursing my stupid ass for taking this challenge.

One line! That was all I had to work with.

A mental freakout sesh was just around the corner, which Tobias must have sensed because his hand landed on my shoulder, grounding me.

"Think," he urged. "You can do this."

I wanted to ask if he already knew the answer, but if he did, that wouldn't help me, so I refrained.

Looking down, because Tobias was distracting at the best of times, I glared at the rocky ground, as if the answer would just pop out of the gravel.

I can do this . . . Concentrate. So, what must you first give in order to keep it?

My eyebrows screwed together. There were so many things in the world to give, but try as I might, I couldn't think of a single object that made sense.

Maybe it wasn't an object.

Love? I scrunched up my nose. Nope, that was stupid too.

The wyvern took a step closer, drawing my attention.

"At a loss?" he asked, eyes glittering with the promise of a chase.

"No," I scowled. Hell, I'd barely been thinking for a minute! What did this guy think, that I was some master riddler or something?

Giving someone my heart? My confidence? My vote? My . . .

"You can't stand here forever, you know," the wyvern said. "Eventually, you'll have to answer."

"How long?"

The creature shrugged his outstretched wings. "Normally, I'd say whenever I feel like it, but I'm feeling generous so . . . five minutes?"

Five minutes?!

I wanted to rail against his judgment but I didn't want to waste time. Or have him to go back on his word—

I stiffened. *Oh my God. His word. I have to make a promise before I can keep it. Is that it?*

Determined not to be rash, I ran through at least a hundred other ideas, both physical and not, that could be given to another person. None seemed to fit the criteria as well as a promise. A word.

That had to be it.

When I looked up, the wyvern was staring me down, ready for a challenge. "Thirty seconds."

"A promise," I blurted out. "You have to give someone your word before you can keep it."

"Are you sure?"

I looked at Tobias, but his face was a mask. Still, I thought I detected a glint of pride in his eyes.

I turned back to the mythical creature. "Positive."

The wyvern let out a long breath. "I almost got my hunt."

"I'm right?!"

"You are. You may proceed."

I pumped my fist in the air and shook my ass to a song of victory heard only in my head. "Yes! Suck it!"

"I'd rather not," the wyvern replied dryly.

A chuckle escaped Tobias, but Benedict didn't seem as pleased. More like irate.

"Are there more tasks?" my familiar asked.

"Go forth and see." The winged creature stepped aside.

Now faced with the possibility of another task, I pulled myself together, and our trio continued on.

But as it turned out, we didn't need to go far at all. The moment we passed the wyvern, a gate appeared, like it had been there all along—though it most definitely had not been. Behind the gate stood a lady with short gray hair.

I sucked in a breath, surveying the woman. I placed her at about seventy, and could easily see her being a strict head-mistress at an all-girls boarding school.

"You're Meredith, I presume?" the woman asked, raising her hand in greeting.

"I am."

"Brilliant. I'm Miriam Black."

"Really? I—"

Tobias stepped in front of me, my vampire shield. "We come here in trust and peace. Do I have your word that you won't harm Meredith? Nor her familiar?"

He didn't ask about himself, which made my heart clench.

When Tobias had first acted as a guard, I hated it, but that was changing. With each passing day I enjoyed his presence more.

"I have no intention of harming anyone in your trio," Miriam said. "Can you say the same, vampire?"

"I shall do no harm."

"Then we're in agreement." Miriam waved her hand, and the gate disappeared. "Which means the three of you should follow me."

Tobias and I shared a skeptical glance, but the woman didn't notice, as she'd already turned her back on us and begun walking down the lane.

In the distance, I thought I caught sight of a house. Figuring that was where Gunner and Silas were being held, I made a choice, jogging to catch up to Miriam.

"Are our covenmates okay?" I asked when I reached her.

Tobias fell in at my side, and Benedict next to him.

"They are," Miriam replied.

"You really are going to let them go, right?"

"After you prove who you are."

I held up my hand, showing her the ring. "Isn't this enough?"

Her eyes latched onto the piece, eyes widening for a moment before she resumed her unimpressed appearance. "It is convincing, but not enough. After all, anyone can wear a stolen ring. We have one simple, foolproof test, however."

"I already took three tests." I gestured back to the lane we'd walked down to get here.

"We can't be too careful."

I huffed. "If that's the case, when does it stop?"

"Is that a serious question?" Pale blue eyes latched on to me.

"Why wouldn't it be?"

Miriam laughed humorlessly. "Because the quest before you is nothing *but* a series of tests, child. Each one is more difficult than the last. If you're looking for an end to trials and tribulations, then you may not be the person we need—even if you prove to be one of the Seven."

"One of the Seven?" The wyvern had mentioned that name. "What does that—"

"*Enough* questions. I will answer no more until you have passed your final test here. So follow me and meet your destiny, Meredith." Miriam's gaze raked over me, as if assessing my every cell. "That is, if you dare."

If I dared? This old biddy was *daring* me?!

I stood a little straighter. No way was I backing down now.

Miriam caught the gesture and nodded her approval. "Good girl."

We walked a ways further down the lane, staying quiet until a manor came into view. At that, all my air left me in one go.

It was exactly like one of those huge homes you'd see in *Downton Abbey*. A true estate, sprawling and magnificent.

"Who owns this?" I breathed.

"Our coven."

"The *Abscondita* Coven?"

"I said no more questions and I already permitted you a freebie."

Scowling, I shut up again as Miriam led us around the home. She didn't stop until she reached a door springing up out of nowhere into what looked eerily like an entrance to a hidden underground dungeon. Or a crypt.

"We will descend now. Watch your step."

I held up a hand. "There aren't dead bodies down there, right?"

Though she'd shown little emotion since first meeting, Miriam's lips pulled up slightly. "I won't answer, but I'm curious: why ever would you think that?" She opened the door.

A damp smell hit my nose . . . which was saying something, because England wasn't exactly a dry climate.

"Uh, because I've seen *Game of Thrones*, and this reminds me of where all the Starks are buried."

"The resemblance to a place of burial was not lost on me either," Tobias remarked.

"Well, it is not. This place is one of a kind, so unless you're too chicken, come with me." She disappeared through the door, down a set of stairs.

Damn, this old lady keeps calling me out!

"What do you think?" I whispered to Tobias.

"If you want to know why your mother left you the ring, and why Ms. Black was listed on your vault at *Le Bastion*, you'll follow." His face turned hard for a moment. "I will have your back, should she try anything."

It wasn't the first time he'd said that, and as before, I took comfort in knowing that the vampire would take on anyone for me. Miriam might look like a granny, but she was far from harmless.

"Let's go." I stepped down the stairs.

Wood creaked beneath me, and my hand sought a rail, which I found quickly. Gripping the cold metal tightly, I continued on, no longer able to see Miriam, but trusting that there would be no detours.

And there wasn't. The stairwell remained straight and true, and slowly, my eyes adjusted to the dark.

No, wait. There was actually light.

A few more steps and the ceiling grew a little taller,

allowing me to see further down the descent. What I laid eyes on ripped a gasp from my lungs.

There was no crypt, but a cavern lit by yellow crystals. Mica shimmered, embedded in the walls, it reflected the glow from the larger gems. In the center, a small blue pool of water spread before me, calm and tranquil and strangely cloudy.

My pace quickened, and I reached the bottom seconds later, eyes never leaving the pool. It was as if I was drawn to it.

"What is that?" I whispered, eyeing the water. Though it was opaque, it also gave off glittering sparks in its depths that when grouped together looked like silver clouds. They were so beautiful, so haunting.

"A magic spring," Tobias breathed, coming to stand beside me with Benedict. "I've heard of them, but never seen one."

He'd been saying that a lot here. Funny how I'd thought since we were coming to England, Tobias would be a good tour guide. So far, he seemed nearly as clueless as me.

"Most are long gone," Miriam spoke in a softer tone than she had when we were above ground. "Lost to the ages. But a few have been protected, just as this one has."

"Why are they lost?" I asked, unable to tear my attention from the pool.

I waited for her to say that she wouldn't answer me. But instead, she humored me.

"People destroy what they don't understand." A burdened breath left Miriam. "This includes much relating to magic. But this land has been privately owned since such a concept existed. And it will remain so for long after I'm gone. I hope."

The sadness in her tone pulled my attention from the spring.

She looked smaller, more fragile than when I'd met her in the gravel lane. And yet, I wasn't about to let my guard down.

"What does this have to do with me?"

Miriam's eyes cleared, like she was coming back to the moment, and she met my stare unblinkingly. "Get in."

I reared back. "But I don't have a swimsuit."

The old witch laughed. "I've seen it all before, child. As has the vampire—probably more times than me and you combined."

My neck grew warm as heat climbed higher, into my cheeks. I refrained from looking at Tobias but could sense him stiffening beside me.

The night in my room, when he'd comforted me in my towel—the mortifying boob slip—came rushing back.

Yes, there was something between us, attraction, certainly, but that didn't mean I wanted to strip and leap into a pool in front of the guy!

"I'll turn around," he said, his tone gruffer than before.

"And I'll make sure he does!" Benedict added, like a proud knight showing up for a lady.

Not saying another word, the vampire presented me with his back, allowing me to breathe fully again.

"I just . . . get in?" I asked Miriam. "It won't hurt me?"

If the pool was clear, and I could see to the depths, I'd be a lot less scared. But there was something about the silver clouds that set me on edge.

"Nothing harmful will occur. This is merely your final test."

"How so?"

"What happens once you're in the water will tell me if your parents were right about you all along—if the stars proclaimed the truth all those years ago." She swallowed, and for the first time, unease flitted across her face. "If we can finally begin the work of a lifetime."

I had no idea what she meant, but I nodded.

Reaching for the hem of my shirt, I waited. When Miriam noticed I was still watching her, she snorted.

"Your vampire is chivalrous, darling, but I will not be turning around. As I said, I've waited a lifetime for this moment." She waved a hand to the pool. "Go on then."

Briefly, I closed my eyes in annoyance, but then I sucked it up and pulled my shirt off. A sharp inhale informed me that Miriam had spotted the scars lining my back, but I didn't elaborate, just got naked.

Slipping my shoes off, my feet touched down on cold, damp stone. I pulled off my pants and placed them on the shoes, hoping to keep them dry. For a moment, I considered keeping my bra and undies on, but thought better of it. If they were wet and I didn't get to change, I'd be miserable, so off they went too. Then, padding softly, I crossed the few steps to the pool, gazing into it as I approached.

"Best to just hop in," she advised, her tone gentler than before. Most people softened after they saw my back. "It won't be warm."

I could have figured that out on my own. It was Autumn in Britain, and we stood underground. This was going to be cold as hell.

Still, it felt so wrong to simply 'hop in,' so I split the difference, kneeling and unfurling my legs quickly into the water.

Goosebumps rose along my skin, but I was already committed and ready to get my clothes back on, so I took the plunge, submerging my entire body.

Underwater, the chill pervaded, but I was instantly aware of something else too. A current of energy.

As I came up for breath, the sensation intensified, lighting me up from the inside out. I gasped for air, wiped the water from my face and blinked my eyes open. But before I could look to Miriam to see if I'd passed the test, her cry of relief cut through me.

I kicked my legs and twisted to find the old woman holding herself up with the help of a rock jutting out from the cavern wall. Tears streamed down her wrinkled cheeks.

"You're here," she choked out. "It's beginning."

"What is?" I asked. "How do you know?"

"Meredith!" Tobias's tone was strained, curious. I looked up to find him staring at me. "Your back."

"I'll explain later," I told him, thinking he was looking at the scars.

"No, I mean, yes, I want to know, but . . . Look at your arms . . ."

Dropping my chin, I immediately saw what he meant. Tattoos, swirling and seeming to glow with white light, ran the length of my arms. There was a pattern there, though it was unlike any I'd ever seen, and it appeared to go over my shoulder, all the way to . . .

"What's on my back?"

"The moon," Miriam whispered. "You're one of the Seven Guardians we've been waiting for."

CHAPTER SEVENTEEN

MEREDITH

A CHILL FROM THE ENCHANTED POOL CLUNG TO MY BONES AS WE trailed Miriam Black toward the manor house. Tobias had given me his jacket, which helped somewhat, but I knew the chill wasn't just from the cold of the outdoors.

What the hell had just happened? The markings that lined my arms while in the spring were in the process of fading. Some were already nearly gone, leaving only the faintest traces of swirls, almost like a white tattoo.

Miriam, though stoic and tough earlier, was trembling now.

I wished I understood what she was so rocked by. The rate at which I inched toward revelations was too slow for my taste.

When we neared the front door, Miriam seemed to find herself again. She climbed the steps and once she reached the top, rolled her shoulders back and flung the door open.

An herbaceous scent flew out at me, only to be forgotten when Miriam clapped her hands together.

I jumped, not expecting the sound, nor the light that flew

from her hands, separating seven different ways and zooming into the darkened home.

"What was that for?" I asked, still not sure I trusted this woman.

My parents listed her name as a trustee of my vault in *Le Bastion*, but did they know she had killer vines, a giant, and a wyvern on the premises? I wasn't sure. After all, if they trusted her fully why hadn't I met her before? Or been offered to stay with her before being sent to the horrible foster family who took me in after Mom and Dad died? I hadn't lasted long with that family before fleeing to the streets, where the Ringmaster found me.

Oblivious to my many doubts, Miriam turned to face me. "We *Arcacustos* are rather old and go to bed early. I'm waking the others."

"I thought you called yourselves something else earlier?"

"The *Arcacustos* are *people*, specifically wardens of forgotten knowledge. Together, we form the *Abscondita* Coven." Miriam replied, much more inclined to answer my questions now that I'd become a Guardian—whatever that meant. "The words are similar, but the meanings are not."

"How many of you are there?" I asked as she stepped into a large, dark foyer and turned down a corridor.

"Eight."

"*Arcacustos* . . . That means secret-keepers," Tobias commented slowly as if he'd been raking through his lexicon of ancient words. "And *Abscondita* means hidden. Fitting, since no one can bloody find your lot out here."

"Except for giants and wyverns," I muttered.

Miriam smiled her first genuine smile. "Jon-Jon and Rygor live in our woods. They were keen for the job of testing you."

"Jon-Jon?" Benedict drawled. "You've got to be joking."

"I take it Jon-Jon is the giant?" The name certainly did not fit the cunning wyvern.

"Yes. You'll find both creatures more amenable, now that we know you're a *Vindix*."

"Oh, good grief." I hadn't been aware that I was in for a vocabulary lesson tonight. "What does *that* mean?"

"Looks like you'll need to invest in a dictionary, if you plan to stay here," Benedict teased.

"Champion," Tobias told me, a hint of amusement in his tone. "I take it you mean a champion of the *lapis caelesti*? In a way it's another word for guardian." He raised an eyebrow at our hostess.

"Precisely," Miriam replied. "But let's wait until my fellow *Arcacustos* meet us to delve further. They should be but a few minutes."

"Actually, I think we should see to Gunner and Silas first," Tobias countered. "In fact, we insist."

"Agreed," I said. According to Luca, Gunner and Silas were being kept in a dark and damp dungeon. "They didn't deserve this to begin with, so they should be released now that I've proven myself, or whatever."

Miriam let out a sigh, but she clearly heard the resolve in our tones, because she stopped and turned around. "In that case, a quick about-face is in order. But we must not dally. The other wardens will be desperate to meet you."

Personally, I was less worried about the other wardens' needs than I was about the state of Gunner and Silas, but I just nodded and allowed Miriam to lead us down another hallway and a flight of stairs.

When we reached the bottom, I scanned the area. It seemed a lot like the hallways above: old, dark, manor-like . . . but also less occupied. A bit unkempt, too.

Not quite the dungeons I'd imagined, though.

"This is the right level?" I asked.

"It is."

"Does someone who lives here stay down here too?" It was the only way I could reconcile the images in my head. *There must be a guard who uses up most of the hall, and the dungeons are at the end.*

"The *Arcacustos* are healthy for our age, but our knees prefer as few steps as possible."

"So, you just keep other people locked up and miserable down here?"

Miriam shot me an amused expression and approached a door, cupping the handle. "I believe you'll find your friends taken care of better than you might have expected."

I didn't reply as she opened the door.

"What's goin' on?" Gunner's voice called out. He sounded half-asleep, and while it wasn't too late, I knew from my stint in an Egyptian jail that time of day didn't matter much when you were imprisoned.

"Meredith and company are here to free you," Miriam said. "You do vouch for this wolf, correct, Meredith? And the fae?"

"Of course, I do," I answered.

Miriam waved a hand, and though nothing visibly happened, I sensed a shift in magical energy in the area. "You're free, wolf."

"Thank the Old Ones!" Gunner barked out, barreling from the room.

He passed Miriam, who sidestepped him just in time to avoid being run over.

"Stoney! Toby! Lil' Ben!"

"*Benedict!*" the cat yowled, but the effect of his anger was dampened by the fact that he darted backward as Gunner rushed us, arms open wide.

"Bring it in, you two!" the wolf howled and scooped us up into a three-person bear hug.

A long sigh rang in my ear as Gunner squeezed tight. Then, to my utter astonishment, he laid a smacker on my cheek.

I blinked and pulled back just enough to see Tobias, stiff as a plank and looking bored. *What's wrong with him?* I mouthed.

"Wolves need connection, touch, and room to roam," Tobias explained. "A lot of each one."

"It appears I wasn't enough for Gunner," Silas smirked, leaving his room next. Apparently, they'd been kept in adjoining cells. "We even held hands!"

Connecting cells? What was this place?

Gunner released us, allowing me to breathe fully once again, and I was shocked to find a tear streaking down his cheek. "'Bout the only thing that kept me sane, Si, my man. Thank you."

Silas smiled. "You're welcome. If I had to be locked up with a wolf, I'm glad it was you."

Confused, because our friends seemed pretty clean and even smelled nice, I peeked into Gunner's room. My mouth fell open.

"There's a king-sized bed and a fireplace in there! Luca said you'd be in a dungeon!"

"I told Gunner that was going a bit far when he talked to Luca." Silas shrugged. "But you can't argue with the results. You two got here fast."

"Yeah, callin' it a dungeon may have been a bit of a stretch." Gunner rubbed the nape of his neck sheepishly.

"I'll try not to take offense to that," Miriam muttered at the same time that Benedict proclaimed that wolves were divas.

I turned on the cat, unable to believe his scorn. "Like you're one to talk. You made me buy a memory foam cat bed!"

"I have a bad back."

"Probably because you sleep half on and half off your bed all night."

"I did tell you to size up."

Oh my Hell. These people . . . and this cat.

Tobias placed a hand on my shoulder. "Breathe."

"I just—"

"I know," he said, clearly holding back a laugh. "But now that we know Gunner and Silas are fine, we have things to do."

"Can we come?" Gunner asked, his tone hopeful but uncertain. He sounded like a little kid, asking if we could be friends.

I stared at the wolf, never having seen him this way. Usually, he was so fun and outgoing and confident, but after a couple of days locked up in a fancy room, all that had changed.

It made me realize I didn't know much about wolves.

"Sure," I agreed, unable to deny Gunner anything when he looked so desperate to be around others.

"Actually," Miriam interjected, "I'm not sure that's wise."

"Well, *actually*, I'm not sure how smart it was to keep Gunner locked up," I shot back. "And they're both a part of S&S, as am I, so what I say goes."

Miriam gave me a sharp look, and I added, "That is, unless you want me to leave?"

"You can't."

"Oh yes *I can*." I propped my hands on my hips. "Prince Orien is trying to take over the world, and I might be fated to fight him and find the missing stones, but that doesn't mean I have to do it your way. I've always worked just fine alone. I could probably figure things out okay."

"Bloody hell. *Fine,*" Miriam huffed in exasperation. "Back upstairs, the lot of you."

We climbed the stairs, and once at the top, Miriam didn't say a word as she led us back the way we'd come, straight to a closed door.

When she opened it, a room adorned with a circular table ringed by ten chairs appeared. In the center of the table, a small tree grew. On the branches, gems gleamed, each one matching a gemstone at the base of my ring.

The hair on the back of my neck stood on end as I looked at the tree, but my attention was quickly diverted as one of the people in the room gave out a little cry.

I tore my gaze away from the centerpiece to find seven individuals. The oldest looked to be seventy-something, like Miriam, and the youngest perhaps in her early forties.

When one stout woman with tightly curled, short, gray hair caught sight of Gunner and Silas, she snorted. "I wondered if they'd release you two first." Her tone was shockingly raspy.

"Damn happy they did," Gunner said.

He didn't look mad at the coven that inhabited this place, just relieved to be released from his 'prison'.

"We'll be needing two more chairs, then," the woman replied. "Stuart?"

The only man among the group hopped to it, rushing into a side room and dragging out a chair.

"I'll help," Gunner said, jogging into the same room for another chair.

"Here we go. Nice and cozy," he beamed as he returned and set the chair down.

"Too cozy," Miriam muttered. "That can be your seat, wolf. Fae, sit next to him. And you, vampire."

"I won't leave Meredith's side," Tobias announced.

"Fine then, she's next to you. Just whatever you do, give the wolf some attention before he jumps on the rest of us."

"I wouldn't," Gunner said, with a frown.

"You won't have to," Silas replied, giving me the impression that, like Miriam, he didn't quite believe his friend. "We can hold hands again."

I almost laughed, but the wolf looked so delighted that I held it back.

The poor guy. I never would have guessed wolves were like this. Harper, the only other wolf I was close to, seemed to like her space. Then again, Shay was always up in her business, so maybe Harper never got a chance to feel lonely.

We took our seats, with me wedged between Gunner and Tobias. Benedict, never one to be left out, leapt up to sit on my lap.

When we were settled, the wolf patted my shoulder, until Silas held out his hand and Gunner took that instead, content to lay his palm on the fae's hand.

"Why don't we go around and introduce ourselves to Meredith?" Miriam suggested as she took her seat.

I stared at the seven new people, who in turn stared at me. There was no way I'd recall all their names, but I didn't want to be rude. I'd worked too damn hard to get here to be cast out for showing a lack of respect. So, I resolved to try my best to commit their names to memory.

"Sure," I said. "But I might need reminders occasionally. Lots to take in."

"Of course." Miriam waved her hand. "We're far past the age of vanity, my dear."

I wasn't so sure about that, but I nodded as the woman next to Miriam leaned forward. "I'm Claire."

"Meredith," I replied, smiling at her and semi-envying her lilting Irish accent and long gray hair. I hoped I could pull off that look when I was older.

The others introduced themselves too, but Claire, Stuart, Gloria, and Aya were the four that stuck out. Stuart, because he was the only man and, at around fifty, younger than everyone . . . except for a British woman whose name had already slipped my mind. Stuart also had flaming red hair, so he was pretty easy to recall.

Aya seemed to be the second youngest. She hailed from Nigeria and wore bright colors that caught my eye. Even though they weren't my personal style, the palette looked great against her ink-black skin. And Gloria was the shorter one with the raspy voice that seemed to boom from her.

Tobias and Benedict introduced themselves too, and when we finished, everyone looked to Miriam in a way that made me think perhaps she was the leader of this little coven.

"Now that that's done," she leaned back in her chair, "you'll want to know what we're here for. What we expect of you as a *Vindix*."

I almost scoffed. *And so much more.* But I simply said, "Yeah."

We had to start somewhere.

"Our coven formed shortly after the *Vindix*, otherwise known as Guardians of the *lapis caelesti*, were chosen."

"Or the Seven," Gunner interrupted. "That's what you called Stoney when we arrived."

"Yes, or the Seven," Miriam echoed, looking irritated. "After your family lines were chosen to guard the sacred stones the angels had created, it was decided that others should be aware of the *Vindix*. These wardens were tasked with knowing what the *Vindix* were entrusted with, who they are, and what the repercussions of the stones are, in case they ever fell into the wrong hands."

"Which the wardens did, for a long time," Claire said softly. "But it didn't work out completely as planned. In retrospect, it was a bit shortsighted to entrust so much to just seven witching families. It was only a matter of time before a *Vindix* went off on their own and others would follow. People gifted with that degree of power and authority do not like to be controlled by anyone, no matter how slight the control"

My eyebrows knitted together. I had a feeling they didn't know where these people were, and that might be where I came in. But first . . .

"The *Vindix* are all witches?" I asked.

"Originally," Miriam answered. "As are we."

"Why?" I asked. "Why wouldn't the angels spread the stones out to other orders?"

"No one can be sure," she said. "But it's said witches were the first supernatural order the angels created. We were easier than some, a mix of magic—which the angels had loads of— and human. But of course, that's just hearsay. No one except the angels can know for sure which order was created first, and the angels don't bless us with their presence often."

I thought of Shay's father, an archangel. Shay was older than she looked, though I'd never asked her exact age. Had Uriel's coupling with Shay's mom been the last appearance of an angel on Earth?

"All we know," Miriam continued, "is that the seven families who guard the stones, and the eight families of this coven, possess witching blood."

"But why didn't the angels just keep the stones?" I pressed. *Did they not trust themselves?*

Every time a morsel of information was presented, a new question arose.

Stuart snorted. "You forget that the angels once counted the Princes of Hell among their number. The heavenly beings know precisely how perfect, or *imperfect*, they are."

"There are seven stones." I was not quite ready to bring the Princes of Hell into the mix. "And you guys know where they are and what they do and who should control them? The *Vindix*?"

The *Arcacustos* once again shared glances, and this time, everyone except Miriam leaned back in their seats, the excitement gone.

"We know what the stones do, we have the texts explaining each one. We know how they interact with one another too," Miriam reiterated. "But we were only certain of the location of the Opal of Heaven."

My stomach sank.

"Which is now with Wrath," Tobias ground out.

"Precisely." Miriam swallowed thickly. "We—"

A massive roar came from outside, followed by a *crack*.

I gripped the side of the table, and Benedict leapt to the floor, taking cover. As one, Stuart, Aya, and the young British woman whose name I'd forgotten shot out of their seats.

"What is that?" Gunner drawled.

"That'll be Jon-Jon," Claire replied.

Gloria pinched the bridge of her nose. "How did you get past him, Meredith?"

"I, uh, sort of knocked him out?"

"Bloody hell," Stuart dashed to the door. "He must have just woken up. We must calm him. Hannah!"

"Very well then." Another chair pushed back, and the forty-ish woman with long, blonde hair ran after Stuart.

Hannah! That was the youngest one's name.

Aya, Claire, and two others followed more slowly, their bodies not as spry, leaving just Miriam and Gloria in the room with us.

"You go too, Gloria," Miriam said. "Jon-Jon adores you, and you know how he gets when he feels slighted."

Gloria stood. "Don't worry, child," she assured me, steel in her eyes as she headed toward the door. "We'll give you a proper introduction to the overgrown baby tomorrow. Set things to right."

A pit formed in my gut. I wasn't sure I wanted that . . . especially seeing as the roaring hadn't stopped, and the cracking sound was becoming clearer; I was pretty sure Jon-Jon was downing trees. And I'd seen the trees around this place, they were huge!

Miriam sighed. "Things are never quiet around here. How can they be, with a forest full of creatures?"

I shrugged, unable to answer that.

"Do you wish to continue?" the secret-keeper asked.

"Kinda. Although, I am tired," I said right as a yawn worked its way up my throat. "I feel like I won't be getting all the information tonight anyway."

She smirked. "Absolutely not. There's far too much."

"Then what I really want to know is what is my part in all this?"

Miriam nodded. "We shall teach you enough about the stones so that you know how to use them. Then, when you're ready, you will be sent to find the other *Vindix*."

I dug my teeth into my bottom lip. Since the moment it was admitted that other *Vindix* had set off on their own, I'd been afraid of this. They didn't know who the others were, and I wouldn't be able to help locate them.

"Seekers can't find people," I said uneasily. "Only things."

"The other *Vindix* have adornments—rings, necklaces, bracelets, and the like—similar to yours," Miriam explained. "And now that you've been dipped in the enchanted spring, the ring has been . . . hmm . . . turned fully on."

I frowned. "But it already worked before that."

Kind of. When it felt like it—which was like once . . . when it wanted to be whole. Come to think of it, the ring was actually kind of a P.O.S.

"So this ring will help me find other pieces like it, because their stones all come from the same place?"

"Precisely."

"But what if other families have lost their jewelry? Or worse, *their stones*? The Pearl was lost. And Wrath has mine!"

I shuddered at the idea of facing the Prince of Darkness again. It hadn't worked out well the first time, and now that he knew who I was, he could strike at any moment.

"It's a possibility, but we have to trust that, one way or another, the *Vindix* will be called to each other," Miriam said. "It's what the angels decreed. And though you're correct that the other gifted families might have misplaced their *lapis caelesti*, the stones will still exist somewhere in the world. They are heaven-made, impossible to destroy. Together you will find them and once they are found, their power will be obvious."

Another roar, followed by shouts, came from outside, and Miriam stood. "I'm sorry, this meeting must draw to a close sooner than I'd hoped. We will pick up again in the morning."

"But I have so many more questions! Like what are the *Vindix* supposed to do? Just watch the stones? And what exactly do the stones do?!"

Miriam swallowed. "Very well. Just a bit to sate your curiosity—and this is perhaps the most important bit." She took a deep breath. "Together, the chosen seven are fated to use the *lapis caelesti* so evil does not devour our world."

Oh, is that all?

"Now, allow me to show you to your quarters so that I might help calm Jon-Jon before he destroys the manor." Miriam waved for us to follow her out the door.

CHAPTER EIGHTEEN

TOBIAS

Our rooms were side-by-side and far from where the *Arcacustos* slept—a layout I appreciated. In our own part of the manor it was easier to relax, to rest.

Not that I planned on sleeping. I didn't need to do so often and I especially wouldn't in a place such as this. Not until I was quite sure the *Arcacustos* were not our enemies.

They might have excellent taste in scotch, I thought, swirling a two-finger pour of amber liquid as I took a seat in the common room closest to everyones' quarters. *Still, I need to know more before I can let my guard down.*

"Just so glad y'all came," Gunner repeated for the third time in five minutes.

I let him prattle on because it clearly made the wolf feel better. In truth, I was just relieved he'd stopped trying to touch me.

Like fae, vampires weren't creatures who particularly loved hugging or touching. That Silas had accommodated the alphablood's physical needs above his own spoke volumes. Particularly since Silas was more reserved than most. In truth, I knew very little about the fae.

Or perhaps it meant Gunner's need to talk all the time drove him to it. The incessant chatter might simply annoy him that much.

Both were believable.

"I was beginnin' to think we'd rot down there," Gunner continued when no one replied. "I owe Si a beer when we get back home."

"Dude, you were in a plush bedroom!" Meredith cocked an eyebrow at him from where she lay on her back in front of a roaring fire. Benedict slept in a tight ball next to her, his black fur likely hot to touch. The witch and her familiar had already been here when I arrived, the former staring at the ceiling lost in thought, the lines of her body illuminated by the flames—a murderous distraction.

What was I going to do about the fading line between us?

"Cooped up!" Gunner barked back. "My kind ain't meant for that, Stoney."

Meredith snorted and shoved up to her elbows. "You're absurd."

"And ya love me."

The witch opened her mouth to reply, but at that moment, Silas swept through the door, wearing new clothes and his long, silver-white hair pulled back.

"Where did that clothing come from?" I asked, slightly envious. Getting out of the shirt the giant had torn would be welcome.

"They brought our bags in from the car the first night. Apparently, someone relocated them to our new rooms," Silas said with a shrug.

"You even had your luggage!" Meredith pointed out to the

wolf, who grinned sheepishly. "They treated you like a prince! No one's brought me my stuff yet."

"I'm sure they will. But if we could move on from Gunner's elevated tastes?" I sipped my scotch, aware of the irony. "I need to know what everyone's thoughts are on this group. Silas? Gunner? You've been here the longest. Aside from your *subpar* accommodations, what do you think of the *Arcacustos*?"

"Really, we only met Claire, Gloria, and Miriam . . . and they're actually alright," Gunner said. "I mean, I dunno what they would have done if you guys hadn't come, but—"

"Probably fed you a five-course meal." Meredith rolled her eyes.

"The food was passable, but not that good," Silas replied. "But I'm with Gunner, the witches are not a danger to us. I'd go so far as to call them good people, even if they did lock me up."

"You believe their purpose justified their actions?" I asked.

"I do," Silas said. "They didn't hurt us, they just couldn't afford to let us go in case we were lying."

"Which means they don't have a witch skilled in mental magic here, or they simply would have checked if you told the truth," I mused. "I wonder what their powers are?"

"Though they did mention memory erasure," Silas said with a frown. "Perhaps they were bluffing. Or perhaps detecting lying is a witching specialty?" He looked at Meredith.

"Don't look at me," she said with a soft snort. "I only know a handful of types of witches."

"Well, one is a warder, for sure." Gunner stood and helped himself to the scotch with a sigh. No doubt, he yearned for a beer. The wolf was a connoisseur of both the craft variety and the swill many Americans seemed fond of. "I bet one's a healer too, 'cause half of 'em are real old, and the nearest hospital is pretty far."

When put that way, a healer seemed a reasonable choice to have on the premise—if they got to *choose* their members from certain families, which I was still unclear on.

"I think I trust them," Meredith said. "They haven't been nearly as forthcoming as I'd hoped, but now that I have an idea of what they guard, I get why they're so cautious. Plus, I'll admit that I want to trust them. After all, my parents allowed Miriam access to their vault . . . I want to think that they had good judgment."

"Undoubtedly, they will feed you information slowly," I said. "Which really does not suit our needs."

The Pearl and the Opal were still with Wrath. Who knew when they might surface again? When they did, we needed to be ready.

"True, but I don't think anything about this scenario can be rushed," Meredith grimaced. "Once I learn more about the stones, I'll still have to find six other people." Her eyes widened as her own words sank in. "Six! That's a lotta small talk."

"And they'll need to be brought here, debriefed." I exhaled.

"Possibly trained," Silas added. "Until recently, Meredith didn't know she was a witch. What if others don't either?"

Bloody hell. This was getting complicated.

"How 'bout we assume the best," Gunner suggested. "That Meredith finds the other *Vindix*, no problemo, and they're all magically trained. Then what? Your little group of seven just takes on Wrath?"

"I . . . guess so?" Meredith's face paled. "Considering I

don't know these people, or how good they are at fighting and magic, that sounds freaking terrifying. What if they're accountants?!" Her pitch rose to a frantic level that might have been comical if the circumstances weren't so dire.

"Naw, don't worry, Stoney," Gunner waved a hand, and the gesture diffused a notable amount of tension in the room. "Even if the other *Vindix* need trainin' up in how to fight, Luca will want in on this and lots of us are good fighters. We gotta all pitch in to get the stones and send the prince back to Hell."

"What if this coven doesn't allow us to tell him?"

"They won't have a choice," I growled. "They've already involved three non-*Vindix* and we aren't backing out now. In our coven, we don't leave people behind."

"I know," Meredith breathed. "And I do feel better hearing you guys say that." She flopped back on to the ground, this time on her stomach, a soft *oomph* leaving her. Mercifully, her long hair fell forward to cover the cleavage that instantly snared my attention.

"I think me and Si should head back to New Haven tomorrow," Gunner said. "Who knows, the witches might be plannin' to kick us out anyway, but I just want everyone to be on the same page. We'll catch Luca up to speed. That way we can be ready to go if you need help finding' the *Vindix*. I betcha you can do it all yourself, but won't it be easier as a team?"

Meredith nodded. "That's something I'm beginning to understand."

She looked like she wanted to add more, but when she opened her mouth next, a giant yawn came out instead.

Her hand flew to cover it. "Sorry. I've been so tired since the meeting."

"I can't imagine why. You traveled a day after you stayed

up all night fighting demons and a Prince of Darkness," I teased.

"'Bout that . . ." Gunner leaned forward. "I wanna hear all about New York. We only read what was on the message boards. We want details."

Meredith rose quickly to her feet. "I hope that you're up for that, Tobias, because I don't want to talk about that night. See you all in the morning."

She scooped up Benedict, who didn't so much as stir. We bid her goodnight, and I watched the witch leave, waiting until I heard her shut her bedroom door behind her.

"Alright, Toby, quit pining for the hot witch and tell me what happened." Gunner scolded, a gleam of mischief in his eyes.

"Yes, I'd like to hear too," Silas added.

I ignored the part about Meredith, and began to relive the danger, the terror, of that New York City night.

* * *

Hours later, I set to putting out the fire. Gunner and Silas had long since retired, leaving me alone with my thoughts, which, upon revealing the story of Wrath and the Ringmaster, had turned dark.

More drink helped, and eventually, I felt as though the scotch had done its work. I was not quite sleepy, but no longer furious at what had happened to Meredith in New York, and felt like I could finally lie down.

Seeing as I'd be able to listen for any sign of foul play just as well from my room as this one, I chose to do so in a bed.

When the last embers died, I let myself into the drafty corridor. Humans romanticized homes built in this period— which I estimated was the seventeenth century—but they were a pain in the arse to maintain and keep warm.

I tilted my head. *Come to think of it, the 1600s are rather recent, compared to how long the Abscondita claim to have been on this land. Did their previous residence burn down?*

Such a fate wasn't uncommon, so I wasn't suspicious, merely curious. I added that query to the heap of them we had on the agenda for tomorrow.

Passing by Meredith's room—wedged neatly between mine and Gunner's—I paused to listen.

Her breathing was a touch fast, but she was still asleep.

"All's well," I murmured, trying not to imagine her plump mouth, slightly open as she slept peacefully. The scotch, while calming my anger, was *not* helping me maintain chaste thoughts.

Not that I'd been having much luck with that since Meredith had dipped into the enchanted pool. I shouldn't have looked, but Miriam had sounded so awed when Meredith had surfaced that I couldn't help myself.

A soft snort escaped me. Who was I kidding? Those types of thoughts had arisen long before our run in with the enchanted pool.

I turned to continue on, when a shrill scream cut through me.

"No! No! *No!*" Meredith's last plea ended in a sob. "Get away from me! Get—"

I spun and burst through her door, my eyebrows pinching together as the scene unfolded before me: Meredith thrashing against the blankets, completely lost beneath them.

I darted over, my keen hearing honing in on her panicked breathing. "Meredith! You're okay. Hold on."

"Tobias?!" the witch shrieked, terror riddling her tone in a way that made my stomach clench. "She's here! Be careful."

I yanked the blankets off to find her with her hands up,

tears streaking down her face. The witch met my eyes, blinking with confusion. When her hands fell, I knew she understood.

"A dream?"

"A nightmare," I corrected, perching on the side of her bed. I wouldn't leave until I was certain she was okay.

"It was the Ringmaster," she whispered.

"I thought as much." And though it went against my instinct to keep my distance, I held out my arm.

She hesitated, but eventually snuck beneath it, leaning close to me as I wrapped my arm around her. Unable to stop myself, I inhaled her scent of jasmine and pine, and nearly groaned. It was even more intoxicating than before. How could that be?

"Sorry if I woke you," she sniffled.

"You didn't," I assured her. "Vampires don't sleep much, and I hadn't planned to while we're here."

She twisted to look up at me. This close, the track marks of her tears were pronounced.

I hated the Ringmaster for making Meredith Stone, a tough-as-nails woman, feel this way.

"We might be here a while," Meredith croaked.

It struck me that she hadn't said *she* might be here for a while. Didn't insinuate that I needn't stay. A month ago, she would have.

"I'll sleep eventually," I promised. "Just not tonight."

A tear brimming in her lashes fell down her smooth cheek, and I reached out, ending its trail.

Her breathing stopped, and abruptly, I realized just how close we were. Our faces, mere inches from one another, our breath mingling. Hers smelled of sweet mint, and beneath her nightshirt her mortal heart thudded hard against her breastbone.

This is a bad idea.

Meredith cupped my face, the touch unraveling my reasoning before I could shield myself with it. "I don't know what it is about you, Tobias. I feel like I know you in a way I've never known anyone."

"The blood you drank," I choked out.

"No," she exhaled insistently. "It's more." Her finger slid to my lips, tracing the bottom one so lightly, so sensually, it was almost painful.

I was powerless to correct her now, to lie again. Instead, the predator in me arose, needing to claim her, to have her. To truly make her *mine* in the way it had wanted to since that one, disastrous training day. A low growl rolled out of me, and she froze.

"Am I in trouble?" she asked softly.

"We both are," I rasped, wrapping my hand around the back of her neck and pulling her lips to mine.

The kiss was hungry, fulfilling every one of those that had never quite come to pass, bringing to fruition nights of fantasizing. With this new connection, my skin tingled, begging me for more, to claim her wholly.

Her tongue swept mine, and I groaned before responding in kind, pulling her closer.

My eyes were closed, but I felt the moment the witch shifted, and the next thing I knew, a weight landed on my lap as she straddled me. Immediately, my heart began to beat, slow and steady, but harder than it had in ages. As if it wished to thrust out of my chest so this marvelous creature could hold it in her hands, claim it.

Down below, I responded too.

Bloody hell.

I hadn't reacted like that to a woman in decades. Hadn't used my manhood for its intended purpose in . . . far too long. Just the thought of doing so with Meredith made my blood burn.

I'm a goner.

"Tobias," Meredith whispered, shifting again, her lips trailing down my neck, offering gentle butterfly kisses. "What is this? What are we doing? Why does it feel like this?"

"I don't know," I said, and my traitorous blood pumped harder through me. I could practically feel it beginning to vibrate. If it started singing now, as it had when Meredith was missing, I didn't know what I'd say.

I was not about to bring up what Giselle believed. *For right now, this is just a kiss,* I lied to myself.

Whatever this was, it was so much more than a kiss.

"It's not just that I drank your blood," Meredith pressed, suddenly mastering herself and leaning back to stare me in the eye. "That might have kicked it off, but my feelings for you have only gotten stronger in time. Even when you piss me the hell off. Which, for the record, is fairly often."

When I barked out a laugh, a smirk grew on her face.

Cheeky, sexy bugger.

"Only you could insult me *and* attract me to you like a moth to the flame," I replied, my tone deeper than usual; more like how it sounded when I'd been a rough and tumble human, a young sailor still learning to be a man and playing the part. I sounded so human, and who could blame me? The woman before me made me feel human again. Alive. Burning. Lusting.

Desperate to taste her again, I licked my lips. From her,

they tasted like honey, as if she were bewitching me. Not that she needed to use magic to do so.

The gesture seemed to captivate her and Meredith leaned closer once again, kissing me, her fingers tangling in my hair.

Gods, help me.

My hands fell to her rear—world-class, if I did say so myself—and I cupped her luscious curves. A man could die happy holding a woman like this.

A seductive laugh ripped up her throat. "So, you're an ass guy?"

"Appears so."

"Well, I have that cov—"

"Oh no, no, *no*! What is going on here?!"

Meredith stiffened, and I closed my eyes, unable to believe this was happening.

The cat, the same bloody cat that had been sleeping while we conversed in front of the fire, the cat that had slept through her nightmare, had woken as Meredith and I *whispered*.

Had I still been a devout man, I would have thought God hated me.

Benedict leapt onto the bed, his amber eyes glaring daggers at me. "Anyone care to explain?"

"Ugh," Meredith groaned. "Why do I feel like my dad just caught me making out?"

"That is not what a protector does, vampire!" Benedict yowled so loudly I was sure Gunner would wake.

Bloody hell, we couldn't allow that to happen. We might be able to tell the cat to shove it, but the wolf would never keep quiet.

"I slipped in my role," I admitted, before looking Meredith in the eye. "And I don't regret it."

Her lips quirked up. "Me either."

"Whereas I very much regret the eyeful I got." Benedict yowled again, and with my keen hearing, I heard Gunner mumble next door.

"Meredith, I don't want to, but I should go," I said, ignoring the fussy feline. "Gunner is rousing, and—"

"Oh my God, leave. I do not want him to ask me a million questions about this!" She leapt off my lap, exposing my excitement. A smug grin crossed her face. "Nice to know what you're working with, Tobias. There would have been no complaints from this girl."

I stood, uncomfortably, and shook my head. Females these days were far more forward than in my times. "You'd fit in quite well on a few of the ships I used to crew."

"Fit in?" she scoffed. "I'd *run* that ship, baby." She tossed her hair sassily.

"Less flirting, more leaving!" the cat yelled, and this time, I heard the floorboards in Gunner's room creak as the wolf got to his feet.

"Gotta run, love." I kissed Meredith on the cheek before striding to the door.

I shot a glance over my shoulder and caught her watching me, her expression a touch more innocent, softer, than before.

I winked, and slipped out the door, zooming into my own room seconds before Gunner opened his door to check things out.

A laugh escaped me as the wolf prowled up and down the hallway a few times before giving up and going back to his room.

For now, our secret was safe. From Gunner, at least.

I crossed the space to my bed and crawled atop the firm mattress to lie flat on my back.

I just kissed Meredith Stone.

Had it been a mistake?

It didn't feel like one. If felt . . . momentous—which I couldn't say for very many instances in my long life.

Before I could get deeper into what had just occurred, how I might have taken a turn with the seeker I'd had no intention of making, my phone lit up. I'd kept it on the side table as our group conversed, but that had been hours ago. It was probably Luca, wondering what the hell we were up to.

Snatching up the device, I glanced at the screen. My stomach tightened. As expected, three messages from Luca flashed at me . . . but those weren't the only notifications I had.

Giselle had tried to call me. Not once. Not twice. *Six* times.

She'd left a voicemail, too. My sire rarely did that, disliking the idea of her voice being recorded.

Swallowing the knot forming in my throat, I clicked on the voicemail.

My maker's voice filled my ear, panic lacing her words. "Tobias, you need to be careful. Earlier today, a woman arrived at the Ordo Aeternum's headquarters. She claims to know of a seeker witch, a woman named Meredith."

Every one of my muscles went rigid, and a long pause filled the air before Giselle spoke again.

"It might not be the woman you're developing feelings for, but I have an idea it is. This other woman—she gave the name Jennifer, but anyone with eyes could tell that was a lie—she wants Meredith's magic, and the OA is willing to help track her down, as long as they get the Pearl. And Jennifer has promised it."

I scoffed. Jennifer—or the Ringmaster, as I was inclined to believe—couldn't pry the Pearl from Wrath. Nor would she want to. Somehow, they were working together and she was playing the Ordo Aeternum to get to Meredith faster. To steal her magic. From there, would she help Wrath find the other stones?

"I think she's very dangerous, Tobias," Giselle continued. "Even for a human. She's convinced the OA to seek Meredith, says that she knows where the witch is already but needs assistance getting to her. I'm trying to get on that detail. I'll do what I can to protect you. And her."

A loud swallow filled the line. "But stay alert. I can't be everywhere at once, and I could tell that, no matter how you tried to hide it, this woman means something to you."

My sire hung up, leaving me staring at my phone in disbelief. The moment S&S had been dreading had finally come.

Meredith's secret had been bound to get out, one day or another. But now it was in the hands of not one, but *two* enemy factions.

CHAPTER NINETEEN

SHAY

The promises had been made, the teams divided, the plan set. We were all systems go, ready to lure in the Prince of Wrath. At the meeting's end, the Covenant members rose from the imposing circular table we'd gathered around.

But my ass remained firmly planted.

We were really doing this?

A lump that had been stuck in my throat for the last half an hour, while the Seats decided my future, threatened to rise—along with my many reservations of being used as bait. I stared at the tabletop, determined to hide my feelings.

Before tonight, before we'd convened and the hour to meet Nicoleta ticked closer, I could fake bravery. In the light of day, it was easy to pretend that I was certain. That this was what I wanted. But now . . .

This was one of the seven Princes of Darkness we were talking about! How did no one see how crazy this was?

"Shaylina?"

At my mother's voice, I swallowed the lump and ripped

my gaze from the table to meet her eyes. She stood behind me, waiting. "Yeah?"

"You'll ride with me, darling?"

She phrased it like a question, but it wasn't. Mom had taken up the mantle of leader in this operation. The other Seats probably thought it was because she worried for me. It was how a normal mother would react, and sometimes, my mother acted that way. My house, the one I'd purchased from her, was well warded at her insistence. But that sort of support was sparse, and I knew the truth.

Mom wanted me to succeed, to bring glory to our family.

"Sure," I replied. "I need to use the restroom first."

Mother nodded. "I'll wait in the car."

Her gaze shifted to Hans. She'd cooled toward him since learning he was Hellblooded, but even now, she managed a smile. How did she do that? It was so fake, but so necessary—though I couldn't do it.

I wished I'd never learned the truth about Hans. Wished we could laugh and talk easily again. But now that I knew what he was, I didn't trust him. Or myself.

How could a part-angel not sense a son of Lilith, Queen of Hell? It shamed me, almost as much as the fact that I'd crushed on him.

"Hans, you'll come with us too."

"Right." He grabbed his jacket off the back of his chair. "See you outside, Shay."

"Yup."

The Covenant members spilled out of the room, and then the house, one by one, waving at friends, imparting air kisses, as if they wouldn't see one another again in a long while.

Already, they were putting on a show for any Darkborn who might be watching the house.

Occasionally, other guests would intersperse with the officials, making it seem as though the party was simply coming to an end. Those who would join us at the meeting spot Nicoleta had specified would arrive in many different cars, taking various routes. The process would be drawn out, which was why we were starting now, at midnight, though Hans and I weren't to meet the demons until one in the morning.

It wouldn't take more than twenty minutes to get to the location, a large park in Washington DC, but we couldn't risk anything getting in the way.

Like a feather being dragged by the wind, I left the meeting space too, aiming for the bathroom. Only when the door latched behind me, and I stood alone in a luxurious, understated half bath, did I feel like I could fully breathe.

My hands found the edge of the vanity, and pressed against the black marble as I leaned forward. Staring into the sink, I forced down my real emotions.

There was still time to get out of this.

No there's not.

My father would come. He'd help, and no one would get any of his blood.

He won't. I'm not that important to him.

Tears filled my eyes. The urge to slam my fist against the mirror rushed through me, but I refrained because I'd need uninjured hands to fight, if I wanted any chance of surviving later.

As if that's going to happen. This is insane.

A long breath dipped into my lungs as I tried to calm myself.

Breaking down would do no good; I'd promised to do this. I was what Nicoleta wanted. If Brons was correct, her actions were on behalf of Prince Orien, and she would do her best not to fail her lord. So Hans couldn't just arrive at the meeting place without me. Nicoleta probably wouldn't even show herself if I wasn't with him. She'd sense a trap.

Won't she already?

That was the prominent question of the night.

We'd spent hours discussing routes, places for teams to hide, how Hans and I would attempt to position ourselves out of the line of fire, but would it be enough? Could the Covenant's plan go off without a hitch?

"Anyone in there?" called a voice I recognized as belonging to Richard Brons as a fist landed on the door.

"Just a sec!" I yelled back, though what I really wanted to do was fling the door open and punch that asshat in his overly-tanned face.

I couldn't believe Egor and Brons had basically forced Hans into making a Vow of Intent earlier. I was having trouble trusting Hans, too, but that was because of what *I* was—the blood running through *my* veins. The vampire and the wizard could claim no such heavenly alliance, and their actions were shady as hell!

Instead of acting on my rash impulses to bash Brons's face in, I went to the toilet and flushed it. After a few seconds, I returned to the sink, turning it on and letting it run as I pulled myself together. I'd show no weakness. That was how the women in the Ramos family did things, and I strove to be just like them. To make my ancestors, and my mother, proud.

Once I deemed it had been long enough, I turned the water off and went to the door.

Brons leaned against the opposite wall, an expression of boredom on his face.

Oh, sorry, is me trying to hold my shit together before I become a devil's sacrifice boring you?

"All yours," I said.

"Hope you used the spray," he replied, shutting himself inside before I could retort.

My fists clenched. *That little—*

"Shay."

I spun, to find Hans entering the hallway.

"Yeah?"

"We need to talk. Now."

"My mother is waiting outside and she *hates* to wait."

"Too bad for her," Hans said. "Come with me."

As much as I didn't like being told what to do, a shiver ran up my spine.

Before I'd known his true nature, I'd had a crush on Hans for months. Okay, *fine,* years. But he was that guy who either always had a girlfriend, or was casually dating a few girls at the same time. I'd refused to be another brief fling. Or worse, a notch on his bedpost. I was all for sexual liberation, but that just wasn't my style.

And though I kept telling myself he was a demon—off-limits, *an enemy*—there were moments when the attraction still struck me like it used to.

Like when he was taking control and bossing me the hell around, apparently.

Heavens, I'm so messed up in the head.

"Hurry," Hans said when I didn't make a move to leave the hallway. "We don't have a lot of time."

"What about using a 'please'?" I snapped.

"Please, Shay. I really need to speak with you. It's about the mission."

Unable to deny our objective, I fell into step behind him as he led me away from the front door, away from the people and their prying ears. We were almost all the way back to the meeting room, when Hans turned and stared me dead in the eye.

"You don't have to do this. We don't. It's too much. I can tell that you're having second thoughts."

I jerked back. "N-no I'm not. I—"

"Don't lie to me, Shay. You're horrible at it."

"Am not!"

"Okay, fine. You're not horrible, but when it's something like this, you do a shit job of hiding your feelings."

He got closer, and though I knew there wasn't a drop of the stuff on him, I thought I smelled that motor oil scent that usually clung to his skin. A manly aroma I loved, mixed with soap.

A study in contrasts if there ever was one, that was the man in front of me.

"We're asking too much of you. My sister . . . she's brain-washed and won't hesitate to—"

"I know what she's like," I cut him off. "In case you forgot, I fought her too. And as much as I appreciate your concern, Hans, you can't make this choice for me. I want to do this."

I do, right?

"There," he pointed at me. "The doubt. It flickered in your face!"

I slapped his hand down.

Dammit! Was I really that bad at lying? I had to lie for missions all the time, and I thought I was pretty good!

"Tell me I'm wrong," he demanded. "Tell me, and I'll drop this."

"You're wrong," I hissed, because not only did I despise being told what I should or shouldn't do, I hated that, out of everyone, it was Hans who could see me so clearly. "I want to do this. I have to, for my family."

He exhaled. "Your mother is pressuring you. I don't understand why, and I don't like it one bit."

"So what?! Parents do that all the time. Can you tell me that your parents haven't pressured you? If you can honestly say that, then I'll consider bowing out." I lifted my chin in defiance and waited.

He looked like he wanted to deny my claim, but when his shoulders drooped, I knew he couldn't. I'd won.

Won a chance to face a crapload of demons. Whooooo. Go me!

"Fine," Hans grunted. "If you insist that you want to go ahead with this—"

"You made a Vow of Intent anyway, dude," I said. "We have to do it."

"No. *I* have to," he retorted. "But you seem determined to put yourself in danger for a little recognition, so let's go, Shay! Let's go make your ridiculous mother proud."

"Don't you dare talk about her like that!"

Unable to deal any longer, I whirled and marched away from him. I stomped through the home, fists clenched into tight balls.

By the time we emerged in the foyer, only a few Covenant members remained, and when they saw me, looks of relief swept across their faces.

"We thought you'd done a runner," one of the siren Seats joked.

"Nope," I forced nonchalance into my tone. "Was just having a few words with my partner." I jerked my thumb over my shoulder, sure that Hans was following . . . even though the smarter thing would be to sprint the other direction.

He wasn't like that, though. He didn't back down from a challenge, or run in fear. Hans faced his fears, including the hard stuff—which, right now, included me.

"Oh, right," the siren said, clearly put off by my tone. "Your mother is outside."

"Got it." I exited the house to find the car waiting front and center, my mom in the driver's seat. I darted down the stairs and slid into the passenger seat, relieved that I wouldn't be forced to sit next to Hans.

"Everything alright, Shaylina darling? You were in there for quite a while. Is your stomach testing you?"

"I'm fine," I said as Hans opened the back door and hopped inside. My shoulders bunched tighter as the car jostled with his weight and the door shut, enclosing us in the small space. "Let's go."

Mother threw a glance at me, then back at Hans, her eyes narrowed shrewdly. "Buckle up."

I nearly scoffed. We were about to battle demons, and Mom was telling me to 'buckle up'?

I didn't make a move to do so . . . and she didn't put the car in drive.

"You need to arrive in one piece, darling."

Oh, right. Surely, the demons would only take an uninjured tribute.

Clenching my jaw, I grabbed the seat belt, slammed the clip in, and Mom began to drive.

We barely made it two blocks before she spoke again.

"I sense tension between you two."

"You don't say?" Hans piped up from the back, and despite how mad I was at him, I almost burst out laughing as Mom twisted to glare at the Hellblooded in the back.

"I do," she said, when her eyes were firmly on the road again. "And as much as I understand there being some . . . discomfort—we are eternal enemies, after all—I don't think it wise that you go into this mission in such a state."

"We're professionals, Mom. We can make it work, no matter how we feel."

"*Angelina*," she corrected me, like this was the freaking time to do that. "I know you are, but if Hans is meant to be leading you there unwittingly, then you should appear like you want to be wherever you are. Perhaps you're on a date?"

Was she joking?

One look told me no, she wasn't joking at all.

"We can't—"

"Actually, that could work," Hans interrupted. "My sister did seem to think I had a bit of a thing for you." Bitterness laced his tone, like he could imagine nothing worse.

That stung. But maybe I really did disgust him. Maybe all those times I'd thought we were connecting, flirting and having fun, he was just a touch too drunk. Or messing with my head.

Ouch.

"Well, she was clearly wrong," I replied, trying to sound just as acerbic as my partner.

Mom shrugged. "Still, there's something to be said for the near-death experiences you two shared in New York. It's not improbable that it would bring two young, attractive people together."

"An angel and a demon?" I prodded.

"Stranger things have happened, Shaylina."

I exhaled. As much as I hated to admit it, she had a point. Our cover would be more convincing if we looked like we were having a fun time—like Hans had managed to convince me to go out with him after we survived New York.

I turned to face him. "If you think you can handle pretending, then I can too."

He stared resolutely out the window. "I'm a pro at playing pretend."

Whatever that meant.

"Then it's agreed," Mom said brightly. "The moment you two leave this car, you're lovebirds on a date." She looked me up and down, her lips tightening a touch at my attire. "Wish we'd come up with this sooner. I could have dressed you more appropriately."

"This is fine," I gestured to my leggings. If we were going into a fight, I didn't want to be forced to wear heels and jeans, all for a fake date. "Everyone in the Covenant changed out of their party clothes, though, right?"

"In our vehicles," my mother nodded. "Demeaning though it was, we needed to keep up the pretense of leaving a party."

Normally, I'd be concerned that the demons would think it odd that my mother was dropping me off for a date, but the Covenant had already put a mega distraction in place. Once *Angelina* gave the sign we were close to the drop-off location, the distraction would go off and likely capture any demon's attention in the capitol. That way, we could slip away from the car toward the meeting location.

We drove a little longer in silence, but as ever, Mom wasn't one to keep quiet.

"I want you to know, Shaylina, that I'm proud that you're doing this."

My anger broke, if only briefly. I craved those words from my mom, and they were so few and far between.

"Thanks, Angelina," I said softly. "I'm a little freaked, but—"

"Do not be. You have your father's blood. Show no fear."

I swallowed. Were archangels never scared? And even if that were true, I was only part pure angel. From my mother's side a small piece of me was human. Was that the part that felt like I was going to pee my pants?

"Do you think he'll come, Mom?" my voice cracked.

"I hope so."

That she didn't correct me for calling her 'Mom' said nearly as much as her words.

She gripped my hand. "But if he does not, know that you will have done something great, Shaylina. Something worthy of our family."

And there went the love I'd felt, crashing to the ground.

My throat tightened, and I nodded, retrieving my hand before looking out the window. "Yeah. Of course."

Silence fell on the car as my mother drove, the discomfort increasing by the second. I swore that I felt heat burning from the back, like Hans had something else to say but was holding his tongue.

Finally, Mom pulled over and parked. "We're here."

I turned and waited for her to hold her arms out, to wish me luck, to say that she loved me.

"Do what you were born to do, Shaylina," she said instead, leaning forward and air-kissing both cheeks.

The almost non-existent affection—something you'd do with a near stranger—might as well have been a slap across the face. Her words went deeper, each pounding through me like blows to my chest.

"I'll make you proud," I managed to grind out before hurling myself out the door and dashing away. I didn't want her to see the tears forming in my eyes.

A second later, a car door slammed behind me. "Hey! Wait up!"

Hans's footsteps came closer, and hurriedly, I wiped the

tears pricking my eyes. When he reached me, he grabbed my hand.

"What the—" I yanked it back, but he held firm, his blue eyes on me.

"A date, remember?" he said softly.

Shit. He was right. We'd been dropped off a few blocks from the meeting place, but still, we needed to be in character.

I didn't take my hand away. "I'm just so—"

"Your mother . . . I know you don't want me to talk bad about her, so I'm not going to, but that wasn't the way she should have behaved."

"I know." I exhaled loudly through my nostrils, trying to blow out the anger and sadness roiling through me. How could I argue with him? Mortal enemy or not, Hans was right, and I couldn't hide it. "She's always been a little cold. And proud."

Hans deadpanned. "I wasn't getting that *at all.*"

Despite the turmoil of emotions rushing through me, I burst out laughing. "You need your eyes checked."

He grinned, and for a moment, it was like it used to be when we were just covenmates. Two people who occasionally had some drinks and a laugh. So simple and easy.

That was, until the very next second, when Hans seemed to realize who we really were and turned away.

My shoulders bunched up. As much as I didn't want to be on this mission with him, or even be around him because it was just too damn confusing, we were here. We had a part to play.

One that could dispel demons from this world.

"Get closer to me," I murmured. "We're on a date."

Hans closed the distance between us an inch or two. "You know, my offer from earlier still stands."

"I'm not backing out," I shook my head. Then I paused. "But I will say that I appreciate the offer. You seem more worried about me than my own mother."

He didn't reply; he didn't have to. We both knew it was the truth.

CHAPTER TWENTY

HANS

Tension riddled the air between Shay and me as we closed in on the meeting spot, a wooded park in DC.

Everyone involved suspected that Nicoleta, or perhaps Wrath, had chosen this area because it was forested and therefore provided many hiding spots. I didn't know about the Prince of Darkness, but my sister was at home in the wilds of the woods. Once we entered the cover of the trees, we'd have to be extra-cautious.

"How much further?" Shay asked, shifting her hand in mine.

Uncomfortable as the situation was, we'd been keeping up the front that we were on a date. We were relying on the idea that Nic would think I'd finally gotten up the guts to ask Shay out—and that the nephilim had been impressed by my willingness to fight my sister, a demon, and had agreed.

Considering how Shay was acting, the idea was ludicrous, but that didn't matter. Nic didn't know that and she probably *would* believe I'd asked Shay out as a pretense to lure her here.

Though the idea that my sister could think so lowly of me

stung, I pushed it aside. If it got us to her and helped us defeat Wrath before he built a greater stronghold in the human realm, then so be it.

"A couple of blocks more and we should see it."

I'd studied the map for so long, the streets were imprinted on my mind. As for the park, it was vast, so we were to approach from a specific side, and take a certain route.

Shay hadn't memorized the way because if she led me by even a half a step, it might look suspicious. After all, she shouldn't have a clue where we were going.

"Have you noticed anything?" Shay asked, smiling brightly at me, though her eyes darted from side to side, searching for threats.

"No."

I hadn't seen a single demon or even a person who might be part of the Darkborn. In fact, though we'd been walking for blocks, we'd passed very few pedestrians.

Is that a bad sign?

I wasn't sure, but it didn't seem right. The streets should be more crowded. Though late it might be, this was a world-class city. Even in New Haven, smaller by almost every measure, humans walked the streets at all hours.

"Me either," Shay said. "It's eerie."

"Agreed."

We crossed an alley, and I peered into the darkness, knowing that two of our people should be in there.

A brief flash of fire gave away their position, reassuring me. The phoenix and Egor were ready and waiting, one having flown, the other having used his super speed to get by any watching demons.

I exhaled softly, relieved to have the backup. Even if one was Egor. I did not want to be out here alone, putting my partner at risk, and up against a Prince of Hell. Neither Shay nor I had fought him in New York, but we'd heard what had happened. Though I thought highly of my magic, I was no match for him. The prince might have retreated at the sight of Luca, but I understood that move. The strategy employed. Outside of Isila, mages were rare, and Orien likely had little experience with them. Surely, he'd do his research before surfacing again. I, however, was a wizard and demon. He knew how to handle both those bloodlines well.

"That's the park, right?" Shay whispered, leaning closer.

I looked down the street and saw she was right. Streetlights illuminated trees in the distance.

I grinned, trying to pretend like my big surprise was finally coming to a head. "You're going to love this!" I said loudly. "This place is magical."

Shay snorted so softly I might have imagined it, but when she spoke, her tone was energetic. "I'm so excited!"

We kept up the charade, chatting about stupid shit, to keep our cover in place for another two blocks. When we crossed the street and entered the woods, we stuck to a cement path joggers used. The trail would lead us to a lake where Nicoleta should be waiting.

My shoulders tightened. With each step deeper into the woods, my instincts urged me to grab Shay and run.

But we couldn't. No matter how dangerous this was, no matter how much I wished Shay had decided to bail because I didn't want her hurt, we'd committed ourselves. I'd made a Vow.

A shiver ran up my spine. I prayed to the Goddess that my promise hadn't been a huge mistake.

"Is it a picnic?" Shay asked coyly. "Where is the basket?"

"Quit trying to guess," I purred as if I were enjoying our

evening instead of scared shitless. "You'll see in just a second!"

"I didn't know you were so creative, Hans."

"Guess you bring it out in me." I gave her a brilliant smile as she met my eyes.

My heart slammed against my ribs. Fuck, she was beautiful. Why hadn't I really seen her before the world began to collapse around us?

That line of thinking wasn't doing me any favors, so I tore my eyes away from the angel, and kept them on the trail. After a couple of minutes, we arrived at a fork in the path. I still hadn't seen or sensed anyone watching us in the park.

The skin on the back of my neck began to prickle. Was it possible we'd gotten this all wrong? That Nicoleta really was going to meet us alone?

"What's that?" Shay asked, pointing.

I looked up, and she squeezed my hand, as if saying *'Get it together, man'*. She must have sensed I was losing myself to thoughts.

The truth was, I really did need to pull myself together. Whether we met only my sister or a hundred Darkborn, Shay's life was on the line tonight. If anything happened to her . . . My throat tightened. I didn't want to consider that.

"A lake," I said, forcing myself to sound normal. Excited. Like a man trying to woo a hot woman. "That's where we're going."

"Oooohhh. Love it!" Her tone was perfect for a date in the capitol, but I felt her muscles tense, saw her eyes narrow as we neared where my sister should be waiting.

I became more alert. By the time we finally arrived at the edge of the small lake, my breath was tight in my chest.

"So . . . what's the surprise?" Shay looked around, eyes wide and innocent.

"It's coming." I released her hand and spun as if searching for someone. One glance at my watch told me we were right on time. "Any minute now. I promis—"

A scream cut through the night and, still in character, Shay leapt closer to me.

"Hans! What was that?"

Another scream shattered the darkness, and my heart rate kicked up in response. Did it belong to friend or foe?

The answer came a moment later when a blaze of fire shot through the sky. The phoenix Covenant Seat was soaring away, a wiry cat-like demon wrapped around her legs as she tried to kick it off.

Fear skittered through me. Our cover was blown before my sister even got here!

"Nicoleta! Where are you?" I bellowed.

"Hans!" Shay hissed, dipping out of character. "Stop."

"Nic!" I shouted, cupping my mouth with my hands. "We're here, just like you asked."

"Not *exactly* how I requested, Brother."

My sister's voice slithered over me like hot oil, and I turned again to face the lake to find her dropping from the sky on black feathered wings. On her chest rested the necklace my father had given her. The Novak family heirloom with a blue-black stone in the center. For a moment, it gave me hope. My sister wouldn't wear such a thing if she had completely forsaken her witch side, right?

She glared daggers at me and that sliver of hope faltered. There was such disgust, such hate in her eyes. "You brought others, more than just the nephilim."

"Nic, I—"

"You acted just as we suspected."

My heart lodged into my throat. "We? Do you mean Wrath?"

"You will refer to him as Prince of Darkness!" Nicoleta roared, her face the embodiment of fury. "And if you wish to save your little angel whore, you'll bow to him."

"I won't do that."

In response, my sister's black ribbons shot out, fast and deadly. They wrapped around Shay like snakes, tightening and constricting.

"Argh!" My partner struggled, dropping to the ground as she tried to unbind herself. Where the Hellborn power touched Shay, her skin grew red, irritated by dark magic.

Heart rate spiking, I fell to my knees, grabbing at the ribbons and trying to rip them off, but they only tightened and more unspooled from Nic, covering Shay's skin with black, gleaming tendrils of magic. Within seconds, the nephilim was completely wrapped in dark magic that I could not pry away.

"Let her go, Nic!"

"If you want her, come and get her." My sister launched herself into the sky, a laugh rippling from red lips as one of the ribbons remained attached to her and whipped a bound Shay into the air.

I lunged after my partner, but Nic was too fast, and Shay slipped through my reaching fingers.

Neck craning, I followed their trajectory and sprinted, around the lake, through the trees. It seemed my sister truly did want me to trail them, because she wasn't going as fast as I knew she could.

In my pocket, my phone buzzed. It had to be the Covenant, wondering what the hell I was doing.

Well, they'd have to just figure it out. I didn't dare take my eyes off Shay and my sister.

For the first time since we'd reunited, I wished I was a bit more like Nic, wished I had wings to chase her down. I couldn't see Shay's face—black ribbons wrapped her up completely, now obscuring her whole body—but she had to be terrified.

Nic veered sharply left, and I leapt over a park bench, then sprinted down a dirt path, and charged toward the gate surrounding the park. Vaulting it, I landed on the sidewalk.

Where was she going?

It struck me that the lake had never been the real meeting place. Nicoleta flew with far too much purpose. She had a reason to change the location, and that reason had to do with Prince Orien.

And she's pulling us away from our allies. Why didn't I foresee this?!

Again, my phone buzzed, and again, I ignored it.

Occasionally, my sister would glance over her shoulder, checking that I was behind them. Whenever this happened, she'd flash me a victorious grin and kept right on going.

"What are you doing?!" A blur of a person zoomed up beside me.

Startled, I nearly fell flat on my face, but caught myself at the last second. I twisted to find Egor running next to me, Brons on his back. Someone had clawed the vampire's face, resulting in deep gouges that were healing before my eyes.

"My sister has Shay!" I pointed to the sky.

"Where is she going?" Brons spoke this time, his voice a low growl.

"I have no idea!"

"Don't you?" Egor demanded.

"Dude," I spat out. "I took a Vow of Intent!"

"But you didn't know you were going to," the vampire countered, annoyingly not out of breath in the slightest. "You might have planned this with your kin."

Anger flooded me, and a retort tipped my tongue, but at that moment, Nicoleta descended, dipping out of sight.

"She's landing!"

We ran harder, but as soon as I turned the next corner, I skidded to a stop. "*Fuck.*"

The Washington Monument rose off to one side, the Lincoln Memorial a distance across from it. Only a street separated us and the historical sites. Why had Nicoleta come here? It was so public. Even at this hour, cars drove by, none of them paying attention but if we used magic that could change in a second.

"She's by the water," Egor spat, his eyes burning with malice.

"Let me talk to her first," I pleaded.

"Better do it fast," Egor replied, and we were off again, racing across traffic toward the Reflecting Pool.

We only slowed when we reached the grass bordering the long strip of water. Nicoleta stood by the edge of the water, Shay on the ground in front of her, still completely wrapped in black ribbons. I winced to think what they were doing to her skin when a faint brush of dark magic irritated her.

Prince Orien was nowhere to be seen, nor were others—Darkborn or demon. But they had to be around somewhere. Nicoleta had lured me here, and there was a reason for that.

I put out a hand, stopping the vampire. He was already too close for my taste. "Stay here. You aren't supposed to be here."

"Angelina would say differently," Brons sneered.

"I can get through to her."

Belief in my sister, in the girl I'd once known, burned through me. I didn't know how, or why—She certainly hadn't proven herself to me—but I couldn't just write her off. I had to go on history.

Nic was family. Once, she'd been a girl who adored me, and while I'd failed her, there was hope. She still loved our father, of that I was sure. She wouldn't harm him. She even wore the Novak heirloom with pride, which I had to believe meant the sister I'd once known was in there, somewhere. And giving up on her sort of felt like giving up on the darkness inside me too, acknowledging it would never be fully tamed.

"Nic! Can we talk?"

My sister snorted out a laugh. "I love how you think you can really change my mind, Hans."

"Well, why not? We're family. The only two of our kind in the world."

"That's where you're wrong."

What? She had to be bluffing. Sure, there were other part-demons, but we were Lilith's only kids.

"Orien has children," Nicoleta continued, chilling my blood. "I'm to be wed to his oldest son, Rikel."

Bile climbed up my throat. Wed?!

"You're seventeen!"

"Nearly eighteen."

"That's basically still a child." I couldn't believe I was saying this. My sister had never once spoken of marriage. I couldn't believe that she actually wanted it. Not now anyway.

Nicoleta shrugged. "All that matters is providing the Prince of Darkness's son with powerful, noble heirs. I will do my duty for the cause."

"B—but he's immortal."

"Anyone can be killed," a masculine voice boomed. "And once we've seen our plans to fruition, the world will only become more dangerous. Insurance is sensible."

Nicoleta smirked, and I followed her gaze to find Wrath walking on water toward us. Clouds of darkness bloomed all around him, coloring the Reflection Pool an impenetrable black.

"Family is so important," he purred, still surfing on his smoke, his palms up, as if in supplication. "It's why you're here, is it not?"

"It's why you can't have my sister, fuckhead."

Wrath laughed dryly. "I don't think she'll agree."

"Nicoleta, please," I whispered.

"Why? You only came here for this bitch." She kicked Shay, and a soft groan came from inside the cocoon of ribbons. "You tried to trick *me*, Hans!" Around her dark eyes, blackness spread, as if the veins were graying.

"What's happening to you?" I rasped, terrified to hear the answer.

"Your sister has tapped into a well of darkness so powerful, so vast, even I am impressed." Wrath stepped from the water onto the cement and came up behind her. "She's a perfect protégé, and one day, she'll be the mother to my grandchildren."

Nicoleta tipped her chin up to the prince, a smile spreading on her face. "As you wish, my lord."

"No!" I roared, thrusting my palms out. I cast a blast of light at the prince, which he deflected with ease.

"You believe that is enough to harm me?" he tutted. "You could be so much better."

"No, he can't," Nic scoffed. "He is weak. Look." She pointed to Shay, and the ribbons curled tighter around her body, so tight I doubted she could breathe. Was she even conscious?

"Nic, stop. I—"

A flash of magic tunneled straight for my sister, but she was oblivious to Brons's incoming attack as she watched Shay with glee in her eyes.

"No!" Instinctively, I deflected his magic.

The magic pinged off to the side.

"I knew it!" Brons spat, he and Egor ran to join me. The wizard shoved me to the ground, a vicious expression on his face. "Traitor! The Vow claims you!"

Horror crept through me, and right away, I felt the clamping down of my magic as it formed a ball inside me and was locked away.

Panic swelled, spiraling wildly through me.

My power was gone, unusable; I was at the mercy of Brons, a wizard who hated me for being Hellblooded.

"No! You have to believe me," I implored. "I didn't mean to!"

But I didn't get to defend myself, for suddenly, smoke filled the area around the Pool. Like a living thing, it crawled over us, thick and choking. The stench of sulfur clogged the area, burning my eyes.

"Egor!" Brons yelled with a cough. "It's burning! My throat!"

I heard footsteps, then the air shifted, and when I reached out to grab for Brons, he was no longer where he'd stood before, looming over me.

Egor had picked him up, saved his fellow Seat. But they'd abandoned me. They'd left Shay too, as if she were nothing, as if she hadn't risked her life for this stupid fucking idea that they'd pushed upon her.

I have to get her.

The smoke had a drug-like effect on me, pulling me ever closer to unconsciousness . . . but I couldn't leave without her.

I also couldn't seem to rise.

Still, I knew where she lay, so on hands and knees, I crawled toward her.

"Shay!" I screamed.

"She's with us," Wrath taunted. "As are you, Son of Darkness."

Suddenly, the smoke pulled in tighter, constricting my every motion until I could inch forward no longer. Until I couldn't draw breath. Until I couldn't see.

Until the smoke was all there was.

CHAPTER TWENTY-ONE

MEREDITH

I woke in a strange bed, remnants of my dreams swirling in my mind. In them, Tobias and I were at a café, just hanging out, talking and laughing. His hand found mine often, his eyes sparkled in a way I longed for but rarely received.

But last night, I had.

My mouth went dry as my body recalled his touch with vivid clarity. The heat of his hands traveling over me, despite the cold of his skin. The fervor that had overtaken me, even if just for a few seconds. How, for that short period of time, the world began and ended with him.

I kissed Tobias, and damn did it feel good.

Not just good—perfect—right.

I sat up and stretched, luxuriating in the expansion as much as the memory that made my toes curl. Who would have guessed someone so stiff and proper could kiss like *that*?!

"Good to see you're finally awake. We need to discuss the events of last night."

I groaned as the part of the night I'd rather forget reared its feline head.

277

"You're such a cock-blocking killjoy." I flopped back down, pulling the pillow over my head.

"We are not going to just brush this under the rug, Meredith." Benedict leapt on my shins, and his tiny claws poked into me.

"*OW!*" I shot back up. "Benedict!"

"Don't you 'Benedict!' me, missy. You're playing one dangerous game with that vampire."

I exhaled. If anyone knew that, it was me. I recalled when he'd threatened me, when he hadn't been able to seem to control himself. I remembered it so clearly I could still practically feel the rake of Tobias's fangs along the tender skin of my neck, but that wasn't the only iffy part of this.

Getting involved with someone *now*? When I was apparently supposed to be looking for others like me and stopping Wrath from dominating this world?

It was the absolute worst timing.

But can I stop myself?

Truthfully, I wasn't sure. Before that kiss, I would have been able to, no problem. Now, though . . . I'd found water after being lost in a vast desert.

"*Meredith!*"

I blinked down at my familiar, who appeared so incredibly peeved that I cracked a smile. "You're right."

"I-I am?"

I shrugged. "Don't act like I've never said those words."

"Honestly, I'm not sure you have." Benedict loped closer, sitting on my legs. "So, you're going to stay away?"

"I never said that." I held up a hand 'cause the cat opened his mouth, clearly about to lay into me. "But it is a dangerous game. Tobias is a vampire, he's powerful."

Benedict snorted. "Don't let it go to your head, but you're

no slouch yourself. I know I said the same as you, but really his power is really the least of my worries."

Huh?

I waited for him to continue, but he didn't.

Did he think his reasoning was obvious? To me it was about as clear as that enchanted pool out back.

"What do you mean?" I finally prodded.

"The vampire is like kryptonite to you."

"Yes . . . That's true . . ."

Benedict smirked, the expression so sure, almost like he knew how I felt.

A thought struck, like a match being lit, and I sat up straighter.

People said animals were sensitive to things humans couldn't discern. Even though I wasn't totally human, Benedict wasn't a regular cat either.

"Do you sense something between Tobias and me?"

The cat looked away.

Busted.

"What can you sense?" I leaned forward and grabbed his tail, which had him whipping his head around to glare at me.

"Lay off." He batted back at my arm.

"Answer me," I urged, not letting go. He was acting too weird. "I can tell you know something, and I'm not taking no for an answer."

"You are quite annoying, you know that?"

"I've been told. Spit it out, Benedict."

A long pause simmered between us, in which we had a stare down. When he blinked and glanced away again, I knew I'd won.

"You two are bound in some way," Benedict ground out, as if each word cost him.

Bound. Yes. I felt that too. Tobias claimed it was because I'd ingested his blood and while that made sense, it wasn't everything. My attraction had started before he saved me from death. It had merely intensified with each passing day after.

How does my familiar know, though?

"Why do you think that is?"

Benedict turned back to me. "I don't know."

I wrinkled my nose. He had to be lying, but before I could inquire further, a knock came at the door.

"Coming!" I called, slipping from the bed and crossing the room.

When I opened the door, I found none other than the vampire himself, leaning against the doorframe and smiling down at me.

My heart fluttered. He looked sexy as hell, but in an effortless, *'I just rolled out of bed'* way.

"Don't get any ideas!" Benedict called out, throwing icewater on the heat that had begun to simmer between us. Freaking cock-blocking cat. He really needed to get his own room.

"Good morning," Tobias said, ignoring my familiar with a grace that I didn't feel for the feline. "I thought I heard you talking."

Oh my God. What if he heard Benedict and me?

"Were you eavesdropping?" I asked, hoping his answer wouldn't kill me from embarrassment.

"I could, but no," Tobias said. "I save my intense spy sessions for when it matters."

I had no clue what that entailed, but I was glad he hadn't been listening in on my conversation.

"Gunner and Silas are already up," he continued. "They

want to get moving, but I have news to share first." The light-heartedness in his face faltered.

Oh crap. Something had happened.

"Is everyone back home safe?"

"I don't know. It's about something else." He swallowed, and a pit dipped into my belly. "Get dressed and meet us in the common room. I expect the *Abscondita* Coven will want to speak with you soon, and I'd like to impart the news before they barge in. We all need to be on the same page."

"I'll be there in a sec." I shut the door, exhaling a long breath.

Damn. How did Tobias look so good all the time? He wasn't even trying to put the moves on me, and I still felt hot under the collar.

Benedict let out a long sigh. "I can see there's likely no chance for me to hide what I've suspected any longer."

"What?!" I darted across the room. "I knew you were keeping something from me! What do you mean?"

The cat stretched out, taking his sweet-ass time to answer. "When supernaturals allow certain people into their lives, and one of them has a familiar, that familiar can smell changes in their person. Since the day we met, I've noticed you smell different when the vampire is around, but of late, the stark difference has grown stronger."

"Okaaaay. Is there a point to this? What does it mean?"

"It means that I believe you've found the person your soul is bound to. The more time you spend together, the closer you get, the more obvious it becomes."

The person my soul was bound to? Did that mean . . .

"Like a *soulmate*?" my pitch elevated. "Those are *real*?"

Benedict nodded. "A soulmate. A fated mate. A bloodbound. The magical community has varied names for it, but they all mean the same thing."

He paused, and I waited, desperate for him to go on, feeling more lost to uncertainty with each passing second. What did this mean? How could I—someone who'd just learned to make friends—bond to someone so intensely? Just the thought made the hairs on my arms stand up.

"Meredith, the vampire is the one person in this world you can love completely. The one person who is meant just for you."

I SHUFFLED TOWARD THE COMMON ROOM, DRESSED, READY FOR MY day, and feeling awkward as hell. And stunned. So stunned.

Benedict hadn't had much more to say besides the teensy fact that he was ninety percent sure Tobias and I were soulmates.

That left him ten percent uncertain, and me one hundred percent reeling.

Not long ago, Tobias and I had despised one another! We were just barely starting to get along.

And yet, Benedict said he'd smelled something funky—eau du soulmate, or whatever—from the first moment he'd stood with Tobias and me. Nevermind that he'd claimed not to want the vampire as my guard, and they routinely fought. I'd deal with those nuggets later. I had to wrap my brain around the big idea first.

More than likely, I had a soulmate. And he was a vampire.

I got to the door, my hand hovering over the handle. Did Tobias know too? Or was he just as clueless as me?

No . . . surely not. I didn't believe Tobias had been clueless a day in his long life. Maybe he wasn't sure though. It was a crazy idea.

Did I dare bring it up?

My throat tightened at the idea of posing such a personal question to anyone, even a person whose soul was supposed to be the other half of mine. I'd rather wear a wool sweater in a sauna.

"That Stoney I smell?" Gunner's jovial voice came through the door. "Whatcha doin' out there, girl?"

Damn these supernaturals and their keen senses!

Unable to deliberate in private any longer, I entered the room, a smile plastered on my face so no one suspected that, inside, an emotional war raged.

"Hey."

I cringed. *Hey? I just learned that I probably have a soulmate, and Tobias already proclaimed he has important news, and all I can muster is 'hey'?*

Thankfully, the guys didn't even blink. Tobias just gave me that small, confident smile as Gunner beamed like a goober and Silas stared into the fire.

"Another fire?" I asked.

Not that I didn't like it; I loved a good fire. Who didn't? But it was morning, and that just felt weird.

"Old homes such as this one are drafty." Tobias replied like he spoke from experience—which he probably did.

Oh my God. My soulmate is so old!

"My room is fine," I protested, trying not to latch on to that thought. I had enough to think about without coming to terms with the fact that Tobias was eight times my age. "Then again, I was snuggled in bed, my favorite place."

At that, Tobias's lips curled up a little more, and flashes of last night, of those lips on mine, forced heat through me.

My cheeks burned.

Why was I talking about my bed? I didn't need any sexy thoughts while Gunner and Silas were around! Why was everything I said right now so stupid?!

"There are lots of covers," I added, trying to pull my own mind from the gutter. "Big. Bulky. *Totally unappealing,* but warm!"

Stop, Meredith. Just. Freaking. Stop.

Tobias's eyebrows knitted together, and his lips compressed, as if he were trying not to laugh. "If you say so." He patted the chair next to him. "Come sit."

It was only then that I realized I'd stopped walking. I was just standing in the middle of the room, like an idiot. This soulmate thing was really screwing with my head.

Trying to muster as much false confidence as possible, I strode over to join the guys. Settling into the chair, Tobias offered me a glass of water. I blinked. Had he felt that I was thirsty? Could soulmates do that?

"I noticed that our rooms had none, but someone set a pitcher in the hallway for us," he explained, making me feel vaguely ridiculous. Yeah, most people did want water when they woke up. It was totally normal. This wasn't some special soulmate thing.

"Wish it was coffee," I managed to get out because I'd just been staring at the vampire in that smooth, smooth way of mine.

Good God, could I just die now?!

Gunner leaned forward in his chair so that his elbows rested on his knees. "We can find some java after you tell us the news, Toby. I'm dyin' to hear."

"I'll get on with it, then. Last night, I received a voicemail from my sire," Tobias began. "I cannot tell you much about her, but she's well-informed in the landscape of various supernatural groups, and she claims that a blonde human woman approached the Ordo Aeternum with information."

He looked at me, his gaze darkening. "She said she knew of a seeker, and wanted to find her. That, if the OA helped her, this woman would give them the Pearl—an artifact that they want dearly."

Ice trickled through me. "Aside from S&S and the *Arcacusto*, only the Darkborn know what I am. Wrath is working with the Ringmaster. If the person was human, that has to be her."

"I believe so too, though she went by the name Jennifer."

"Has a sweeter ring to it than 'Ringmaster,'" Gunner said, drawing a chuckle out of me.

"If she gets the OA's help, she'll have access to surveillance across the globe," Silas commented, catching everyone's attention.

"What do ya mean by that, Si?"

"The OA have many hackers in their group. They'll be able to find Meredith's passport, and from there, hack into cameras that can follow her." The fae met my stare. "It won't be hard for them to find you. Perhaps not even here."

"But how did she know to go to the OA?" Gunner asked.

"She has supernatural connections," I replied. "When I was captive, she told me the man who wanted Denz was magical. Obviously, that's his sire—who we know to be super strong because Tobias couldn't fully compel Denz when he tried."

"Not just strong," Tobias corrected. "Of the vampire royal line. Otherwise, I would have been able to compel him with no issue."

"Right," I said. "But even though she's human, the Ringmaster realized it right away, and somehow, she formed an alliance with him. She gave up Denz and got introduced to this world."

"The man is likely Darkborn as well as a royal vampire," Tobias mused, his chin tilting up. "But who could it be?"

"My question is how'd your boss convince a powerful supernatural to ally with her?" Silas asked.

"She has so many associates who are powerful and lots of money." I shuddered. "She's a force to be reckoned with, don't underestimate her."

"Hmm." Silas sounded as if he didn't quite believe it.

Then again, in regards to my old boss, he hadn't seen what I had.

"Gettin' back to the point," Gunner said. "Basically, someone's comin' for Stoney. But even if they can track your passport, I expect you're pretty safe here."

Normally, I'd be inclined to agree. The *Arcacusto* had a giant and a wyvern and who-knew-what-else roaming the woods, protecting them.

But again, my old boss had a network of dangerous people, and now that network included Darkborn and, above all, Wrath. He'd want someone he could control to wield seeker magic. He already had two stones, and I'd bet that they would make finding the other *lapis caelesti* easier.

Not if I get there first.

I exhaled. "Is that all, Tobias?"

"Isn't that enough?"

"Definitely," I agreed. "But there's nothing I can do about it now. There's really nothing I can do about *anything* until this coven teaches me about the stones, and I find the other *Vindix*. If I can find them, then maybe we can band together with their stones and shoot Wrath back to Hell."

"What a vision," Silas chuckled.

"I try." I grinned, rising to my feet. "But if there's no more bad news, I say we get breakfast."

"I'm game." Gunner rose too. "I think I smell bacon fryin'."

As a group, we made our way down the hall, Gunner following his nose—which proved spot on. We found the dining room, complete with one of those long tables I always saw lords and ladies eating at in the shows. It was brimming with food, complete with a platter of bacon that made me salivate.

"Oh good, you're up." Mirim swept in through a side door. Behind her trailed Claire and Hannah—the youngest *Arcacusto*. "It's late morning, so everyone else already ate, but we saved food for you. I trust it will be enough?"

I gaped. "Uh, yeah."

"You look shocked, but the wolf has been eating us out of house and home."

Turning, I assessed Gunner, who just shrugged.

"Wasn't much else to do but eat, and I've always had a healthy appetite."

Admittedly, he was one of the biggest guys I'd ever seen. I had absolutely no trouble picturing him devouring a whole rack of ribs or something equally enormous.

"Well, then, what are you waiting for?" Miriam waved at the spread. "Sit down and eat. Meredith, make sure you get enough. We have much work to do today."

Wondering how much she'd reveal, I took a seat. Tobias claimed the one next to me, and the moment we were both sitting, I felt a hand land on my knee, hidden by the tablecloth.

Electricity zinged through me, igniting my every nerve and hurling fire through my body as a gasp parted my lips, drawing the attention of Gunner. He looked at me over a plate somehow already piled with bacon, potatoes, and what looked to be beans.

"You okay, Stoney?" He sat across the table from me. I wished he was further away.

I swallowed. "Yeah.

"Bit jumpy today."

"Just all the new stuff, I guess."

I didn't dare look at Tobias, but I felt his smug smirk all the same as he squeezed my knee and then removed his hand.

Its absence opened a hole inside me, one I didn't understand but that I wanted filled with him—his touch, his attention, his presence.

What was going on with me? Would this only get more intense?

Can I handle that?

"Your plate." Though it had been sitting right in front of me, Tobias lifted the plate, handing it to me.

Gunner didn't miss the interaction, and as if that small thing clicked the pieces into place, a knowing little smile tugged at his lips. For what I was pretty sure was the first time in his life, though, the wolf managed to stay quiet, if only by stuffing a whole piece of toast into his mouth.

"Dude, you're going to choke," I said, frantically searching for anything that could pull my attention from the vampire.

The one who'd just touched my leg.

The one I'd kissed.

The one who was apparently my soulmate.

What the actual hell . . .

Had one kiss really changed everything?

"You know, Stoney," Gunner replied, chewing noisily, that aggravating, teasing grin still crinkling the corners of his eyes.

CHAPTER TWENTY-ONE

"I might not be the only one about to choke. Somethin' is up with you, girl."

I didn't reply to that, didn't know how to. So I just loaded up my plate and prayed to get through this breakfast without making a total fool of myself.

CHAPTER TWENTY-TWO

HANS

PAIN SLICED THROUGH ME AS I OPENED MY EYES AND QUICKLY shut them again. The light was too much, too blinding, and the world spun so violently that my stomach began to revolt, threatening to empty itself. I felt like I'd been run over by a Hummer.

What happened to me?

My face was pressed up against something hard and cold. A window? I shifted, and my cheek made a sucking sound as I peeled it away from the hard surface. Only then did I notice that I was moving up, not to the side. I inched my hand out, felt the vague impression of squares.

Tile? Was I on the floor?

The last thing I recalled was crawling across cement to help save Shay from Nic and Wrath. But this wasn't cement. While being cold and hard and smooth, it also had raised portions, like it was painted.

Though I wanted to see where I was, the intense vertigo I'd already experienced stopped me from looking again. Any motion on my part would probably result in me spewing my guts out.

Breathe. Just breathe, and the spinning will stop.

It took a disturbingly long time, but eventually, I was proven right. The spins stopped, and finally, I was able to chance opening my eyes.

When I didn't immediately want to hurl, I went a step further and pried myself off the cold floor.

What the hell . . .

I was in a circular room with stone walls. The place was fairly bare, containing only a bed, a rocking chair, and a side table. The most ornate feature was the floor I was so well acquainted with, the tiles painted in an elaborate style that was probably stamped on my cheek.

Whatever fucking asshole had stowed me here, they'd apparently tossed me just a few feet inside the door.

The sound of a motor from outside hit my ears. Was I still in DC? It didn't seem likely. This room, with its shape, almost like a castle turret, was too Old World for Washington. Then again, maybe it wasn't. People there had stupid amounts of money and they could make their homes look however they wanted.

Still, I needed a clue, anything to help pinpoint my location. Once I did that, I could make a plan to find Shay, and we'd escape.

Struggling, I pressed my body off the tile, wondering why I felt so awful. Once standing, I took a step and immediately wobbled.

Fucking hell. What happened to me?

I ground my teeth together, tightening my muscles and holding firm so I wouldn't topple. That I couldn't remember all of the events that led me here infuriated me. I suspected I'd hit my head—probably when my captor threw me on the damned ground. A quick check revealed no bumps or bruises on my skull, so I had no way of knowing for sure, but a head injury would explain a lot.

Balance renewed, I walked toward the only window in the room. It was small and the glass looked dirty and, if the wavy appearance of it was any indication, old. When I finally reached it, I grabbed at the wall to steady myself before peering outside.

What the—?

A lake, vast and deep blue, spread out before me. Trees bare of leaves waved in a faint breeze as the sun beat down on them. From the sun's position, I guessed that it was midday.

Though I tried my best to spot a person, there wasn't a soul in sight. In fact, the only indication that I wasn't in the middle of nowhere was a home on the other side of the lake, and even that seemed out of place. It looked more like an old European mansion rather than a modern American home.

Since I didn't see a road, it was likely the motor I'd heard hadn't been a car, but a boat.

"Where the hell am I?" I whispered, trying to reason where Wrath could have gone that looked like this.

Another scan of the room provided no more information, nor did a more formal search, which consisted of checking the underside of the rocker and mattress and opening the single drawer in the side table.

As those were the only places to hide anything, the search took all of two minutes. When it was done, I strode over to the door, which was old and wooden. Being optimistic, I tried the handle; it was, of course, locked. Wards likely gripped the door too.

But would their wards be able to stand against my spells? There was only one way to find out.

"*Rekia.*"

I spoke the spell that allowed its caster to open doors with force, hoping it would be sufficient to break whatever ward might be placed on this one, then tried the handle again.

Nope.

"Hmmm. How 'bout this?" I held my hand out, certain now that I was dealing with a stronger-than-average warder. "*Disol.*"

Normally, when I used the spell to dissolve other magic, I felt the shift as it worked, but there was no such indication here. Which only left me with one interpretation: some of the Darkborn knew demonic spells. Wrath would have taught his people. If he hadn't, he was an idiot.

Unfortunately for the Prince of Darkness, the demon spell for opening doors and portals was among the few Mom had taught me

"*Otkrx.*"

BOOM!

I was thrown backward, my arms and legs flailing before I slammed into the far stone wall. I groaned, my head pounding as blood began to pour from a cut along my cheek.

"*Mother fucker.*"

Quickly, I inspected the injury with my fingers. It wasn't large, only a half-inch or so, but dammit, now I'd be a bloody mess too.

Not about to be defeated, I hauled myself up again and stared at the still-intact door. The old wood now glowed red, as if the door itself was screaming, "*Ye shall not pass!*"

I snorted. "Watch me. Just gotta put a little protection in place so you don't try to kill me this time. *Baestu.*"

The moment the charm left my lips, I realized something was terribly wrong. My power was often invisible, unless I was working with light or specific spells whose effects could be seen, but I could still *feel* it.

And yet, I hadn't.

Not now, when the protection of a shield should be wrapping around me, and not before either—though I hadn't even noticed because I'd been so preoccupied with solving the mystery of how to get the hell out of here.

My heart rate kicked up. What was going on?

"Baestu," I cast again, thinking maybe I'd misspoken. Casters had to be exact in our pronunciation. Even being a syllable off could render a spell useless. Or different, perhaps even a disaster.

Again, nothing happened, and this time, I was certain I'd spoken correctly, used the right inflection, the right word. I'd done everything right. Yet, my magic was acting as though I'd said nothing. As if . . .

Like a suped up Bugatti racing down the track straight at me, my recollection of last night returned, stopping my heart.

The Vow of Intent.

My power was gone! Bound to Richard Fucking Brons! That's why nothing had happened when I'd spoken the words, why I felt nothing . . . Because I had nothing.

"Noooo!" I roared, spinning and marching to the bed so I could pummel the pillows, which I did with a vengeance. "This can't be happening!'

The pillows were old, like everything else in this damned place, so after a few dozen punches, they split open. Feathers flew into the air, the smallest ones tickling my nose.

I took a step back, chest heaving. "Where the hell am I?" I demanded to the room at large and stomped back to the door.

It had ceased to glow, and I still had no idea why it had reacted to me earlier when I'd used the demon spell. It's not like I had any freaking power to break it open with, so the door must have just been angry with me for trying to escape.

Well, if that was the case, I was about to push its limits.

My fists slammed against the wood again and again and again. "Let me out! Let me the fuck out!"

I pounded on the door until my knuckles cracked and started to bleed, and even then, I kept it up, yelling and demanding to be released until my voice was hoarse. Only then did I stop, fists and forehead pressed against the wood. Up this close, the gray of my veins was front and center. It also looked darker than when I'd last noticed it. Was it because my sister and Wrath used their power on me?

Nic . . . My teeth ground together.

Why was the world so unfair? I'd broken my Vow of Intent to save Nicoleta. I'd done so on pure instinct. And now I was here while Shay was probably being tortured by my sister.

And I had no magic!

Rearing back, I hurled all my weight at the door, both fists slamming down simultaneously, before I dropped bodily to the floor.

I was so pissed, I really couldn't think straight. What was I going to do?

For as long as I could remember, I'd had magic, both demon and witching. Some wizards couldn't call their power until puberty. That had never been an issue for me. Though I'd viewed that as a curse because it drew unwanted attention in my village, the fact remained that I'd never been without.

Now, however, here I was, on the floor in a mystery room, bleeding like a little bitch.

Tears brimmed in my eyes, but I wiped them away. Crying

would only make me feel weaker. I needed to get my shit together and think because my partner was . . . Somewhere . . . Probably being tortured. I had to get to her.

But how? I'm nothing now. Human. I—

A knock came at the door, and my head whipped around so fast, droplets of blood that had been lodged in my hair sprayed on the walls.

Not waiting for my answer, the door opened, and an older man with a dark olive complexion and shining black hair peppered with gray at his temples peered inside. His nostrils flared.

"I heard a ruckus." His brown eyes roved over my head and hands, which were covered in blood from wrist to fingertip. "You must clean up. I'll bring water."

"Wait!" I shot up. "Where am I?"

The man pursed his lips. "I cannot say."

I darted forward, prepared to overpower him, to make him tell me our location and then escape and find Shay. But the moment I grabbed his shoulders, the old man did the same, stopping me with an iron-clad grip and forcing my back up against the nearest wall.

This guy had to be in his fifties. Maybe even his sixties. He didn't look that strong.

"What are you?" I rasped.

He smiled and his fangs had dropped a little, probably because he was excited from showing dominance, revealing his true nature. Slowly, he leaned in and licked my cheek, lapping up the blood dripping down my face from my head wound. I tightened.

Vampire.

"Do not make me hurt you, *Signore*." his voice was light but threatening.

Signore! This dude was Italian!

Was I outside of Boston? New York? They had a large Italian community there. What lakes were near those cities?

"Stay here, I will bring you water to wash," the man repeated when I made no move to fight back.

Mostly because I was pretty sure I couldn't. With my magic, we'd be more evenly matched. Actually, I'd cream his ass. But at the moment, I was as weak as I'd ever been, and it sucked.

"Can't I just use the bathroom?" I asked.

"No. My master has proclaimed that you are to remain here until we have need of you. I shall bring you a chamber pot."

A what?! Who has chamber pots just lying around?!

Pushing those perplexing questions aside for more dire matters, I pressed harder. "When the hell will that be? And why am I here? Who is your master? Prince Orien?"

"I do not serve the demon prince, but my master's identity is of no concern to you. All you need to know is that when my master says you can leave this room, you will. In the meantime, you'll do well to remain quiet so my master does not come up here himself and take care of you."

I scowled. "I'd like to see him try."

It was big talk for a guy who probably had a concussion and definitely possessed no magic, but I couldn't stop myself. I hated feeling weak. Useless.

I thought I saw a flash of pity in his dark brown eyes. "He learned discipline from vicious lords. You would not survive such measures."

I swallowed. Okay so this guy's master was no aristocrat with a penchant for rough discipline, but a brute. Any other time, I'd be begging for a fight, but not now. Now, I needed to really consider my plan of attack. I was weaker than normal, which meant I had to be smarter than usual.

"Understood," I said.

Apparently appeased with the fear he'd struck in me, the vampire released my shoulders. "I'll return with a chamber pot and a basin of water so that you may wash."

I didn't reply as he let himself out the door, which glowed red once again, locking me inside.

CHAPTER TWENTY-THREE

MEREDITH

WE STOOD AT THE ENTRANCE TO THE MANOR HOME AS TOBIAS gave Gunner and Silas the rundown on what the Ringmaster looked like and exactly what to tell Luca.

After learning that the OA was searching for me, the idea that our phones might be being monitored soon, if they weren't already, meant we needed to be careful with the information we sent.

Yet another reason for Gunner and Silas to vamoose—not that the *Abscondita* Coven would allow them to stay for long, anyway. During breakfast, Miriam had made at least three thinly veiled comments that the wolf and the fae needed to be on their merry way.

She said nothing of the sort to Tobias, which made me wonder if Miriam, like Benedict, could tell there was something between us?

Once Tobias finished relaying the particulars, Gunner caught my eye, his own twinkling with mischief. "He thinks we don't know a thing, doesn't he?"

I snorted. Tobias *was* a little overbearing at times. It was just his way.

"I'm thorough, wolf," Tobias said. "Luca will be wanting to know what's happening here. I'm actually surprised he isn't calling every five minutes."

"I'm not," I scoffed. "We left New York in a post-apoc state, and Hans and Shay are trying to swindle Wrath. He's probably way more worried about them."

"Or something else crazy has happened," Gunner added. "You never know what's gonna pop off in S&S."

"Point taken," Tobias replied.

"Well, I guess we should get going," Silas chimed in, rocking from his toes to his heels and generally looking ready to leave.

"Safe travels," I said.

The pair waved and saw themselves out, their car waiting just outside the front door. The one Tobias and I arrived in was there too.

Apparently, one of the *Arcacustos* had brought them both up their drive so no one would start investigating the vehicles left on the side of the road. That shouldn't have come as a surprise; these people had been in hiding for centuries; they knew a thing or two about taking care of matters on the sly.

Kinda like me, I thought. As an ex-thief, I'd had to hot-wire a few cars in my day. *Maybe I'll fit in better around here than I think.*

"To the library, then?" Tobias prompted.

"Yeah, but first . . . I have a question for you."

There hadn't been time or the privacy to ask him about being soulmates earlier, but I had both now. I needed to seize it.

"What's that?" He came closer, until there was only a few

inches of space between us, and his scent of leather and spice and something fresh all mixed together in an aroma I found hard to resist.

I inhaled deeply, the pleasing aroma making me weak in the knees. It had always had an effect on me. Was that because we were soulmates? Or just 'cause he smelled scrumptious?

"If I didn't know better, I'd think you were a vampire," Tobias teased, tucking a stray lock of hair behind my ear. "Scenting me so deeply."

I swallowed, slightly embarrassed. "Well, you smell good."

"As do you."

"Like what?"

He tilted his head, a slow, devastatingly sexy smile curving his lips. "Like jasmine and pine and rain."

"Jasmine is so . . . floral." My nose scrunched up.

I was a rocker and a once-thief, and black was my favorite color. Jasmine reminded me of prom queens and Stepford wives.

A low, growly chuckle left Tobias's throat. "It's merely a hint of jasmine, though to me, it's stronger because I have a superb sense of smell. But mostly, you remind me of the woods and rain, but with a bit of sweetness—more when you use your magic, of course."

"Magic smells like something?"

"Like honey. The more powerful the witch, the sweeter it is."

"That's . . . unexpected."

Tobias's hand found the small of my back, pulling me closer as he leaned forward, softly brushing his lips against mine. "*You* were unexpected."

I savored the kiss, the surprising gentleness of it after we'd claimed one another so thoroughly last night. This vampire kept surprising me, and I wasn't sure when that would end. *If it would end.*

Did I want it to end?

When I pulled back, I looked into his eyes and the question I was dying to answer filled me again. It pressed into my every nook and cranny, demanding to be answered.

"Benedict thinks we're soulmates," I blurted before I could stop myself.

Tobias's eyebrows pinched. "He does?"

"This morning. He says people smell different around their soulmates." I cleared my throat. "Did you know that?"

He paused. "I was aware that some have said that, but I cannot smell if someone has found their bloodbound love."

Bloodbound . . . That must be how vampires preferred to think of soulmates.

"You didn't know?" Relief sailed through me that I hadn't been the only one totally oblivious.

But the vampire frowned, and my relief halted.

"Tobias?"

"The idea was presented to me by my sire," he said finally. "I didn't think it could be true."

I took a step back, confused, and a sliver of hurt plunged into my heart. "Why not?"

I thought back to all the times he'd mentioned his sire, and latched on to one in particular.

"Did she tell you that when you went to Paris? After you returned, you were different."

Had he had a notion that we might be connected all this time? And he hadn't brought it up, even when it was clear things were shifting between us? After I drank his blood . . .

Don't get ahead of yourself. Give him time to explain.

CHAPTER TWENTY-THREE

So I waited and watched. I searched for any clue as to what he was thinking.

The vampire, however, wore a mask that was difficult to read. One honed by years of hiding who he really was to the world.

"Giselle, my sire, did bring it up in Paris," Tobias admitted, looking away, which I took as a hint of guilt. "She saw that I was different, but I did not want to believe it."

That sliver of pain deepened, grew into a laceration that began to creep through me. "You hated me that much?"

Though it was painful to think about right now, I supposed I could see that. When we'd first met, I hadn't liked him much, either.

"Well, actually . . . I had reasons other than our general dislike of one another."

The question of what those other *reasons*, plural, could be was on the tip of my tongue, when someone walked around the corner.

"There you are, Meredith." Miriam's tone was clipped. "This has taken quite a while. Are you ready to see our library?"

I took a step back, because Tobias and I were intimately close, and wrenched my gaze away from the vampire. "Can we have just a moment, Miriam?"

"Of course." She folded her hands and remained standing where she was.

Okay, so no privacy. Fine.

"Give me one reason," I whispered.

Tobias cleared his throat, probably acutely aware that Miriam was still there, even though he hadn't turned around since she arrived. "I—well, I didn't like the idea of being bloodbound to a mortal, because it would take away your options."

"Like what?"

"Bearing children."

My lips parted in shock. *Children?! Back the eff up.*

"I cannot have children in the usual manner," he added equally softly. Clearly, he didn't want Miriam hearing this either.

"Okaaay," I murmured, waving that mind-blowing detail away for just a moment. "But did you really suspect that we were soulmates, bloodbound or whatever, before last night? Even if you didn't want to believe it? And like how strongly on a scale of one to ten?"

"I did. My suspicion has been growing for a while now. I cannot give you a number for it changed constantly."

For weeks, I hadn't known what to do about my growing attraction and feelings, and he'd had an explanation all along? And he hadn't told me because of some hypothetical kids?

I huffed out a breath.

I was so *not* on the path to motherhood right now, and I wasn't sure if I ever would be. After a childhood like mine, that wasn't a given, like it seemed to be for so many other people.

And honestly, I didn't appreciate Tobias making a choice like that for me before I even knew there was a choice to make.

"Meredith, are you well?"

I cleared my throat, not prepared to talk about this further until I'd sorted out my ideas on the matter. "I'm ready for the library."

Rounding him, I went to Miriam, but the vampire caught me by the wrist. I pulled away quickly, as if he'd scalded me.

"Meredith." Tobias swallowed, the gesture not lost on him. "I didn't mean to upset you."

"I know you didn't. But you also didn't intend to give me a choice."

"That's not fair."

Maybe it wasn't. I wasn't sure yet.

I shrugged. "I just need time to figure this out. I think I deserve that—you've had plenty."

A wounded look rippled across his face when he released me. "To the library, then."

Miriam didn't say a word about our interaction, and I chose to believe she couldn't hear us, because I didn't want to explain. What she'd witnessed was already embarrassing enough. Instead, we just followed her in silence, the six inches of space between Tobias and me feeling more like a mile.

"Here we are," Miriam announced, as we reached the end of a corridor. "Our personal library. In here, you'll find tomes the rest of the world has never seen. I'll be with you, but I ask that you please take care when touching them."

"Of course," I said.

"I'm trained to work with ancient texts," Tobias assured her, but his comment only earned the vampire a raised eyebrow.

"You, Tobias, are not allowed in here."

"Pardon?" he stiffened.

"This area is for those in my coven and the *Vindix* only." Miriam crossed her arms over her chest. "You're welcome to explore the grounds of the manor, but you may not enter this sacred space."

Tobias's green eyes narrowed. "You're aware that I hold membership in the Beinecke's supernatural section and have handled tomes that are likely just as rare, if not more so, than those behind this door?"

"I don't really care. Our rules are our rules." Miriam's chin tilted up. "Now, if you please, Meredith and I have much to get done. Unless you'd like to waste more of her time arguing with me out here?"

Tobias glowered but shook his head. "Might I speak to Meredith alone before she's in there for hours?"

In answer, Miriam let out an annoyed huff but opened the library door. I caught the faintest whiff of old books and candle wax wafting out of the room. "I suggest you find one of my covenmates and have them introduce you properly to Jon-Jon before you go anywhere, vampire. If you two are here for long, you'll require time to take the air. If he knows who you are, and trusts you, the giant will not attack again." Miriam shifted her attention to me. "Be but a minute, my dear."

At my nod, she slipped inside the library, closing the door behind her.

The moment Tobias and I were left alone, I swallowed.

He reached out and grabbed my hand. My skin there burned, wanting more of his touch, but I was not ready to deal with what I'd learned, what he'd known but not thought to mention to me.

"I'm not going to say a word about it," Tobias assured me. "You can have your time. As much as you need. I only wanted to let you know that I intend to explore the grounds, perhaps even go into the village and see if there are signs of the OA there already. Silas made an excellent point about the OA having gifted hackers. Someone might have already arrived in the village and could be sniffing their way here."

"Maybe you should take Benedict?" I suggested, glad he

wasn't going to press the matter that I was not ready to speak of yet.

His eyebrow arched. "Why's that?"

"I feel like you two need to bond. And two sets of eyes are better than one."

He didn't reply right away, but when he did, he nodded. "Very well. Your familiar and I will get some quality time together. Listen to Miriam and learn all that you can." He cupped my cheek. "Many lives depend on it."

I stared into his eyes, wanting to kiss him, but in the end, I merely placed my hand over his, entwining our fingers and guiding them down until I released.

"I'm here because fate decreed it," I said, because while I didn't fully understand my place in all this yet, that much was certain. "I started this by finding the Pearl, unleashing it, and I don't intend to let anyone down."

With that, I pressed the door to the library open and slipped inside.

True to his word, Tobias didn't follow, but the feeling of him did. He lingered in my skin, my breath, my heart as I shut the door behind me. His presence was near suffocating, but in a way that I didn't want it to end.

What the hell?

I'd never been this girl, but one kiss, a mention of a soul-mate, and the truth splitting me open wide had irrevocably altered me.

I still wasn't sure how I felt about Tobias basically making the choice for me of whether we'd be together or not, but one thing was for damn sure: the vampire had wormed his way into my heart, my life . . . and from this day forward, I wasn't sure I could live without him.

"Did you two finish your lovers' quarrel?" Miriam asked, making me jump.

I'd been so deep in my own head I hadn't even noticed she was watching me from the end of an aisle between rows of shelves.

"It's best to leave all issues at the door," she added. "Else, you will not absorb all that you must."

"We did the best we could."

There was no point in telling her that Tobias and I were not lovers.

Not when we might be so much more.

The old woman gave a nod. "Hannah will be here soon to assist. She may be the youngest of all of us, but the girl has a mind like a sponge. I believe she's read nearly as many of these books as myself, Gloria, and Claire, if you can believe it."

Considering the older trio had thirty years on Hannah, it was surprising. But then again, nothing about this place was normal; there was a freaking giant roaming around outside!

Speaking of the giant . . .

"Is Jon-Jon okay? I forgot to ask at breakfast."

Mostly because some vampire had rubbed my thigh and kept sending sneaky sexy looks my way, but I wasn't about to say boo about that to Miriam.

"He's fine. The big baby does not like to be bested. We'll have to give you a proper introduction later, after you've completed your studies for the day."

"Can't wait," I muttered, before scanning the area properly for the first time.

It was nothing like I would have thought. Plainer, for sure. There was something about a place that housed ancient knowledge few could access that brought to mind luxury.

Gold and marble and glass, paired with soaring ceilings and books climbing high to fill that space.

None of that existed here.

The room was about the size of Tobias's and my bedchambers put together—not that I should be thinking about us or our bedchambers.

Get your mind out of the gutter, Mer! I averted my attention to distract myself.

The library shelves were plain wood and heavy with books. Most did look old, but also worn, like they hadn't been taken care of properly. This was nothing like the library at Yale with its temperature and moisture-controlled climates.

"So, how many of those am I going to have to read?" I asked. There had to be at least a thousand books in here.

"In time, I hope you will read all of them."

"So that will take me, what? Just eighty years?"

Miriam snorted. "Luckily, we don't need you to read them all now. There are a mere ten tomes of vital importance to the *Vindix*. I've set them aside for you and bookmarked the pages that will most help ease you into this world.

"We'll start with the Pearl of Hell, since you have some personal knowledge of it already, then move on to the Opal, your family stone. From there, you will learn of the other *lapis caelesti*. Finally, you'll learn of the families who should wield these weapons gifted by the angels."

She gestured to a table large enough to seat six, a stack of books—red and blue and black in color—sat atop it.

"So, Meredith, are you ready to begin?" She gave me a look like she wasn't quite sure I was up for it. Like I hadn't traveled across an ocean, hadn't found this hidden freaking place, and hadn't taken on all their tests to get here. What more did a girl have to do to get some respect?

"Well?" Miriam pressed. "Or are you still thinking about the handsome vampire?"

It was unlikely that Tobias would ever leave my mind, but for a few hours, a few days, even a few weeks, if I had to, I could prioritize this—my destiny.

I rolled my shoulders back and forced the vampire to the corners of my mind. "No, I'm ready. Let's begin."

CHAPTER TWENTY-FOUR

MEREDITH

I took a seat at the table Miriam had set out for me and looked at her expectantly, ready to do what she thought was best.

We'd traveled far for this information, and it might help save the world, so I needed to shut up, listen, and learn. If there was one thing the Ringmaster had imparted on me that I wouldn't forget, it was the importance of research and learning from the past.

Miriam sat next to me, approval in the set of her lips, and opened the top book on the stack to a pre-marked page. Slowly, she turned the book to face me.

I recognized the painted illustration right away, though it looked different from when I'd seen the stone I'd stolen from a tomb in Egypt. The *lapis caelesti* sat on a pillow of black silk, not set into a necklace meant to glorify the Egyptian Goddess Isis.

"That's the Pearl of Hell," I said.

"Yes. A black pearl of extraordinary power."

"In real life, it looks almost blue-black," I corrected. "And opalescent, like a pearl, so sort of purple-y too. It was . . . unlike anything I'd ever seen."

I hadn't thought much about the day I'd found the Pearl. Hadn't had time to reflect after fate threw me into S&S, but now, the memory of finding it, of holding one of the sacred stones, sent chills up my spine.

"Really?" the old witch asked, picking up a pen and scratching a note in the margin.

I gaped at her. "Is that kosher?"

"I'm an *Arcacusto*, child—this is my job. My reason for being is in these books. I would never defile them, and your account is the only firsthand one we've had in centuries."

She set the pen down. "I must say, it is miraculous that you found it without any training, setting all this in motion."

"I used to think it was by chance," I admitted. "My partner and I had overheard people talking about a necklace in a tomb. We were in Cairo for another artifact, but once we told our boss about the necklace, she pivoted, wanting to acquire it for a client. I was happy about it too. The tomb was guarded, but not as much as the first location we'd scouted. I thought the job would be easy." I snorted. "Little did I know."

"Was she supernatural?"

"No," I said, "just ambitious. Though, she is trying to become supernatural now."

I didn't elaborate. We hadn't brought up the Ringmaster or the OA at breakfast, and I didn't want to right now either. Both Tobias and I were of the mind that maybe his sire would send more information.

Not to mention, I didn't want to show her the scar along my collarbone where Josiah had cut me to steal my power. It was fading, but the attack was still fresh in my mind.

If word came that the OA was nearing, we'd tell the coven.

But for the time being, I just wanted to focus on learning about the *lapis caelesti.*

"Interesting." Miriam arched an eyebrow.

When she realized I was not going to give more information, she pointed to the page she had open, her finger straying to a line at the end.

The Pearl of Hell was the first stone the angels used to create the supernaturals of Earth, Isila, and Hell. The holder of this stone is said to be a leader among the Vindix.

That was a relief. The Opal of Heaven was my stone. Obviously, the Pearl's holder probably had no idea they were connected to all this. They hadn't even held their stone, but that would change. When I found whoever could claim the Pearl, they could take the lead.

When the time comes for the seven Vindix to defend those of Earth against evil . . .

I paused in my reading and looked up. "This doesn't say the Darkborn by name?"

"Of course not, dear. The Darkborn are a threat now, but they have not always been so. There have always been supporters of the Princes of Hell, but not under such a name."

"What name?"

"Too many to count." She waved her hand. "These tomes are filled, not only with the information you require, but the names and histories of your enemies."

"Why not name the Princes of Darkness though?"

"As I said, you have many enemies. The princes are not even the worst."

I gaped at that, and she added. "They have always been nuisances, and quite powerful, but they are far from the only evil plaguing our world." Miriam exhaled a long, troubled breath. "And though no one but the *Arcacustos* know it, this is not the only time the sacred stones have been called to do away with such evil. The previous time was millennia ago. Now keep reading."

I had more questions but did as she said, bending my head, and picking up at the sentence where I'd left off.

When the time comes for the seven Vindix to defend those of Earth against evil, it will be the Pearl of Hell that makes the first play.

"The first play," I whispered, recalling how the air had shifted in the tomb when I found the Pearl, and how the snakes—those damned snakes!—had started hissing louder. "This book makes me think the stones have personalities or something. Are they sentient?"

"Perhaps. I cannot know if the stones have a will. To my sadness, I've never seen one, nor held them. All I know is that, by finding the stone, *you* put it in play after it had been dormant for many years. It fits."

"Hmmm. I guess so."

I read further and learned that not only did the Pearl of Hell cause madness in another person if the wielder so wished it, but once the wielder mastered the stone, it also submitted people fully to the holder's will.

"It takes away free will," I said. "And those who are evil, like Wrath, would use it to create chaos, with or without the madness attached."

"If he masters it," she amended, "which is no easy feat."

"But he's powerful."

"I'm not saying he won't," Miriam replied. "In fact, I'm sure he's actively trying to do so. It works so well with his sin."

"How so?" I wanted to be sure we were on the same page.

"Chaos often brings about, or hurries, war. That is a state

that Prince Orien loves, and he will try to amplify the sin of wrath in the areas he controls," she answered seriously.

"Areas? You don't think he'll try to take over everywhere?"

"I believe he will split the world with his brothers."

"Why is that?"

"The Princes of the Underworld not only control their sin, they *feed* upon it," Miriam explained. "They like the taste of their own sin best. If they succeed in breaking through the Eyes of Darkness, as my coven has feared for years, they will form kingdoms in which their sins reign. In that way, their own sins can dominate the area in which they live. There's plenty of the world to split up."

I shuddered. "Like a city of lust, envy, greed, and so on?"

Just thinking about New York—which wasn't totally lost to wrath so much as it was in epic disarray—was frightening, but to witness a place in which certain sins were the default was horrifying. What would they look like? How would people live? Would they merely be playthings to the princes?

"Precisely," Miriam said. "Continue your studies, child."

I read about how the angels blessed the Pearl and used it, though none of that was pertinent to me, seeing as I was not an angel. There were also hints of its use in history, and the approximate date it was lost.

But nothing was as important as knowing that the Pearl caused people to give up free will, granting us a glimpse into the Prince of Darkness's plans.

Once I reached the fifth page, Miriam placed a hand on the book.

"Now we move on to the Opal. You know nothing of it, correct?"

"That's right, but there's still a lot on the Pearl I don't know too," I pointed out. I'd barely made a dent in the massive tome.

"There is, but we do not have time for you to read it all. You need a working knowledge of all seven stones before you set out to find the other *Vindix*. As the Opal is *yours* to control, it is the most important to you."

Realizing she had a point, I leaned back, and she took the first book, replacing it with another, and opening to the correct page.

Since I'd learned I was the 'owner' of the Opal, I had been pretty curious about the stone. No one knew a thing about it besides what sort of gem it was.

To be fair, no one knew anything about any of the gems besides the Pearl.

It was sort of nice to know I wouldn't have misconceptions —and that I'd finally know what the heck to expect when I retrieved the Opal from Wrath.

Positive thinking for the win!

"Here." Miriam pointed yet again to a portion of the page she wanted me to read.

I was impressed that the woman knew the manuscripts so well. Then again, what else did they have to do here besides keep the manor in order, study, and wait for the *Vindix* to arrive?

I read the passage she indicated, holding my breath until I reached the last word, when I snorted.

"You've got to be kidding."

"These tomes are no laughing matter, Meredith. What confuses you?"

"All of it! How could I be in charge of a stone that creates joy?!" I understood the promoting free will part, I'd always had an independent streak a mile wide, but joy? That felt alien.

And what the heck would Wrath do with such a stone? I left that question unspoken, more focused on myself at the moment.

Miriam's eyebrows pinched together. "How do you mean?"

My reason stuck in my throat. It would sound too pathetic, too weak, to voice. And yet, I viewed this as a cruel joke from the universe.

"I believe I understand," Miriam sighed after my silence continued. "What happened to you after your parents died must have been awful. I know I do not know the half of it—"

"No. You don't," I snapped, not wanting her pity.

The foster home I'd lived in for only a short week, before the foster father made an advance on me that forced me to flee to the streets. The nights of living in a cardboard fucking box, fending off creepers who tried to take advantage of me. The brief happiness of being taken in by someone who seemed kind, only to realize too late that they were a psycho who used the less fortunate for their own means.

No one knew everything about my past, and I intended to keep it that way. It was too painful to share. Or to even think about. So, while Shay and Harper—and more recently, Tobias—were wiggling their way into my guarded heart, I still didn't think I could spill all that I'd endured. Some things I'd just have to be fine with taking to the grave.

"And I won't ask," Miriam whispered. "But I assure you that the Opal, a stone meant to spread joy and free will—the antithesis of the Pearl, if you didn't notice—is yours to protect. It has been in your family for as long as the *lapis caelesti* have existed. You, and you alone, are meant to use it when the time comes. I've known this since the day of your birth."

She sighed. "You are, in fact, the only *Vindix* I was certain about, and when I lost track of you . . . I felt great remorse. I'd failed in one of the only important tasks in my life."

"Why didn't my parents name you as my legal guardian?" I blurted.

So much of my suffering could have been relieved by that, and I wouldn't have been clueless about my fate now. Maybe then, the idea of being stuck with the 'happy' stone wouldn't seem quite so absurd.

"We spoke of you coming here to learn of your heritage. Of staying for some time, so that you might get to know our coven. Then, after you'd met me, they would have named me a guardian. But your parents wanted to put it off for as long as possible."

Miriam smiled, seemingly not at all upset by the delayed meeting. "They wanted you to have your full childhood. Not to lose their daughter to a destiny so large, it might threaten to swallow a wee one whole. No one can blame them for that."

"And then normality ended with a bang."

"It did." She shuddered. "You might not want to discuss it. Being English I understand keeping emotions close to the vest, but I couldn't help but notice your scars when you entered the enchanted pool."

The lines on my back would be impossible to miss. They spanned the length of my spine, a constant reminder of my shitty past.

"I . . . worked for someone. Not a very nice person," I said. "They did that. I didn't know where else to turn when I left foster care—which was traumatic, let me tell you. I thought the person I worked for was the answer. I was wrong."

Miriam nodded slowly. "I am so sorry for that. Had I known about your parent's deaths I would have tried to intervene with the foster system. But I am very far away from your home and did not learn of their fate for months. Then I couldn't find you. For that I am sorry, Meredith. Your parents were good people."

She knew them better than she was letting on. I could feel it. A part of me wanted to ask questions, but another part knew it would be too painful. Not all of my memories had returned, and I wanted them to do so before I heard stories. I wanted to see the past play in my head like a movie, not have to reconstruct it from what others told me.

I said nothing, and we stayed quiet for a few moments, me staring at the book, at the drawn image of the Opal.

I'd almost convinced myself it was time to suck it up and move on, when the door to the library opened. I glanced up, daring to hope that it was Tobias, even though Miriam would probably flay him. Instead, Hannah smiled at me.

"Am I too early?" she asked.

"Not at all," Miriam replied. "In fact, why don't you sit in while Meredith reads up on the rest of the stones? So far, we've covered the Pearl and the basics of the Opal."

The old woman stood, brushing herself off. "I think I'll make myself scarce for a few moments."

I exhaled. Yes, that would make things easier. At the very least, I wouldn't feel the urge to ask about my parents. Hannah was too young. She couldn't have known them.

"What do you say I prepare you two some tea?" Miriam offered, perhaps sensing that I wished for her to leave, if only for a few minutes. "It will fortify you through your studies."

She spoke so lightly, Hannah didn't seem to notice the heaviness in the room.

The young witch nodded. "Happy to help with the research in the meantime."

She approached, and there was something about her that

was less familiar and weighted than Miriam, which made my shoulders loosen.

"Do you want to go over the history of the Opal next?" she asked. "We have quite a lot of it, since your family held it for so long and we knew where they were. Far more than the other stones."

Hannah's blonde ringlets fell around her shoulders as she pulled out a chair next to mine. "Or the Pearl, but most of that is rumors—stories we can't be sure about. Still fun to read, though, don't you think?"

"Yes," I said as Miriam slipped out the door, presumably to give me space. "But I'd love to learn more about the Opal first."

CHAPTER TWENTY-FIVE

TOBIAS

I HEARD THE GIANT BUT COULDN'T FIND HIM AMIDST THE TREES; an admittedly impressive feat for someone so large even in this thick of a forest.

Then again, he did sneak up on us last time, the brute . . .

"Are we sure this is a good idea?" Benedict asked, his tone tense, just like it had been when I went by Meredith's room to invite him on this outing.

He wasn't pleased about the situation between me and his witch. Not that I could blame him. I was still coming to terms with it. And Meredith . . .

"Did you hear me, vampire?"

I laughed dryly. "How could I not, with a yowling tone such as yours?"

"I'll show you yowling when I leave you to fight off that giant *alone* this time." Benedict scanned the woods. "This is a horrible idea."

I shrugged. Maybe it was, but Stuart and his coven seemed to think it was smart. Seeing as I had little better to do, I decided to take my chances and follow the ginger wizard into the woods. Otherwise, I'd merely sit outside the library door like a sad puppy, and Tobias Blake Aston Laurent was many things, but a sad puppy was not one of them.

"We can't be certain how long we'll be here. Do you want to be confined to the house all day?" I asked, eyebrows raised.

The cat didn't reply, which was no surprise. Meredith's familiar liked to run about in New Haven. Here would be no different. It might even be more enticing. More wild. More alive.

I, for one, felt my predator side emerging strongly as Stuart led us through the trees to where Jon-Jon liked to relax.

Just knowing that the Ringmaster had told the Ordo Aeternum of Meredith and that they could be closing in was enough to set me on edge. I did not like that we had to be here when they came looking, rather than in New Haven. Back home, we'd be guarded at all hours. We'd have people we trusted around us.

Of course, the *Arcacusto* Coven had protections, but would they be enough to stop the supernatural organization? Meredith, Benedict, and I had gotten through, and we were only three people. The Order known for disliking humans and attracting the worst kind of supernaturals could bring many more with them. Being in New Haven, with the protection of S&S, would be far less worrying.

But alas, that was not our reality. For the foreseeable future, we were here, and then . . . Who knew?

Wherever Meredith thought a *Vindix* might be was where we'd go, because one thing was certain—if we departed from this manor, these woods, I was not going to leave her side.

Images of Meredith bombarded me. The way her lips parted in shock when I'd squeezed her knee earlier, the way she'd looked in the seconds before we'd kissed, her expression this morning, when she'd entered the common space and hadn't been sure what to do or think—they all made me happy.

But then there were the bad moments. Like how hurt she'd looked when I admitted to knowing about soulmates, and that I'd had a hunch we might be connected in that way. It was enough to make my smile falter.

I should have told her earlier . . . but it hadn't felt right. Deep down, I hadn't wanted to believe it, because who wanted to bring someone so important to them into a world where they'd always have a target on their back? A world where she couldn't have a family? A world in which a possessive vampire would always be there?

Would she want that?

I snorted at the too little too late query. Did it matter? I couldn't leave her now, even if she was angry with me.

I wondered what she was learning in that library, and the abrasive sense of annoyance that I was not allowed inside filled me once more. I could only hope the witches were giving Meredith exactly what she needed to succeed. To survive.

"Jon-Jon?" Stuart's call brought me back to the moment. "We're just stopping by!"

A low growl filled the air in the woods, and I still could not see the giant. But how?! The creature was so enormous I should be able to spot him a mile off. Where the bloody hell was he?

The answer came a second later when a mound of earth up ahead rose and the giant appeared, wet dirt crumbling off his face.

His eyes narrowed, latching on me, and he roared.

Stuart turned as the giant began taking large, gulping breaths. "Just a mo' okay? He was pretty irate last night."

So sorry for not rolling over and dying for you.

I didn't say the words I thought, just nodded and stopped my trek.

"He looks like he wants to make me cat-popcorn," Benedict whispered, edging closer to a tree. "If he charges, you really are on your own this time."

"Glad I came and got you."

"Why did you, anyway? It couldn't be just for this."

"Meredith wants us to bond," I admitted.

The cat didn't reply. I got the sense that he was thinking it over.

That was fine. Vampires rarely needed to rush things, and I'd rather focus on the giant, who still looked like a bull ready to rush me. If he moved so much as an inch, I'd be ready.

See how he likes his shirt mangled.

Minutes passed in which Stuart tried to calm Jon-Jon. To my great surprise, it seemed to work, so when the ruddy-faced wizard waved us over, I did as requested, slightly less hesitant than before.

The stink of a large, unwashed body grew more apparent as we neared the giant, and I was all too happy when Stuart motioned for me to halt ten feet away.

"Jon-Jon," the wizard said softly. "You met Tobias and Benedict, Meredith's familiar, last night. Then, they were intruders, and you did well to protect our coven against them." The giant grunted, and Stuart smiled in response. "But now they're guests. Would you like to say hello?"

Jon-Jon's brows dug together, as if he were still contemplating beating us to a pulp, though he was no longer growling or breathing deeply.

Stuart was something of a giant-whisperer, it seemed.

"Cat hurt Jon-Jon," the giant said after a moment, using a

beefy finger to point at Benedict, who remained a good five paces behind me. "Bad cat."

My lips twitched in a smirk. Apparently, the big lout was fine with me, but Benedict would have to grovel.

Seemed about right. After all, I had been the one thrown through the woods—not digging my claws into Jon-Jon's face.

So I turned and gave Benedict a serious look. I was going to love every minute of this. "That's true, you know. I expect you do owe him an apology."

"Scar!" Jon-Jon pointed to his face, where Benedict had landed. There were actually no markings to be found—likely thanks to a healer witch—but the giant didn't seem to know or recall that tidbit. "Hurt me!"

"Is this a joke?" Benedict muttered, and though we were working on becoming friends, that made my lips spread wider.

"Best to get on with making amends," I said. "Meredith needs everyone to play nicely."

The cat huffed out a breath and loped closer, caution in his amber eyes. When he halted, he was still notably out of Jon-Jon's reach.

"Hello," Benedict said to the giant. "I feel horribly for scratching you—even if it was to save my own fur—can you forgive me?"

At the half-assed apology, I nearly let out a chuckle, but stopped my mirth just in time. Jon-Jon seemed to be considering Benedict's words, and surely, laughing would only further confuse the oversized man.

After a prolonged silence, in which Benedict seemed to stiffen by the second, the giant took a step closer.

The cat darted backward, stopping at my feet.

"Hold on," I hissed.

Jon-Jon didn't appear threatening, and when he held his meaty hand out in a familiar gesture, I knew I'd judged his expression correctly.

"Friends?" he asked. "No more hurt?"

I nodded and extended my own hand, wrapping it around one of his fingers. "I accept. Benedict does too, right, chap?"

"I do, but I'm not great at shaking." The cat held up a trembling paw.

A roar of laughter burst from the giant, nearly bowling me over, it was so forceful. When he stopped, Stuart approached, looking relieved.

He'd seemed so sure that Jon-Jon would accept our apology before, but judging by how much his shoulders had loosened, I now suspected he'd been putting up a front.

"Very good! Now that you're all friends, you can patrol the woods safely," the wizard said.

"We won't happen upon any other surprises? You haven't got, say, a manticore roaming about that might eat Benedict? Or perhaps a werewolf?"

I felt the cat's glare but chose not to meet his eyes. He'd been scared of Jon-Jon eating him, so really, I'd said nothing wrong.

"Manticore? Of course not! Those only live in Isila!"

"Like giants," I commented.

"I suppose that's true," Stuart mused. "But no. We have Jon-Jon, the wyvern, and a few other creatures that take refuge in our woods, but none as dangerous as the two you've already met. You should be just fine!" He waved a hand dismissively. "So I'll let you get to it."

"Alright," I said, somewhat stunned that he was fine with just leaving us. But by the determined glint in his eyes, he had something he wanted to do. "Are you going to assist Meredith?"

To me, that was the most important thing any of the *Arca-custo* could do. I hoped they felt similarly.

"I was planning on going to the library," Stuart said, a blush filling his pale cheeks. "So yes, I'll check on her."

"Good. Tell her I'm thinking of her."

Stuart froze, eyes widening.

I couldn't blame him. I sounded like a besotted fool, not like the vampire guardian most of these witches knew me to be.

"Sure," the wizard said with a slow nod. "Now, if you two are certain you won't need help in the forest, I'll be going."

"We can find our way back," I assured him. Now that I was more familiar with the land and how things smelled, I'd be able to track a path back to the manor.

"See you around, then." With a bob of his head, Stuart left Benedict and me with Jon-Jon, who watched the exchange with interest.

I turned my face up to the giant. "We're going to patrol the woods. That okay with you, mate?"

Jon-Jon nodded slowly. "I help?"

Should have seen that one coming.

I now trusted the giant not to snap my neck between his fingers, but that didn't mean I wished for him to join.

"How about we divide the woods so we can cover more ground?" I suggested. "The cat and I will go this way, and you take that direction." I gestured to the back of the property last, determined to scout the front and see if anyone had tried to breach entry yet.

"Good," Jon-Jon said as he turned. "Bye-Bye."

"Best of luck," I replied, relieved it was that simple with the creature, and began to stride through the undergrowth toward the road.

"So. *'Tell her I'm thinking of her,'* huh?" Benedict said, running up next to me.

I'd hoped that comment would sail past him. How foolish of me.

"What are you two going to do, vampire?" Benedict pressed when I didn't answer.

I turned to him. "I can't answer that question without speaking to Meredith."

"But you agree you're her mate, correct?"

"I . . . I do." Fully admitting it out loud was still difficult, but the longer I thought on it, the more sure I became.

Giselle had been right all along, and she'd never even witnessed Meredith and I together—only the effect the witch had on me. How had I been so changed then and not seen it? That had been before I'd given her my blood to save her life.

And more importantly, how would I be strong enough to protect Meredith from what would come her way? Could she really forsake the life she wouldn't have, a more normal, safer existence?

We needed to talk, that much was clear.

Benedict craned his neck up at me. "Good, I'm glad you're on board. Because I don't think there's going to be any going back, for either of you."

My step hitched. "Can you smell the difference on me?"

He gave me the smuggest look I'd ever seen on his feline face. "There's *something*. I can't be as sure with you as I am with her, but you are different."

It was true, and I couldn't pinpoint the exact moment I'd shifted. When I'd given her blood to save her life? When I'd seen her in the infirmary after she went to Hell? When we'd barely stopped someone from stealing her magic?

Bloody hell, she doesn't need me to find trouble, does she?

Not that that made me feel any better. I'd just have to make it clear what being in a relationship with a Laurent meant when we finally spoke. I'd be explicit, and hope she didn't downplay the dangers in her head.

"Do you thin—"

The words died in my mouth as, in the distance, a trio of ravens swept through the trees, racing away from us.

"Benedict!"

I scooped the cat up before he could respond. With my vampiric speed, I caught up with the ravens quickly, but sensing a predator at their backs, they simply veered skyward, up up up and away.

I watched them go, furious I hadn't gotten a look at their eyes. Had they been milky? Had Josiah been controlling them?

Benedict hissed, his claws cutting into my arm. "Put me down!"

I ignored him and instead, continued to scan the forest, on the lookout for ravens, or the necromancer who controlled them.

After a few moments, I had to admit that the woods were silent. I couldn't even hear Jon-Jon's thundering steps anymore, so I set down an indignant Benedict.

He shook, then glared up at me. "Not every raven belongs to Josiah, you know."

"Obviously. But it's not a common skill, even among necromancers, and in regards to Josiah, I'm on edge." I swallowed thickly. "You would be too, if you'd seen her that day."

"I would have died to be there with her."

A breath dipped into my lungs. The cat was usually sassy

and a bit annoying, but I'd be damned if he wasn't serious as the grave right then.

I respected him for it.

"We should have brought you," I said quietly.

"Yes, you should have. Now, are we going to continue?"

I nodded, but hadn't even taken a step when my phone pinged.

Hastily, I pulled it out, thinking it might be Meredith. But the number that blinked up at me from the screen was unfamiliar.

The hair on the back of my neck rose.

"What is it?" Benedict asked.

"I don't know." Tamping down the fear rising inside me, I opened the message.

A photo stared back at me, of Heathrow Airport, and the pieces clicked together. This was a burner phone; the message had to be from Giselle.

She was warning me. The OA had landed in England. They were following Meredith's trail, and it wouldn't be but hours —days, if we were lucky—before they arrived here.

"Bloody hell," I swore. "It's from my sire. The OA is on their way."

Benedict's hackles rose. "Then we'd better hurry and search the woods."

"And afterward, I'll demand that the witches strengthen their protections," I growled. "The Ringmaster will not be getting anywhere near Meredith again."

CHAPTER TWENTY-SIX

MEREDITH

HANNAH AND I SPENT THE BETTER PART OF TWO HOURS COVERING the *lapis caelesti*, which included their history and individual powers. Thankfully, most of the sacred stones were not that hard to understand.

The Emerald of Earth, Sapphire of Seas, Amethyst of Air, and Ruby of Flames were all elemental-based, their gems' colors correlating to their respective magic.

The angels, apparently, weren't very creative, though Hannah was quick to assure me that being the master of any of these stones would be like being an elemental on steroids. The likes of such power, the world hadn't seen in a long-ass time.

The specific example she'd used was that the keeper of the Sapphire could, once trained up, act as powerfully as Poseidon had in Greek myths.

Just thinking about that made me squirm. I'd read many of those myths, and Poseidon had done some real shit, which made me determined to become besties with all of the elemental *Vindix* once I found them.

The Diamond, like the Pearl and the Opal, was different.

Its full name was the Diamond of Souls, and the wielder of this specific *lapis caelesti* could call upon ghosts, astral travel, and journey to the spirit realm, just to name a few of their abilities.

I had a million questions about the spirit realm, but Hannah told me we'd have to tackle those later. She had a basic understanding of the spirit realm, but not enough to feel comfortable teaching me. Aya was their resident spirit expert.

And though all of the stones held my interest, and each was powerful and terrifying in their own right, the two that I'd learned of first still held the most intrigue for me. Perhaps because they were the only two posing a threat at this very moment.

The Pearl and the Opal. Diametric opposites. One could undo the power of the other. And the Pearl and the Opal affected people the most directly, in their hearts and minds.

The same could not be said for any of the other stones to the same degree. The people who wielded the first two had too much power—which was probably why the Darkborn had gone after those first.

Though, if they get the others . . . That will suuuuuck.

"Are you ready to move on to the families?" Hannah asked.

"Sure." I set down my teacup, the dainty, flowery kind that I'd never used in my life because it seemed pointless.

Miriam kept bringing tea in, and I didn't have the heart to ask for a mug. But, come on! The teensy cups held precisely three gulps of tea—which, come to think of it, was probably more a reflection on my un-ladylike table manners than anything else.

Tobias probably loved these stupid little cups in his human life, I thought, and immediately shook the vampire from my mind for what felt like the millionth time.

"Let's get back to business."

"Okay." Hannah smiled and went to a shelf.

"I thought Miriam pulled all the books out already." I pointed to the stack. It had dwindled, but there were still five we hadn't touched.

"Those are all wonderful resources, but if I'm to introduce you to the royal covens, I like to start with when they were formed."

Royal covens?

"I haven't heard the term," I admitted.

Hannah twisted. "No? It's what we call the families of the seven *Vindix* and their closest supporters. Besides the *Arcacustos*, of course—we're our own little club." She smiled brightly.

"The cool kids."

"For sure," she laughed musically.

"So the families were all in the same coven?"

"Well, no really. Back in the day, families in general were much larger and often made up their own covens. Including extended family and all that. Then those of the other *Vindix* would marry in—to keep the secrets, you know. So in a way they were of the same coven, but only when they chose to be."

"Wouldn't that cause incest eventually?" I cringed, not liking where this was going.

"It wasn't quite that strict," Hannah assured me. "However, had the families been smaller and the marriages more restricted, then you'd likely be correct. I don't think it ever got to that, though, seeing as the last time the *Vindix* protected Earth was shortly before they split. After that, bloodlines were lost—killed, actually . . . two of them, to be exact. And of course, after that happened, the other families hid, so we can't be sure what happened then."

"The family who held the Pearl of Hell and the one that held the Diamond of Souls are the ones that were murdered, right?"

We'd gone over it briefly while discussing the latter, but I'd also learned approximately six hundred other facts since then. A refresher couldn't hurt.

"Exactly." Hannah looked pleased that I remembered.

"You think the rest are all still alive?"

"I do."

"What makes you think that? Have you guys felt something?"

I recalled when I found the Pearl, and Luca's claim that unearthing it had had a ripple effect felt by supernaturals around the globe.

"Call it hope." She shrugged.

Hope did not seem like enough to me.

"What happens when the *Vindix* are not around anymore? Like with the families that died out. What happens to their stones?"

"They will choose worthy replacements," Hannah said with a shrug. "We don't know how."

Again, the way she spoke made me think the stones had a mind of their own.

I hoped that soon I could get my hands on one and learn if that was true or not.

"But that will make it much more difficult for you to find them," she added after a moment, as if she didn't quite want to admit such a thing.

As if finding six other random people in the world wasn't

going to be difficult enough! Seeker magic applied to objects only. Not people.

Ugh, one thing at a time.

"So, why are those families called royals?" I asked. "I thought witches didn't have royalty like other orders. Isn't that more of an Isila thing?"

"It is. And we don't, but that doesn't mean that we did not have them at one point."

Hannah pulled out a book and opened it to an image I recognized right away: seven people dancing beneath an over-large moon, holding hands.

In a very similar image my mother had hidden the final stone in my ring—the ring that would eventually, we hoped, help me find the other *Vindix*.

"I've seen this," I whispered.

"Have you? It's a representation of the leaders of the royal covens. This was one of the ceremonies the witches partook in, twice a year, at Beltane and Samhain. It was a time to revere our supernatural order and the responsibilities we'd been given. According to our books, each festival was one of great joy."

She smiled, and for a moment, I thought I smelled flowers in the air, almost as if I were dancing around a maypole at Beltane, celebrating witching kind.

"Your family was once looked upon as angel-chosen, and hence, royal," she told me. "The concept was lost as witches spread out and lived in new lands, but the stones recognize the blood. Or, in the case of the lost families, certain characteristics. That is the hypothesis, anyhow."

I leaned back. As someone who didn't know a lot about her family, it was weird to hear that I'd descended from leaders, royalty.

"I—"

Suddenly, my vision clouded. This time, I recognized the signs of a memory returning, so instead of freaking out, I just allowed it to take hold of me. And when I found myself in a backyard with my father, I was glad I had.

We were kicking around a soccer ball. I was probably around ten at the time, and on my head, I wore a pink tiara.

Cringe! Little Meredith, what were you thinking?!

My questionable color choice aside, I smiled as Dad and I laughed. This was a rare memory I'd seen where we just looked happy and free.

"Ready to head in soon, princess?" Dad asked as he stopped the ball from soaring behind him with a quick catch.

"You can't use your hands!"

"Right. Sorry, my lady."

A soft exhale gusted out of me. Was he just doing that thing dads did? Or had I known we were of royal blood all along?

That felt like a stretch, but I had to have received some grooming as a child, right?

"Dad, can you tell me about our castle again?"

Okay, hold the phone! Was this real?!

"We don't have one anymore, princess, but we used to. It—"

The vision dissipated, as it so often did, at the worst possible second, and I found myself sitting in the library again, Hannah watching me with concern on her face.

"Are you well?"

I blew out my lips. "My memories were lost when my magic was bound—long story—and they're slowly coming back. A lot of times, it seems like the conversation I'm having triggers them. Like now, I just saw one in which my father told me that our family had a castle!"

CHAPTER TWENTY-SIX

Hannah smiled. "Interesting! I'd love to hear more."

"That's really all I've got." I pulled the book closer. "I bet I'll learn more about my family's heritage from these pages than from my memories. They appear at the most random times, and usually in snippets."

"I see." Hannah sounded a little disappointed, which I could relate to. My memories often disappointed me too. "Go on, then. I'll be here if you have any questions."

I dug in again, ignoring the crick growing in my neck and trying not to wonder what Tobias was up to now. Was he in the village? Was he—

Back to the book, Mer.

I found the sentence that had lost me, a whole three lines down from the top, and I began to devour the excerpt on the royal covens.

As Hannah said, they were families, many from Britain. Two were more friendly toward one another than the others, the ones who held the Pearl and the Opal.

From what the history said, there was always strife between fire and water and air and earth. I tucked that away for later, wondering if the modern *Vindix* would be the same.

Finally, I got to the point when the families began to migrate to other parts of the world. My own stayed in England the longest, until eventually relocating to the U.S.

The families who held the Pearl died out first, and then the clan in control of the Diamond eventually died out too. As a result of those fates their sacred stones were untraceable. The rest of the families were simply lost to time and an ever-growing world.

When I finished two pages, I looked up at Hannah. "How did you know the families died? They could have just gone rogue or lived in hiding, right?"

"When the final *Vindix* in a line passes, we get a sign. Just like when the new *Vindix*—the ones fated to take on evil—were born, we received signs."

"Which was?"

"A shower of stars rained from the sky the night of each of your births. They all happened within a relatively short span—seven years, I believe, though I was younger then and not in place in the manor, so I might be off."

I doubted it. Hannah did not seem to be the type to be 'off' about anything. She even set her teacup precisely in the center of her saucer. Every dang time.

I was thinking about what I'd just learned, and was about to read some more, when the door to the library opened.

Half expecting to see Miriam arriving with more tea, I blinked when Stuart appeared.

"Hey there," he said. "Thought you two might want some lunch? You've been at work a while."

He was speaking to both of us, but his eyes remained locked on Hannah, who was blushing.

Ooooo!

A grin spread across my face as I felt the heat in the room ratchet up a little.

"I'd love lunch," Hannah admitted.

"Me too. Maybe you two can go get it for me?" I suggested.

Apparently, Shay was rubbing off on me, if I was trying to play matchmaker. That normally wasn't my thing, but the way these two were looking at each other was fire!

"I couldn't leave you all alone in here," Hannah shook her head. "It's my responsibility to be of service to you."

"I'll get it," Stuart assured her. "Ham sandwiches alright, then?"

"Sure," I paused. "Have you seen Tobias?"

"I introduced him to Jon-Jon earlier, but he's been exploring the grounds since," Stuart said. "If he returns, I'll let you know. In the meantime, I'll be back shortly with your food."

He left, and I punched Hannah lightly on the shoulder. "You like him!"

"I—" Her red cheeks gave her away. "He's kind and funny."

"But?"

Although she hadn't said it, I totally sensed a 'but'.

"I'm not sure it's proper for us to be together. The coven must always stay united. We have a sacred duty to guide the *Vindix* when they arrive. What if we date and it doesn't work out?"

The concern was valid. It wasn't like just anyone could do what the *Arcacustos* did.

But, then again, were they so strict that they'd confine people to loveless lives? This wasn't a nunnery. Or, in the case of Stuart, a monastery.

"What if you never try," I countered, "and you have to live with the torture of him always being around, and not knowing if you could have been magic?"

Okay, it was official. Shay's optimism was definitely rubbing off on me. But I couldn't deny that I really felt that way.

What was more, something in my words struck a cord deep within myself.

I needed to take my own advice.

It wasn't like I had been wanting to cast Tobias off like a bad smell—not even close—but his reasoning for not telling me that we were, in all likelihood, soulmates lurked around me, unshakable. It distracted me, made me doubt myself, and made me worry that he wouldn't want to even try and I'd get hurt.

I'd even begun to wonder if it wasn't just easier to pretend this bond didn't exist.

As if that is possible.

It wasn't. I knew it deep in the core of my being. My advice to Hannah applied to us too. Tobias and I could be magic, and there was no way in hell I could give up on that.

I glanced out the window, an exhale parting my lips as I resolved to convince him that, no matter what sort of restrictions he wanted to put in place, we were going to give this a shot, because we truly felt like something worth fighting for.

CHAPTER TWENTY-SEVEN

HANS

I'D BEEN CLEANED UP AND STUCK IN THE SAME ROOM FOR HOURS, and still, no one had returned. Eventually, because I had nothing better to do, I lay down on the bed and stared at the ceiling, reliving last night and wondering where I was now.

The feeling of being lost was so all-encompassing that, when the Italian vampire finally returned, I was actually happy to see him.

That was, until I caught a peek at the trio of demons behind him.

"Is all that necessary?" I gestured to the muscle-bound goons, my nose wrinkling at the faint stench of brimstone wafting off of them. They had large, black bat-like wings and noses that belonged on pigs, but their bodies were human looking. Unlike me, these creatures weren't Hellblooded—part human, or another magical order—they were all demon. Though I couldn't pinpoint which type. I hadn't seen these demons in Hell, there were probably a hundred species I hadn't seen. "You handled me pretty well by yourself earlier."

The vampire smiled coolly. "And I could do so again. These

. . . compatriots weren't my choice. My master and the Prince of Darkness deem you a volatile adversary worthy of a brawny escort." He arched his brows. "Not that I understand why. As you said, a butler who rarely sees action could take care of you."

Pain at losing my power gripped me, but I kept my face a mask of indifference as the vampire butler assessed me, trying to determine why others would think I was a threat.

I sure as fuck wasn't going to mention that my magic was gone. Seeing as I was being kept here, it seemed no one suspected that yet. I doubted even Shay knew. She'd been tied up in black magic when it happened.

I shuddered as I rose slowly from the bed. Somehow, I had to get them to believe I still had my power . . . otherwise, what would stop Wrath from making me his plaything? Or killing me?

I needed to keep my secret for as long as possible. And in the meantime, I'd do my damndest to try and figure out where the hell I was being kept and save Shay.

If she isn't already dead.

My jaw clenched.

Nicoleta hated Shay, but I had a growing suspicion that the nephilim was here for more than just my sister's amusement. Nic must have mentioned Shay's sword of fire and light—a dead giveaway that she was related, or at least blessed by, the archangel Uriel—and Wrath knew how to use Shay's lineage to his benefit. It was the only thing that made sense.

"Hurry up," the middle demon grunted, his red eyes narrowed.

"What's in it for me?" I tilted my chin up, though I didn't stop striding toward the door.

Pushing my luck was sort of my thing, but this guy didn't

seem like the sharpest tool in the box. He might rage out on me even if his boss wanted me unharmed—which I could only imagine was the case, since Wrath hadn't paid me a visit yet.

"You have two legs." The demon cracked his knuckles. "The snapping of bones is one of my favorite sounds."

"You make a convincing point." I shrugged as if I wasn't scared at all. "Lead the way, Muscles."

Bat-boy looked as if I'd insulted him, which only made me smirk.

Too bad Wrath wasn't an idiot like this guy. I wouldn't even need my powers to defeat him.

My escort, with the vampire in the forefront, led me down a spiraling flight of stairs. While the room I'd been locked inside hinted that this home was old, the stairwell made me even more certain; no modern builder would install steps this steep. They were a lawsuit waiting to happen.

At the bottom of the staircase, we entered into a hallway that was basically an alternate reality from my barren room. Marble sculptures dotted the corridor every few feet, and chandeliers marched down the length of the hallway. Tapestries hung from each wall, one of which I was damn sure was a work of art I'd seen an image of in a book in the Beinecke. It depicted witches and a unicorn.

"I didn't know they made such convincing replicas." I pointed to the wall hanging in question.

The vampire glanced my way. "That's an original."

I stiffened. "Your master has an original tapestry from the Middle Ages? But that must be worth . . . hundreds of thousands of dollars."

Obviously, people in and around DC had money, but that was beyond extravagant.

"Over a million," he corrected. "Master deemed the investment worth it, though, as it used to belong to the Medicis."

"As in the family from Florence?"

I was no history wiz like Tobias, but I knew enough to get by, and who *hadn't* heard that name?

"Who else?" he scoffed.

Oh, right. Who the fuck else?

Instead of asking more questions that would probably seem stupid as hell, I decided to take in the home as I walked. At the very least, I needed to figure out where the exits were located.

But the deeper we went, the less I concerned myself with exits. Partly because we didn't pass any, and partly because more signs of immense wealth stole my attention and made me wonder who the hell I was up against.

"Is that a Fabergé egg?" I asked as we strode past a room in which an ornate gold and amethyst egg was perched on a coffee table, like it was nothing more than a candle.

"It is," the vampire servant replied without even looking at what I'd referenced.

"A real one?"

He turned, stared at me blankly. "Why would it not be real?"

I stopped walking. This was all too much. "Am I in a castle or something?"

I didn't know why it hit me then, but the stone, curved walls of my tower came rushing back, bolstered by all the finery that we'd seen.

"Of course you are." The servant paused, stopping our group. "Did you think you were in a shack?"

Touché.

"To be honest, man, I had no idea—still have no idea—

where I am. My room was clearly a tower, but I couldn't see much out the window. I don't know of any place in the U.S. like this—"

"That's because you're not in the United States."

I didn't know why he was giving up this information now, other than perhaps I'd find out in a few seconds anyway, but what the hell?! I wasn't in the U.S.?

I frowned. "Canada makes even less sense."

One of the demons sniggered. "Idiot."

My muscles tensed, primed to punch the crap out of him, but I remembered that I had nothing more than strength to back up an attack. And no doubt they would expect me to use magic rather than physicality.

Best not to start something that would hint at my secret.

"You're not in Canada either," the vampire said impatiently. "You're in Italy. Lake Como, to be precise."

Italy?! But how?

Since my realization that I had no magic, my memories of the night had returned slowly. I recalled Wrath's black smoke enveloping me, choking me into darkness, and then I'd woken up here.

How could they have gotten me to Italy? By private jet?

"Customs just let them come into the country with an unconscious person?"

Probably two, actually. I doubted they'd treated Shay any better. How much did you have to pay off customs for them to be down with that?!

The demons busted up laughing, and this time, it took all I had not to slam my fist into their chins, one after the other.

Unlike the goons, the vampire's face shone with pure pity. "You didn't fly. You appeared on the lake front."

All at once, my stomach tightened as things clicked

together. Little was known about the Princes of Hell, but I seemed to have just learned something important.

Wrath's smoke could just . . . *poof!* . . . transport him places? No wonder he'd left no trace when he retreated from New York. There wasn't a path to follow.

"Yes," the servant said softly, clearly reading my shock. "There's much we don't know about the Prince."

"No talking about our boss!" one of the demons grunted. "Get a move on!"

For a moment, the vamp appeared irritated, but then a mask slipped over his face, no doubt well-practiced, and he nodded to me. "*My* master awaits."

Hmm. From the sounds of it the butler was not totally aligned with Wrath. He had a different master, likely a vampire. I was about to learn of yet another enemy.

We continued walking through the home, the *castle*, until we reached a door. The butler opened it, and I was shocked to see stone steps leading outside.

The lake I'd seen earlier glinted beyond a vast expanse of lawn. No boats traveled its waters, and the sun was setting fast. Outside, everything was calm, peaceful.

The vampire descended, and I was nearly shoved down after him by one of the demons. The others chuckled at their pal's brilliant attack.

Rolling my eyes, I followed the bloodsucker, and when we got to the bottom, he cut across the lawn, aiming toward a wooded area.

Not breaking a step, I glanced over my shoulder, pointedly ignoring the demons snarling at me. My heart skipped a beat. Yup, the whole time I'd been in a legit fucking castle, and it looked even larger from the outside than it had felt inside.

"How much land does your boss own?" I thought I

spotted a building through the trees behind us, but wasn't sure. The trees were dense and, if a structure was there, it was far away. In the direction we headed, there were just trees.

The vampire didn't answer right away, as if he were determining whether or not the question was safe. "Many hundreds of hectares, most of it on this side of the castle is his land."

Had I been American, I would have been clueless at the term, but I wasn't originally from the U.S., so I knew that was a lot of land.

I looked across the lake. The manor I'd seen earlier stood out to me, and now that the tower's stone walls weren't cutting off my view, I could clearly see homes tucked in the trees on either side of it. Though they all looked large, qualifying more as mansions or villas, they didn't have much land around them. Not like this castle did. Whoever lived here was a real power player.

As we entered the woods, I stayed quiet, still observing. Though, to be honest, escape seemed less and less like an option.

Could I swim across the lake? No . . . Even if I did that, at least three of the demons on-site had wings. Nicoleta was sure to be here too. She had wings but could also just fish me out with her dark magic.

Not to mention that if Shay was worse off than me, which was probably the case, could she swim? Run?

Dammit, think, Hans! Think.

I did, and all the while, we trekked through the woods to Goddess only knew where.

I still hadn't come up with a solution, or even an option that seemed reasonable, when voices hit my ear.

I stiffened. One of them was feminine. Was that Nicoleta?

"Don't try anything, Hellblooded," one of the demons said. "No magic. If you do, we attack."

I exhaled slowly. Yet another excuse not to use my power. "Wouldn't dream of it."

Mere minutes later, we exited the trees into a clearing about as large as my home back in New Haven.

My eyes went first to my sister, hanging onto some dude who looked a few years older than her—Wrath's heir, no doubt. About twenty demons and a dozen other supernaturals milled around them, acting as guards.

Though, knowing Nic, she didn't want them. Nor did she need them. If my sister had proven anything to me since our reunion it was that she was vicious and could take care of herself.

I swallowed thickly, wishing that she was still the sweet, carefree girl I'd once known. The one who lived in books and ran wild in the woods.

Off to the side, Wrath spoke with a tall, olive-skinned man. Italian like the other vampire, if I had to guess. They were so engaged in their conversation, they didn't even notice my arrival until the servant who'd escorted me called out.

"Master, the Hellblooded."

The other vampire's attention snapped to me, and Wrath followed, taking me in with as a slow, cunning smile spread on his lips.

I jerked my chin up. "Where's Shay?"

"You'll see soon enough," Wrath replied smoothly, shifting his black feathered wings. "It appears that you've recovered from our transport. Most smoke-travelers can't move for days afterward. Even my brothers Levi and Belhor are not that adept. It was your first time?"

I nodded.

"Lilith's blood truly does work wonders. Few are stronger than her."

I swallowed, not liking that he knew about my mother. Surely, he was using my sister only because of the power that ran through Lilith's line.

"Hans, is it?" The vampire master walked toward me, not at all deferring to Wrath. His body language insisted they were equals—or at the very least, the bloodsucker thought so.

But does Wrath?

"It is," I replied.

"My brother has spoken of you. Vaguely, of course, as befits the secrecy of your little coven."

"Your brother?" My eyebrows pinched together. This guy had a connection to S&S? "Who's that?"

"He goes by Tobias Aston." The man's nose wrinkled. "He should use his royal title, but my brother does not see the value in it."

My blood froze. This was Tobias's brother?!

"I didn't know he had a brother," I said, though that wasn't entirely true.

Tobias had spoken of his Laurent family from time to time. Never publicly by name, but I knew because once, his blood had saved me and I'd been conscious enough to glimpse the truth of who he was. During the times that he'd spoken of his family, he'd mentioned two siblings, just not their genders.

"Yes, well, until lately, we did not speak often." The man's eyes glittered dangerously, making my heart drop to my knees.

Was Tobias the traitor in S&S? Was he working with Wrath and . . . I lifted my chin. "You never gave me your name."

"Raphael Laurent, but you may call me Master."

Like hell I would.

I was saved from flinging a retort that would likely have earned me a beatdown, or fangs to the neck, by Wrath, who circled the vampire, smiling like he owned the world.

"Now, now, Raphael. I'm not sure 'Master' is correct for this one. He, like me, like *you*, is of royal blood."

"A half-breed and a bastard," Raphael sneered.

"In Hell, we do not associate bastards with being less than true-born heirs." Wrath tilted his head. "In fact, they're more often celebrated for their viciousness. A characteristic I can see in this one's family."

My lips pressed together. "Neither my sister nor I are vicious."

"Hold your tongue, Hans!" Nicoleta yelled.

I hadn't even been aware she was watching us, but why wouldn't she? Her lord was here, and she was devoted to him.

"You're not, Nic. Not deep down. I know the real you."

"The girl you knew is long dead." As if to prove it, Nicoleta pulled the young man I assumed to be Wrath's heir in for a kiss.

My stomach roiled as he grabbed her butt, pulling her closer, deepening the kiss. His tongue flicked out, trailing her lips.

Wrath chuckled. "Soon enough, I will have more family to welcome." He looked at Raphael. "But if an heir is born before they claim one another in unholy matrimony, all the better."

Raphael snorted. "I would not tolerate bastards in my line."

"You can't even make kids," I snapped, because I had to take my anger out on *some*one. "You're made, not a natural-born Laurent."

Tobias's brother lunged, and the next thing I knew, my feet were dangling and my throat was on fire.

I kicked, but Raphael had lifted me at least three feet from the grass.

If I ever needed my magic, it's now.

"*Release him!*" Wrath boomed.

Raphael growled, red ringing his dark brown irises. The pressure on my windpipe didn't let up.

"If you wish for me to make good on our bargain, you will do as I say, vampire."

I fell to the ground unceremoniously, the squeezing force of Raphael's grasp still burning a ring around my neck.

Bastard! If I had my magic, he'd be drowning in the lake by now.

"I think that's quite enough for introductions," Wrath segued. "Unless there are objections, shall we begin?"

Raphael made a show of looking out over the lake, as if assessing. "The sun will fully set soon," he said, which apparently meant something to Wrath, because he nodded.

"Then the timing is right." Prince Orien snapped his fingers. "Bring the sacrifice."

My heart leapt into my throat. The Prince of Darkness could only mean one person.

I was proven correct a few seconds later as, on the opposite side of the clearing, Shay emerged from the trees, her eyes firmly on the ground, hands and feet bound in golden chains held taut by two hulking demons.

They'd dressed her in a short dress, all white and gold, and some asshole had placed a magical golden halo over her head.

All around, the Darkborn laughed and pointed as the demons led Shay to a raised stone altar that I hadn't noticed before because at least twenty people, maybe even thirty, crowded in front of it.

My jaw clenched as one Darkborn leapt in front of Shay, spitting in her face.

They were making a mockery of Shay's angel blood. And I hated to think who had put those clothes on her, because I knew the woman well enough to know she would not have done so herself.

"A tamed angel," Wrath cooed. "All bark and no bite."

My stomach dipped at what that could mean. Had Shay, like me, been stripped of her magic?

I looked around. Most of the people in the crowd were demons from Hell—winged and horned and red-eyed. True monsters. But there were others who could easily be Hell-blooded like me, or vampires, witches, fae . . . or worse. Sorcerers.

I grimaced. Sorcerers were just witches who'd gone dark, but with that shift, they also generally went a little crazy. That made them dangerous. If Shay could not wield her magic, had they forced the change on her violently? Was it permanent?

Does it matter?

From the look on Wrath's face, I had sincere doubts that he would let Shay live through the night. He had plans for her, and I needed to get her out of here before he could enact them.

I glanced around, only to be hit on the side of the head by one of the demons that had escorted me here. "Go."

I blinked and found Wrath and Raphael approaching Shay. Apparently, I was supposed to do the same.

With each step I took, I felt more ill.

Not only was Shay dressed in the most ridiculous manner, but she looked paler than I'd ever seen her. Sickly.

That cemented the idea that they'd given her something to stifle her magic.

She lifted her head for the first time since entering the clearing. Her eyes locked on me and widened.

"Hans," she whispered, the sound of her voice so raw, so full of emotion.

She didn't look as if she despised me at all, even though she should. It was because of me that we were in this mess.

Wrath twirled to face me. "Yes, Lilith's spawn is here too! He has a part to play, just like you, my dear." Prince Orien grinned, a promise of danger and blood and violence. "I had thought to use Nicoleta, but this is much better. She needs to keep her strength for breeding, and this is more poetic, don't you think?"

"There's nothing poetic about this," Shay growled. "You're a monster, and that's all there is to it."

"Even the darkness holds beauty, little nephilim. You'll see. Soon, you'll see."

Wrath nodded to the demons carrying the ends of her chains. "Bind her!"

Shay struggled, but it was no use. The monsters flanking her were three times her size, and without her magic, she was as powerless as me.

Of course, no one had questioned the fact that I had not used magic yet, but why would they? I'd been surrounded by vampires and demons this entire time. They were formidable foes, and I was greatly outnumbered. I'd get my ass kicked within seconds.

So how the hell was I going to get us out of here without getting both Shay and me killed?

As the demons pulled her to the center of the raised stone altar, a ticking began in my head.

I wasn't sure how I'd manage to save us, but I needed to figure it out fast. Time was running out.

CHAPTER TWENTY-EIGHT

SHAY

MY SKIN BURNED FROM WHERE THE DEMONS HAD TOUCHED ME, and I wanted nothing more than to wipe off their prints. Even just their eyes lingering on me made me feel gross, like I needed a shower.

The chain shackled to my right wrist was clipped to a metal ring on one side of the stone altar, and the left side followed a second later, sealing my fate with two resounding *click*s.

"Let me go," I growled, as I had many times before.

My words earned me a snarl from the demon and a nose full of sulfuric stench as he jerked closer, baring his rotting teeth.

I held my breath, deciding not to speak again. It wasn't working anyway. The only thing I'd gotten out of my threats and pleas was a sore throat and a slap across the face.

That assault had been courtesy of Wrath himself, after I'd talked back too much.

But that wasn't the worst of my injuries. The moment we'd arrived in Italy, a vampire had shaken me awake and forced a potion down my throat. That elixir had nullified my magic.

So really, it was up to Hans to save our butts—which I was finding hard to deal with. Not only did I hate being the damsel in distress—on a sacrificial altar, no less—but he was a demon too.

No, he wasn't a Darkborn, nor did I really believe he was evil, but even Wrath had separated me and Hans.

Upon our arrival, only I'd been woken up and given the elixir to stymy my magic; I was pretty sure some part of Wrath hoped Hans would join their group and become one of the people who would hurt me until my father came.

Or until I died. I didn't believe for a second that there was a line they wouldn't cross.

I cast a glance at my covenmate, standing some twenty feet away. He wasn't even bound, but he just stood there. He just watched me, like he couldn't do a damned thing.

Why? Sure, it would be difficult for him to fight through all these people, but he wasn't even going to try?

Shadows and Secrets had rules: we didn't harm one another, we didn't allow others to harm our covenmates, and we never left a person behind.

Did Hans not understand the severity of this situation?

No . . . One look at his face, so pale, and his eyes, so filled with pain, and I knew that he had to get it.

So why not act?

"Hans!" I yelled, hoping to jumpstart him into doing something.

"He won't save you, whore!" Nicoleta, his charming sister, sang. "You're not leaving that altar alive, so get used to it."

"Nicoleta, darling," the demon next to her purred. He was young, maybe twenty or so, and Wrath's heir. Annoyingly, with his long black hair, silver eyes, and built body decorated with tats, he was hot too, which did not escape Nicoleta's notice. They'd been all over each other while rooms were prepared to contain me and Hans. Disgusting.

"We might need her later," Wrath's heir said. "She's of strong blood."

Nicoleta shrugged. "Once the Eyes of Darkness are open, why do we need angels at all? Darkness will reign."

"I love the way you say that," the young man growled and tilted her chin up to take her mouth in his. Tongues licked and fingers traveled to private areas, as if this were a strip club, as if they were the only two around.

Gag!

I looked away, only to find that Wrath and the vampire who owned this place—a pompous asshole who insisted that everyone call him 'Master'—were standing right next to me.

"You must excuse Rikel." Wrath spoke slowly, as if he had all the time in the world to kill me. "He's quite enamored with Nicoleta."

Rikel. So that was the devil spawn's name. It fit.

I wrinkled my nose. "Maybe they should think about saving some of the PDA for the bedroom."

"Does your angel blood make you more prudish?" Wrath smirked. "In Hell, we are not so . . . virginal."

"Can we just get on with it?" the vampire beside him barked, clearly irritated I wasn't already dying.

"For a Laurent, you really have no patience, Raphael," Wrath remarked dryly.

I froze. *A Laurent?*

Before, I hadn't merited an introduction—not that I wanted one. But I knew that name. Almost everyone in our world did. Tobias was a Laurent, a member of the clan of royal vampires that largely lived in Isila.

"Ah, you recognize my family name?" The vampire's chest

seemed to puff out at little. "So my brother confided in you as well. That's unlike him to share with so many. Why did he do so? Are you his whore? His Source?"

I recoiled at the thought of a vampire drinking from me. Though I respected and liked Tobias, there were some things my kind just didn't do. That this jerk would suggest such a thing was vile.

And yet, he waited for my answer. As if my response was a given. He was so sure of himself that it made me sick.

I could withhold the information . . . I wanted to, just to spite him. But then again, this man—Raphael—could simply compel me to give it to him, so my resistance would be pointless.

"I'm none of those things, asshole. We went to *Le Bastion*."

"Ah, and *Le Tête* would have outed his bloodline anyway," Raphael shook his head. "Accola always did love to flaunt his connections."

I had no argument to that point. Anyone who had spent more than ten minutes in Oskar Accola's presence knew it to be true. Plus, I had more important things on my mind.

"Is Tobias in on this?"

Raphael quirked his brows. "Does it matter? You won't live to get revenge."

"It matters to me."

Not only would it surprise me, but Tobias was with Rooms right now. If he was a traitor, he could do so much more damage. Was she safe with him? My throat constricted at the idea of my friend in danger.

"Hmmm," Raphael mused. "You should really prioritize better."

He turned to Wrath, still not having answered me, which I took to mean the worst.

Tobias had to be involved with this. Was he the traitor in the coven? The person who had allowed the shade inside headquarters? As the one who'd retrieved her from Egypt he had known about her, and he'd been one of the only ones . . .

Before I could go too far down that path, Wrath procured a blade from a sheath he wore on his hip, the silver glinting in the sunset, wrenching all of my attention to the dagger.

"Any last words, nephilim?"

I swallowed but said nothing. If I was going to die at the hands of a demon, I'd go out stoically. I'd die in a way that would make Mom and Dad proud.

Ever so slightly, my gaze went to the heavens. Dad was up there, and I'd soon be joining him.

"I'll take that as a no." Wrath stepped closer, grabbed at my right wrist, and sliced.

A strangled scream tore up my throat, and it wasn't but a heartbeat later when my second wrist was flayed open.

Blood poured from my wounds, spilling onto the gray stone, which suddenly began to glow a brilliant white.

Wrath's lips curled up. "Perfect. Confirmation of a pure line. Now . . ." He drew the same blade across his own wrist.

Blood darker than my own, nearly black it was so red, poured to mix with mine. The blood pooling on the stone began to hiss and simmer, and a spiral of light and darkness appeared, swirling around me like some boiling whirlpool. The colors danced around each other, not mixing, and where the blood met, it boiled.

"The blood of the underworld, mixed with that of the heavens," Wrath hissed. "I call forth a champion for this Daughter of Heaven. An angel worthy of taking on a Prince of Darkness. I beseech you, Archangel Uriel—if you have any love at all for this girl, save her soul!"

He loosed a roar and shot his hands up, while black tendrils of magic scooped up some of the mixed blood and sent it flying skyward, like a geyser.

Holding my breath wasn't an option. I needed every gulp of air to stay alive, and though I didn't believe in my heart that my absentee father would come, I waited. I dared to hope, when before, I'd told myself that I wasn't worth it.

Everyone else seemed to watch too, and soon enough, the mixed blood spiraled out of sight, into the darkening sky, the sun nearly gone.

And yet, as if he could see our blood, Wrath's face remained tilted to heaven, expectant, until finally, he dropped his arms, then his chin, and eyed me. "You are of noble heavenly blood. The sword you wield, the way our life-force, our magics, battle even outside our bodies . . ."

He frowned. "But you are clearly not important enough."

I winced at that, even though I knew it was true.

"Which makes my plan all the more difficult," Wrath continued.

"Good," I rasped, the words barely tripping off my tongue. "I hope you fail. Meredith will see to it that you do."

Wrath snarled. "The seeker will join you soon enough, nephilim. She—"

Blasts of lightning rained down from the sky, striking the two demons who had chained me. They fell to the grass, dead.

Others in the crowd threw up cries and darted into the woods, a few calling on their magic to prepare for battle, but Wrath spun, a bark of a laugh tearing from his lips, as if nothing could delight him more than the chaos breaking out all around.

"Uriel! Have you finally come to face me?!"

"Release her," a voice boomed from nowhere, making my breath catch in my throat.

I'd only met my father a handful of times, but that was his voice. I'd know it anywhere.

As if to prove that point, light enveloped me, but instead of striking me dead, it healed me. The wounds on my wrists closed up, and an energy ran through my veins as my father's angelic powers burned away the potion nullifying my magic. The powers I couldn't reach sprang back to life inside me, lighting my blood on fire, begging to be used.

I drew a sharp, hopeful breath. Yes! If I could just get free of these chains, I could help!

"*HANS!*" I bellowed. "Break the chains!"

As if my words acted like a catalyst, Hans broke into a run in my direction. Demons leapt at him, but he managed to disarm them—though each time, using only his fists, not his magic.

What the hell?!

Hans could blast those suckers away, no problem. Why wasn't he just doing it? We were wasting time!

More lightning surged from the sky, snagging my attention. Five more foes fell, two of them vampires.

"Oh come now. Show yourself, Uriel! Face me!" Wrath challenged, leaping off the dais and into the clearing. For the time being, I'd been forgotten, thank the heavens. Still, I kept an eye on the devil prince as he spun, searching the area, as if he expected my father to be hiding amongst the trees.

"Prepare to meet your doom, Orien!" My father blasted down from the sky and slammed into the rock I stood upon.

"Dad!" I gasped, the ground shaking beneath me.

"Stand still, Shaylina." His sword of fire and light materialized, and with two swipes, my father cut the chains in half.

They dissolved upon impact, the power of his magic too much to stand up against.

Freed, and the angelic magic he'd sent into me having done its work, I called my own sword, my wings bursting from my back. "I'll help."

"Go to him." My father pointed to Hans, who was no longer charging my way but facing off with Nicoleta and her betrothed.

"But, Dad—"

"Go, Shaylina." He pulled feathers from his wings, and I watched in total awe as golden light wreathed his hands and from the feathers grew people. Twelve armed people. Warriors.

The conjured fighters rushed Prince Orien's demon subjects, engaging them in battle. They were strong and skilled with the blades that they'd been born with too.

He had to show me that trick.

"Shaylina, go," my father urged.

"I want to stay with you. To fight Wrath!"

"No. Go to your friend. He is one of us, a warrior for the light, and I have business to attend to." My father hurled himself at the Prince of Darkness.

Struck by my father's words, but not about to contradict him a second longer, I raced across the grass, mercilessly cutting down anyone who approached me.

When I finally reached Hans, his sister and Rikel were playing with him, like they were two cats who had caught a mouse between them. I was thankful the feather-soldiers seemed to be taking care of everyone else, but confused. Hans ducked and leapt out of the way, but didn't fight back with magic or fists.

"Hans! What the hell!" I shouted. Why was he just

allowing this to happen?

He pivoted, barely avoiding one of his sister's strikes as he danced out of the way on light feet. His eyes widened when they latched on to me. "The Vow!"

I froze. *No.*

That had to mean he'd broken the Vow of Intent he'd made to Brons. His magic was gone? But what had he done?

A blast of dark magic snapped me out of my thoughts, and I found Rikel watching me, murder in his eyes.

"Time for you to bow to your betters, angel." He stalked closer, graceful as a cat, and suddenly, my knees bent, and my back bowed.

I gritted my teeth. So, this douchebag had dark compulsion—a power like angelic influence or vampiric compulsion, just way more vile.

"Too bad I don't see any of those," I spat, surging back up and arcing my sword at him.

The devil whirled out of the way, dark smoke spinning from his body. I ran backward, not about to get close to that shiz. I couldn't be sure, but I suspected the smoke was part of why I'd been so violently ill when I arrived here.

Behind the heir, Hans fought his sister, and with each strike, he tried to talk sense into her. It wasn't working in the slightest, and when Nicoleta got too close to her brother with her ribbons, I shot a blaze of light at her.

It hit her thigh, and the demon hissed.

"Bitch!" She clutched her leg, and because she was wearing an absurdly short—dare I say *skanky*—skirt, I noticed her skin turned livid red and irritated where I'd struck her, just like it had the last time we fought. It was the most violent reaction to my power that I'd ever seen.

The question as to why that happened burned through me,

but there was no time to explore it before Wrath's heir lashed out again, this time with a dagger made of glowing red metal.

It grazed my arm, and I roared in pain, leaping toward him with my sword.

This time, he didn't get out of the way soon enough, and my fiery blade sliced his forearm clean off.

"*Aggghhhhhhh!*" Rikel screamed as blood spewed from his arm, now amputated at the elbow. "Help!"

"I'm coming!" Nicoleta shouted back a second before her ribbons twined around my adversary, lifting Rikel into the air.

She beat her wings and threw me a glance of pure loathing as she flew off. "Next time, angel trash, you're mine!"

Before I could retort, they disappeared over the trees.

"Shay!" Hans limped up to me, a dagger in his hand. Only then did I notice his thigh was bleeding.

"Are you okay?" I asked.

"Fine," he assured me. "It's a surface wound. I can move, which we might want to consider." He pointed over my shoulder. "Look."

I turned, and a gasp ripped up my throat. The sounds of fighting filled the woods. The feather soldiers had pushed Wrath's demons and the vampire's supporters into the trees. However, now that my attention was directed properly, it was clear that most of the clamor was coming from my father and Wrath.

They battled over the lake, each soaring with ease, the archangel with white wings and the devil with black.

My father had likely lured Wrath away from the clearing, but what about the humans who lived on the edges of the water? Surely, they would see!

I swallowed, realizing it only mattered if my father won. If he didn't, Wrath planned to bring Hell to Earth, and he wouldn't be quiet about it. The humans would soon know that the devils in their holy texts were real, if not entirely how they imagined them.

"We need to help." My wings snapped out, ready to catch the wind.

"I don't know what I can do." Hans's tone was bitter, and though I wanted to learn how he'd broken his Vow, there wasn't time.

Just like there wasn't time for my prejudices right now. No matter what was in our blood, Hans was clearly on my side.

"If I give you my sword, do you think you can handle it?"

His eyes widened. "Yeah. Can other people hold it, though?"

The question was reasonable. Uriel did not give his sword of fire and light to others, and I never had either. But we *could*; all I had to do was wrap his hand in angel magic, and Hans wouldn't burn.

"Hold out your sword hand," I instructed. "And once you have the weapon, don't let go, or it will disappear and return to me."

Hans did so, and I flooded his arm with magic, creating a shield that would allow him to hold my magical sword without injury. Once the protection was in place, I offered the sword hilt-first.

He took it, awe on his face that humbled me.

I gave a small smile. "All yours. I'll—"

A distant roar of pain stole the words from my mouth, and I whirled again.

My heart stopped.

My father was falling toward the water, a violent diagonal slash atop his heart. The Prince of Hell had landed a serious blow! Above, Wrath appeared untouched, and ribbons of darkness spooled out of him, catching the archangel before he hit the water.

"No!" I lunged to help, but Hans grabbed me.

"Shay! Look!" He pointed to a few errant ribbons that seemed to have formed a cup and were flying our way—toward the dais.

I held my breath. What was happening?

The answer came a second later when the cup crafted of ribbons stopped above the altar and tilted. Gold liquid—pure angel blood—spilled out.

The instant it hit the stone, it cracked, and the stench of sulfur filled the air.

"Join me, Brothers!" Wrath howled, wrenching my attention back to him only to find the most horrific sight I could have imagined.

The Prince of Darkness cradled my father in his black tendrils, and below, the lake was boiling, disappearing.

Dread mounted in me as the reason presented itself.

We weren't at this location by chance. No . . . Lake Como was significant. This place was one of the seven Eyes of Darkness, and the lake was about to split open, unleashing Hell on Earth.

CHAPTER TWENTY-NINE

HANS

"Shay! We have to get out of here." I grabbed my partner's slender wrist as, not far away, Lake Como bubbled viciously.

On the opposite side of the lake, humans spilled from their homes to crowd the shoreline, oblivious to the horror they were about to witness. To the danger that was about to befall them.

A part of me wanted to wave and yell and make sure they got the hell out of here, but another part knew it would do no good. They were too far away, the sound of the boiling lake too loud . . .

We didn't have much time. If Shay and I were going to live, we had to leave. Plain and simple.

"Shay!" I tugged on her, trying to break the spell the lake had over her.

"I can't leave my father."

My stomach sank. I'd been afraid she'd say that—though I would say the same thing about Nicoleta or Dad. But how the fuck were we going to save Archangel Uriel from the clutches of Wrath when he wasn't even on land?

Sure, Shay could fly, and she was powerful, but I didn't believe she could handle Prince Orien on her own. Her father, a freaking archangel, couldn't defeat Orien on his own.

Luca might have scared the prince off in New York, but Wrath hadn't had backup and there were so many demons here. If Shay managed to get a leg up there was no way they'd stand by and let a nephilim pummel their master.

And I was basically useless. Thank the Goddess that Uriel could make feather soldiers, or whatever the fuck those things were, because if there had been more demons around we'd have been screwed.

"Shay," I said, determined to talk sense into her before I lost her. "I get that but we need a pla—"

She yanked her arm from my grasp, and knowing what she was about to do, I lunged for the nephilim.

But I was too late. She leapt into the air, soaring toward the lake.

My heart lurched, watching her get closer to Wrath. Worse, I still held her sword of fire and light. She was without her best weapon! The Prince of Darkness hadn't noticed she was coming, not yet, but when he did . . .

A roiling sensation inside me made me feel ill, and I clenched my stomach—but quickly realized the feeling was in my chest, circling from front to back.

Fuck. My magic.

How? It should be bound to Brons, but seeing Shay barrel forward without backup was making it react. More than that, it felt weird, different, but also vaguely familiar, like a lost memory coming to light.

My magic pulsed through me, a lion trying to break out of its cage. The sensation was even more visceral than the pain I'd felt when I'd watched Shay bleeding out on the altar. I hadn't thought she would survive that, but she did, and now she was throwing away her second chance at life.

I found the nephilim again, and the rush of my magic intensified to the point I nearly fell over.

I blinked. What the hell!? I'd heard that bindings like this were painful, and while this was, it was also uncomfortable and . . .

Like my body was trying to tell me something.

"Daughter of Heaven! Returned to avenge your father?" Wrath lashed out at Shay with a cloud of black smoke and a laugh, as if this were all just a game to him. "Let us all hope that you're a better warrior than your sire!"

She dodged, soaring upward and pivoting in the air. I foresaw a dive-bomb attempt.

While I admired her bravery, I really wished she'd stay the fuck away from him.

"Shay!" I waved the sword, hoping to lure her back and talk sense into her. But neither the nephilim nor Wrath heard me.

The boiling of the lake was growing louder, and now I swore I heard cracking, like the Earth was opening beneath it. Goosebumps raced up my arms.

An Eye of Darkness was threatening to gape open right in front of me. The instant they could do so, the trapped creatures of Hell would spill onto land, they'd infiltrate our world.

Desperate to help because the sooner we saved the archangel, the sooner we could get out of here, I darted forward. Her father was wrapped up in so many ribbons, I couldn't spot a sliver of skin. If only I could fly, I could use the sword to cut through them, and—

The odd feeling of my magic trying to push its way out

rippled along my back in two distinct lines, and I sucked in a breath, finally placing the sensation.

My *demon* magic, not the power of my wizarding blood, was trying to emerge. Was it possible that the Vow of Intent had not affected my Hellblooded powers?

Wrath's words came roaring back.

"Lilith's blood truly does work wonders. Few are stronger than her."

He was right, and strong as he was in the witching community, I was sure that Richard Brons was not powerful enough to best my mother. Lilith was an equal to the Princes of Darkness, a legend in her own right. An immortal queen. Was this a loophole neither of us had anticipated?

Did I dare test it? Did I dare give in to the demonic magic inside me?

The last time it appeared had been an accident—and I'd been determined for that not to happen again. Each time dark magic was used, it grew more powerful, and I didn't want to be controlled by the darkness within me.

So for years, I'd kept it locked up so tightly that I hadn't needed to worry about a slip. I was a pro at confining it, so good others didn't even sense I had demonic powers.

But now . . . Was the demonic power in my blood our only chance? If I set it free, could I trust it?

Another roar from Wrath redirected my attention. Shay had just barely escaped his clutches, and blood poured down her face from where a ribbon had cut her cheek.

Below, half the water in the lake was gone. More humans lined the shoreline than just minutes before, pointing and gawking when they should be running for their lives.

Shit was about to go down, which meant one thing: No

matter how terrified I was to give into my demon magic, I had to try.

I closed my eyes. *I submit. Take over.*

For the first time since I was a boy and I learned how to control my demon magic, I intentionally released my hold over the darkness. I gave in to it, and confirmation that I'd been right immediately presented itself. Like before, my veins darkened, telling me the demon magic was surging.

Wrath had spoken true. Brons was a strong wizard, strong enough to bind my wizarding power, but he couldn't contain the blood of Lilith. Compared to her, and the power she gave her children, Brons was nothing.

Standing before an Eye of Darkness, I allowed the power born of that vile realm to run through me, to well up from some hidden, shameful place inside me so strongly it nearly took my breath away.

The tickling on my back intensified, and I knew what would happen seconds before wings sprouted from my shoulder blades, splitting open my skin to grow and unfurl.

A groan was wrung from my lips, and I clung tightly to Shay's sword, not about to give it up, hoping to use it in just a moment.

When the pain stopped some seconds later, I twisted to stare at my new form.

Midnight black feathered wings, nearly as wide as Wrath's, expanded from my shoulder blades. They were brooding and beautiful. Breathtaking.

Never before had I possessed wings; I hadn't thought it was possible. But all my darkness needed was for me to allow them to come into being, to accept them.

I snorted at my stupidity. I hadn't really mastered my darkness at all. It had always been there, waiting for when I had needed it. For when I could no longer deny its presence and who I really was.

"Let's see what you can do."

I leapt into the air, beating my new wings. Unsurprisingly, gravity took me right back down to the fucking ground.

No. This was not happening. I couldn't afford to spend time learning to fly. We might be murdered at any second. I had to learn *now*.

"Get your shit together," I growled, glaring first at the right wing, then the left. Had my witch magic been free, I would have used a levitation spell to help me rise into the air, but that wasn't possible. Right now, I was like a baby bird being shoved from the nest, except I was the one doing the shoving.

Still on the ground, I gave them a test flap. One beat. Two. Then three. Okay, we were synced, and surprisingly, they felt strong, like they'd been just waiting to sprout out of my back and be used all my life.

If that's the case, buck up and perform, bros. Time to try this shit again.

I pushed the wings harder and jumped. This time, they caught on a faint breeze, and I surged up, just a little higher.

Ha! I was fucking flying!

A scream cut my elation short, and I sought Shay. She had just narrowly escaped an attack.

Time to get us the hell out of here.

Again, I beat my wings, and some semblance of instinct took over. The next thing I knew, I was flying, albeit a little shakily, but still going in the right direction, straight for the Prince of Darkness.

Wrath's back was turned to me, largely because Shay was soaring toward him from the center of the lake, a blazing ball of angel magic in her hand. The water beneath her was almost gone, and the cracking of the earth under the surface was louder than before. The ground shook, and with it the trees swayed.

I approached from land, as silent as the grave so as not to give away the fact that Wrath now had one more adversary to contend with. We'd only have one great shot at freeing the archangel. So with Shay's sword of fire and light extended, I zoomed toward the cocoon of ribbons holding the Archangel Uriel captive.

The tendrils of darkness gleamed prettily in the light of newly born stars, forgotten by the prince as the nephilim advanced. The instant I reached them, I swiped, cutting through the ribbons supporting her father, and before my eyes, the rest of the ribbons of darkness dissolved into nothing.

The angel dropped, unconscious, but I released Shay's sword and dove to follow the archangel, catching him with an *oomph* before he hit the boiling water below.

Carefully, I situated him in my arms; it wasn't pretty. The angel was big, and slick with gold blood so we dropped a few more feet. My wings weren't even used to my weight, let alone that of a rider. Nonetheless, I had to make it work. Adrenaline pushed me to course-correct quickly, and we rose up by the force of muscle and pure energy.

"*Noooo!*" Wrath screamed, and I looked up just in time to see a bloom of smoke coming straight for us.

My eyes narrowed, and I called on my demon magic, wishing pain on Wrath.

The smoke stopped, as if it had run into an invisible wall, and dispersed to the winds as Prince Orien loosed a howl of agony. My veins darkened so much they were nearly black and, internally, I cringed. This was everything I hated about my power to inflict torture. But I wasn't going to stop. In fact, I doubled down, allowing my dark magic to wash over him in waves, pummeling him.

Immobilized by pain, Wrath wrapped his arms around his body, screaming and screaming and screaming.

Shay appeared at my side. "What are you doing?!"

"We'll talk about this later," I grunted. "We need to leave."

She looked down at her father, gold blood smeared across his chest, and gave a small nod. "Follow me."

The nephilim took off, soaring across the lake. I held my dark influence over Wrath for as long as possible. We were halfway across the lake when I could no longer maintain my thrall and had to release him.

I cast a glance back, hoping he wouldn't follow, and my heart leapt.

Prince Orien was no longer in the air, but on the shoreline, flat on his back. Others gathered around him, clearly concerned by what I'd done, though none followed. Maybe they were too injured to do so. The feather soldiers were nowhere in sight, but from what I'd seen they'd been vicious fighters. Whether from fear over what I'd done to their leader, or injury, not following was a good call on the demons' part. From past experience, before I shoved my dark magic deep inside me, I knew that my magic could render a normal man motionless for days. It wouldn't affect a Prince of Hell that strongly, but there was no way he'd be following any time soon.

"Hurry!" Shay called, and I pushed my wings, putting on speed.

As we neared the opposite shore, people pointed at us, gaping in wonder. I wished they'd run, but we didn't have time to help everyone. We couldn't control what they—

Goosebumps lined my arms.

CHAPTER TWENTY-NINE

Or could we?

Pain was a great motivator for action, and for once, I might be able to use this power for good.

Harnessing my dark magic, I threw a small amount of it toward the onlookers, hoping it would hit just a few and scare the others, spurring them to seek refuge. I felt when the magic struck, once, then twice.

Immediately, cries of anguish rose up. Two men fell to their knees, shaking violently. I watched with relief as the humans did as I'd hoped. They grabbed the two men who were afflicted, turned, and ran back into their homes.

I waited until they were out of sight before letting go of my hold over them. I had no idea if walls would save them, but that cover had to be better than standing out in the open on the lakeside as six Princes of Darkness arose from Hell.

"Hans!" Shay banked a hard right, veering toward the thick forest.

I followed, less steady in flight than she was, and holding on to her father, who seemed to grow heavier by the second.

What the hell do they eat in Heaven?!

We flew over the tops of the trees, deeper into the forested area that surrounded Lake Como.

And not a second too soon, for behind us, I heard a monstrous *crack*. The treetops swayed, and the birds that had been nesting in branches took flight, soaring in our direction.

That could only mean one thing.

I knew I wouldn't like what I saw, but I couldn't stop myself. I looked back the way we'd come.

The lake was bone-dry, and a gaping chasm had opened in its bottom, from which smoke—in black and a poisonous red —surged.

Figures poured out of the fissure, all of them winged, some

horned, some big, others small. But aside from the black wings that lifted them into the air, the most frightening ones didn't look like brutish monsters at all. They were human in form, likely striking to behold, and their power was legendary. Dangerous. Deadly.

A shiver ran through me, and I pushed my wings harder, desperate to put as much distance as possible between us and the seven Princes of Darkness.

CHAPTER THIRTY

MEREDITH

WE ROSE FROM THE TABLE, MY STOMACH FULL AFTER INDULGING IN a roast made by Claire.

"That was great, thank you," I said, placing my hand on my belly. "I'm going to pass the heck out tonight."

"Of course, love," Claire said, looking pleased that I'd enjoyed the meal. "After such a full day of studies, you need something that will keep you fueled. I'm sorry we didn't have sustenance for you, Tobias."

Next to me, the vampire shrugged. He'd been tense since I met up with him after researching, and he'd shown me the photo his sire sent. It made me nervous too, but for now, there was nothing to be done. Just because the OA was in the same country as us, didn't mean they'd be knocking on the manor house door any time soon.

"I didn't expect anything and will be fine for a few days," Tobias assured the witches. "But perhaps locating a blood bank soon would be a good idea? Just in case?"

"Already done," Gloria rasped. "Aya and Stuart will go tomorrow and pick up bags for you."

"Do you have . . . a preferred type? O? A? AB?" Stuart asked. "Does negative or positive matter? We've never had a vampire guest."

"Whatever is available will be fine," Tobias replied, though I suspected that he did, in fact, have a type. He was just that kind of guy. "You lot will strengthen the protections around your property tonight, correct?"

The topic of the photo and Giselle's voicemail had also been discussed with the *Arcacustos*. Their coven wasn't pleased that someone was looking for me, but they also didn't seem too shocked by the idea.

"Correct," Miriam assured Tobias. "We'll head into the forest now and be outside for hours. Should you need anything, Meredith has my phone number."

I nodded. I'd been just as surprised that Miriam had a cell phone, as I had when she demanded to put her number in my phone after Tobias shared word of the OA. She just didn't seem to be the type to use technology.

"We'll be fine," I assured them. "Like I said, I'm beat. I'll probably fall fast asleep."

Miriam's gaze bounced from me to Tobias and back again, her eyebrows arched like she didn't believe a word I'd said.

Then again, now that I thought about having some alone time with the vampire, I didn't either. We might not be getting it on, like Miriam was probably thinking, but we had a lot to talk about.

"We'll see you in the morning, then," Miriam said. "Olga, you're fine to clean up and then meet us outside?"

The old Russian woman nodded, already grabbing the plates, so one by one, the *Arcacustos* filed out of the dining room.

"I can help, Olga," I offered, because it felt wrong to leave.

She was ancient, her hands shaky. Could she even carry all the plates?

She just waved me off. "Go, girl. You need your rest. This is up to me."

"Come, Meredith," Tobias caught my elbow. "We need to speak."

We did, and I'd been dying to do just that for hours, so I didn't press Olga, but waved goodbye and left the dining room.

The hallway was empty, open for conversations of even the most private nature, and we didn't make it far before Tobias grabbed my hand, slipping his fingers through mine. The feel of our skin touching sent waves of heat through me.

"I want to say that I'm sorry for earlier," he breathed. "About the soulmates. I should have said something, even just hinted at what I thought was growing between us."

"It would have been nice," I agreed. "But I can understand your hesitation. We weren't exactly best pals at the start."

A dry laugh echoed off the walls as the vampire squeezed my hand. "At each other's throats every other second."

"Some of us literally," I teased, recalling my first training session with him.

He shook his head. "I told Luca I wasn't fit for helping you that day, but he insisted."

"I wonder if he knew?"

"No," Tobias said. "I'm sure he couldn't have. Benedict is one matter, but Luca is not connected to you in the same way. He's merely a mage. Their senses aren't even particularly good, little better than a human's senses."

"And your sire?"

"She and I are connected and always will be. Giselle must have sensed the change in me. Or perhaps it was just that I was unlike how I was with most people. Giselle has seen me in love—and maybe she sensed this was even more."

"Was it our dislike for one another that stopped you? Or something else?" I didn't have the whole story yet, but I wanted it. I needed to understand.

"More," he said, halting his steps and turning to me. "I loved a woman once, Meredith. What we had is nothing compared to how I feel for you. Our bond is more primal, more etched in my body, and while I loved the other, I didn't feel it as deeply." He paused, as if not wanting to admit the next words.

"What happened to her?" I asked, needing more information, even if it was bad news. The urge to know as much about Tobias as I possibly could was growing, just like my sense of belonging with him.

"She perished at my hand." Tobias met my eyes as he spoke, as if wanting to make sure I understood just how serious this matter was. "I didn't mean to kill her. I was protecting her, but I was a much younger vampire then, and less in control of my urges. Those who attacked the compound we lived in at the time hurt her, and she probably would have died anyhow, but it was me who ended her life."

"How?" I whispered, trying to piece it all together.

"I thought I could change her, could save her by doing so, but she didn't want that. When she awoke as a vampire, she barely lived three days before taking her own life." He looked away, swallowing thickly.

"So you didn't kill her."

"I as good as did."

I stepped closer to him. "She made a choice. Perhaps you shouldn't have changed her, but after that, she was alive. Not as she wanted to be, but she was. In the end, her death was her decision."

"She wouldn't have had to make that choice at all if we hadn't been together." He met my eyes again. "Meredith, you're new to this world, so you might not know what it means, but I'm a royal vampire. It is dangerous to be with me, and it always will be. That is how Cecilia died."

Cecilia. So that was her name.

"Enemies of the Laurents knew they could affect me, sway me, get me to do things for them if they harmed Cecilia. They, however, went too far. Her death certainly did not put me on their side," he pressed. "I do not know if I could live if someone would harm you in that way." His chest rose with a breath that I knew he didn't need to live.

I waited, sensing he was building up to something.

"I-I tried to kill myself after Cecilia passed."

"You did?!" Just the idea made my heart crack in half.

"Giselle stopped me just in time. But for years, I thought of trying again. The pain was too much. For the same fate to befall a bloodbound mate . . ." He shuddered. "I would not be able to survive."

"You don't have to worry about that," I assured him. "Cecilia was human, but I'm a witch—and I'm not about to be a damsel in distress. I can take care of myself. And with you at my side, I'll be even safer. Plus, we have S&S at our backs too."

Nevermind that I'd basically been the picture of a damsel in distress when a demon had scooped me up off the sidewalk and taken me to the Ringmaster, but that wouldn't happen again. I refused to believe it and would make sure I was ready for the next attack.

"You're different from her, that's certain." Tobias came

closer so that our noses were inches apart. "But there are forces at work that even you cannot control. Those you cannot know, Meredith. Dangers beyond your wildest dreams."

"So teach me," I murmured, tilting my head so that my lips hovered over his. "Because I'm not going anywhere, Tobias. I'm yours and you're mine and that's that."

Before he could argue, I pressed my lips to his.

A hungry growl was his response, and suddenly, his hands were at my back, pulling me close. The next second, I found my back up against the wall, my hands running through his dark hair, smooth as silk.

This time, we explored each other more slowly than the night before, more deliberately, with hands and tongues and breath that came ever faster.

It felt like I'd known him all my life, like I'd never been with someone more in tune with me, more made for me.

I pressed myself into him, felt the hard length of him on my leg, and smiled.

Desperate to get closer, I wrapped my arms around his neck and leapt. He caught me as my legs cinched around his waist.

"Meredith," he rasped. "We need to get to a room."

A laugh bubbled out of me. We hadn't made it far from the dining room at all, and at the rate we were going, we'd definitely need privacy, but I didn't want to move. Not yet. I couldn't bring myself to break the spell of euphoria washing over me.

"Wait," I whispered, breaking my lips from his and trailing kisses along his jaw.

He moaned, low and rumbly, which made pleasure trill inside me. That sound, the feel of his stubble, and the scent of him was enough to drive me mad.

And then he slid one hand from my butt up my back, until he lodged it in my hair, and teased my lips back to where they belonged. On his.

"Mmm," I hummed savoring the kiss, the feel of this strong man holding me up with one arm, my body pressed against his.

"If you keep making those sounds," he growled, "I can't promise that what I do next will be proper."

"Screw proper." I tossed my head back, offering him my neck.

When I realized what I'd just done, I sucked in a breath. But I didn't move. Had to think.

Did I mind if he bit me? Before, I had, but now?

I wasn't sure, but when I opened my eyes and found him looking at me with such hunger, I didn't think I did. I wanted him to look at me like that. Wanted to be the one who could feed that hunger. The only one.

"Meredith, did you mean—"

A scream cut through the hallway, and as one, since we were still stuck together, we whirled.

"It came from the dining room," I said breathlessly.

Tobias set me down. "Perhaps Olga fell."

"That didn't sound like a fall."

We rushed to check on her, but were met halfway there by Olga herself, shuffling as quickly as her legs would allow toward the front door.

"What's wrong?" I asked.

"This!" she pointed to a band of light—magic—that glowed on her wrist. "It means one of our wards has been breached. Child, you should hide."

I drew myself up. It had to be the Ringmaster. She was already here? With who else? A small army?

"We're coming with you," I said firmly. "This is my battle."

Perhaps it was my tone, or perhaps she simply didn't think she had the time, but Olga didn't try to convince me otherwise. She merely shuffled out the door and down the drive, scanning the area for her covenmates or the threat.

Tobias and I followed.

The moment I was outside, my ring began to heat up. I looked down. What the hell?

"Are you alright?" Tobias asked.

"My ring is warm. It hasn't acted like this since we looked for the missing base-stone in the Beinecke."

The vampire's green eyes widened. "Perhaps it is affected by the attack? This place is sacred to you just as it is to the *Arcacustos*."

That could be it. But then again, I'd expected my ring to show me the way when we'd first come here, but it hadn't. Now I knew that was largely because the *Abscondita* Coven had been testing me. But now . . . this was no test. This was a true attack. The start of what would, if we couldn't stop it in time, blow up into a war.

"We need to search for her and Josiah," I said to Tobias. "The Ringmaster can't hurt these people."

"I'm with you, every step of the way."

I smiled at him. "Back at you. Let's go."

We entered the woods side-by-side, searching for the person who'd made my life a living hell—determined to bring her down once and for all.

ALSO BY ASHLEY MCLEO

<u>Coven of Shadows and Secrets</u>

Seeker of Secrets

Hunted by Darkness

History of Witches

Marked by Fate

<u>Spellcasters Spy Academy Series (Magic of Arcana Universe)</u>

A Legacy Witch: Year One

A Marked Witch: Internship

A Rebel Witch: Year Two

A Crucible Witch: Year Three

The Spellcasters Spy Academy Boxset

<u>The Wonderland Court Series (Magic of Arcana Universe)</u>

Alice the Dagger

Alice the Torch

<u>Standalone Novels</u>

The Alchemist of Silver Hollow (Magic of Arcana Universe)

<u>Fanged Fae Series - A Bonegates sister series</u>

Blood Moon Magic

Faerie Blood

<u>The Bonegate Series - A Fanged Fae sister series</u>

Hawk Witch

Assassin Witch

Traitor Witch

Illuminator Witch

The Royal Quest Series

Dragon Prince

Dragon Magic

Dragon Mate

Dragon Betrayal

Dragon Crown

Dragon War

The Starseed Universe

Prophecy of Three

Souls of Three

Rising of Three

The Starseed Universe (five-book boxset)

ABOUT THE AUTHOR

Ashley lives in the lush and green Pacific Northwest with her husband, Kurt, their dog, Flicka, and the house ghost that sometimes makes appearances in her charming, old home.

When she's not writing urban fantasy and portal fantasy novels she enjoys traveling the world, reading, kicking butt at board games (she recommends Splendor and Dominion), and frequenting taquerias.

For all the latest releases and updates, subscribe to Ashley's newsletter, The Coven. You can also find her Facebook group, Ashley's Reader Coven.